THE PALE DOOR

DEATH OF A LADIES' MAN

ROBERT MARTIN
WRITING AS LEE ROBERTS
Introduction by Jim Felton

STARK
HOUSE

Stark House Press • Eureka California

THE PALE DOOR / DEATH OF A LADIES' MAN

Published by Stark House Press
1315 H Street
Eureka, CA 95501, USA
griffinskye3@sbcglobal.net
www.starkhousepress.com

THE PALE DOOR
Originally published by Dodd, Mead & Company, Inc., New York,
and copyright © 1955 by Lee Roberts. Reprinted in paperback by
Bantam Books, New York, 1956.

DEATH OF A LADIES' MAN
Originally published by Gold Medal Books, Greenwich, and
copyright © 1960 by Fawcett Publications, Inc.

"Robert Martin: Too Good an Author to be Forgotten" by Jim Felton
copyright © 2004 and originally published by *Mystery*File*, issue
#43, April 2004; reprinted by permission.

ISBN: 978-1-951473-83-9

Book design by Mark Shepard, shepgraphics.com
Cover design by Steven Ray Austin, enigma media, Austin TX
Proofreading by Bill Kelly

First Stark House Press Edition: July 2022

ROBERT MARTIN: TOO GOOD AN AUTHOR TO BE FORGOTTEN

by Jim Felton

Often it is easy to understand how some once-popular writers have been forgotten: just read some of their work. Or try to read it. At times it is hard to understand how they could ever have been popular. Better to let *Unsolved Mysteries* take a shot at some of these cases – and for some of the "remembered" writers as well. Inevitably, though, some worthy writers become forgotten, pushed from memory when there is nothing new forthcoming for previously loyal readers, overwhelmed by the unending flow of books by other writers. One author quite worthy of being remembered is Robert Martin (1908-1976). And not merely because he lived down the street from me when I was a kid.

By all appearances, Bob Martin was a very popular writer in his day. As far as I know he published only mysteries, mostly featuring a private detective as the leading character. Larry Estep of Pulpgen fame provided me a list of some 51 pulp stories plus reprints – and there were a few more to discover. Martin's name appears thirty-seven times on the covers of U.S. magazines with his stories (plus one issue without a story by him). Martin easily made the transition into the hardcover and paperback novel markets, eventually publishing 22 novels.

Starting off slowly, Martin's pulp career went back to 1936 with "A Case for the Morgue" appearing in *Scarlet Gang Smashers*. A total of three stories appeared in *Double Action Gang Magazine* in 1938 and 1939. Discounting the 1942 reprinting of his story "Getaway Double-cross" by the Canadian *Private Detective* pulp, we don't find him again until 1944 when the first of his four stories published in *Mammoth Detective* appeared when Howard Browne had taken over.

Martin broke into *Dime Detective* in 1945 with the first of his 23 that would appear in that magazine, and he also made an appearance in *Thrilling Detective* that year. He would break into *Black Mask* the following year for the first of eight stories he had published there. A story by Robert Martin, "Passage a Tabac," appeared in the French-

Canadian pulp *Loup Noir*, another Popular Publications title, but it has not been confirmed that this is "our" Robert Martin.

In contrast to that slow start, 1947 would see seven stories published, nine in 1948, thirteen in 1949, and nine in 1950. Most of these were in titles produced by Popular Publications. I suspect this may have been due in part to the fact his agent was the fabled Joseph T. Shaw. During that time frame, Martin's name would often be featured on the cover, even as mentioned earlier, once when no story of his appeared in that issue (*Dime Detective*, January 1949).

Just two of his short stories saw print in both 1951 and 1952, and only single stories appeared in 1954 and 1955. This last short story was published in the first issue of the short-lived *Justice* magazine. Beside the Canadian reprints, at least eight short stories were reprinted in Great Britain, three in Australia, two in Finland, and two in Sweden.

As far as I have been able to discover, Robert Martin did not write for the pulp magazines under any pseudonyms, nor in other genres. Martin graduated from high school in 1927, so it is possible for other early stories to be uncovered.

It is not clear to me how he went from being a sporadically published writer to becoming a regular almost overnight. Perhaps it was a matter of getting someone's attention when fresh writers were sought. I have read his 1936 story "Midnight Call," and it is well-written crime and suspense tale. After one of the bank robbers is shot during a hold-up, they pick a doctor out of the phone book to treat the wounded gang member. The doctor is taken to the hideout and told he will be killed if he does not save the wounded man's life.

As the short story market was drying up, Martin turned to the longer novel form, a natural progression, since a number of his pulp stories were novelettes or called novel-length. Between 1951 and 1965, Martin published fourteen novels as Robert Martin and eight as Lee Roberts, a pseudonym which incorporated his middle name. His books were part of the Red Badge Detective mystery series published by Dodd, Mead.

As many writers did, he relied on his body of published pulp stories for characters and plots. In both 1955 and 1957 he published three novels, and two novels per year five other times. Three novels were reprinted in Detective Book Club editions. Toward the end of his career, his novels began to appear as paperback originals, and eventually he found no publisher for his final stories.

Martin's novels were read around the world. Canadian editions exist for several titles in paperback. There were British editions in both hardback and paperback. In fact Martin's last four novels were published first in Great Britain many years before the American

editions. All were translated into German and went through several editions in paperback with a few titles also coming out in hardback. At least seventeen of the novels appeared in Italian translations. There were French editions for seven of the novels, and Swedish editions of two. Spanish and Japanese translations may also exist.

He even made it into television. His novel *The Widow and the Web* was the basis for the episode by the same name on *77 Sunset Strip*. One of his stories was used for *Surfside 6*, another series by the same producers.

For the most part his main characters are either private detectives or small town family doctors. In the pulps he used Jim Bennett or Lee Fiske as PI's, as well as a couple of others; Clinton Colby usually appeared as his doctor.

Jim Bennett was his most well developed detective character. He heads up the Cleveland, Ohio, branch of a New York-based private detective agency. Bennett has a college and law school background, but he likes the action this choice brings to his life over the sedate practice of law. Perhaps his WW2 experience bears on this. Bennett is in love with his secretary, Sandy Hollis, and Bennett he realizes that one of these days he ought to marry that gal and settle down.

Dr. Clinton Colby from the pulps became Dr. Clinton Shannon in the novels, all of which came out under the authorship of Lee Roberts. Shannon is married, while Colby is single. In each instance, Colby/Shannon has an attractive, competent female office assistant. The relationship between them is professional but the potential for love and romance is recognized, if not realized.

This last statement needs some explanation. Shannon is definitely married with a young son and much is made of the 60s style family life, but the nurse/secretary in love with the doctor/boss dynamic is very much present. It is particularly evident in *Suspicion* in a scene where his nurse disrobes in Shannon's presence to tempt him (unsuccessfully). As if Shannon didn't have enough trouble with just about everybody else suspecting him of killing a former flame...

Robert Martin's stories usually feature a doctor, and not just the Colby/Shannon stories. Since private detectives always get themselves beat up, knocked out, or gun shot, the medical angle could be expected. In several stories this doctor is also a coroner.

Most of Martin's stories take place in Northern Ohio. With the agency based in Cleveland, naturally some stories will take place in that city, but some cases take Bennett or Fiske to Columbus. At the time the stories were written, Cleveland was among the nation's largest cities and a leading financial, industrial, transportation, and cultural center.

Its professional sports teams were in their glory years, and the city's slogan was "best location in the nation." In contrast, Columbus was important mainly for being the state's capitol city and the home of a major university.

Not all of Martin's stories take place in an urban locale. Small towns, Lake Erie and even rural locations offer circumstances and plot possibilities not found in big cities. One pulp story takes place at a country club turned dude ranch. Martin's detectives handle the usual (dare one call them classic?) kinds of cases: called on by the rich to clean up their messes. Prodigal children, unfaithful or runaway spouses, the unapproved romantic attachments of offspring or siblings – the usual things.

A good many cases are business- or industry-related. In one pulp story Bennett breaks up a ring of thieves responsible for the in-transit disappearance of valuable machine tools. Is sabotage behind the fatal failures of the company's products? What is causing patrons of a fancy beauty shop to lose their hair? Was that worker's death accidental, or murder? Loaned out to the state's Worker's Compensation Bureau, Bennett investigates not run-of-the-mill malingerers but cases where disabled workers' causes of death do not jibe with their documented illnesses.

Dr. Colby/Shannon doesn't go looking for trouble; bad things just happen to occur around him, and it's like an extension of the Hippocratic Oath for him to jump in and make things right, whether the bad things are medical or not. This is juggled into the normal routine of treating patients in his office, making house calls and hospital rounds, performing surgeries, or responding to medical emergencies after hours.

Starting some twenty-plus years ago, I have read all of the Robert Martin/Lee Roberts novels and all but a half dozen or so of the pulp stories. In my opinion, the writing is still fresh, and the stories hold up pretty well. Remove the inevitable World War Two references in his stories from the Forties, and have his leading characters give up tobacco, drink more responsibly, and these stories would be contemporary. Quality-wise, I would say he wrote as well as early Ross Macdonald and John D. MacDonald. The emphasis is on early. While those two other guys went on to bigger and better things – and you have heard of them – Martin's writing lacks the extra dimensions found in the mature works of those two masters. He certainly lacks JDM's agendas.

Martin gives the clear impression that he knew what he wrote about and was confident in that knowledge. Have you been reading along in a mystery and hit the spot where the author tries to be cute by inserting some esoteric subject then glibly spills all he "knows" about the matter?

That immediately exposes the writer as a phony, because so often he has gotten it wrong. Stories that rely on such devices ought to bear warning labels to protect the consumer. On the other hand, Martin never insults the intelligence of his readers by skirting away from technical or specialized matters. He didn't go into excruciating detail but told his readers enough to understand what was necessary.

He did not fall prey to that somewhat epidemic fad among some writers who find it necessary to insert at least one word that is so archaic, so obscure, so obsolete and rarely used, that an abridged dictionary is useless in determining its meaning. Nor was he an author who scattered foreign language phrases without regard for his reader who may not be as adept with other languages.

As I said earlier, when I was a kid, Robert Martin lived down the street from me in Tiffin, Ohio. When the leaves are off the trees his Victorian frame house is easily visible from my folks' home. He had a daughter a few years ahead of me in school, a son two years behind me, and a second daughter younger still. One summer I mowed his next door neighbor's very large yard (without benefit of a riding mower). I never met Robert Martin, I am positive, and I am fairly certain I never laid eyes on him. Maybe I had some awareness that a writer lived in town – it was not a secret – but it didn't mean anything to me at the time. I left town in 1966 for college and moved back about twenty-five years later. Not too many people in Tiffin are left who knew him. There are some who knew of him, but most people have no idea who he was. Maybe he should have worked out a deal with Welcome Wagon to hand out copies of his paperbacks.

Another person who never met Robert Martin is writer Bill Pronzini. After his own writing career was well under way, Bill wrote to Martin and Bob Martin replied, leading to a correspondence ending with Martin's death in 1976. Pronzini recounted his relationship with Robert Martin in a column for *Mystery Scene* #41 many years ago [reprinted as the introduction to *Little Sister*, also published by Stark House Press]. Pronzini included Robert Martin's name in a list of favorite authors to whom he dedicated his novel *Undercurrent*.

His most successful novel appears to have been *Little Sister*, a paperback original. It went through six U.S. printings. The "little sister" is a precocious bit of what is known in the vernacular as jailbait, the circumstances being a variation on *The Big Sleep*. As far as I know, this title did not appear as a British edition, although there are Canadian and Australian editions.

Despite the successes he achieved as a writer, Robert Martin did have a day job, a responsible position as personnel director for a

manufacturing company, as well as a wife and three children. Previously he was a bank teller. This work experience was a fruitful source of story material, but it also meant that writing could not be his highest priority. Though Martin's output sounds impressive, no full-time writer could have survived on that kind of income.

I have found several sources which either claim or at least suggest that Robert Martin lived in Cleveland (such as *Bluebook* for March 1954; *Mercury Mystery Book Magazine* for July, 1956; Bill Pronzini's tribute mentioned above; and certain editions of the German paperbacks). My research in Tiffin, Ohio city directories and phone books shows him to have always lived here. The Tiffin factory where he worked was owned by Cleveland-based interests at times, so that may be the source of the residency claims. And it might have been much easier to tell strangers he was from Cleveland, a place people knew about, rather than Tiffin of a more select fame. Tiffin is about 60 miles southeast of Toledo, and about 30 miles from Lake Erie. One of Martin's novels, *Killer Among Us*, centers around a factory 60 miles from Toledo.

I urge you to read a Bob Martin story. Discover for yourself that he's too good a writer to be forgotten.

[This article first appeared in *Mystery*File* #43, April 2004.]

THE PALE DOOR

ROBERT MARTIN
WRITING AS LEE ROBERTS

Once Again for VERTI

And travellers now, within that valley,
Through the red-litten windows see
Vast forms, that move fantastically
To a discordant melody,
While, like a ghastly rapid river,
Through the pale door
A hideous throng rush out forever,
And laugh—but smile no more.

FROM THE HAUNTED PALACE
BY EDGAR ALLAN POE

1

It was ten o'clock in the morning when Chad Proctor parked before the home of his friend, Dr. Walter Kerry. The sun was high and it glinted on the turning September leaves of the two maple trees on each side of the front walk. As he moved to the iron-railed stoop, Chad noticed that the doctor's black Packard sedan was still in the garage. He opened the front door, knowing that it would not be locked, and was about to enter when he heard the whine of a vacuum sweeper inside. He hesitated and then rang the bell. The sweeper sound died and a woman came to the door.

She was elderly and scrawny, with bright lipstick on her thin puckered lips. Her eyebrows were impossibly arched and penciled, and the brassy dyed tendrils of red hair protruded from beneath a gaily flowered bandanna tied around her head.

"I want to see Dr. Kerry," Chad said.

"I expect he's gone," she said in a cracked voice. "He's usually gone before I get here."

"What time do you get here?"

"Nine o'clock, mostly."

"His car is still in the garage," Chad said.

"Oh, is that so? I really didn't notice." Her bony hands fluttered to the tendrils of red hair. "I ain't cleaned his room yet. Sometimes he sleeps late—if folks get sick at night."

"Would you see?" Chad asked patiently. "It's rather important."

She smoothed the thin house dress down over her hips and arched her back so that her sagging breasts wearily lumped the material in a ghostly reminder of attractions long gone. "Are you sick?" she said curiously.

"No, I'm not sick. I just want to see the doctor."

She sighed dramatically. "The poor man needs his rest. Really—"

Chad pushed the door wide and stepped inside.

She stepped back and fluttered her eyelashes. "He's going away," she said hurriedly. "Him and the missus. He told me yesterday. But she ain't here. I already cleaned her room."

"Damn it," Chad blurted. "Call him. If you don't, I will."

She shrank from him like a maiden with her virtue menaced. For the first time Chad noticed that she was wearing scuffed saddle oxfords and bright green ankle socks. Her thin bare legs were lumpy with varicose veins. "Well!" she gasped. "Really—"

"Call him," Chad said grimly.

She hesitated, regarding him with old shrewd eyes. Then she smiled, showing the perfect teeth of her upper plate, and tossed her head airily. "Well, all right." She turned and undulated down the hall with her hands on her thin swaying hips.

Chad stepped into the living room and lowered himself into one of the two white leather chairs by the stone fireplace. An electric sweeper stood in the middle of the room, with various attachments scattered about. From down the hall he heard the woman's knuckles rapping on a door. Then her cracked voice called, "Dr. Kerry, Dr. Kerry ... Yoo-hoo."

There was silence then, and in the silence came a sound—the click of a door latch. Then more silence, perhaps thirty seconds of it. Chad stretched out his legs and closed his eyes. From the hall came a new sound, something which started on a low guttural note and climbed fast to a soprano screech.

Chad opened his eyes and jerked upright. It took him a small space of time to realize that the woman in the hall was screaming with a violence that threatened to split her wattled throat. He jumped to his feet, entered the hall and ran to where the woman was standing before an open door. She had stopped screaming and was making low whimpering sounds and gnawing at the back of one hand. Chad moved past her into the room. He stopped suddenly, numb with a wild mixed feeling of shock, of outrage, of sadness.

Dr. Walter Kerry lay on his back on the bed. He was wearing no coat, but was otherwise fully dressed, complete to black shoes and a neatly tied bow tie. There wasn't a lot of blood, but enough, and it stained the left side of his white shirt. His eyes were half open and the pupil of one was slightly off center. They held a glazed pulpy look. His jaw sagged open and Chad could see the dull glint of lower teeth. He lay peacefully, his arms at his sides.

Chad heard a thudding sound behind him. He turned slowly, pulling his gaze from a horror he felt could not be real. The woman was slumped to her knees against the far wall of the hall. As he watched, she slid slowly forward and doubled over. He stared at her dumbly, and then returned his gaze to what lay on the bed. Slowly he moved forward and bent down and his fingers felt a cold wrist. He saw at close range where the bullet had gone in and he knew that Dr. Kerry had been dead for several hours.

A jangling sound let loose from the hall. He started, and then took a deep shuddering breath, remembering that the telephone was in the hall. He moved out of the bedroom and down the hall, ignoring the woman on the floor, and the sadness and the bitter outrage flared

stronger within him. The telephone was on a small table near the front
door. He lifted the receiver, said, "Yes?" in an unsteady voice.

A woman's voice said, "Darling, darling, come and get me."

He knew the voice. "Where are you, Virginia?" he asked.

"At Sally's Harbor—it's a bar on Dorrence Street ... Darling, I need you.
I—I'm sorry about last night. I want to go with you."

He started to say, "All right," but his voice was a croak and he tried
again. "All right. Stay there. Do you hear?"

"Yes, yes, Walter. Please hurry."

He hung up slowly, trying to organize the turmoil of his thoughts. He
had talked to Virginia Kerry, the wife of the doctor, who thought she had
been talking to her husband. But Dr. Walter Kerry was dead, already
cold, with a bullet in his heart.

He became aware of a thick sighing behind him, and he turned.
Down the hall the woman was stirring a little and moaning, a thin eerie
sound. He moved to her, pulled her to her feet. She sagged against him,
her head lolling, and he almost gagged at the musky smell of heavy
perfume. Roughly he grasped her chin and shook her head. She opened
her eyes and her mouth and began to scream, the sound bleating
obscenely against his ears. He slapped her and shook her until she
stopped. Then he swung her around and pushed her down the hall. She
stumbled ahead of him, making thin whimpering sounds.

In the living room he guided her to a fawn-tinted divan where she
collapsed, her legs outspread, her eyes squeezed shut.

"Stay there," he said harshly and went to the kitchen. In a cupboard
he found some Scotch, and he carried the bottle and the two glasses back
into the living room. He poured a drink for the woman and one for
himself. She drank it avidly in one swallow, shuddered, and sank back
on the divan. The thin dress was twisted up over her wrinkled and
knobby knees.

Chad sipped at the Scotch and regarded her with distaste. Then he
said, "You arrived here at nine o'clock?"

"Yes." Her gaze was on the bottle in his hand.

He poured her another drink. "You didn't see the doctor or hear
anything?"

She cuddled the glass in her hands and shook her head. "I didn't hear
a peep from his room. She was gone and I thought he was gone." She
raised the glass, drank too fast and began to cough.

He placed the bottle on a low table near the divan and went out to the
telephone. He called the police department and asked for Lieutenant
Abner McKinney of Homicide. The Lieutenant was in his office and
Chad told him where he was and what he had found. He hung up before

the questions began. Then he returned to the living room, thinking bleakly of Virginia Kerry's desperate voice on the telephone: *Darling, come and get me.*

He said to the woman on the divan. "My name is Chad Proctor. I've got to leave now. The police will be here shortly. Tell them that I'll be back. Can you remember that?"

Her eyes were wide with terror. "You gonna leave me here—alone?"

"It won't be long," he said impatiently, trying to decide what she would look like without the lipstick, the eyebrow pencil and the phony red hair. Like a debauched grandmother, he thought, and said sternly, "Don't move around or touch anything."

As he left the room she reached for the bottle with a trembling hand.

It began a number of evenings previously when a man came around to Chad Proctor's apartment and sold him some life insurance. Chad felt that a private detective, and a bachelor at that, didn't have much use for life insurance, but the salesman was young and eager, with a wife and four small children to support, so Chad signed for a policy. Then he had to take a physical examination, and that is how he happened to see Dr. Walter Kerry on a certain night in September.

There were three women in the waiting room in addition to Ann Travis, Dr. Kerry's combination nurse, receptionist and secretary. Ann had long slim legs, a generous red mouth, brown eyes, shoulder-length black hair and a figure that a white starched uniform could not hide. She was twenty-three years old.

Chad knew Ann pretty well. In fact, for over a year they had been seeing each other often. They laughed a lot together and liked the same things. It had been more or less understood, Chad thought, that sooner or later they would get married, although he had never actually asked her to set a date. Looking at her now, he suddenly decided to bring up the subject that evening, if he got around to it. He hadn't seen her for two weeks because he'd been abruptly called out of a town.

As he sat down in a chair beside her desk, she said, "Well, hello."

"Hi," he replied happily. "I've been working in Akron—a rush job. I meant to call you, but—"

"I understand," she said coolly.

"It was a good job," Chad said, not noticing the coolness. "A rubber tycoon's wife was chasing around with a nineteen-year-old shipping clerk in her husband's factory, and the tycoon wanted evidence that would hold up in a divorce court, and I really got it for him. You see, the tycoon was nuts about his red-headed secretary, and—"

"I see," Ann broke in, her voice still cool.

Chad noticed it then. "What's the matter, honey?"

"Nothing."

"How about a drink when you get through here?" he asked. "There's something we should talk—" He stopped abruptly. For the first time he saw the diamond ring on her left hand, third finger. A big diamond, too big.

She saw his gaze on the ring and flushed faintly.

"You double-crossed me," Chad said, trying to keep it light, but feeling a sudden tightness in his chest and a bleak sense of loss. "I thought that we ..."

She looked down at some papers on her desk.

"A fine thing," he said stiffly. "I go away for a couple of weeks and you let some jerk sell you a bill of goods. A fine thing." He didn't know what else to say. It was a shock, that was certain. He had considered Ann his girl, but maybe he'd been too satisfied to let things pleasantly drift.

"Chad ..." She raised her eyes.

"You can't do this to me," he said. "Tell him you've changed your mind. Give him back his damned ring."

"Chad, I—"

A bell wired to the side of her desk tinkled gently. She stood up and nodded at one of the women sitting across the room. "You may go in now, Mrs. Bowers."

Mrs. Bowers, a squat heavy woman, heaved herself out of her chair and waddled to the door of the doctor's office. The two remaining women peered at her over the tops of magazines. Ann ushered Mrs. Bowers inside, returned to her desk and nervously began pushing papers around. Her eyes avoided Chad's.

"Who?" he asked.

"Jay Lawton."

"No!"

She looked at him defiantly. "Why not?"

He knew Jay Lawton. He knew a lot of people in Lake City and he had quite a few friends, but Jay Lawton was not one of them. Lawton dressed and acted like an aging sophomore, was big and blond with blue eyes and a disarmingly friendly smile—if you didn't notice the measuring coldness behind his eyes. He had drifted into Lake City a few months previously, and no one seemed to know his roots or background. Although he didn't work, as far as Chad knew, he seemed to have plenty of money. He drove a red Buick convertible, played the races out at Drake Park, was often seen in the better cocktail lounges, belonged to the second-best country club and shot sub-eighty golf. He was an expert poker player and frequently won, although Chad had seen him drop

several hundred and laugh it off. Gossip had it that Lawton was from California and had once been married to a movie starlet whose chief claim to fame was her startling mammary development. Chad knew Lawton slightly and the latter's breezy patronizing manner had never failed to irritate him.

"I didn't know you knew Jay," he said to Ann.

"I haven't very long. I met him at a party—get that look off your face."

"What look?" He tried to smile.

"That disapproving look. You'd like Jay—if you really knew him."

"Oh, sure," he said dismally, wondering what the hell was going on. It had happened too quickly. He was fairly certain that she hadn't been seeing Lawton before he went away—or had she? He and Ann had been together two or three times a week and their relationship had been pleasant, easy-going, sometimes passionate. But she was not promiscuous, he was certain of that, and he realized that he had assumed too much and that he did not want anyone else to have her.

"Chad," she said softly, "you—"

The bell on her desk tinkled again. Dr. Kerry had apparently treated Mrs. Bowers and had let her out of his side entrance. The two remaining women peered at Ann expectantly. She smiled at them, got up and opened the door to the doctor's office. They laid their magazines aside and stood up. As they moved side by side into the office, Chad saw that they were angular and dried-looking. Ann closed the door after them, returned to her desk and sat down. She sighed, removed the starched white cap perched on her black hair, and took a cigarette from a package in a drawer. Chad held a match for her.

"Sisters," she said, referring to the angular women. "Maiden ladies. They always have the same ailments, at the same time." She sighed again. "I hope that's all for tonight."

"What about me? I'm a patient."

She smiled. "There's nothing wrong with you. You probably bought some more life insurance."

He nodded. "That's right. A fellow got me in a weak moment."

"Chad, what do you have against Jay Lawton?"

"Not a thing. A charming personality."

She frowned. "Be serious. We've known each other—how long? Ever since I came to work for the doctor. I was a small town girl, just out of nurse's training. The first week I was here you came in, remember? I helped the doctor dress a bullet wound in your side. I was scared—I thought you were a gangster. Afterward the doctor told me who you were and what you did. I—I guess I fell a little in love with you that night ..."

"A fine time to tell me," he said, thinking sadly and at last that she was

all a man could want for a wife. But he had never considered marriage seriously. The kind of life he led wasn't the kind he wanted a wife to share, and he had been a bachelor so long that he instinctively shied away from marriage responsibilities and ties. He had his life, he thought. Maybe it wasn't much of a life, but it was his and he was reasonably happy. A wife would complicate things, might even make him ambitious and drive him to work harder, to get out of the business he was in, perhaps force him to yearn earnestly for a bigger and costlier automobile than his neighbor.

As head of the midwestern office of a national investigation agency he made enough money to satisfy his fairly simple needs. But with a wife, he thought, and maybe kids, it would be different. He wouldn't be working for just himself any longer, but for a family, and he would lose all his selfish pleasures and cease to be an individual. He would become a breadwinner, a husband, maybe a father, drowned in a sea of smothering responsibilities, and he couldn't reconcile such a life with the around-the-clock job of investigation for the private citizens and corporations who desired the services of the agency.

Maybe someday he would marry and settle down. But now he had nothing to offer a wife, nothing but irregular hours, a collection of odd friends, a three-room apartment, a couple of dozen books dealing mostly with criminal investigation, a liking for martinis and rare steaks and a job that often required him to be away from home days on end. Marriage wasn't for him, not yet, he had thought; but now as he gazed at Ann Travis he felt again the sense of loss. Maybe he could talk her out of it, but not right now. He would think about it and give it a try. Maybe he could still have his cake and all that. But why had she picked a man like Jay Lawton?

"I want you to like him," she said.

"Sure." He tried to grin at her. "Like a brother."

Her lips parted as if to speak and then she lowered her gaze and crushed out her cigarette. "Chad," she said in a low voice, "I—I guess I'm just too normal. It seems that I want a home and kids, like twenty million other girls."

"Sure," he said again. "All the best."

She looked at him and he saw the tears in her eyes.

Suddenly he leaned across the desk and kissed her. She didn't draw away, and it was a nice kiss, warm and clinging, warmer than many kisses she had given him, and his resolution wavered; maybe now was the time for him to ask her. If he waited, he might really lose her. A sudden odd panic seized him. He moved his lips away from hers, intending to speak, to say something, and it was then that he saw the

man standing in the doorway.

There was an amused smile on the man's face as he closed the door quietly and leaned against it, his hands in the pockets of a plaid jacket. He wore gray flannel slacks and a midnight blue sport shirt. He was hatless and his blond hair was neatly combed and parted on the side. His eyes were a clear blue, his chin firm and square beneath a full-lipped mouth that held a suggestion of looseness.

He said pleasantly, "Hello, there, Proctor, old boy."

"Hello, Jay."

Jay Lawton sauntered over to the desk. "I love you very much," he said to Ann Travis, "but I'm afraid I don't approve of ex-boyfriends kissing you." He winked at Chad to show that he really meant no ill-will. "I don't blame you, Proctor, but I came to take her home. Is that all right with you?"

"She doesn't work for me," Chad said.

Lawton's faintly contemptuous gaze took in the neat and plainly furnished waiting room. "I've been trying to get her to quit this two-bit job."

Ann Travis said quickly, "I've told you, Jay—the doctor needs me and I'm staying until he can find another girl."

Lawton smiled tolerantly, lifted his wide shoulders and said to Chad, "You can see who's boss."

"Jay," Ann said, "I—"

The door to the inner office opened and Dr. Walter Kerry stepped out. He was a short man, nearing forty, with the thick body of a wrestler. His hair was black, thinning on top, and he had a strong, tough-looking face, with keen brown eyes behind dark-rimmed glasses. His buttoned white jacket seemed to accentuate his thick stature. Light glinted on his glasses as he nodded to the three persons in his waiting room. "Is that all for tonight?" he asked Ann Travis.

"All except Chad."

The doctor grinned. "He looks healthy. How about some golf Sunday, Chad?"

"Sorry," Chad said. "I'll be out of town."

Jay Lawton said, "How about me, Doc? Ten bucks a hole?"

The doctor shook his head. "Too steep. Ten cents is more my speed."

Lawton laughed. "Hell, you can't make any money that way. I'll spot you twenty strokes."

"For nine holes?" the doctor asked innocently.

"Hey, Doc, wait," Lawton protested. "I'm not that good. Twenty strokes on eighteen holes, a hundred on the round. Okay?"

"Jay," the doctor said, "I'm afraid you're too mercenary." He turned to Chad. "You wanted to see me?"

"Just an insurance check-up," Chad said, handing him a form the insurance salesman had given him. "Got time?"

"Sure. Go on in and sit down."

Chad moved into the doctor's office, not looking at Ann Travis. She said softly, "Good-night, Chad."

"Good-night," he said without turning, and sat down in a leather chair beside the doctor's neat glass-topped desk.

Behind him he heard the soft voice of Ann speaking to the doctor, and the loud laugh of Jay Lawton. The outer door slammed and Dr. Kerry entered the office and closed the door. He sat behind the desk, spread out the form Chad had given him, and unscrewed the cap of a fountain pen. "More insurance, huh?"

Chad sighed. "I'm afraid so."

"Again?" the doctor said, smiling. He began to write on the form.

Chad said, "What about Ann and Lawton?"

Dr. Kerry lifted his heavy shoulders. "They're in love, I guess, but I rather thought that you and Ann ..."

"So did I," Chad said ruefully. "He must be a fast worker. I leave town for a couple of weeks and when I come home she's engaged to the guy."

"Too bad," the doctor said. "Or aren't you the marrying kind?"

"Hell," Chad sighed. "I don't know. I never thought much about it. I liked her fine, but—"

"I know," the doctor broke in wearily. "I like her, too, and I hate to lose her—but I can always get another nurse."

"I can get another girl, too," Chad said bitterly. "But—oh, to hell with it."

"Chad," the doctor said quietly, "I'm sorry."

"When did it begin? This big affair with Jay Lawton?"

"I don't know exactly. A couple of weeks ago he began coming here to take her home, and Ann introduced me to him. And then, three or four days ago, she showed me a ring and said she was going to marry him. I was surprised and thought it rather sudden. She said she'd stay as long as I needed her, so I haven't been in any hurry about hiring another girl."

"She said she met him at a party," Chad said.

Dr. Kerry smiled. "I doubt that. Ann isn't much of a party girl—especially when you're away. I think she met him right here. He came to me first as a patient—sinus trouble, he said. But he just had a slight nasal congestion, like most people have at one time or another. I treated him twice, I think, and then discharged him. After that he began to call for Ann almost every night." He poised his pen over the insurance form. "Do you use alcohol?"

"Occasionally," Chad said, grinning. "At wakes or weddings, when it's

forced upon me."

Dr. Kerry sighed. "They could lift my license for this." Chad saw him write *Moderately* on the form.

The telephone on the desk jangled. The doctor picked it up, said quietly, "Dr. Kerry."

In the quiet office Chad heard a voice coming clearly over the wire: *Doc, it's bad news again. I'm sorry, but we picked her up driving without lights over on the east side. We've got her here at the station and she's in bad shape, not fit to drive ...*

The doctor's thick shoulders seemed to sag. "All right," he said in a tired voice. "I'll be down. Thanks, Sergeant." Slowly he replaced the phone and screwed the cap back on his pen. "I'm sorry, Chad," he said, averting his gaze, "I've got to leave."

"That's all right, Walter."

The doctor stood up and unbuttoned his white jacket.

Chad hesitated and then said, "Look, it's none of my business, but I heard what the sergeant said. If I can help ..."

Dr. Kerry removed the jacket and laid it on the desk, his expression bleak and remote. He removed his glasses and rubbed his eyes slowly with a thumb and forefinger. His hands were big and clean-looking, with blunt fingers and coarse black hair on the backs of them. "Thanks, Chad," he said wearily, "but I'm afraid this is my personal little hell. There's nothing you can do, or anybody. I—I don't know what's happened to Virginia—it's been very bad this past year." He sighed and hooked the glasses over his small flat ears.

Chad knew about Virginia Kerry. She was a gray-eyed blonde, about ten years younger than her husband. A year ago, he remembered, their first child had been born dead. Dr. Kerry had told him about it, briefly, and had never mentioned it again, but Chad knew that it had changed Virginia Kerry, or something had. Ever since, she had been drinking heavily and had been seen alone in many of the bars around the city. He knew her slightly, having met her but a few times at stag poker parties at the doctor's house. On several occasions he had encountered her on the street or in a bar, but she had not recognized him, or had pretended not to; and since she had been obviously drunk, he had refrained from speaking to her. He felt sorry for her, but he felt sorrier for his friend, Dr. Kerry.

He said gently, "Walter, you'll need someone to drive her car home, I can do that."

The doctor moved to a closet and took out his hat and coat. "All right, Chad," he said. "If you're sure you don't mind."

2

The police were discreet about it. Dr. Walter Kerry was liked and respected in the midwestern metropolis of Lake City. In the days when he was starting practice he had served as medical examiner for the county. He and Chad got Virginia Kerry out of the station and into his black Packard sedan without much trouble. She hung limply between them, her head down, her ash blonde hair falling over her face. She was wearing gray flannel slacks, brown moccasins and a tight turtle-neck black sweater which clung snugly to her small high breasts and slender waist. As they put her in the front seat of the Packard, she mumbled something thick and meaningless, and Chad thought sadly that drunks were pretty much alike, no matter who they were.

The desk sergeant followed them out to the parking area behind the station and said, apologetically, "I'm sorry as hell, Doc, but we had to pick her up. She might have had a bad accident. You know in this state drunk driving carries a mandatory jail sentence, but we didn't book her ..."

"Thanks," the doctor said in a tight voice. "I appreciate it. I'll try and keep her out of trouble."

"I wish you would, Doc," the sergeant said in a worried voice. "Some night she's gonna—"

"I know," the doctor said sharply. He got behind the wheel of the Packard.

The sergeant pointed to a Plymouth station wagon parked nearby. "There's her car. The keys are in it."

"I'll drive it home for you," Chad said to the doctor.

"All right." The Packard moved slowly down the ramp to the street.

The sergeant looked at Chad and shook his head. "A hell of a thing. Doc's such a swell guy. You've been friends with him a long time, haven't you?"

"Yes."

The sergeant sighed. "What makes 'em do it? She's young, good looking, got a man like Doc for a husband, a nice home, plenty of money ..." He sighed again. "She's gonna get plastered some night and kill herself and maybe somebody else, too."

"Yes," Chad said again, and got into the Plymouth.

The sergeant leaned in the window. "There was a bottle of bourbon on the seat, half full. We got it in the station."

"Keep it," Chad said.

The sergeant grinned. "Thanks, Chad. Maybe I'll have a little snort

when I go off duty."

"Do that." Chad drove the Plymouth down to the street.

Dr. Walter Kerry's moderately-sized white frame house was on Ridge Road in a new development not far from the lake and surrounded by well-kept lawn and shrubbery. The houses were spaced far apart and the nearest neighbor was almost a block away. As Chad turned the Plymouth into the drive, he saw that the doctor's Packard was already in one side of the two-car garage. Its lights were still on and the doctor was lifting his wife from the front seat. Chad got out and went to help. Between them they carried Virginia Kerry up a flagstone walk to a rear door. As they entered and crossed a brightly lighted kitchen, Chad noticed that the refrigerator door was standing open and that beside the sink there was a tray of melting ice cubes, a glass and an empty whisky bottle. They went through a darkened dining room and entered a long living room with a bare polished floor partially covered by shaggy white rugs. A huge window took up most of one wall, and at the far end was a stone fireplace with two white leather chairs beside it.

Sitting quietly in one of the chairs was a dark young man with thick black hair combed straight back from a broad white forehead. He had a rather long nose, slightly aquiline, heavy black brows, a full red-lipped mouth. He wore a dark gray suit, a white shirt with a stiff collar, a plain black necktie and polished black shoes with pointed toes. A black Homburg lay on the floor beside him.

As Chad and the doctor entered the room, the young man got quickly to his feet, his eyes widening at the sight of the limp figure in their arms. He stood still and smiled a little uncertainly. Chad saw he was tall and slender with wide spare shoulders. The dark suit was ill-fitting and his shirt collar looked too tight.

Dr. Kerry said, "Hello, Sam," and kept moving toward an archway beyond the fireplace. His wife's pale hair fell away from her face and her eyes were closed. At the archway the doctor said to Chad, "I can handle her now."

Chad released his hold on the woman. Across the hall, through an open door, he saw a softly-lit bedroom. The doctor carried his wife into the bedroom and closed the door. Chad turned and faced the dark young man, who was still standing by the chair.

"Mrs. Kerry is ill?" he asked Chad. He had a soft rich voice with a whisper of accent,

"Yes," Chad said.

The young man opened his mouth as if to speak, and then closed it. Chad said, "My name's Proctor."

The young man smiled hesitantly, and held out a hand. "I am Dr.

Hamid. I have been waiting to see Dr. Kerry." He pronounced each word carefully and slowly.

Chad took the offered hand. It was smooth and soft, but the fingers held a firm pressure. He guessed Dr. Hamid to be about thirty, his own age. At close range he saw that his eyes were brown, large and liquid-looking. His skin was smooth, but the roots of his beard showed bluish-black. He offered Chad a long, oval gilt-tipped cigarette from a tooled leather case. Chad took one, and Dr. Hamid flicked flame from a silver lighter of a curious Oriental design. Chad inhaled and coughed a little. It was Turkish tobacco, strong and sweet.

"Thanks," Chad said. "Walter will be back in a few minutes."

Dr. Hamid said in his soft rich voice, "I hope that Mrs. Kerry ..."

"She'll be all right," Chad said.

A door opened and closed and Dr. Kerry stepped into the room. He lowered himself into a deep chair and sighed. There was the pallor of fatigue and worry on his broad, heavy face.

Dr. Hamid stooped and picked up the black Homburg. "I wanted to see you, Doctor," he said, "but some other time will do. The front door was open, and I thought that you would be home soon ..." He moved toward the hall.

"Don't go, Sam," Dr. Kerry said. "Virginia never locks doors, or turns off lights." He nodded at Chad. "This is my friend, Chad Proctor."

Dr. Hamid smiled. His teeth were strong-looking and very white. "We have had the pleasure of meeting."

"What's on your mind, Sam?" Dr. Kerry said, smiling a little. "Get hold of something that isn't in the book?"

"It is not important," Dr. Hamid said with a deprecating smile. "Tomorrow, perhaps ..."

"All right, Sam—I am tired. I'll be making house calls in the morning, but I'll be in the office after one o'clock. Call me then." He smiled again. "Will your patient live that long?"

"I am sure she will," Dr. Hamid said, smiling. He nodded at Chad and went out.

Dr. Kerry slumped deeper in his chair. "Poor Sam," he said. "He worries too much. Probably got an overdue maternity case. Young doctors never seem to realize that women usually figure their last menstrual period wrong, but he'll learn. I'm afraid that part of his trouble is that he isn't much interested in general practice."

"No?"

"He wants to specialize in the fields of psychiatry and psychology, a worthy ambition. But he must earn a living first, like all of us. He has a rather unusual background."

"What's that?"

"Well, for one thing," the doctor said, "he's a devout Mohammedan. He was born in Istanbul and got his degree at a medical college in Ankara. He came to the States about two years ago, took some psychiatric work at Columbia, and came out here. A friend of mine on the staff at Columbia wrote me to kind of look after him. His name is Mustapha, but I call him Sam. I've sent him a few patients, and I don't mind helping him, but tonight ..." He made a helpless gesture.

Chad said, "Well, I'll be running along."

"No, don't go yet. I'll make us a drink."

Chad looked at the doctor's haggard face. "You're working too hard, Walter."

The doctor took off his glasses and rubbed his eyes. "I know it," he said wearily. "Most of us do. But people depend upon us and I can't get hard-boiled enough to say, 'No.'" He smiled faintly, but Chad saw the naked pain and worry in his eyes. "Bourbon?"

"All right." Chad sat in the chair vacated by Dr. Hamid.

The doctor got up and left the room. Chad crushed out the Turkish cigarette with a grimace of distaste. He gazed across the hall at the closed bedroom door. No sound came from behind it. In a few minutes Dr. Kerry entered carrying two tall glasses. He handed one to Chad and sat once more in the deep chair, his short thick legs stretched out before him. He drank from his glass and then leaned his head back and closed his eyes. "Chad," he said, "what the hell am I going to do?"

Chad lit a cigarette. It tasted much better than the one Dr. Hamid had given him. "She's a grown woman," he said carefully, exhaling smoke. "If she wants to keep on drinking as she has been, nothing will stop her—unless you keep her locked up."

"I can't do that," the doctor said miserably. He paused and opened his eyes. "I—I don't know what happened to her. Ever since she lost the baby ..." He took another swallow of his drink.

Chad didn't say anything.

The doctor finished his drink and the ice clinked in the bottom of his glass. He stood up and took Chad's half-empty glass. "I'll sweeten it up," he said, and started out of the room. At the door he turned, his face worried and grave. "It started right afterward—almost as soon as she left the hospital—and it got worse. If it was just liquor—well, I think I could handle that. But something makes her drink, maybe the loss of the baby ..." He moved an arm helplessly. "It's driving me crazy. When she's sober, she won't talk to me about it—I can't seem to get to her. She's like a woman in a dream world of her own. She makes promises to me, and then I'll get a call from some bar, or from the police ..."

"I know," Chad said gently. "I've seen her around."

"I suppose you have," the doctor said bitterly. "A lot of others have, too. It's bad for my practice, but I'm helpless." He looked down at the glasses in his hands. "Virginia and I have been married for twelve years—ever since I graduated from Ohio State."

"How about her parents? Couldn't they help?"

The doctor shook his head. "They're both dead, and she has no brothers or sisters. Her only relatives are a few cousins and a couple of aunts and uncles." He sighed deeply. "Once I talked her into seeing a psychiatrist, a good one, too. But it didn't work. I think she hated me for it. The only thing I haven't tried is a mental hospital, and that would kill her. I'm at the end of my rope. I can't let her go on the way she has, and I don't know how to stop her." He looked at Chad and smiled crookedly. "Well, this isn't getting a drink for us." He turned abruptly and left the room.

Chad sat quietly smoking. People, he thought, people and trouble. Everybody had trouble, no matter how carefree they seemed to others. Why did trouble have to be a part of living? Was anyone completely happy? Was he, Chad Proctor, happy? He thought of Ann Travis and decided that he was not. Maybe he could talk her out of marrying Jay Lawton, but did he want to do that? Would he be happy married to Ann? Would she be happy with him? He didn't know; he only knew that he was unhappy now. And why had she picked a phony like Lawton? He stabbed out his cigarette with a vicious motion.

Dr. Kerry entered the living room carrying a glass and a saucer bearing a cup of steaming coffee. He handed the glass to Chad and said, "I changed my mind—decided to have coffee instead of whisky. It's a habit that dates back to medical school, when I used to study all night. Want some?"

Chad shook his head and lifted his glass. "This is fine."

The telephone began to ring. The doctor sighed, placed the saucer on a table and moved into the hall. Chad heard him say, "I'm sorry, but I'd rather not tonight. If you can get someone else ..." He came back into the room and sat down. "I don't often turn down a call," he said to Chad, "but it wasn't an emergency, and I'll probably have to go out later tonight anyhow—got a woman in the hospital who may need surgery before morning." He looked at Chad. "You see?" he said. "I can't look after Virginia."

"I know."

The doctor sipped his coffee and said thoughtfully, "We damn near starved the first year, Virginia and I. But she helped me. I don't know what I would have done without her—probably taken a staff job in some hospital. That was a bad year. I was in debt for my instruments, drugs,

car—everything. Some months we went hungry so that we could pay the office rent. We lived in one room above the office, a fire trap on the north side. What patients I had couldn't afford to pay me, but we stuck it out. She was wonderful." He paused, a glow in his eyes, remembering.

Chad waited silently.

"But it was fun," the doctor went on, "in those days. Virginia took nurse's training so that she could help me more, and she never lost faith in me. Later on, when things got better, I moved the office uptown. I got busier and busier and was able to hire a nurse, and I didn't need Virginia anymore. We built this house and for a time she seemed fairly happy taking care of it, but it wasn't the same. I suppose it was my fault. My practice became more and more demanding and she was alone much of the time. She became nervous and restless, and we thought that a baby would help, and it did—until it was born dead, and she knew that she couldn't have any more. After that ..." He lifted his thick shoulders.

Chad said, "Can I do anything?"

The doctor took off his glasses and began to wipe them with a handkerchief. "Chad, I've been thinking—I don't blame Virginia, really. As I say, it's probably my fault for neglecting her. She used to know the symptoms of all my patients, the case histories, when little Joey Smith was due for his typhoid shots, when babies were due, what house calls were necessary—all the stuff that Ann handles now. Maybe if I asked Virginia to help me again ..."

Chad shook his head. "I'm afraid it's too late for that. Why don't you take her away for a while? Just the two of you." He paused and smiled. "Pretend that it's a second honeymoon."

The doctor smiled grimly. "Maybe it's too late for that, too."

"But you can try it," Chad said. "You need a vacation yourself. Go up to that cabin you've got on the lake. There's wooded land there and squirrel season will be in pretty soon. Just relax, do a little hunting, and—"

"No hunting," the doctor broke in, smiling. "I never shot a gun in my life. Don't know a damn thing about them. Never had the time for that sort of thing—hunting, fishing or any hobbies. I play a little golf now, but that's all. Virginia keeps a pistol in her dresser drawer—God knows why. Her father gave it to her, years ago, before he died." He drank coffee and said quietly, "I'd be happy just to be alone with Virginia for a while—but I'm afraid it's not possible."

"Why not?"

"Oh, I've thought of it, but I never seem to be able to get away. My patients ..."

"To hell with them," Chad said. "What would they do if you broke a leg?

They'd get another doctor, wouldn't they? Your wife comes first. Take her away, get acquainted with her all over again."

"It's easy for you to say that," the doctor said, "but I've got appointments for months ahead."

"Cancel 'em."

"I can't do that."

Neither of them spoke for several minutes. Then the doctor said, "Chad."

"Yes."

"She's getting worse, Chad. It's either take her away—or put her away. I just can't let her run around loose anymore."

"No," Chad said.

The doctor said slowly, "I've got an idea—how about you watching her for a week or two, until I can take her away? Just keep track of her and head off trouble. Does that come under the head of investigation?"

"You mean sort of a bodyguard?"

"Something like that, although I wouldn't want her know it. Could you manage that?"

"I think so, but—"

"At your agency's regular fees, of course. This would be strictly a business arrangement."

"It isn't that," Chad said. "I'd do it for you, if I could. When would you want me to start?"

"Now— tonight. I'll wind things up in a week or ten days, arrange for one of the other men to take my practice, and then we'll go away, for as long as necessary. If that doesn't work ..." The doctor shook his head hopelessly.

"Maybe this Dr. Hamid would take care of some of your patients? You've helped him."

"Sure he would, and he's competent, too. But there's more to it than that. It means closing my office, notifying everyone, arranging things at the hospital—I'm chief of staff at Lakeview, you know, and president of the County Medical Association. God knows how long I'll be gone. I just can't walk out on everything."

"I see," Chad said.

"Will you watch Virginia until I can get away?" There as almost a pleading note in the doctor's voice. "You're the only one I would trust."

"Walter," Chad said, "I'm sorry, but I can't. Not right how. I've got to be in Detroit tomorrow—personally. A special job for the Treasury Department. It'll take a week, at least. After that, I'll be glad to help."

"I can't leave her alone for a week," the doctor said bleakly. "I'm afraid to leave her alone for another hour."

Chad hesitated, and then said, "How about one of my men watching her—until I get back?"

Dr. Kerry looked at him quickly. "A reliable man?"

"Yes."

"You'll vouch for him personally?"

"Yes."

"Get him," the doctor said.

Chad got up and went to the telephone in the hall.

3

Edward Stewart Doyle looked a little like a Cherokee Indian. He was slender, six feet tall, with a lean face, black eyes, high cheek bones and closely-clipped black hair. At Michigan State he had been an All-American halfback, a fact which did not prevent him from graduating from law school. For a year he had been legal counsel for a trade union, and had served four years in the U.S. Navy as a commissioned officer on a mine sweeper. After the war he worked for the F.B.I., and became acquainted with a field man of the agency employing Chad Proctor. The work of a private investigator on a national scale interested Doyle, and he applied for a job. Because of his law degree, his F.B.I. experience, and his general qualifications he was hired and sent to the agency training school in Pennsylvania. He had built up a good record in the east before he had been assigned to the Lake City office six months previously. Chad liked him and had found him intelligent, courageous and efficient. He was not married and lived in a small hotel on a side street near the center of the city.

When Chad called him, he answered the phone immediately. "Doyle speaking," he said in his quiet voice.

"Ed, this is Chad."

"Hi, boss."

"What're you doing?"

"Relaxing."

"Alone?"

"Well, not exactly." Doyle laughed softly. In the background Chad heard the sound of music. "We're just playing records and having a few drinks."

"I don't suppose you feel like working?"

"Now?"

"Yes."

Chad heard Doyle sigh, and he said, "I'm sorry, Ed. Give my apologies

to the lady."

Doyle sighed again. "Okay, boss."

"Business before pleasure, and all that," Chad said, thinking that if Ed Doyle had a weakness, it was women, preferably blondes. He gave him Dr. Kerry's address. "Do you know where that is?"

"I'll find it, if I must."

"Right away."

"Give me twenty minutes."

"Thanks, Ed."

"Right-o," Doyle said, and hung up.

Chad returned to the living room, told Dr. Kerry about Ed Doyle and said that he was on his way over. The doctor appeared satisfied and offered Chad another drink. Chad refused, but said he'd have some coffee. The doctor went to the kitchen to make more and Chad helped him. They had two cups each while they waited for Doyle. Twice the doctor entered the bedroom to look at his wife.

Presently Doyle arrived and Chad introduced him to the doctor. As always, Doyle was immaculately dressed. He wore a gray flannel suit, a dark blue knit tie and dark brown shoes. In his hand he held a brown felt hat. He stood quietly in the living room, the light slanted down on his lean Indian-like face.

Dr. Kerry shook hands with him, smiled, and said to Chad, "He doesn't look like a detective."

"He's not supposed to," Chad said. "That's what fools people. Did you expect him to have a bottle of rye in a coat jacket and a blonde hanging on his arm?"

"Perhaps," Dr. Kerry said dryly. "After all, Chad, you're the only detective I know, and you look like a high school football coach."

Chad reached out and plucked a long golden hair from the sleeve of Doyle's coat. "I take it back about the blonde," he said, "but I'm sure you'll never see Ed with a whisky bottle in his pocket." He grinned at Doyle. "Anyhow, not when he's on duty."

Doyle smiled, watching Chad for the tip-off. Chad told him quickly and as tactfully as possible about Virginia Kerry, and what was required of him. When he had finished, Doyle said quietly, "I understand. I watch this house. If Mrs. Kerry goes out, I follow her, no matter what time of the day or night. I don't speak to her, or let her know that I am following her. I just stay with her, and approach her or interfere with her actions only if the situation demands it. If I think it necessary, I call Dr. Kerry."

Chad nodded and looked at the doctor questioningly.

Dr. Kerry said grimly, "I guess that's about it."

Chad said to Doyle, "I'm going to Detroit in the morning—expect to

be gone about a week. Ben Durstin is due in from Toledo sometime tonight. I'll leave word at the office to relieve you. The two of you will have to work twelve-hour shifts until I get back. Call the office around noon tomorrow and tell Ben where you are. Mrs. Kerry will probably not leave the house tonight, but if she does, stay with her. Dr. Kerry may be called out before morning, but pay no attention. Your job is to stay with Mrs. Kerry. Got it?"

"Right-o," Doyle said.

Chad had learned that Doyle's "Right-o," spoken with a faintly affected English accent, was a sort of unconscious habit acquired, Doyle had once explained, from a friend in Washington who had been attached to the British Embassy.

"Where did you park?" Chad asked him.

"Across the street—down a little ways."

"Where you can see both the front and rear entrance of this house?"

"I think so."

"Good." Chad hesitated, and then said, "Ed, I want to tell you that Dr. Kerry is a close friend of mine. We're both counting on you."

"I understand."

"Any questions?"

"Could I have a description of Mrs. Kerry? Or a photo?"

Chad looked at the doctor. "Do you have a photo?"

The doctor shook his head. "I'm afraid not—no recent ones, anyhow. Why not let him take a look at her? She's sound asleep now."

Doyle said, "If you're certain that we won't disturb her ..."

"We won't," the doctor said grimly. "This way." He moved across the hall to the bedroom door. Chad and Ed Doyle followed him. Quietly the doctor opened the door and stepped into a dark room. He turned, motioned the two men to enter, and whispered, "I'll turn on a light."

Chad and Doyle stepped into the room and waited silently in the darkness. They heard the movements of the doctor and could vaguely see him groping for a lamp. Then there was a faint click and a shaded lamp on a low dressing table came on, filling the room with a soft glow. Against one wall was a bed covered with a pale blue silken spread. Virginia Kerry lay on top of the bed. She was no longer wearing the black sweater, the gray flannel slacks, or the moccasins. They were scattered on the floor besides the bed along with a small wispy head of underclothing and a light blanket with which the doctor had evidently covered her. She lay on her back, one leg slightly bent, her arms at her sides. Her lips were parted a little and she was breathing deeply and steadily. She slept relaxed and peacefully, like an exhausted child sleeps, and the light made a soft sheen over her long slender legs, the

firm white thighs and the small high breasts. A faded white scar ran the length of her abdomen.

Chad and Doyle stared at her dumbly, too surprised to speak or move. Dr. Kerry turned away from the lamp, saw his wife. With a smothered exclamation he hurried to the bed and folded the silken spread over the naked loveliness. He turned to the two men with an embarrassed smile and spoke in a low voice. "I'm sorry. She was dressed when I looked at her last, but she's in the habit of sleeping nude and I suppose she aroused sufficiently to take off her clothes—an instinctive subconscious action."

"Yes," Chad said, remembering the vision of Virginia Gerry.

Ed Doyle said nothing.

The doctor said to Doyle, "Well, there she is. I can probably dig up a snapshot, but it won't be recent."

Doyle gazed at the face of the sleeping woman. "I'll remember her," he said shortly. He turned and moved to the door. Chad followed him, and the doctor turned off the light.

In the living room Doyle said to Chad, "Well, I'll go to work."

Chad said, "I'll be at the Book-Cadillac in Detroit if you want me."

"Right-o." Doyle nodded at the doctor and went out.

"Chad," the doctor said, "your man impresses me favorably."

"You can count on Ed."

"What about this other fellow you mentioned? The one who will relieve Doyle?"

"Durstin? Hell, Ben's with me for five years. They don't come any better."

"Good." The doctor sighed. "That was a hell of a thing—about Virginia. I never thought that she'd be—"

The telephone rang again. Dr. Kerry entered the hall, spoke briefly, and returned. "It's the hospital—the call I've been expecting. I've got to leave. You can drive Virginia's car home, if you like. I'll have it picked up tomorrow."

"Thanks but I'll get a taxi."

The doctor put on his coat and hat and gazed thoughtfully at the closed door across the hall. "I hope she'll be all right."

"Don't worry," Chad said. He called a taxi and then walked out to the garage with the doctor. Across the street he could see the dark bulk of the agency Ford parked beneath a maple tree. He touched Dr. Kerry's arm and pointed. "That's Doyle. He'll be there all night, unless she leaves, and then he'll stay right with her."

"It's a load off my mind, Chad, and I appreciate it. I—"

"You'll get a bill," Chad said, grinning.

"You can't put a price on a thing like this," the doctor said soberly. "Whatever the cost, it'll be cheap." He held out a hand. "Thanks, Chad— and be careful in Detroit."

"Walter," Chad said, "I'm sorry I can't do this for you personally, but everything is set in Detroit, waiting for me. It's something I can't duck."

"I understand," the doctor said. "If you say your man is reliable, that's good enough for me."

"I'll be back in about a week. If you still need me, I'll take over then."

"It doesn't matter. Just so somebody looks after her—until I can."

The doctor got into the Packard and Chad watched him back out of the drive and disappear up the street. Then he crossed the lawn to the agency Ford parked at the curb and leaned in the window. Ed Doyle had the radio turned softly to a dance band and was smoking a cigarette.

"Doc had to leave, huh?" Doyle said.

"He went to the hospital. You all set?"

"Sure."

"Plenty of cigarettes?"

Doyle nodded. "And a chocolate bar besides."

"Gun?"

"Yep." Doyle laughed softly. "Do you think I'll need it—on a soft job like this?"

"No, but the book says you've got to carry one. What do you think of Mrs. Kerry?"

"Nice."

"She's a dipso."

"I gathered that. Too bad."

"I was sorry to drag you away from your lady friend," Chad said.

"That's all right," Doyle said carelessly. "She'll keep."

A car with a yellow dome light came slowly up the street. "That's my taxi," Chad said. "Take it easy, son."

"Sure."

Chad stepped out and waved at the taxi.

As he rode across town, he thought of the naked body of Virginia Kerry with disturbing vividness. She had strongly attracted him, even though she was the wife of his friend. He had never seen her like that, so completely defenseless and so peaceful, and it had reached out to him. He remembered Dr. Kerry's embarrassment, and he felt embarrassed for him. But why should he? She was the doctor's wife, not his, and it was very strange.

He thought of Ann Travis, too, and of Jay Lawton, and he had a sick, sad, uneasy feeling. Suddenly he wanted to talk to Ann, to tell her that Lawton was not the kind of man for her, not for Ann. But that would be

juvenile, he thought. Ann was mature, wise enough to know her own mind. Maybe he could call her, tell her that he was going away in the morning and say good-bye. It would be a reason for calling her, and no harm in it.

The taxi took him to where he'd left the agency Ford, the twin of the one Ed Doyle was driving, parked outside Dr. Kerry's office, and he drove it back across the city. He came to an intersection, saw the lights of an all-night drugstore and pulled over to the curb. He called Ann from a booth in the store, but she didn't answer. He stood in the booth, feeling the disappointment and the ugly stirring of jealousy. She's with Lawton, he thought, somewhere. He looked in the book for Lawton's number, found that it wasn't listed, and dialed information. A crisp female voice told him that Mr. Lawton lived in an apartment house at 689 71st Street and gave him a phone number. Chad thanked the voice and started to dial. Then he stopped, jeering at himself. If Lawton was home, and Ann was with him, what would he say? Is my girl there, you bastard? What's the idea? It's midnight and she needs her sleep, and I don't like it ...

He left the booth, feeling the jealousy and the sense of loss. He'd had her, and he'd lost her, and to hell with it. Buck up, Proctor, there are a million other women, around every corner, in every bar, just waiting to meet you. How about a drink, Proctor? Just to drown your sorrow? Go ahead, if you really want to be juvenile. To hell with that, too. Proctor, the thing for you to do, in a situation like this, is to go home and get the hell to bed. You're going to the metropolis of Detroit in the morning and when you get back maybe they'll be married and all best wishes to the happy couple. Why don't you worry about a client for a change? Dr. Walter Kerry, for example, your friend who really has bad trouble. Maybe when you return from Detroit that situation will be cleared up, too, all tied in a pretty bow, like the ribbon on a wedding present. Ed Doyle will do a good job, you can count on that, and Doc understands why you can't handle it yourself.

Go to bed, Proctor, and get some sleep, for the dawn is coming.

He drove slowly through the streets and when he came to 71st he turned right. It was located on the northern fringe of the city close to the lake in an area known as The Flats. In years gone by it had been a genteel residential section, but with the coming of industry and lake shipping the fine old Victorian houses had been converted one by one into apartments for the dock and mill workers. The once green lawns were now rutted and weedy, littered with stacks of rotting lumber and odd pieces of rusty metal. On almost every block there was a tavern, built mostly with drab cement block, and all were lighted and filled with

customers. Number 689 was at the far end of the street, a towering, gabled, frame structure with peeling paint and sagging steps leading to a wide front porch and a glass door opening into a lighted vestibule. The number was painted on the glass and Chad could see it from where he parked across the street.

He sat for a while, watching the place where Jay Lawton lived, wondering if he were there, if Ann was with him. He knew he was acting badly, like a lovesick kid, and he was faintly ashamed, even though he knew that up until now he had never really realized what Ann Travis meant to him—now that he had lost her. He reached for the ignition key, intending to leave, and then he paused. As long as he was here, he thought, he may as well see what kind of a dump Lawton lived in. No harm in that, he told himself, not letting himself think that Ann might be there with him. He gazed up and down the street. There were a number of parked cars, but none of them were Lawton's red Buick convertible.

He got out of the car and crossed the street.

4

The vestibule smelled of disinfectant and stale cooking. On one wall was a row of metal mail boxes bearing the names of tenants. Lawton's apartment was on the second floor, number five. A stairway covered with a threadbare carpet curved upward. Chad went up and down a musty hall. From somewhere a baby was crying fitfully. The door to number five was closed and a light glowed behind a dusty transom. Chad paused. Well, he told himself, you've seen where he lives. Why don't you get the hell out? What're you doing here, anyhow? What would you say if Lawton came out and caught you? He turned abruptly, feeling anger at himself, and started back down the hall.

Behind him, behind the door of number five, there came a small sharp sound followed by a woman's sobbing. A man spoke gruffly and the sobbing stopped abruptly. Chad turned slowly, moved back to the door, and he thought, *If the bastard's got Ann in there …*

The sobbing began again, low, muffled, and the man muttered something and laughed. There was a thudding sound, like a chair falling over, and the man laughed again. Chad made up his mind and rattled knuckles against the door. All sound within the room stopped. Chad knocked again.

The man's voice came out to him. "Go away."

Chad tried the knob. To his surprise the door wasn't locked. He kicked

it open and stepped inside. Jay Lawton faced him from across the room. He still wore the gray flannel slacks, but had removed the midnight blue shirt. He had a broad white torso and powerful shoulders. A soft roll of fat bulged above his belt and light glinted on a golden mat of chest hair. He held a brown bottle in one hand and swayed a little as he gazed at Chad.

A woman lay on her side on the floor by the bed near an overturned chair. She was facing Chad and he saw that she was not young, but not old, either, with a hard handsome face. Her full red mouth was quivering and mascara streaked her cheeks. A tight black dress was twisted up over curved white thighs and she wore no shoes or stockings. Her toenails were covered with gilt lacquer. She put a hand to her cheek and said plaintively to Chad, "He hurt me."

Chad looked at her and he felt happy. It's not Ann, he thought, and he smiled at Lawton. "Sorry," he said. "Excuse me." He backed away, toward the hall, toward clean air.

Lawton moved swiftly behind Chad and slammed the door. Chad stood still, his gaze sweeping the room. It was cluttered with articles of clothing, crumpled newspapers, racing forms, filled ash trays. An open closet revealed an array of men's suits and bright sport jackets. A pair of women's red high-heeled shoes were on the floor beside the bed. The top of a dresser held a bowl of melting ice cubes, two glasses, a little pile of bills and silver, a scattered deck of playing cards, an open package of cigarettes, a blue steel .38 revolver with an ivory grip, three sets of dice— and a photo of Ann Travis in a gilt frame. The room smelled of whisky, cigarette smoke and woman.

Lawton said thickly, "What's the idea, Proctor? Afraid I had pure little Ann in my lair?"

"Shut up," Chad said pleasantly. "I told you I was sorry." He moved to the dresser and gazed at the photo. It was the same one she'd given him a few months previously, a soft-focus print showing her smiling into the camera. He gathered up the playing cards and shuffled them absently, looking at the photo. His thumb caressed the edges of the cards and he felt the tiny notches and he smiled to himself. He put the cards down, picked up two of the dice and rolled them in his fingers. They weren't apparent at first, but they were there, the microscopic snags designed to trip on the green felt of a dice table.

"Snooping," Lawton said sullenly. "A goddamned snooper."

Chad put the dice down beside the marked cards, and he said to Lawton, "You must be good at switching decks, and the dice. No wonder you don't need to work."

"Listen," Lawton said, taking a step toward Chad.

The woman pushed herself to her feet and sat heavily on the bed, not bothering to pull her dress down over her knees. She sat spread-legged, her toes curling, and looked at Lawton with sad, wet eyes. "You hurt me, honey," she whined. "You didn't have to slap me."

Lawton took his gaze from Chad and said to her, "Women need slapping. They love it." He swung toward Chad again. "Isn't that right, Proctor?"

"I wouldn't know," Chad said.

"I suppose you'll tell Ann about this," Lawton said thickly, waving a hand at the room in general. "You'll run to her and squeal, but it won't make any difference. She won't believe you—I got the inside track now. Anyhow, Alice is just an old friend. We were merely having a few drinks together and discussing cultural subjects, like the opera and Van Gogh and the essence of James Joyce. Merely a friendly, platonic association, isn't it, Alice?" He peered at the woman on the bed. "What's your last name, dear?"

"Smith," she said. "Alice Smith. I told you in Al's Cafe, don't you remember? When you bought me them drinks, and—"

"Ah, yes," Lawton said. "Miss Alice Smith." He bowed and stumbled, regained his balance, and pointed the bottle at Chad. "Miss Smith, allow me to present Mr. Proctor, who is my dear friend and a sonofabitch."

"Please to meet you, Mr. Proctor," the woman said. "What line of business are you in, may I ask?"

"Snooping," Lawton said. "He gets paid for snooping, don't you, Proctor?"

"Do you have a permit for that gun?" Chad asked, nodding at the .38 on the dresser.

"Is it any business of yours?"

"No, but I can make it my business. Where did you come from, anyhow?"

"To hell with you," Lawton said. "Just because I took your girl—"

"Shut up," Chad snapped, and he reached for the doorknob.

Lawton grasped Chad's arm and held it tightly. "Not so fast. You haven't told me what you're doing here."

"You're drunk," Chad said. "Let go of my arm."

The woman giggled happily. "Let's you and him fight," she said. "Mix it up, boys."

"You thought Ann was here, didn't you?" Lawton said. He grasped Chad's arm more tightly and peered at him with bright hot eyes. "I suppose you can't wait to tell her about my lady friend, can you?"

"Maybe. Let go of my arm."

"She won't believe you," Lawton said thickly. "She trusts me. Maybe

you had her once, but I got her now, and I want you to stay away from her." He swung Chad around, swayed a little, and regarded him from beneath heavy lids.

"For the last time," Chad said wearily, "Let go."

"When I'm damn good and ready. Listen, you—"

Chad hit him then, a short jolting right to Lawton's jaw. Lawton stumbled backward, dropping the bottle. It rolled over the floor spouting whisky. The woman scurried to retrieve it. Lawton hit the wall, shook his head, and then charged, his right fist drawn back. He was wide open and Chad hit him again, putting his weight behind it. Lawton hit the floor heavily and lay still. Chad gazed down at him, rubbing his knuckles, realizing that he'd gotten pleasure from hitting the man, and wanting to hit him again. It was something he had needed, he thought, and Lawton deserved it.

The woman said admiringly, "Gee, honey, that was swell." She offered Chad the bottle, "Have a little drinky."

Chad grinned at her. He felt good. "I'm sorry I had to hit your friend."

"Him?" she said scornfully. "Friend? Hell, I just met him tonight." She smiled at Chad and rolled her hips a little "What're you doing the rest of the evening?"

Chad smiled. "Thanks, not tonight."

She shrugged and drank from the bottle. "If you ever get lonesome, go to Al's Cafe and ask for Alice. It's on—"

"I know where it is," Chad said, "and I'll remember—if I ever get lonesome." He looked down at Lawton, who was stirring a little. "Some cold water on his head would help," he said to the woman.

"The hell with him," she said sullenly. "Give me a lift over to 68th, will you?"

"Sure." Chad moved to the dresser, carefully took up the .38 and put it in a coat pocket.

The woman capped the bottle, sat on the bed while she put on the red shoes, picked up a loose black coat and moved to the door. "I look a mess," she said, "but I can fix up when I get back to Al's." She gave him a sly smile. "I guess you wanna get out of here before he comes around, huh?"

He smiled faintly. "I think it would be best." They went out and Chad closed the door.

Down in Chad's car, the woman said, "He was a mean bastard—likes to slap people. I hate them slapping kind. You'd be surprised how many—"

"Yes," Chad said.

"I'll bet you ain't that kind."

"I hope not," Chad said, aware of her heavy perfume.

As they drove away, she moved over until her thigh touched his. "I like you," she said softly. "I could show you a real good time. Sure you won't change your mind?" Her fingers pressed his knee.

"Some other time."

"Oh, sure," she said carelessly, and moved away from him. "You married?"

"No.

"Got a girl? A steady girl, I mean?"

"I had one."

"And that bastard took her away from you? I heard what he said."

"That's right."

"That ain't no credit to her," she sneered. "Ditching you for a guy like him. He—"

"Never mind," Chad said sharply.

She patted his knee. "Sorry, honey. But you'll get over it."

"Sure."

They were on 68th Street and Chad saw the lights of Al's Cafe ahead. He pulled to the curb and stopped.

"Thanks," the woman said, opening the door.

"You're welcome."

"I could help you forget that babe," she said. "Just try me."

"I'm sure you could," Chad said. "Good-night."

She sighed. "Good luck, honey." She got out to the sidewalk and entered the cafe, carrying the whisky bottle beneath her arm.

Chad rolled down the window and drove away. The cool night breeze felt good on his face and swept away the cloying scent of Alice Smith. It was one o'clock in the morning when he reached his apartment. He went to bed and slept restlessly. He dreamed, too, not about Ann Travis and her sudden decision to marry a man like Jay Lawton, but about Virginia Kerry.

5

In the morning he spent an hour in his office clearing his desk with the help of Marjorie Betts, his secretary, a serious plain girl who lived at the Y.W.C.A. At ten o'clock Ben Durstin reported in from Toledo. He was a short wide man with a fat red face and a lot of gold teeth. He and Ed Doyle were Chad's assistants, and most of the time the three of them were busy. The Lake City territory took in three states, and sometimes Chad was compelled to hire extra help in the form of various specialists, both men and women, who were experts in the many phases of

investigation—accountants, photographers, safe and vault men, actors, fingerprint and laboratory technicians—all the oddly assorted crew of persons needed in the never-ending business of a private detective agency. But ordinarily Chad relied upon himself and Ben Durstin and Ed Doyle, with Marjorie Betts to handle the office routine.

He told Durstin about Dr. Kerry's wife, and explained that Doyle was to be relieved at noon, and that Durstin was to wait in the office until Doyle called in. Durstin nodded and retired to a corner of the office to read the morning paper. Chad called Dr. Kerry's office. Ann Travis answered.

"Good morning," he said lightly. "Is Doc in yet?"

"Not yet, Chad."

"How's the blushing little bride-to-be?"

"Chad, I ..."

He caught the break in her voice and he felt again the sense of loss, and a kind of slow rage against Jay Lawton. He was glad that he had hit Lawton, but he couldn't tell Ann about it; there was nothing he could do about it, not now, and he said gently, "Don't mind me—I'm just jealous. Is Walter making house calls or at the hospital or what?"

"House calls, until noon."

"Thanks, Ann." He hesitated, and then said, "I tried to call you last night."

"You did?" Her voice was cool.

"I just wanted to say good-bye and to wish you happiness—in case you are married when I get back."

"That was sweet of you. Where are you going?"

"Detroit, for a week or two."

"I stayed at the office until late last night," she said. "The books hadn't been worked on for weeks."

"I see," he said. "I didn't think to call there. I thought you were with your fiancé."

"I wasn't." There was a faint sharp edge to her voice.

"I know you weren't," he said. "Well, good-bye, Ann."

"How did you—?"

"I've got to go," he broke in. "Tell Walter I'll see him when I get back."

"All right, but—"

"Good-bye," he said, and hung up.

He sat there a while, a tall slender man in a gray tweed suit. His hair was straight and black, parted on the side, a faint touch of gray showing at the temples. His eyes were an odd shade of brown, almost amber, and his jaw held a stubborn look. Maybe he should have told her about the trouble Dr. Kerry is having with his wife, he thought, and about the

encounter with Jay Lawton. But why should he? The sooner he forgot about Ann Travis the better.

He stood up, took a hat and topcoat from a rack, and entered the outer office. His bag was by the door. "I'm off, honey," he said to Marjorie Betts. "Hold the fort. You know where to reach me?"

She looked up from her typewriter, nodded at him and smiled. "Yes, Chad. Have a good trip."

He grinned at her and said to Ben Durstin, "How about running me out to the airport?"

"Sure thing." The legs of Durstin's chair hit the floor.

The job in Detroit took longer than he had anticipated. It was ten days before he returned to Lake City on a plane arriving at three o'clock in the morning. The work had been unexciting, mostly tedious digging through contacts the agency had that the Treasury Department did not. But it ended with enough evidence to indict a ring of Dearborn real estate operators for income tax evasion. The government men were satisfied, and so was Chad. But it had been a long ten days and he was tired. He took a taxi to his apartment and slept until noon. After lunch he spent most of the afternoon at the office cleaning up an accumulation of desk work.

When he asked Marjorie Betts how Edward Doyle and Ben Durstin were getting along with their job of keeping Virginia Kerry out of trouble, she said, "All right, I guess. It's tied them up, though, and we've had to turn down a number of other jobs. Ben took a few, but it meant several times Ed had to work without sleep. But he offered to do it, and we all thought that you'd want us to take care of all the business we could."

"That's right," Chad said. "You kept track of their overtime?"

"Of course. The payroll vouchers for last week have already gone to New York."

"Good." Chad grinned at her. "I've got a swell team here."

At five o'clock Ben Durstin came in. His tan suit was wrinkled and his eyes were red-rimmed, "Hi, boss," he greeted Chad. "God, I'm glad you're back."

"How's it been?"

"Rugged," Durstin sighed. "As quick as we get short-handed, all hell breaks loose."

"What about the Kerry deal? Ed's out on that now?"

"Who else? I was supposed to help him, but all these other jobs came up, and Ed said go ahead ... That boy must be dead for sleep."

"I'll relieve him tonight," Chad said. "You go get some sleep yourself,

Ben." He turned to Marjorie Betts. "Has Ed called in today?"

"Yes, a little before noon, from a bar uptown. He said Mrs. Kerry was drinking as usual, but not too much, and that he expected her to head home shortly. It's the first he's called in two days."

"Listen, Chad," Ben Durstin said, "the poor guy hasn't had a chance to call in. I tailed that blonde and I know. She's nuts, I think. She drinks and drinks, all alone, all day and all night. And she keeps moving, as if she can't stand to stay in one place. Guys make passes, but usually she don't pay no attention, and pretty soon she'll scoot for another bar. And then all of a sudden she'll head for home in that Plymouth station wagon and you don't see her for four, five hours. Then out she comes, all dressed up and looking like a million, and starts all over again. Damnedest thing I ever saw. I felt kind of sorry for her. Once, in a joint on the south side, a man and a woman come in with a little girl, about the age of my Mary Janice. She went over and kissed the kid and then she began to cry, and she ran out of the joint crying and drove like crazy for home. Had a hell of a time keeping up with her." Durstin sighed heavily and crushed out a cigarette.

"Go on home, Ben," Chad said. "Get some sleep."

"Hell, I forgot how to sleep."

"Then get a sitter and take your wife out to dinner. Relax and put it on the expense account."

Durstin's broad red face cracked into a grin. "Does that include a couple shots of rye?"

"Sure. We'll say you were entertaining a client."

Durstin reached for the telephone. "I gotta call the old lady."

While Durstin was talking, Chad finished dictating a report to New York on his work in Detroit. "Mail it tonight," he told Marjorie Betts, "and then you go home, too."

Durstin turned away from the phone, said happily, "I'm off, folks," and went out.

A short time later Marjorie Betts finished her typing and left with a bulky envelope under her arm. Chad sat at his desk and watched the sun go down behind the city's skyline. Dusk came very quickly, and he remembered that it was September, almost October. After a while he stirred, picked up the phone, and called the office of Dr. Walter Kerry. Ann Travis' cool voice answered.

"Hello," he said.

"Chad, you're back!"

"Yes. Am I speaking to Mrs. Lawton?"

"No, Chad. I told you that I would stay until the doctor—"

"Is he there?"

"No, no. We're terribly busy. The doctor is closing the office for a
while—today is the last. He's going on a vacation tomorrow, he and Mrs.
Kerry."

"Tomorrow?"

"Early in the morning, he said. He had two patients to see, and then
he's attending a medical association dinner. He's president, you know.
No office hours tonight. He's been working very hard preparing to get
away ... Chad, how was Detroit?"

"I missed you." It was the truth, but he said it without thinking.

She didn't answer for a second, and then he said, "What're you going
to do? I mean, while Doc's away?"

"He wants me to stay here—to answer the phone, work on the
records—stuff like that."

"Are you?"

"Of course."

"When's the wedding day?"

"Not until the doctor returns, I'm afraid."

"Won't the groom become—uh—impatient?"

"Jay is very considerate," she said crisply. "I explained to him, and he—"

"Yes," he said wearily. "Good-bye, Ann." He hung up and stared out of
the window at the darkening sky. After a while he stood up, put on his
hat and went out.

In a hotel lounge filled with chattering pre-dinner drinkers he had
three lonely martinis, followed by ravioli at his favorite Italian
restaurant on a nearby side street. Afterward he stood on the sidewalk
and smoked a cigarette. A stiff wind was blowing in from the lake,
making the canvas of the marquee snap briskly. A few dried leaves
skittered across the sidewalk. A taxi cruised slowly past him, the driver
eying him hopefully. Chad shook his head and the taxi zoomed angrily
toward the light of Northern Avenue.

Chad snapped his cigarette over the curb and walked slowly along the
sidewalk. The leaves blew past his feet and the wind grew colder. When
he reached Northern Avenue he turned into a bar and ordered a brandy.
Two of them failed to help his restless mood. He left the bar, thinking
that he should try and make contact with Ed Doyle. If Dr. Kerry was
taking his wife away in the morning, the job was practically finished,
but he could at least relieve Doyle until the doctor came home, and he
welcomed any activity that would take his mind away from Ann Travis.
Swiftly he walked the four blocks to his office.

The elderly night man on the elevator said, "'Evening, Mr. Proctor. You
been away?"

"Yes."

At his floor he walked down the empty corridor to his office. Gold letters on the glass door read: *Investigations, Inc. Lake City Branch. C. E. Proctor, Mgr.* He unlocked the door, stepped inside, turned on the lights. He had a drink from the water cooler and then sat down at Marjorie Betts' desk and called Dr. Kerry's home. No answer. No use trying his office, he thought, because Ann had told him he was attending a medical association dinner. The thing for him to do was to go out to Dr. Kerry's house and wait for Ed Doyle to show up, if he wasn't already there. Maybe Virginia Kerry was again asleep on her bed and did not hear the phone. And Doyle would be camped outside. He should have asked Ann where the medical dinner was being held—not that it made any difference; he would see the doctor before he left in the morning.

He had made up his mind to drive out to the Kerry residence, when the phone jangled. He picked it up, said, "Yes?"

"Chad?" The voice was low and guarded.

"Yes," he said, realizing that the voice belonged to Ed Doyle. "Hi, Ed."

"When did you get back?"

"Early this morning. I was just coming out to Dr. Kerry's house to see if you were there."

"She hasn't been home all day. Listen, Chad—I tried to get Ben, but the gal watching their kids said he and his wife were out. Then I called your place, thinking you might be back. Marge wasn't at the Y, either, and so I called the office on the off chance that—"

"What's the matter?"

"I've got a little problem here, Chad. I'm in a bar, a dive called Sally's Harbor, on Dorrence Street, close to the ore docks. Mrs. Kerry is in a back booth and she's in bad shape—been drinking all day. And now a couple of yokels got her cornered. I know I'm not supposed to tip my hand, but, hell, Chad, she's drunk and scared, and those two bastards are pawing her ... What do you want me to do? Call the cops?"

"No. Keep an eye on things. I'll be right over."

"I can handle it myself, if you give the word. But you said I wasn't to interfere unless—"

"That's right," Chad broke in. "We don't want any trouble now. Sit tight." He hung up.

Before he left he took a loaded .38 Colt revolver from a desk drawer. Beside it lay the ivory-gripped gun he'd taken from Jay Lawton's room. He had forgotten it, and he wondered now why he had taken it. He carried it into the outer office, laid Lawton's gun on Marjorie Betts' desk and wrote on a pad: *Marge: Please send this gun over to Lieutenant McKinney for fingerprinting. Tell him I'll see him about it later. Chad.*

He left the office, locked it, and went down in the elevator to the

basement garage where the two agency cars were kept. A sleepy Negro attendant shuffled back into the shadows and drove out a black late model Ford sedan. Ed Doyle was using its twin. Ben Durstin drove his own car mostly and collected mileage expense.

Chad tipped the Negro, gunned the Ford up the cement ramp and merged with the evening traffic on Northern Avenue.

6

Sally's Harbor was a stone building on the shore end of a dock which stretched out to the blackness of the lake and the looming skeletons of ore chutes. It was at least sixty years old and until the coming of the ore boats it had housed a weighing station and a fisherman's supply store. A small neon sign over the door read: *Sally's Harbor. Food-Liquor.* The front door was slightly ajar and the smooth seductive music of a famous dance band seeped from a juke box and floated out over the black water.

Chad parked on the opposite side of the street and walked across. A dozen cars were in the cindered area in front of the place and he spotted the agency Ford that Ed Doyle was driving. Virginia Kerry's Plymouth station wagon was there, too. Yellow light gleamed through the cracks of the closed Venetian blinds, and as Chad grew closer he could hear loud laughter and voices above the music.

He was about ten feet from the door when it burst open and two men came out supporting a woman between them. Chad stopped. The woman was Virginia Kerry. She dropped between the two men, her head down and her pale hair falling forward over her face. She was wearing a plain black dress and a light loose topcoat. The men were dressed in overalls and soiled and tattered leather jackets. One of them had an arm around the woman, his hand cupping her left breast. The other man said thickly, "I'll open the door," and lurched for an old and battered sedan with most of the windows broken out. He carried a beer bottle in his hand. When he reached the car he stopped, tilted the bottle to his mouth, and then flung it across the street, where it shattered against the curb. The other man stumbled forward, almost dragging the woman.

A fourth figure stepped out of the bar and stood in the light from the doorway. It was Ed Doyle, and he said in a voice cold with rage, "Let her go, you sonofabitch."

The man stopped, half turned and stared stupidly. Then he said something obscene and spat on the cinders. Ed Doyle moved toward him. The man released Virginia Kerry and she slumped down, and the loose coat billowing around her. There was a small click and a knife

glittered in the man's hand.

Standing in the shadow beyond the lane of light, Chad started to speak, but in that instant the man with the knife sprang forward. Ed Doyle moved, too, and there was a flurry of movement, a sharp slapping sound, and the thud of a fist on flesh. The knife glinted in an arc toward the street, and the man who had held it sank to his knees. Doyle's right fist came around and the man pitched sideways and lay still.

The other man, the one by the sedan, started for Doyle.

"Come on, you bastard," Doyle said from between his teeth. "I'll kill you."

The man hesitated. Then he turned and ran to the sedan, dived in and raced away with a clattering sound of loose pistons.

Doyle stepped forward, lifted Virginia Kerry, and held her in his arms. Chad moved up and touched his shoulder. "Nice work, Ed."

Doyle whirled to face him, his face white with rage. Chad grinned at him. "Relax."

Doyle managed a tight smile. "The dirty bastards—they were all set for a little raping party."

"Yes," Chad said, "I saw it." He gazed at the man on the ground. He was moaning a little and his mouth was bloody.

Doyle carried Virginia Kerry to the agency Ford and laid her gently on the rear seat. Then he turned to face Chad.

"Take her home," Chad said. "I'll follow in her car."

Doyle nodded and got behind the wheel of the Ford. Chad leaned in the window. "You've had a pretty rough time, haven't you?"

Doyle sighed. "Oh, it hasn't been too bad. Tonight was the worst. Those filthy—"

"Yes," Chad said. "Well, tonight is the last. Doc is all set to take her away in the morning and try and straighten her out. After we get her home, you can knock off. If Doc isn't there, I'll stay until he shows up."

Doyle started the motor. "Okay, you're the boss—but I'd just as soon finish the job. I've followed her around so much that I feel, well—sort of responsible for her." He gave Chad a crooked grin. "And besides, I like that time-and-a-half pay."

"You've earned it," Chad said. "Suit yourself. It'll just be until Doc gets home anyhow." He stepped back.

Doyle backed the Ford from the parking area and headed slowly up the street. Chad got into the station wagon and followed. As he drove away, the door of Sally's Harbor opened and two men and three women came out. They were all laughing loudly. Chad wondered if they would notice the man on the ground and maybe call a doctor, but he didn't

really care, and he smiled to himself as he remembered Ed Doyle's rage. A good man, he thought, who was serious about his responsibility to a client.

There were lights in the Kerry house, but the doctor's Packard was not in the garage. Ed Doyle carried the limp form of Virginia Kerry into the house, while Chad opened the unlocked doors. In the bedroom Doyle gently laid her down, removed her black high-heeled shoes, and covered her with a blanket. Chad hoped that she would not again arouse herself and take off her clothes—at least, not until her husband arrived. But there seemed little likelihood that she would stir for hours. She was breathing heavily, her lips parted, a faint troubled frown on her smooth forehead. She mumbled something incoherently, and then resumed her deep breathing.

Doyle shook his head sadly. "It's a shame," he said in a low voice. "She's fighting something, God knows what."

"Yes," Chad said. "Let's hope that Doc gets her squared away."

They left the room and quietly closed the door. As they moved across the hall to the living room, the front door chimes tinkled gently. Chad went to the door and opened it.

Dr. Mustapha Hamid stood there, an apologetic smile on his red lips. He was dressed exactly as he had been when Chad had last seen him—severe dark ill-fitting suit, black tie, stiff white collar and the black Homburg. The light slanted across his pale face with the dark beard beneath the skin, and Chad smelled the sweetish odor of Turkish tobacco. "Hello, Doctor," he said, thinking that the man would look quite natural in a turban.

"Dr. Kerry is not here?"

"No."

Dr. Hamid hesitated. He seemed embarrassed. Then he said, "I do not wish to interfere, but as I came up the street I saw you carry Mrs. Kerry into the house. Is she—ill—again?"

"She'll be all right," Chad said shortly. He didn't ask Dr. Hamid to come in.

Dr. Hamid made a faint apologetic gesture with a slim white hand. "I did wish to see Dr. Kerry. Will he be home shortly?" There was almost a pleading look in his liquid brown eyes.

Chad relented a little, aware that Ed Doyle was standing behind him. "I don't know," he said, "but if you'd care to come in and wait ..." He stepped aside.

"Thank you," Dr. Hamid said gratefully. He stepped into the hall and removed his Homburg. His gaze strayed to Virginia Kerry's closed

bedroom door, and then he looked at Chad. "You are Mr. Proctor? We met here some days ago, did we not?"

"Yes," Chad nodded at Doyle. "This is Mr. Doyle. Ed, meet Dr. Hamid."

The two men shook hands gravely, and then the three of them moved into the living room. Dr. Hamid sat down stiffly, his black Homburg on his knees. Chad said to him, "Look, Doctor—I've got to leave. While you're waiting, perhaps you wouldn't mind driving me to where I left my car?"

"I am sorry." Dr. Hamid spread his pale hands. "You see, I do not drive. I have never learned. In Turkey I did not have the opportunity ..."

"Never mind. I'll call a taxi." Chad moved to the phone in the hall.

Ed Doyle followed him, jerked his head toward the living room and asked in a low voice, "What's his angle?"

"Why?"

"Well, in the past ten days I've spotted him a few times with Mrs. Kerry. Once she went to his apartment and stayed a couple of hours. I saw his name on the door. Twice he showed up, after she was settled in a bar, and tried to talk to her. She listened the first time. The second time she was too drunk to listen, and he just looked at her with a sad look on his face—like a dog with a master who kicks him. The bastard gives me the creeps."

Chad said, "He's supposed to be a protégé of Dr. Kerry's, but I suspect he's in love with Doc's wife. I could be wrong. Anyhow, I think he's harmless."

"Okay," Doyle said. "I've kept some notes on my adventures and travels these last ten days, and I'll turn in a report tomorrow."

"No hurry," Chad said. "We were just supposed to keep her out of trouble until Doc could take her away and, thanks to you, we've done that." He picked up the phone and called a taxi.

Doyle said, "I'll move the Ford around in front." He grinned. "I feel right at home parked out there."

"I'll bet you do," Chad said. "See you in the morning."

Doyle went out the front door and Chad returned to the living room. Dr. Hamid said in his soft rich voice, "Do you think Dr. Kerry will be long?"

Chad gazed at him thoughtfully, and then said in a quiet voice, "Let's face it, Dr. Hamid; you don't want to see the doctor—you're worried about Mrs. Kerry."

Dr. Hamid's pale skin darkened. He avoided Chad's gaze, took one of his oval gilt-tipped cigarettes from the leather case and placed it between his lips. His hand trembled a little as he offered the case to Chad.

Chad shook his head, watching him.

Dr. Hamid took a deep breath, flicked flame from his silver lighter. The sweetish smoke drifted past Chad's nose. "Mrs. Kerry is a wonderful person," Hamid said quietly, "and she is suffering greatly. I have been attempting to help her, in my insignificant way. Dr. Kerry has been very kind to me. He is a fine gentleman, a brilliant physician and surgeon. I am very fortunate to have him for a friend. I am grateful to him and I want to help his wife. It happens that I have interested myself in mental illnesses, and—" He paused and spread his pale hands. "Surely, you realize that Mrs. Kerry ...?"

"Drinks too much?"

"Yes," Dr. Hamid said softly. "But what makes her do it? That is the problem we face, not the alcohol. I have learned that she lost a child. She needs something to replace the child. She feels that she is—is inadequate, not a whole woman, you see? If I could convince her that another child would wipe out the tragedy of the first ..." He drew on his cigarette and his eyes seemed to burn with an almost holy light. "But she is afraid," he whispered. "We must take away the fear."

"She's not afraid," Chad said harshly. "She can't have any more children."

Dr. Hamid stared, and his pale face seemed to grow paler. A wild haunted look crept into his eyes. "That can't be true," he said hoarsely. "She never told me ..."

"Of course she didn't," Chad said bitterly. "You're going by the book. I'm just a dumb bastard, but I think she's afraid to admit to anyone, even herself, that she can't have another baby. That's her trouble. Damn you, you've been making it worse for her, with your silly talk of another baby. Why don't you get the hell out of here and let her alone?"

Dr. Hamid looked stricken. There was sweat on his broad pale forehead. He ran a pink tongue over his red lips. "I must make it up to her," he whispered. "I must, I must. I did not know ..."

"You know now," Chad said. "Tomorrow Dr. Kerry is taking her away, and—"

"But he cannot do that!" Dr. Hamid broke in desperately. "Not yet, not now. I know her trouble now, and I can help her. I must talk to her." He stood up and started for the hall.

Chad moved swiftly and stopped him with a hand on his chest. "No, you don't," he said grimly. "She's in no shape to talk to anyone."

"But I must." Dr. Hamid's eyes were a little wild. "This is the crisis. I must arouse her, plant the correct thoughts in her subconscious. She is on the borderline. She—she—" He stopped and passed a hand over his forehead. "I cannot explain to a layman," he said in a tired voice, "but

you must believe me. It is imperative that I talk to her, before she goes away ..." He took a long drag on his cigarette and gazed beyond Chad, as if he were seeing something that Chad did not.

"Why is it imperative?" Chad asked softly. "What do you mean?"

Slowly Hamid's eyes focused on Chad. "I cannot say," he said.

Something like a chill touched Chad's shoulders. "You mean she's— crazy?"

"Not yet," Dr. Hamid whispered, "but any little occurrence can push her over the line. Sometimes madness comes slowly, and then again it comes in a rush, after a long mental strain, or unhappiness—or self-reproach. If I had known that she was not physically capable of bearing another child, I could have helped her. But she did not tell me, and I assumed—that is where I made my mistake." He slapped a palm against his forehead. "I failed her— I should have guessed." He looked at Chad. "You are the police? Instead of arresting her, you brought her home?"

"I'm just a friend of Dr. Kerry's, trying to help."

"Let me see her," Hamid pleaded.

From out in front of the house a car horn tooted. "That's my taxi," Chad said. "Come on— I'll take you home. You can come back when Dr. Kerry is here. Maybe he'll let you talk to her."

Dr. Hamid said quietly, "Dr. Kerry is my friend and benefactor, but he does not understand. I must talk to her alone—now."

"Damn it, she can't talk," Chad snapped. "She's too drunk." He picked up the Homburg and handed it to the doctor.

"But—we can't leave her here alone!"

"She's not alone," Chad said shortly, thinking of Ed Doyle parked outside.

"But I do not understand ..."

Chad grasped his arm firmly. "You're not supposed to understand, Doctor," he said as he led Dr. Hamid out the door and down to the curb. Hamid got into the cab with Chad without speaking.

"Where do you live?" Chad asked him.

"Just a short distance." His voice was dull. "Four blocks, on this street. My apartment is in a building called the Clermont."

Chad spoke to the driver and sat back in the seat. They passed the agency Ford parked on the opposite side of the street, but it was too dark to see Ed Doyle at the wheel. They reached the Clermont, a four-story brick building on a corner with a short flight of steps leading to a small lighted foyer, and Dr. Hamid got out.

"Thank you," he said stiffly.

"You're welcome. Good-night, Doctor."

He stood on the curb, his Homburg in his hand, a bleak sad look on his long hook-nosed face. "Good-night, Mr. Proctor."

As the taxi pulled away, Chad said to the driver, "Sally's Harbor, on Dorrence Street."

"My God, Mac," the driver said, "you got your brass knuckles with you?"

7

It was after ten o'clock by the time the taxi dropped Chad at Sally's Harbor. He paid the driver and walked to where he'd left the agency Ford. The night was colder and the wind from the lake whipped at his trousers. There were more cars in the cindered parking area now, and the music from the place was louder, a raucous hillbilly tune. He wondered if the man who had tangled with Ed Doyle was still lying on the cinders, and he walked idly across the street to look. The man was gone and cars were parked over the place where the scuffle had taken place. He stood in the wind and toyed with the idea of entering the bar and having a drink, and then decided against it. He didn't really want a drink, and the job for Dr. Kerry was finished. There was no point now in backtracking over Virginia Kerry's tragic trail. She was in her husband's hands now, or she soon would be, and he hoped that it would work out.

He thought of Dr. Hamid's hints as to Virginia Kerry's mental condition, and he tried to shrug them off. She was a dipsomaniac, probably because of a feeling of loss and inadequacy due to the death of her baby, and he wished that he knew her better. His friendship for Dr. Kerry had flourished on the golf course, at stag gatherings, over a poker table. Being a bachelor he had not had much opportunity to take part in the Kerrys' social life, but the few times he had met Virginia Kerry, before she had lost her baby, she had impressed him as a woman of beauty and charm, and obviously in love with her husband.

He drove the Ford slowly away, leaving the lights and the twanging music of Sally's Harbor behind him. He avoided the parkway leading into the heart of the city and headed for the section where Dr. Kerry lived. Twenty minutes later he was on Ridge Road passing the Clermont, where he had left Dr. Hamid. Only a few of the apartment lights in the building were on and the foyer appeared deserted. As he approached Dr. Kerry's house he saw that the other agency Ford was still parked in the shadows across the street, and he was glad of that. It meant that Virginia Kerry was still sleeping, that she hadn't left the

house. He stopped behind the Ford, cut the lights, and walked up to the window on the driver's side. Ed Doyle said softly, "Hi, boss."

Chad leaned on the window and in the faint light he saw the glint of a gun cradled in the crook of Doyle's left arm. The muzzle was tilted upward just below the edge of the window. Chad grinned in the gloom. "Ready for me, huh?"

"I thought it might be you," Doyle said, "but I wasn't certain."

"I can see that the agency trained you good. And you did a nice job on the knife-toting boy at Sally's Harbor."

Doyle shrugged. "He was awfully slow."

Chad nodded at the house. "All quiet?"

"As the grave."

"I wanted to see Doc. Is he home yet?"

Doyle shook his head. "Nobody in or out." He yawned.

"Look," Chad said, "let me take over the rest of the night—or until Doc shows up. You're dead for sleep."

"Not a chance," Doyle said, yawning again. "I'll stick it out now to the bitter end. Besides, I can sleep tomorrow, and you've got to be at the office."

"All right," Chad said. "When Doc comes home, tell him you're checking out, and let him take over. He's supposed to leave with her early in the morning. Tell him I want to see him before he goes, and that I'll be out here around six. That ought to catch him."

Doyle laughed softly. "What do you want to do—give him the bill?"

"That, too," Chad said. He moved away. "I'll see you around six."

Doyle's soft voice came to him in the darkness. "Right-o."

Chad had a sandwich and coffee at an all-night diner and then drove across town to his apartment. He set the alarm for five o'clock and went to bed. When the alarm awoke him, he made a pot of coffee and then shaved and showered. After a breakfast of canned peaches and toast he dressed, transferring the Colt .38 to the suit he had put on. It was still dark when he went down to the Ford parked at the curb, but the dawn was just beyond the tops of the buildings and there was the smell of frost in the air. He turned on the car's heater for the drive across the city to Dr. Kerry's house.

Before he reached Ridge Road, a wet fog began to roll in off the lake. It delayed the dawn and cut visibility. Chad switched on the bright lights, decided that the dims were better, and drove at a cautious speed. The fog cleared a little by the time he reached Dr. Kerry's house, but it was still difficult to see objects more than twenty or thirty yards ahead. Across the street from the house the agency Ford loomed out of

the fog. Lights still burned in the living room of the house, and Chad had a small moment of worry. Hadn't Doc come home yet?

As he stopped behind the parked car, he saw that Ed Doyle was standing on the boulevard smoking a cigarette. Chad walked up to him, and Doyle said, "Hi—I'm still awake. Just stretching my legs a little."

"How's everything?"

Doyle shrugged in the swirling grayness. "She hasn't left, and the doctor is still out." He yawned and rubbed his eyes. "I'm glad you're here, Chad. I don't even care about the overtime anymore."

Chad frowned and gazed at the house. He knew that Dr. Kerry, like most doctors, was frequently obliged to be out at night, but not to come home at all, especially when he planned to go away with his wife early this morning ...

He said, "Anything happen at all?"

"A little," Doyle said. "Enough to keep me awake. About three o'clock a red Buick convertible drove up. A man and a woman got out and went into the house. They stayed about five minutes and then drove away. I figured it was somebody wanting the doctor, but I sneaked over and got the license number anyhow." He reached into his pocket and handed Chad a slip of paper.

"Thanks," Chad said, taking the paper.

"After they left I went into the house," Doyle went on, "and everything was okay. Mrs. Kerry was still sleeping."

"With her clothes on?"

Doyle's teeth showed in the mist. "Yes—this time. I came back out to the car and played the radio a while. A police prowl car came along and asked me my business. I showed them my card, and I'll say this, Chad—the cops in this town seem to like you. Anyhow, they didn't bother me anymore."

"Good. Anything else?"

Doyle shook his head.

"I thought that maybe that Dr. Hamid might come back. He was all hot to stay and talk to Mrs. Kerry, but I shooed him out."

"The sad Oriental M.D.," Doyle said.

"He's worried about Mrs. Kerry," Chad said, "he's real sincere. Thinks she's on the borderline, or something—and he's trying to keep her from drinking."

"Hah!" Doyle said.

"He gave me a story tonight about wanting to help her because he feels indebted to Doc, but I told you that I think he's in love with her."

"She'd be easy to love," Doyle said, "if she'd sober up."

"Yes," Chad said, remembering again the disturbing sight of Virginia

Kerry's nakedness. "You've done a good job, Ed, and I know it hasn't been easy. Let's see—you've been with me about six months, haven't you?"

"Yep—the twenty-fifth of September."

"About time for a raise. I'll put it through the first of the month."

Doyle grinned. "Thanks, boss." He opened the door of the Ford and slid behind the wheel. "Give my regards to Mrs. Kerry. She doesn't know me, but I sure as hell got acquainted with her." He paused, and said soberly, "I hope she makes it."

"It's up to Doc now," Chad said.

Doyle drove slowly away. He turned at the next corner and through the fog and the darkness Chad saw the Ford's lights streaking for the city. He got into the second Ford, smoked a cigarette, and listened to the early morning news. The lights in the Kerry living room burned on. After a while the fog lifted a little and he could barely make out the garage in the rear, with the Plymouth station wagon parked in one side of it. The other side, where Dr. Kerry kept his Packard, was a yawning darkness.

Chad thought of entering the house and waiting for Dr. Kerry there, but decided that he'd better stick to his post. He wondered what circumstances or emergency was keeping the doctor out all night. At six-thirty the September morning was almost full born, but the fog still clung close to the earth. And then a car came up the street, a black Packard sedan. It turned slowly into the drive of the house and stopped in the garage beside the station wagon with a blink of red tail lights. A door slammed and Chad saw a figure emerge from the garage carrying a small bag and enter the back door of the house. Lights came on in the kitchen, and then went out, and the living room suddenly darkened. Chad was about to get out of the car when he saw a light come on in the window of Virginia Kerry's bedroom. He stopped then, his hand on the door latch.

Abruptly the light went out, and the whole house was in darkness. Chad settled back in the seat and he thought: *He's had a long hard night, and he's with his wife now. Perhaps she's awake at last and he's telling her about his plan to take her away. Now is the time to leave them alone, to let them bicker, or make love, or to lie in cold silence. I can't disturb them now ...*

For a time on Ridge Road there was nothing but the gray fog and the slow creeping of the day. And then the first faint glow of the sun was abruptly gone and dark clouds rolled in from the east, and a soft rain began to fall down through the fog. Chad sat watching the darkened house and suddenly it seemed to him that something was moving on the front lawn. He sat up straight and peered through the mist and the rain.

A man was hurrying across the grass from the rear of the house. He crossed the intersecting street under the nebulous halo of a street lamp and Chad saw that he was tall and was wearing a dark suit and a Homburg hat.

Chad slid out of the Ford, quietly closed the door, and moved up the street in the rain and the gray light, walking swiftly on the grass along the sidewalk. For four blocks the man stayed ahead of him, a tall hurrying figure in the grayness. When he reached the apartment building called the Clermont, he went up the steps and entered the lighted foyer. Chad began to run, but when he reached the steps he saw that the foyer was empty. He went inside and stood silently, listening. From the floor above he heard rapid footsteps and he went up the stairs on tip-toe, reaching an alcove in the upper hall. The footsteps stopped and he heard the jangle of keys on a ring, and then the sound of a key entering a lock. He peered cautiously around the corner. The light was dim and he had just a quick glimpse of the man in the Homburg entering an apartment. The door closed. Chad waited a few seconds, and then moved down the hall to the door. A card tacked on it read: *M. Hamid, M.D.* The sweetish odor of Turkish tobacco was strong in the still air.

Chad stood uncertainly before the closed door. No sound came from beyond it. Presently he turned, went back down to the foyer, and looked at his wrist watch. It was ten minutes before seven o'clock in the morning.

He walked back to the Ford and resumed his vigil. It was still raining, but the fog was thinning, dissipated by the rain. It was quite light now and he could see the dirty white of the sky above the trees. He sat in the car watching Dr. Kerry's house, and he thought bitterly, *He came back to see her, after all. The sonofabitch was with her, and Doc came home and scared him away. But how did he get in without Doyle or me seeing him ...?*

He sat for an hour, wishing that he had some coffee, and thinking that it was slightly ridiculous for him to be camped there. But the agency was still officially responsible for Mrs. Kerry, and if the doctor was sound asleep he could not prevent her from leaving the house. He was reluctant to go in and awaken Dr. Kerry, and he thought that if Ben Durstin and Ed Doyle could keep the vigil for ten days, he could do it for a few hours. He began to idly compute what the doctor owed the agency, not counting the expense incurred by Durstin and Doyle. It would be a stiff fee, he knew, and he was sorry that he could not have done it as a personal favor. But it was agency business, and the New

York accountants were very fussy about the branches reporting all jobs—and collecting for them. He also knew that the doctor would not object, no matter what the fee; they had kept his wife out of trouble, and that was what he had wanted.

He stirred restlessly and wished that some sign of activity would show around the house, so that he could see Dr. Kerry and get to the office. Ed Doyle was off today, but Ben Durstin would be reporting, and he wanted to see the morning mail and get started on the rest of his desk work.

Presently he became aware that the rain had stopped and that the sun was making a yellow glow through the heavy air. He smoked another cigarette and watched the cars pass on their way into the city, the occupants headed for jobs in factory, store and office. Then, suddenly, he saw Virginia Kerry come out of the back door of the house and walk swiftly to the garage. He heard the whine of a car starter. The Plymouth station wagon backed out of the drive and headed up the street. As it passed him, Chad saw her clearly. Her face looked pinched and white, without lipstick or any make-up, and her eyes were like dark holes in her face. She was staring straight ahead, racing the Plymouth's motor. Chad cursed silently and fervently, started the Ford, made a U turn, and followed her.

She drove fast, edging the lights. Before long Chad guessed where she was going, and he wasn't surprised when she skirted the downtown traffic, turned into Dorrence Street and stopped at the place called Sally's Harbor. Before Chad had shut off the Ford's motor, she had left the Plymouth and was entering the bar. He saw that she was wearing the same black dress and light loose topcoat she'd worn the night before.

Chad left the Ford at the curb and got out. It was then that he saw the red Buick convertible nosed up against the wall of the building. Something stirred in his memory and from his pocket he took the slip of paper Ed Doyle had given him. The license number written on it checked with the Buick's plates. Chad sighed and gazed out over the lake. The choppy water was the color of granite and gulls were winging around the ore chutes at the end of the dock. A few small craft were bobbing at their anchors and far out an ore boat was making a black smudge of smoke on the horizon. The sun was bright now, burning through the last wisps of the fog. Chad made up his mind, walked across the cinders and entered the bar.

It was no better and no worse than he had expected. It smelled of stale beer and dead cigar butts and the rancid fat of a million hamburgers. There was a long bar, a row of wooden booths, a single line of tables and

chairs, a gaudy juke box, a serving window to a kitchen at the end of the bar, two doors side by side labeled *Gents* and *Ladies*. Most of the chairs were on the tables and a weary and scabrous old man was slowly pushing a soggy mop around on the floor. Behind the bar a thin hollow-cheeked man was sullenly washing glasses. Virginia Kerry sat in the back booth. All he could see of her was one nylon-clad leg and the top of her blonde head. Jay Lawton sat facing her. There was no one else in the place.

Chad walked back to the booth. The mop-pusher and the glass-washer paid no attention to him. As he approached the booth, Lawton hurriedly took something from Virginia Kerry and placed it in the pocket of a green corduroy jacket. His yellow hair was neatly combed and his blue eyes were bright and clear, with faintly amused crinkles at the corners. There was still a faint blue bruise on his right jaw where Chad had struck him. He was drinking coffee, and he had seen Chad from the moment he had walked in.

Virginia Kerry sat erect, her hands clasped on the table, and she gazed at Chad without expression or recognition.

Lawton smiled and said pleasantly, "Hello, there, Proctor. Haven't seen you for a while. Up kind of early, aren't you?" He nodded at the woman. "You know Mrs. Kerry?"

"Yes," Chad said. "Hello, Virginia."

Faint surprise showed in her eyes, and she peered at him closely. "Chad—Chad Proctor? Is that right?" Her voice was low and a little husky, a pleasant sound.

Chad nodded.

"A friend of Walter's, aren't you? It's been a long time ..."

"That's right," he said, thinking that even with what must be a wicked hangover, and without makeup, she was one of the prettiest women he knew.

She avoided his gaze and coughed nervously into a fist. There were soft purplish hollows beneath her eyes and her lips were bloodless. "Jay," she said to Lawton, "please ..."

Something like a sneer crossed Lawton's face, and then was gone. He smiled engagingly. "Of course, Virginia." He called to the man behind the bar. "Double bourbon, water on the side." He cocked a blond eyebrow at Chad. "Drink, Proctor?"

"No, thanks."

"Coffee?"

Chad shook his head, although he would have liked some. Virginia Kerry gazed at the tabletop and coughed into her fist again, delicately. The hollow-cheeked man brought the whisky and water. She lifted the

whisky with a trembling hand, drank half of it, coughed again and sipped at the water. A soft glow showed in her eyes and she seemed to be contemplating something mysterious and very wonderful. She drank the rest of the whisky.

Jay Lawton pushed his coffee cup away and stood up. "Nice to have seen you again, Virginia," he said, smiling down at her. "I've got to move along."

She didn't answer or look at him, and stared at her empty glass.

Lawton winked at Chad and shook his head sadly.

Chad said, "So now you're leaving?"

"Yep," Lawton said cheerfully. "I'm on my way to Akron. I stopped for some coffee, and who should walk in but Virginia." He smiled down at her. "Good-bye, Virginia."

She didn't answer.

Lawton winked at Chad again, tossed some silver on the table and moved toward the door. Chad followed him. Lawton turned and fingered the bruised spot on his jaw. "You've got a nasty right," he said. "My jaw still hurts."

"Sorry," Chad said.

"Oh, I asked for it. The truth is, I should never drink. I guess I owe you an apology for the way I acted the other night."

"Forget it," Chad said shortly.

Lawton sighed. "That's generous of you. But I was feeling low that night. Ann said she had to work at the office, and I went to a bar. Then that woman came up to me and—oh, hell, you know how it is."

"Sure," Chad said.

"By the way," Lawton said, "I seem to be missing a gun."

"You'll get it back."

"That's my property," Lawton said reproachfully. "Why did you take it?"

"It seemed a good idea at the time—under the circumstances."

Lawton eyed Chad a moment, and then he shifted his gaze to the booth where Virginia Kerry sat. "It's a damn shame about her," he said in a low voice. "Tough on Doc, too."

"Have you known her long?"

"Not long," Lawton said carelessly. "Ann introduced us one night at the office."

"I see," Chad said. "And you just happened to see her in this dump this morning?"

Lawton's gaze swung back to Chad. He was smiling a little, but something had shifted behind his eyes, like a shadow moving, or a cloud crossing the sun. "I could ask you the same question," he said softly.

"What were you doing at Dr. Kerry's house at three o'clock this

morning?"

Lawton continued to smile. "You get around, don't you?"

"A little."

"Checking up on Ann, huh? Like you were doing at my place that night? You may as well forget her, pal."

"Was she with you last night?"

"Sure she was. We were on an errand of mercy. The hospital was trying to locate Doc Kerry, and they called Ann. We had been out dancing and I had just taken her home. She tried to call Doc, but didn't get an answer, and she asked me to take her out to his house. We went in, but he wasn't there." He nodded at the rear booth. "She was, though, passed out on a bed." He looked at Chad mockingly. "Does that explain everything satisfactorily?"

"Sure. Give my regards to Ann."

"I'll do that, Proctor." Lawton held out a hand. "No hard feelings?"

Chad took his hand, said shortly, "No."

Lawton gave him a two-fingered salute. "See you around." He went out.

Chad went back to the booth and sat down opposite Virginia Kerry. Her eyes were closed and her head was resting against the back of the booth. Chad said, "Why do you do it?"

She opened her eyes and gazed at him dully. "I'm no good."

"Let me take you home."

She closed her eyes again and said in a tired voice. "Go away. Let me alone."

"Walter wants to take you away. He's waiting for you."

"I know—poor Walter."

"He wants to help you."

"Nothing can help me."

"Walter can. Like you used to help him."

"She helps him now. He doesn't need me."

"Who?"

"Ann is her name. Miss Travis." Her lips twisted with a faint bitterness. "She does the things for Walter that I used to do."

Chad remembered his conversation with Dr. Kerry. Maybe this was the answer, after all. Maybe all that Virginia Kerry needed was to help her husband, as she had in the early struggling years. He must tell Doc, he thought, and he had a feeling of excitement. She wanted to feel that she was needed, and it wasn't the loss of the baby. To hell with Dr. Mustapha Hamid.

He said, "Walter needs you, too. He's waiting for you." He reached out and touched her hand. "Come with me, Virginia."

She moved her head slowly from side to side. "No, no," she whispered. "Go away."

He felt anger then, and he said harshly, "Lawton?"

She opened her eyes then, and he saw the tiny flicker of fear, of alertness. He also saw the smooth whiteness of her throat and the soft swell of her breasts beneath the black dress, and he remembered once more how she had looked lying naked on the bed. "Just an acquaintance?" he asked.

"Yes. What else?" She leaned forward and the front of her dress fell away slightly. "I just happened to meet him here."

"Your stories jibe," he said.

"How nice," she said carelessly, but her hand trembled as she fingered the empty whisky glass.

"Let's go," he said.

"Where?"

"Anywhere you say. My apartment?"

A kind of coldness crept into her eyes. "You, too?"

He shrugged. "Why not?"

"Walter's friend," she sneered.

"What he doesn't know won't hurt him." He tried to smile convincingly.

"Oh, stop it," she said wearily, leaning back so that he could no longer see her breasts.

"You can't blame me for trying," he said.

"It won't work," she said in a brittle voice. "I'm not leaving with you. And don't bother to tell Walter where I am. I won't be here long. And tell him I'm not going away with him." She pushed the glass toward him. "Before you go, order me another drink. Bourbon, double."

He stood up. "Order your own," he said shortly.

"I will, never fear." She smiled up at him, but there was something cold and ugly in her eyes.

He left her and walked to the front door. The telephone was on a counter behind the bar and he knew that he couldn't use it without the risk of Virginia Kerry hearing him. He went out. Diagonally across the street was a gas station. He walked over. Inside, along with stacks of tires and shelves of auto accessories, was a telephone booth. He called the home of Dr. Kerry, waited for ten rings and hung up. Then he called the doctor's office. No answer. He looked at his wristwatch. Nine-fifteen. From where he stood in the gas station he could see Sally's Harbor. The Plymouth station wagon was still there. He called his office.

When Marjorie Betts' quiet voice answered, he said, "Marge, has Ben come in yet?"

"Yes, but he's left for that job in Port Clinton."

"Oh, yes," Chad said, thinking that Port Clinton was forty miles away. "I forgot. I'll be in as soon as I can."

He made one more call. He hated to, but there was no help for it. The clerk on the desk at Ed Doyle's hotel told him that Mr. Doyle did not wish to be disturbed. "I'm sorry," Chad said, "but this is an emergency. Call him."

It took three minutes for Doyle to answer. Chad heard him yawn before he said, "Doyle speaking."

"Ed, I'm sorry as hell, but I need you again. I'm at that bar called Sally's Harbor. Can you come down here right away?"

"Where?"

"The bar on Dorrence Street—where we were last night."

"Oh." Doyle yawned again. "What's the matter?"

"She's starting all over again, and I can't reach Doc. Ben's gone to Port Clinton and somebody's got to watch her while I see what the hell the score is."

Doyle sighed. "Okay, boss."

"Hurry, Ed. She's liable to take off any minute."

"I'm on my way."

"Thanks—I'll make it up to you."

Doyle laughed. He seemed wide awake now. "All in the line of duty, boss." He hung up.

Chad left the gas station and stood on the curb watching the bar on the opposite side of the street. The Plymouth was still there. At exactly nine-thirty the black agency Ford came down Dorrence Street and stopped at the bar. Ed Doyle got out and Chad walked down to him. Doyle's eyes were red-rimmed and he hadn't taken time to shave, but he was neatly dressed in a blue flannel suit, a crisp white shirt and a regimental striped tie. He grinned at Chad. "Job not over yet, huh?"

"Hell, no. Doc Kerry came home a little while after you left this morning and went to bed. I didn't have the heart to wake him, so I waited around. Around eight o'clock Mrs. Kerry left and I followed her here. She won't let me take her home—or any place." Chad paused, and then added. "Our melancholy friend, Dr. Hamid, was hanging around last night. He left the house early this morning, right after Doc Kerry came home, and I followed him to his apartment. I don't know how long he'd been inside. I didn't see him enter, and neither did you."

"No," Doyle said. "He could have sneaked in from the back, I suppose."

"Yes." Chad sighed. "He was determined to see her," he said, remembering Dr. Hamid's reluctance to leave the Kerry house the evening before. He patted Doyle's arm. "You can go back to bed pretty soon."

"Hell, I'm wide awake now." Doyle's yawn belied his words.

Chad nodded at the bar. "When she leaves, stay with her, and call the office when you get a chance. Ben should be back by noon, and he can take over—if we still need him."

Doyle yawned again, lit a cigarette and gazed thoughtfully at the entrance to Sally's Harbor. "Right-o," he said.

Chad drove back to the house on Ridge Road with the white-painted front door, the pale door to death, and he talked to the woman who looked like a debauched grandmother. He found Dr. Walter Kerry dead on his bed, and Virginia Kerry telephoned from Sally's Harbor and pleaded, "Darling, darling, come and get me ..."

8

He headed back to Dorrence Street, driving fast, with the ugly memory of Dr. Kerry like a flame inside him, but when he slid the tires on the cinders surrounding Sally's Harbor he saw that he was too late; both the Plymouth station wagon and the agency Ford were gone. He went into the bar. The floor-mopper was gone and the chairs were in place at the tables. Three men were drinking beer at the end of the bar, and in one of the booths a shabby white-whiskered old man was sopping doughnuts in a cup of coffee. The hollow-cheeked bartender was reading a newspaper.

Chad went up to him. "The blonde," he said. "How long ago did she leave?"

The bartender lowered the newspaper and gazed at him blankly. "What blonde?"

Chad sighed and laid a dollar bill on the bar.

"Oh, that blonde—she left about ten minutes ago." The bartender picked up the dollar.

"Alone?"

"I guess so. She came in alone."

"Did she make a phone call from here?"

"Are we still talking about the same blonde?"

Chad nodded grimly.

The bartender cradled his chin in a palm and looked dreamy. "Well, now, I just can't remember."

Chad laid another dollar on the bar.

"It's coming back to me now," the bartender said. "Yes, I believe she did make a phone call. Then she had another double shot and went out." He reached for the bill, but Chad kept his hand on it.

The bartender looked hurt.

"The man she was sitting with—was he here first?"

"Yep. Then she came in. Then you." He gave Chad a yellow-toothed leer.

"Your memory is getting real good. How about remembering if the two of them have been here before?"

The bartender glanced at the bill beneath Chad's hand.

"Another buck is all I'm paying for memories this morning," Chad said.

The bartender coughed delicately and spat behind the bar. "Since you mention it," he said, "I seem to remember the two of them here before— maybe two, three times in the last few weeks."

"Thanks," Chad said. "Where's Sally?"

"That's me. Short for Salazar."

"That's a hell of a name." Chad grinned at him.

"Ain't it, though? What's yours?"

Chad flicked the bill across the bar. "Doakes," he said.

"Cop, huh?"

"You know better. Cops don't pay for anything."

"Husband, then," the bartender sneered.

Chad went out.

As he drove up Ridge Road, headed again for Dr. Kerry's house, he passed the apartment building called the Clermont. A Plymouth station wagon was parked in front. A short distance behind it was the black agency Ford Ed Doyle was driving. Chad abruptly swung to the curb and stopped behind the Ford, the twin of the one he was using. There was no one in it. He got out and moved up the sidewalk to the Plymouth. It, too, was empty. He went up the steps to the ornate entrance of the Clermont.

Ed Doyle was standing inside the foyer with his back to the door. His hands were in the pockets of his blue flannel jacket and he was gazing at the row of mail boxes on the wall. Beyond the mail boxes was a door labeled OFFICE.

As Chad entered, Doyle said in a low voice, "Hi, boss." He didn't turn around.

Chad stood beside him. "Where is she?"

"Upstairs." Still Doyle didn't look at him.

Chad said, "Relax, Ed. Nobody's on my tail."

Doyle turned and grinned. "I'm going by the book. How does Section Four go? *When contacted by another operative while on duty do not immediately betray your acquaintanceship, but—*"

"Quit showing off," Chad broke in. "She's in Dr. Hamid's apartment?"

"Yep. What brings you here?"

"Death," Chad said wearily, "and a phone call from Mrs. Kerry. Her husband was murdered last night."

Doyle stared at him. Then he said quietly, "While I was on duty?"

"You—or me," Chad said bitterly. "But we couldn't tell what was going on inside the house from a car parked outside." He looked up the stairway.

"How?" Doyle asked.

"Shot," Chad said, "in the heart."

"I didn't hear any—"

"Neither did I." Chad nodded at the stairway. "I'm going up. You stay here."

"I'd better go along."

Chad shook his head. "You've done your part. This is my worry. You go outside and wait. I don't know if he's got a back door, but if either of them leave, stay with them."

"Right-o." Doyle went out.

Chad went up the stairs quickly, moved down the hall to Dr. Hamid's apartment and pressed the bell button. He didn't get any response and he tried the knob. It turned loosely and the door swung inward. Chad let go of the knob and waited. Nothing but silence. He smelled the sweet pungent odor of Turkish tobacco. The silence grew and seemed to hang around him like a cloud. All he could see of the room was a rug and the end of a divan. He shifted the Colt .38 from the inside pocket of his coat to the right pocket and kept his hand on it. Then he kicked the door gently. It swung wide open.

Dr. Mustapha Hamid's soft brown eyes looked at him. He was standing in the center of the room. The beard beneath his smooth pale skin looked blacker than ever, and his full red lips were moist. He was wearing the same dark gray suit he'd worn the night before, or one just like it. A black Homburg lay on a table.

"Good morning, Mr. Proctor," he said in his whisper of accent.

"Good morning, Doctor. Didn't you hear the bell?"

"Yes. I called to you to come in, but I was in the bedroom and perhaps you did not hear me. The lock on the door is broken." He turned and picked up the Homburg.

"Going out, Doctor?"

"I was just leaving for my office. I have an appointment with a patient." He smiled ruefully. "They are not too plentiful as yet."

"Don't be in a hurry," Chad said. He closed the door and gazed around the apartment.

From where he stood he saw three doorways leading to what he guessed were a bedroom, a bath and kitchen. The living room was small

and furnished like a—he searched for a word—like a harem, he decided. Silk cushions were scattered on the floor and a flowered tapestry was held against a wall with bronze-tinted spears. A yellow five-foot vase stood in one corner and the divan was draped with a fringed red silk shawl. In addition to the tobacco odor the place smelled of stale coffee and a heavy incense.

Chad said, "Where is she?"

Dr. Hamid's expression changed. The eyes were no longer liquid, but as hard and as dry as a cobra's. The smooth skin of his face darkened a little and he ran a pink tongue over his red lips. "Who?" His voice was almost a whisper.

"You know who. Mrs. Kerry."

"She is not here."

Chad moved past him to one of the doors. It was the bedroom. From the corner of his eye he saw Dr. Hamid walk slowly toward him. Chad stepped into the bedroom. Behind him Dr. Hamid's tall form filled the doorway.

There was an unmade bed, with pink silk sheets trailing on the floor, a marble-faced dressing table with a gilt-framed mirror over it. A silver box filled with long, oval, gilt-tipped cigarettes was by an ivory ash tray on a teakwood table beside the bed. Chad moved around the bed and opened a closet door. He saw a dark gray suit on a hanger, a black overcoat, a black Homburg on a shelf, a pair of black pointed shoes on the floor. A metal rack fastened to the inside of the door held three neckties—all black.

Chad closed the closet door, skirted the bed, aware that Dr. Hamid still stood in the doorway quietly watching him. There was an open screened window in the far wall and Chad could see part of a black fire escape railing. The screen was hooked from the inside. As he turned back to the door, an object on the bed caught his eye, something small and half-buried in the tangled pink sheets. He leaned over and picked it up. In the doorway, Dr. Hamid stirred a little, but he made no other move. Chad glanced at him briefly, and then examined the small object in his hand.

It was a doll, not an ordinary doll for babies to pat with sticky hands, but a special little doll, modeled by an artist. It was about eight inches high, with silky ash blonde hair framing its delicately moulded face, a miniature face which looked vaguely familiar to Chad. He felt the hair with his fingers. It's human hair, he thought, from a living person's head, a person he suddenly realized he knew. The doll was dressed in a little white silk frock which could have been tailored in Paris. On the feet were tiny white sandals of soft leather, with silver buckles the size of dimes. There were two tiny pockets in the front of the dress and stitched in blue

on one of the pockets were the initials, *J.K.*

Chad held up the doll and said to Dr. Hamid, "Yours?"

A faint flush showed beneath Hamid's pale skin. "Yes. I've had it for a long time. It—it belonged to my wife, in Istanbul."

"Your wife?"

Hamid hesitated, his gaze on the doll. "Her name was Kizza—Josephine Kizza—before we were married."

"That's fast thinking, Doctor," Chad said. "The initials check. Where is your wife now?"

"She is—dead."

"Sorry," Chad said shortly.

Dr. Hamid turned away.

In that moment Chad heard a metallic scraping sound from behind him, from the direction of the window. He turned quickly, but as he turned the room rocked with gunfire. A hot whispering sound fled past his ear and there was the thunk of a bullet against plaster. He dove headlong behind the bed and hugged the floor while the silken sheets above him rustled with the impact of bullets. He squirmed sideways and got his gun in his hand, but he did not dare lift his head above the bed.

And then another gun spoke, a new sound, and it came from behind him. Trapped, he thought wildly—that damned Hamid, a cross-fire. He wiggled desperately under the bed, smelling the bitter gun smoke.

No more shots came and he heard a scrabbling sound on the fire escape. An unsteady voice from the bedroom doorway said, "Chad—you all right?"

He rolled out from under the bed and stood up, the gun in his hand. Ed Doyle weaved in the doorway. One of the agency's .38 Colts hung limply in his right hand, a wisp of blue smoke still curling from its muzzle. The collar of Doyle's shirt was a soggy red, and the right shoulder of his blue flannel jacket was darkly stained. "The window, boss," he said, grimacing in pain.

Chad jumped to the window then, saw the ragged holes in the wire screen where the bullets had ripped through. He unhooked the screen and leaned out over the fire escape. He could see the street below and the small court with cars parked there, and from somewhere beyond his line of vision he heard a car roar up the street. There were a few bright drops of blood on the grating below the window. He ducked his head back inside, moved to Doyle, put an arm around him and helped him to the bed. Doyle sat down heavily, his head sagging. There was sweat on his forehead and it glistened on his white scalp beneath the short black hair.

"Take it easy," Chad told him. "He got away, but you winged him.

There's blood out there."

He heard a soft sound behind him and he whirled. Dr. Hamid stood in the doorway. There was a shiny cast to his pale face and he was trembling a little.

"This man's wounded," Chad snapped at him. "Do something."

Dr. Hamid turned quickly and went away. Chad lowered Ed Doyle gently to a reclining position. The doctor returned carrying a black leather bag. He knelt beside Doyle and his long white fingers moved swiftly and deftly. He wasn't trembling now and there was a remote intent look on his long hook-nosed face. "Cold water," he said to Chad without looking up. "And a towel. In the bathroom."

As Chad left the room he saw that the front door was open and that a little group of persons was standing in the hall peering in. "Something wrong?" a man asked. "We heard some noise ..."

"Nothing wrong," Chad snapped, slamming the door. He propped a chair beneath the knob, moved to a door opposite the bedroom. It was locked. He rattled the knob and pushed with his shoulder, but the door held. He looked around at the doctor in the bedroom. "It's locked," he said.

Dr. Hamid turned to gaze at him bleakly. "Force it," he said quietly.

"Haven't you got a key?"

"It is on the inside. Force it. Quickly."

Chad heaved a shoulder against the door. On the second try the lock gave away and he stumbled into the bathroom. Virginia Kerry was sitting on the floor with her back against the tub. Her pale hair hung over her face, and her long slender legs were stretched out before her. The black dress was twisted up over her white thighs, exposing the tops of her stockings. One stubby high-heeled black shoe lay on the floor beside her. There was a whisky bottle in her lap.

Chad stepped over her, grabbed a towel from a rack, soaked it with cold water from the bath tub tap. As he went out, the woman on the floor muttered, "Darling, come and get me ..."

In the bedroom Chad saw that Dr. Hamid had removed Doyle's coat and shirt. He took the towel from Chad and began to tenderly bathe the wound at the base of Doyle's neck. Chad leaned over and saw the smooth red groove, just above the collar bone.

Dr. Hamid said tonelessly, "The bullet missed the bone."

Chad said to Doyle, "How do you feel?"

"Not too bad. Arm's getting stiff, though." He grinned up at Chad. "Do you suppose the good doctor has a drink around?"

Dr. Hamid, busy with antiseptic, gauze and bandage, said, "There's some fig wine in there." He jerked his head toward the living room.

Doyle grimaced, said, "Thanks just the same, Doc."

Chad went back into the bathroom. Virginia Kerry had not moved. He took the bottle from her lap and held it up to the light. The label said bourbon and there was still an inch of whisky in it. He carried the bottle to the bedroom and handed it to Doyle, who lifted his head and drank. "Thanks, boss," he said, resting the bottle on his naked chest.

Dr. Hamid worked swiftly, his face expressionless.

Chad entered the living room, saw the telephone on a small table, and called Dr. Kerry's office. Ann Travis answered. At the sound of her voice, his heart quickened a little, but he said coldly, "This is Chad."

"Yes, Chad."

"Have the police been there yet?"

"Police? Why would—?"

"Walter is dead."

There was silence on the wire for maybe a second. "Dead? W-what do you mean ...?" Her voice faltered.

"Murdered," he said. "Last night."

He heard her quick intake of breath. "Dr. Kerry?" Her voice sounded choked.

"Yes," he said impatiently. "I can't explain now. I need your help or somebody's. I'm at the Clermont, an apartment building on Ridge Road. Do you know where it is?"

"Yes, but—"

"Can you come over here? Right now?"

"Of course, if you want me."

"Good girl." His voice softened a little. "Ann, I'm in a mess. I had to leave Doc's house before the police arrived. One of my men is here. He's wounded. Virginia Kerry is here, too—dead drunk. The police are looking for her, I'm sure of that, and me, too. I want you to take care of her, get her in as good shape as possible, and take her home—for Doc's sake. We can do that much. She's got a tough time ahead of her. Will you do it?"

"Virginia?" she said, and he caught the coldness in her voice. "Did she ...?"

"I don't know," he said. "I hope not." He gave her the number of Dr. Hamid's apartment.

"I'll take a taxi," she said and hung up.

Chad returned to the bathroom. Virginia Kerry was still in the same position. A black leather purse protruded from beneath one leg. He picked up the purse and opened it. Inside were the usual female articles—compact, lipstick, cigarettes, matches, a small coin purse, a thin leather wallet. He flipped open the wallet. The first thing he saw was

a state driver's license. He read it quickly: *Virginia Fern Kerry, 120, 5' 4", Blonde, White, Housewife.* In the currency compartment he counted seventy-six dollars. A slip of paper was nestled between the bills. Scrawled in pencil on the paper were the words: *You know where. 9:00 tomorrow. $500. or else.* He put the paper in his coat pocket, returned the wallet to the purse, and gazed moodily at the woman on the floor.

She moved her head slowly from side to side. "Walter," she mumbled, "darling ..."

Dr. Hamid appeared in the bathroom doorway, his long pale face impassive. Chad pointed a finger at him. "Talk," he said.

The doctor looked at the woman on the floor and his liquid brown eyes grew sad. "I have been trying to help her," he said in his soft rich voice. "I told you that, Mr. Proctor. She is sick—in her mind. But I did not know that she could never have another baby—until you told me. She lied to me because she did not want to admit it, not even to herself. It is a common trait with the mentally ill—not to face the truth. But I was blind. After you told me, I wanted to talk to her again, to approach her illness from the proper angle, and—"

"And so you sneaked back to her house last night to see her?" Chad broke in harshly.

Dr. Hamid shook his head quickly. "No, I did not. She came to me this morning. She was incoherent and she babbled to me about money and about Dr. Kerry's failure to come and get her at a place called Sally's Harbor. She said he didn't love her or want her, that he was ashamed of her, and begged me to help her. I tried to calm her, but—" He shrugged his wide spare shoulders. "She ran in here and locked the door, and then you arrived."

"Did Dr. Kerry know of her visits to you?"

"I hope not," he said sadly. "He is my friend, and he might— misunderstand. I truly want to help her."

"Because you're in love with her?"

Dr. Hamid didn't speak, but looked at Chad with haunted eyes.

"To hell with you," Chad said bitterly. "No wonder you didn't want Dr. Kerry to know that she was sneaking up here and—"

Hamid's eyes flamed and he took a quick step forward, his right fist clenched.

Behind him a soft voice said, "Take it easy, Doc."

Dr. Hamid turned slowly. Ed Doyle stood in the bathroom door with the .38 in his hand. He was naked to the waist and the bandage against the base of his neck looked very white against his skin. "No rough stuff, Doc," he said.

Dr. Hamid swung toward Chad. "Dr. Kerry is my friend," he said

fiercely.

"Was," Chad said. "Dr. Kerry is dead."

A kind of sighing scream filled the bathroom. Chad started, and turned his head. Virginia Kerry was staring up at him. The fingers of both hands were spread across her mouth and her gray eyes held a look of madness.

"Damn you," Dr. Hamid said to Chad from between his teeth.

The woman began to scream again. Chad shouldered his way roughly past the doctor. "She had to know sooner or later," he snapped. "Do something for her."

He stood outside with Ed Doyle and closed the bathroom door to soften the sound of the screaming. Doyle stuck the .38 into a hip pocket. His lean Indian-like face was white. "I wish I had some more of that bourbon," he said, grinning.

"What happened downstairs?" Chad asked him.

Doyle lifted his broad naked shoulders. "I'm standing out in front when I hear a car door slam from the court around at the side. I peek around there and I see a guy going up the fire escape. He stops at a window about where I figure this apartment is. So I come up, thinking I'd better tip you off. When I'm outside the door I hear the gun and I bust in. This guy, Hamid, is standing outside the bedroom door scared blue. I push him away, see the guy slinging lead at you through the screen, and I open up on him."

"And a good thing," Chad said. "He had me like a duck in a rain barrel. What did he look like?"

"I didn't have time for details, but he was big, light hair, no hat. Wearing a green jacket, I think."

"What kind of a car?"

"I saw it in the court—a red Buick convertible."

Chad sighed. "Okay. Now tell me again about last night; around three o'clock a Buick stops at Dr. Kerry's house, a man and a woman go inside, stay a few minutes, then come out and drive away. Right?"

Doyle nodded.

"Then you went into the house, checked on Mrs. Kerry, and she was still sleeping?"

Doyle nodded again. "Let's sit down. I feel a little rocky."

The screaming inside the bathroom had stopped, but the two men could hear the soft tones of Dr. Hamid's voice. Chad entered the living room, tossed some cushions from a chair, and sat down. Doyle stretched his tall form on a divan. His naked torso made an oddly appropriate picture against the oriental background.

"At six o'clock this morning I relieved you," Chad went on, "and you

left. At six-thirty Dr. Kerry came home and entered the house. Right afterwards Dr. Hamid left the house and walked away."

"You're certain it was Hamid?" Doyle asked.

"Yes. I told you that I followed him right here, to his apartment. Then I went back to the house and waited. About eight o'clock Mrs. Kerry left and I followed her to Sally's Harbor." He paused and then went on, "So Dr. Kerry was killed sometime between six-thirty, when I saw him come home, and ten o'clock, when I returned to the house."

Doyle said softly, "Hamid?"

"Or Mrs. Kerry. She was there all of the time."

"Why would she kill him?"

Chad shrugged. "She's a dipso, and he was taking her away today, away from whisky—and away from Hamid. I'm certain he's in love with her. Maybe the feeling is mutual."

"Maybe," Doyle said, "but it looks like Hamid is our boy."

"The coroner's report will help us on the time of the killing," Chad said, thinking with a faint uneasiness of the persons who had visited the Kerry home at one time or another during the night and early morning. Jay Lawton and Ann Travis had been there, and Dr. Hamid, and Virginia Kerry had been inside the house all night. But Dr. Kerry hadn't come home until six-thirty, after Doyle left, and he had been killed some time after that ...

Doyle said, "You haven't told me who the character is who pumped lead at you."

"That's another story, I think." Chad stood up. "I'll tell you about it later. Right now there's a cop named Abner McKinney who's probably got a dragnet out for me. I've got to get back to Doc's house." He looked at his watch. Ten minutes after eleven in the morning. Where was Ann?

"What'll I do about Hamid?" Doyle asked.

"Can you keep him here until McKinney can pick him up?"

Doyle took the .38 from his pocket, held it across his chest, and grinned. "A pleasure," he said.

"And Mrs. Kerry, too," Chad added.

"Yeah," Doyle sighed. "I know."

The doorbell buzzed. Chad removed the chair from beneath the knob and opened the door. Ann Travis stepped inside. She was wearing a light tan gabardine topcoat over her white nurse's uniform and carried a small leather bag under one arm. Her face seemed pale and her eyes looked tired. Chad remembered that she hadn't had much sleep, if any, the night before, because she'd been out with Jay Lawton. He felt a sudden cold jealousy, but he tried to keep it from his voice. "Hello, Ann. I'm glad you're here."

Ed Doyle got up from the divan and stood quietly, holding the big revolver behind him.

Chad introduced him to Ann, and Doyle smiled and bowed slightly. Ann's eyes widened at the sight of the bandage on his shoulder. Chad said to her, "Ed stopped a bullet intended for me."

She looked at Doyle and then said quietly, "Thank you, Ed."

Chad shot her a surprised glance, but she turned away, not looking at him. Doyle said, "I'd better get dressed," and entered the bedroom.

Ann took off her coat, laid it over a chair, and turned to Chad. "Where is she?"

"In the bathroom with a Turk named Dr. Hamid—this is his apartment." He hesitated, and then said, "You know about Mrs. Kerry's—trouble?"

"Her drinking?" There was contempt in Ann's voice. "Yes, the doctor talked to me about her. She worried him very much... Chad, can you tell me about ...?"

"Not now. Later. Doyle will keep an eye on Dr. Hamid until the police get here. You take Mrs. Kerry home as soon as you can."

"All right. But why must Mr. Doyle watch this Dr. Hamid?"

"Never mind," he said gently.

"How—how did the doctor die?"

"A bullet—in the heart."

She put a hand to her eyes and swayed a little. He moved to her and placed an arm around her, aware of the familiar clean scent of her, a scent of soap and starch and the perfume of her hair.

"But why?" she said brokenly, "Walter Kerry was the finest man..."

Chad looked over her head and saw Ed Doyle standing in the bedroom doorway. He had managed to put on his blue flannel jacket and button it over his naked chest. The bathroom door opened and Dr. Hamid came out. He gazed at the three of them with brooding eyes, and showed no surprise at seeing Ann. "She is calmer now," he said. "She needs rest and quiet." He looked down at his pale slender hands and bunched them into fists and his full red lips quivered. "And peace," he said brokenly. "Peace and understanding and love ..."

Chad said to him, "Doctor, this is Miss Travis. She was Dr. Kerry's nurse."

Dr. Hamid raised his eyes. There were tears in them. "I am honored," he said.

She stepped past him into the bathroom and immediately her crisp voice came out to them. "Will someone help me get her to bed?"

Dr. Hamid turned silently and entered the bathroom.

Chad said to Doyle, "Are you sure you'll be all right?"

He grinned. "I only need one hand to hold a gun."

Chad entered the bedroom. The doll was lying on the floor, half out of sight beneath the bed, where he'd dropped it when the shooting began. He picked it up and put it in a coat pocket just as Dr. Hamid came in carrying Virginia Kerry in his arms. He laid her gently on the bed. Ann Travis came in and bent over her. Chad turned and went out. In the living room he said to Ed Doyle, "Ann will take Mrs. Kerry home. It'll be better than having the cops pick her up here. I'll be back as soon as I can."

"Right-o," Doyle said.

Chad went down to the street, got into the Ford and put the little doll in the dash compartment. Then he lit a cigarette, sighed deeply, and drove once more to Dr. Kerry's house.

9

The area immediately surrounding the house was clear, but crowds of curious neighbors and people who had been passing by were standing in droves along the opposite side of the street. A small but efficient crew of uniformed policemen kept the crowd at bay and an officer was at each intersection diverting lines of motorists away from the street in front of the house. When Chad reached the intersection he was waved impatiently away, but he drove to the center and stopped. The policeman came toward him with an angry expression, and Chad grinned at him. "Keeping you busy, Dan?"

The policeman recognized him then. "Hell, yes, Chad. Go ahead. I got orders to let you through." He blew a whistle and waved viciously at a motorist who had sneaked out into the middle of the intersection behind Chad.

Chad parked behind two squad cars with a uniformed officer at the wheel of each. They were young and he didn't know them. They gazed at him impassively as he went past them up the walk. A police laboratory truck was parked in the drive and a plainclothesman leaned lazily against the front door. As Chad approached he grinned maliciously. "Well, well, so you finally showed up. McKinney's inside chewing the rug." He stood aside and bowed elaborately. "Go right in, Mr. Proctor."

"To hell with you, Clady," Chad said as he entered the house.

As he crossed the hall he saw that the door to Dr. Kerry's bedroom was open and he caught the lightning-quick reflections of flash bulbs. Still shooting pictures, he thought grimly, although he knew that they must

have taken the body away long ago. He entered the long attractive living room.

Lieutenant Abner McKinney turned away from the wide front window. He was a slight short man with a round head, thin dark hair and tired blue eyes behind rimless glasses. His wrinkled blue suit looked more like a uniform than a suit. "About time," he snapped.

"I'm sorry, Mac," Chad said, "but I couldn't wait here for you." He told him quickly about how he had left the house to go to the bar on Dorrence Street in response to Virginia Kerry's pleading telephone call, and about the work his agency had been doing for Dr. Kerry. He told him of the events leading up to the finding of Dr. Kerry's body and of his suspicion of Dr. Hamid. He omitted the visit of Ann Travis and Jay Lawton to the doctor's house at three o'clock that morning, and the shooting at Dr. Hamid's apartment. Time enough to tell him about those things, he thought, when the reasons for the events were more clear in his mind.

When he finished, McKinney nodded. "All right, Chad. I figured you had a good reason for pulling out. You say that Doc Kerry's nurse will bring Mrs. Kerry here shortly?"

"If not, you can pick her up at Dr. Hamid's apartment. My man is riding herd on him for you."

"I appreciate that," McKinney said. "I want 'em both—Mrs. Kerry and this Hamid. She's a drunk and a screwball, and Doc was taking her away today. Both of 'em had the opportunity and the motive—maybe they were in cahoots." He paused and gazed at Chad thoughtfully. "You've always played along with us, Chad, which is a hell of a lot more than I can say for a couple of other private dicks in this town, and I don't mind telling you that I've done some digging already. Doc Kerry carried a hundred grand life insurance policy, and his wife is the beneficiary. We found that out, and we haven't even started. She traveled fast and there'll be a boyfriend in the wood pile—maybe this Hamid. I always liked Doc—worked with him a lot when he was medical examiner. His wife's a bitch, but the department covered up for her many a time— because of Doc."

"I know," Chad said. "What time did he die?"

"Sometime between three and seven o'clock this morning. That's as close as the coroner can place it for now, but he'll narrow it down after he does the autopsy. From what you tell me, Doc's wife was here all that time, and you saw Hamid sneaking away a little after six-thirty, right after Doc got home." McKinney picked up a gray felt hat from a chair. "Let's go."

"Wait a minute," Chad said. "Doc was alive at six-thirty, when I saw

him come home, so that narrows it down."

"Let's wait and see what the coroner says," McKinney said.

"What happened to the woman I left here?" Chad asked. "She does housework for Doc, and is the one who really found him."

The lieutenant laughed. "The glamorous grandmother? Hell, when we got here she was passed out on the floor with an empty Scotch bottle in her hand. We put her to bed and she's sleeping it off." He moved down the hall to the front door. "Come on."

Outside McKinney spoke briefly to the man at the door and moved out to the first squad car at the curb, Chad following him. "I'll ride with Chad," the lieutenant said to the young cop at the wheel. "You follow us."

As they drove away in the agency Ford, a taxi came slowly up the street toward them. Ann Travis and Virginia Kerry were in the rear seat. Chad pointed them out to McKinney, who said, "All right, let 'em go. Mrs. Kerry will keep. I left orders with Clady. We'll collect this Dr. Hamid first."

They reached the intersection and McKinney said, "Hold it." Chad pulled to the middle and stopped. The policeman came over.

"Did you let a taxi go through just now?" McKinney asked him.

"Yes, sir. Two women—a Miss Travis and Mrs. Kerry. I figured you'd want Mrs. Kerry."

"Good work, Dan."

Dan grinned and went back to his job.

As Chad drove on, McKinney said, "I like a cop who uses us head. A lot of 'em would have stuck to orders and caused a stink."

"Maybe Dan wants to get on the detective detail."

"We need some good men."

"The department doesn't pay enough to attract good men," Chad said.

"You're not telling me anything," McKinney said gloomily.

They left the young cop in the hall of the Clermont and entered Dr. Hamid's apartment. Ed Doyle and the Turkish doctor were sitting quietly in the living room. Doyle was holding the .38 loosely in his lap. Dr. Hamid stood up and gazed at Chad and McKinney uncertainly. Doyle remained seated, but he kept a weary eye on the doctor.

McKinney showed his shield and said, "Dr. Hamid?"

The doctor looked at Chad, his brown eyes soft and reproachful. "I have been telling Mr. Doyle," he said, "that I know nothing of Dr. Kerry's death."

"I'm sorry," Chad said, "but you were seen leaving his house a little after six-thirty this morning."

"But it is not true! I was at a patient's house at that time this morning."

"Doctor," Chad said gently, "I personally followed you here from Dr. Kerry's house."

McKinney said, "You're certain, Chad?"

"I'll swear it under oath."

McKinney nodded in a satisfied manner and said to Dr. Hamid, "Come on."

Dr. Hamid made a hopeless gesture. "This is a grave mistake. My patient will verify—"

"All right," McKinney broke in wearily. "You can make your statement downtown. You are not under arrest at this time." He moved to the door, opened it and the young cop came inside. Dr. Hamid, his face pale but expressionless, picked up his Homburg and put it on. He didn't look at Chad as he moved to the door. The young cop said politely, "Excuse me," and slapped the doctor lightly for weapons. Then he stepped back.

McKinney said to Chad, "I'll want to see you later. Thanks for your cooperation." He nodded at Ed Doyle, "Thank you, too, son. How about a job on the force?"

Doyle smiled. "Thanks, Lieutenant, but I'll stick with Chad. He pays for overtime."

"All you guys think about is money," McKinney said. He nodded at Doyle's naked chest. "You lose your shirt?"

Chad said quickly, "That's a long story, Mac. I'll tell you later."

McKinney gave him a quizzical look. Then he said, "Do that, Chad. I'll remind you." He went out with Dr. Hamid, followed by the young cop.

Doyle said to Chad, "You took me off a hot spot. I didn't know how much you'd told him."

"I skipped the fracas we had here, and I'm glad he didn't see the bandage on your shoulder." As he spoke, he thought uneasily, *Why didn't I tell McKinney about Jay Lawton? Because of Ann?* He asked Doyle, "How do you feel?"

"Not bad. It hurts some, and my arm is pretty stiff."

"You better have another doctor look at it."

"Hamid did all right—I'll say that for him."

"Ready to shove off?"

Doyle nodded, stuck the .38 into a hip pocket, and turned his jacket lapels up over his bare chest. "I'm not exactly dressed for the street." He moved to the bedroom door, leaned down and picked up his brown felt hat from the floor. Chad saw the jagged bullet hole in the brim close to the band. Doyle saw it, too, and poked a finger through it thoughtfully.

"Close," Chad said.

Doyle grinned. "I didn't notice at the time."

"Ed, I won't forget what you did for me."

Doyle seemed embarrassed and said carelessly, "It's not the first time I've had a look at my hole card. All in the day's work." He lit a cigarette, and as he blew out the match Chad saw that his hand trembled slightly.

"Get a girl, Ed," he said, "and maybe a bottle. Relax a little."

"I don't know many girls," Doyle said. "After all, I've only been in this town six months."

"That's plenty long enough. What about that one in your room when I called you to come out to Dr. Kerry's house—that first night?"

Doyle grinned. "That was Isabelle. We both like Brahms."

"Scare Isabelle up. Play some Brahms. Take tomorrow off. You've earned it."

Doyle blew smoke at the ceiling. "What's the catch, boss?"

"Just fifteen more minutes' work today. Is it a deal?"

Doyle smiled at him through the swirling smoke. "What can I lose?"

They left the apartment and went down to the small foyer. Chad opened the office door and asked an elderly lady behind a desk to have the lock on Dr. Hamid's door repaired. "The doctor may be gone for a while," he explained, and closed the door. Ed Doyle waited while he entered the telephone booth and called his office.

"Is Ben back from Port Clinton?" he asked Marjorie Betts.

"Yes—he just came in."

"Good. Tell him to go over to 689 71st Street. It's kind of a ratty old house converted into apartments. Ed Doyle will meet him there and give him the story. Got it?"

"Yes, Chad, but listen—Mr. Harrington has called three times from Toledo. He says it's a crisis and that it's absolutely imperative that you come today."

"All right. If he calls again, tell him I'm on my way." He left the booth and went outside with Doyle. They stood on the sidewalk in the noon sun and Chad said, "There's a man named Jay Lawton. He lives over on 71st Street. He may be there now, and he may not; he may not even go back there, but I want to know it if he does. He and I have a little business."

"What does he look like?"

"Tall, about your height, but heavier. Blond hair, blue eyes. Drives a red Buick convertible."

"And wearing a green jacket?" Doyle asked softly. "Probably corduroy?"

"When last seen."

"I remember him," Doyle said. "On the fire escape." His eyes glinted.

"He's armed, so don't take any chances."

Doyle reached under his jacket and tenderly touched the bandage. "It'll be a pleasure," he said, "and I won't take any chances. I promise."

"All right," Chad said grimly. "It's not far from here, but the hell and gone across town from the office. You go there now and wait for Ben Durstin and give him the story as I gave it to you. I've got to go to Toledo now on a rush job, but I expect to be back early this evening, maybe by nine or ten o'clock. Tell Ben if Lawton shows up this afternoon to stay with him until he can get in touch with me. After Ben comes, the first thing you do is get another doctor to check that wound."

"I thought the first thing was to call up Isabelle."

"That's the second thing. The main idea is for you to relax—and sleep." Chad grinned at him. "Are we all squared away?"

"Right-o."

10

Mr. H. Gerald Harrington was president of a Toledo auto accessory manufacturing company and the crisis he had mentioned on the telephone to Marjorie Betts involved a long-legged secretary who had threatened to turn over certain lurid and startling photographs to Harrington's rich wife, who really owned the auto accessory company, unless he paid her the sum of twenty-five thousand dollars by five o'clock that afternoon.

The threat had been hanging over H. Gerald Harrington's head for a month, and two weeks previously he had called Chad's office for help. Chad had spent a day in Toledo investigating the long-legged secretary, and then had returned to Lake City and sent out inquiries to contacts in a number of cities, including other branches of his own agency. The replies had come in while he had been in Detroit, and he had just read them the day before. He had all the evidence against the secretary that he needed, and it didn't take long to persuade the secretary to relinquish the photographs, plus the negatives. It seemed that the secretary had married and divorced men in Los Angeles, Memphis and Wapakoneta, Ohio, and was currently collecting alimony from each of them. Chad was polite with her and permitted her to leave Harrington's private paneled office, but he'd had the foresight to call the Wapakoneta police, who were waiting outside the office door.

H. Gerald Harrington was almost tearfully grateful and insisted that Chad come home and meet his wife and stay for dinner. Chad was gratified to note that Harrington displayed a touching affection for his wife, who was really quite attractive in a matronly way, and he was also

grateful at the size of the cash bonus Harrington privately pressed upon him. It was almost nine o'clock when he left for Lake City, feeling a little mellow from pre-dinner martinis and after-dinner brandy.

Three miles from the city he stopped for a traffic light at one of the roads crossing Route 20 just outside a village called Seneca Falls. A red Buick convertible edged away from the side of the road on the green light and turned into the lane next to Chad's. It was coming slow—too slow, Chad thought—and it was in the wrong lane. At first he thought the driver was drunk, and he tapped his horn to scare him off, but the Buick continued to head straight for the Ford. Then suddenly it veered off. Chad breathed easier and let up on the horn. Luckily, traffic was thin at the moment, and he decided that if the Buick kept on its course it would pass him with room to spare. And then he had an uneasy feeling.

At the last second, just before the Buick came abreast of him, he gunned the Ford and swung the wheel to the right. The Ford jumped like a greyhound and in the same instant a gun barked and the windshield splintered in front of Chad's eyes. He fed gas and circled in a wide arc, the tires screaming on the rims. The Buick sped away, headed for Lake City. Chad prodded the Ford after it.

At the next intersection a batch of cars was waiting for the green light. Traffic with a few holes in it was streaming across the highway. The Buick swung out into one of the left lanes, picked a hole, and roared through against the light. When Chad hit the intersection there weren't any holes to squeeze through. He slammed on the brakes just short of the solid line of traffic, gunning the Ford and edging the light. But when he jumped ahead on the amber, the Buick was out of sight.

He slackened his speed to the legal limit and drove into Lake City. The wind made a whistling sound through the hole in the windshield.

It was almost ten-thirty when he parked at the curb in front of 689 71st Street. Ben Durstin was loitering on the sidewalk with a newspaper under his arm. He strolled over to the Ford, the vestibule lights of the building casting a squat shadow before him. Chad got out and stood on the sidewalk beside Durstin, who had observed the hole in the Ford's windshield.

"Trouble, Chad?"

"A little. Somebody tried to gun me out on Route 20. He got away."

Durstin pursed his lips. "Any ideas?"

"You're damn right. He drove a red Buick convertible."

"Hmmm," Durstin said. "A little while ago a red Buick parked around in back and a guy went inside. A woman was with him."

"Lawton," Chad said, more to himself than to Durstin, and he tried not

to think about who the woman might be.

"Hefty guy," Durstin said. "He checks with what Ed Doyle told me. Light hair, wearing a green jacket." He squinted his small blue eyes at Chad. "The sonofabitch plays rough, huh?"

Chad nodded, his gaze on the house. "I'm going up. You stay here and watch the front door." He started for the steps.

Durstin plucked at his sleeve. "I'll go with you."

"No."

Durstin's eyes gleamed wickedly. "I'd better, Chad. I don't know what the play is, but I'd better be in on it."

"No," Chad said. "This is kind of a private party. But if you hear a ruckus, come on up. Number five, on the second floor."

Durstin sighed. "You're the boss."

Chad turned away.

"Boss," Durstin said.

Chad turned impatiently.

"The old lady says to thank you for last night. We had a swell time."

"Good. You earned it, Ben."

"You got a gun?"

"Sure." He left Durstin and went inside. The vestibule was deserted. He went up the steps quickly and down the hall to number five. A brawny kid in a T-shirt was on a stepladder fussing with a screwdriver at a light in the ceiling. He looked down at Chad, grinned, and said, "Hi."

"Hi," Chad said absently, stopping before the door to Jay Lawton's apartment. Turning away from the kid's gaze he switched the .38 to his right outside coat pocket and kept his hand on it. Light showed over the transom, but no sound came from beyond the door.

The kid on the step-ladder said cheerfully, "Go right in, mister. I just saw 'em come home."

Chad knocked on the door and waited. Nothing happened. He knocked again. From inside he heard a woman's voice.

"Go on in," the kid urged. "They're home."

"Shut up," Chad snarled.

The woman stopped speaking. More silence. He pounded the door and stepped back a little, his fingers tight around the gun in his pocket. He heard the woman's voice once more, louder now, as if she were close to the door. A man said something harshly, and the light showing through the transom went out. Then he heard the soft click of a lock and he stiffened. Slowly the door began to open, and a man said, "Damn you—!"

Chad kicked the door wide open, stepped quickly inside into blackness and moved along a wall. In the dim light from the hall he saw a vague

white figure near him, and was aware of faint movement.

"Ann," he said softly.

"Here, Chad." Something like a sigh escaped her. "Be careful—he's got a gun."

He knew she was standing somewhere on his right. With his left hand he groped behind him for a light switch. He found one, but he didn't turn it on. "Close the door," he said to Ann Travis.

The door swung shut, leaving the room in almost complete darkness. "Lawton," Chad said.

There was a faint scurrying sound from across the room. Chad flicked the light switch then, and an overhead chandelier blazed. Jay Lawton was caught in the act of backing through a doorway leading to the rear of the small apartment. There was a crude bandage around his right wrist with brownish stains on it. The hand below the bandage looked red and swollen. In his left hand he held a black automatic pistol. The muzzle was pointed at Chad's chest. His yellow hair glinted in the bright light and his blue eyes looked almost black. He was still wearing the green corduroy jacket he'd worn that morning when Chad had met him at Sally's Harbor. There was a blond stubble of beard on his cheeks. He blinked in the light and smiled. "Oh, hello, Proctor." He lowered the gun. "I guess I thought it was one of my—uh—business associates."

"You must have real friendly associates," Chad said.

Lawton shrugged, still smiling. "You know how it is."

"In the rackets? With marked cards and crooked dice? Sure, I know how it is."

"Racket isn't a nice word, Proctor. Let's say it's my business."

"Let's," Chad said. "You tried to kill me today—twice. Was that all in the course of your business?"

A puzzled frown crossed Lawton's face. "You're mistaken, Proctor. I've got nothing against you. What kind of business are you talking about?"

"Blackmail."

Lawton smiled blandly. "Oh, come now. There is no need for you to talk like that. I know why you're here and I don't really blame you. I'm sorry about Ann, but after all the best man won, and all that."

Chad said, "Leave Ann out of it. I came here because you tried to shoot me at Dr. Hamid's apartment this morning and tonight out on Route 20. You've been blackmailing Virginia Kerry, and when I showed up at Sally's Harbor this morning and caught up with her, you guessed that Dr. Kerry was suspicious and had hired me to tail her. You got scared and followed me to Dr. Hamid's apartment, where you knew Virginia had gone. You were convinced that I was after you and you came up the fire escape and tried to kill me. But one of my men came to my rescue

and nicked you—on the wrist, apparently." As he spoke, Chad was aware that Ann Travis, still in her nurse's uniform, was standing rigidly along the wall a few feet from him.

Lawton said mildly, "You're being melodramatic, Proctor. I'll admit that my business has its hazards, but—"

"What is your business?"

"Investments, mostly," Lawton said with a thin smile. "Perhaps occasionally I wager small sums on games of chance or at the track. What's wrong with that?"

"I suppose you hurt your wrist shooting dice?"

Lawton gazed at his bandage wrist with an amused expression. "As a matter of fact, I was changing a tire, and—"

Ann Travis said quickly, "It's a bullet wound, Chad. He picked me up and brought me here, saying he wanted me to meet some friends. Then he asked me to dress his wrist. I told him that he should see a doctor. He became angry, and then you knocked on the door."

Lawton looked at her and something ugly gleamed in his eyes. "Thank you very much, my dear," he said softly.

Chad spoke to Ann, but kept his gaze on Lawton. "I'm sorry," he said.

"Don't be, Chad. Please don't be. I—I deserved it ..."

"My darling, my betrothed," Lawton said in the same soft voice.

"Shut up," Chad said harshly. "The only reason you made a play for her was because of Virginia Kerry. Through Ann you could keep track of Dr. Kerry's movements and know when it was safe to contact his wife, and the doctor would never suspect that the man who was engaged to marry his efficient and loyal nurse was blackmailing his wife—in case he became suspicious of his wife's expenses. You found out that Mrs. Kerry was seeing Dr. Hamid, and you didn't have any trouble convincing her that it would be to her advantage to keep her visits secret from her husband. And so she paid. Five hundred at Sally's Harbor this morning, for example."

"Fantastic," Lawton jeered. "Really, Proctor, you've been reading too many mystery novels."

"I've got the note you wrote to Mrs. Kerry telling her to meet you at Sally's Harbor this morning—with five hundred dollars."

"You can't prove it," Lawton said.

"I don't have to," Chad lied. "I also have your fingerprints from the fire escape outside Dr. Hamid's window, and from the gun I took from your room the other night. The bullets I dug out of Dr. Hamid's bedroom wall will check with that gun in your hand. And on top of that, Mrs. Kerry spilled the whole story to me."

"You're lying," Lawton said flatly. "Why should she tell you—?"

"Because her husband is dead," Chad snapped. "She has nothing to gain by paying you any longer."

Lawton's pleasant veneer cracked a little. "Doc's dead?" Tiny drops of sweat appeared on his forehead and he steadied the gun on Chad.

Chad said, "Did Dr. Kerry get wise to your little blackmail game with Virginia? Is that why you killed him?"

"Talk sense, Proctor. I didn't kill him. I don't know anything about it. What happened?"

"Drop the gun and we'll talk about it."

"I can't, Proctor. I need this gun." Lawton paused and took a deep shuddering breath. "You've got me with the fingerprints, and you probably saw me anyhow. I was sure I wouldn't miss, but that other guy, your helper, he showed up in the bedroom door and screwed it up."

"You hit him," Chad said. "I owe you something for that."

"Sure you do," Lawton said quickly. "I don't blame you—there's nothing personal in this. Give me a break, that's all I ask. Maybe I did take a shot at you this morning, but I couldn't help it. When you took my gun I knew you'd have it checked for prints and, well, I can't afford that. I admit I'm fancy with the cards and dice, but if I didn't take the suckers, somebody else would. I'll leave town and I won't come back." He smiled at Chad. "You win, Proctor."

"It isn't that simple," Chad said. "You tailed me in your damned red Buick and laid for me at Seneca Falls tonight and tried to gun me again."

"No," Lawton said quietly. "I didn't do that. But it doesn't make any difference. If you want the truth, I spent the whole afternoon in a woods along the lake, waiting until it was dark so that I could get to Ann and have her fix my wrist. I couldn't go to a doctor, and it hurt to beat hell. Maybe I was taking Virginia Kerry for a little money, but—" He stopped and smiled, a friendly smile, without malice, oddly open and engaging. "Well, you understand. A man has to turn a fast buck wherever he can, and I knew she was seeing Dr. Hamid on the sly. I figured she wouldn't want her husband to know about it, that it would be worth something to her for me to keep quiet. You see?"

"Yes," Chad said. "Now you'd better drop that gun."

Lawton shook his head. "No, Proctor. Right now I need Ann. My whole arm is hurting—infection, I think. She can fix it until I get to a doctor I know in South Bend. Ann will go with me."

"No," she whispered.

"You must," Lawton said in a ragged voice. "Let us go, Proctor. I'll be good to her, and she can get a train back from South Bend. I need her."

"No," Chad said.

Lawton sighed and braced himself against the wall. "All right," he said

wearily. "Let's get it over with. If that's a rod you're holding in your coat pocket, start shooting."

"I will, if I must."

"You're afraid, Proctor. All you squares are afraid when the chips are down." He waggled the gun in his hand. "You know damn well that I can shoot first."

"That's right," Chad said calmly, and he squeezed the trigger of the gun in his pocket.

Lawton's gun answered, even as he staggered with the impact of Chad's bullet, but Chad had dropped to a crouch before Lawton's shot hit the wall behind him. Lawton slumped against the wall and his gun thudded to the floor. Chad jumped forward, scooped up the gun and stood erect. Behind him he heard the dying whisper of Ann Travis' scream, and he smelled the burned odor of scorched fabric where his bullet had torn through his coat pocket.

Jay Lawton stood hunched against the wall, both arms hanging limply before him. There was a small black hole in the green corduroy of his jacket above his left elbow. He lifted his head with an effort and his white teeth showed in a smile. "Nice shooting, Proctor. Just like in the movies."

11

There was a commotion in the hall and the sound of excited voices. The door swung open and Ben Durstin stepped quickly inside. He had a gun in his hand and his little blue eyes glittered. With a heel he closed the door and stood with his back against it, his gaze sweeping the room. A pounding started on the door.

"All under control, Ben," Chad said. "Keep the mob out while I call the cops."

Durstin's broad red face broke into a lop-sided grin. "Just wondered. Heard the shooting and came a-running." He dropped his gun into a coat pocket and went out, closing the door firmly behind him. They heard his voice in the hall, "Just stand back, folks. Everything's all right. Just stand …"

Chad looked at Ann Travis. She was gazing at Lawton, who had lowered himself to the floor and now sat with his back against the wall, both arms limp beside him. Ann took a step toward him.

"Stay away," Chad snapped. "We'll get him to a hospital."

She stopped and looked at him uncertainly. Her face was pale.

"Are you all right?" he asked.

She nodded slowly. "I—I'm fine now, Chad."

Suddenly he felt happy and he touched her arm as he moved to a telephone hanging on the wall. Lieutenant Abner McKinney was not at the station, but the policeman on the desk said he'd put Chad's request on the radio and that someone would be there in a few minutes. Chad hung up, aware that Lawton was watching him.

"The law," Lawton said bleakly.

Chad nodded.

"No chance for me?"

"I'm afraid not."

"Listen, I can scrape up maybe two thousand. It's yours, if you'll drive me over the state line. If I can get to South Bend ..."

"No."

Lawton's eyes glittered. He twisted painfully until he faced Ann Travis. "Help me, honey."

"Jay," she said, "please ..."

Lawton looked at Chad and said savagely, "What more do you want? You've got your girl back now. What difference does it make to you? If the cops pick me up, I'm finished."

"Why?"

"Never mind," Lawton said. "Let me walk out of here."

"Did Virginia Kerry pay you off this morning? At Sally's Harbor?"

"Yes, sure she did. It's in my wallet. Take it. I'll get the rest of the two thousand, I promise." A gleam of hope flared in Lawton's eyes.

Chad moved to him, reached into the inside pocket of Lawton's jacket and took out a wallet. It contained five one-hundred-dollar bills and six tens. He put the wallet in his pocket.

"Keep it," Lawton said breathlessly. "Hurry. There's a fire escape in back." He struggled to his feet and stood swaying against the wall. His eyes were wild.

"What about the murder of Dr. Kerry?" Chad asked.

"I don't know!" Lawton cried. "Damn it, I've told you."

The door opened and Ben Durstin came in followed by two policemen. In the hall a group of people stood gazing into the room. The kid with the screwdriver stood in the doorway. Durstin slammed the door and said to Chad, "All set?"

Chad nodded.

One of the policemen said, "Hi, Chad," and pointed at Lawton, "Him?"

"Yes. Get him to a hospital first. I'll be down in the morning to make charges. If you need any now, you can start with blackmail and attempted murder."

"That's plenty." The policeman advanced toward Lawton.

"Thanks, pal," Lawton said bitterly. He didn't look at Ann Travis as the two policemen helped him to his feet and led him out.

Chad told Ben Durstin to go home, and he and Ann Travis went down to the agency Ford. They sat quietly for a moment. Then she said in a faint voice, "What happened to the windshield?"

"Bullet."

"Intended for you?"

He nodded gloomily.

"Jay? Because he was afraid of you?"

"Yes." Chad sighed. "He tried twice today."

"Chad, I—I'm sorry ..."

"About Lawton?"

"Yes."

"Because you can't marry him now?"

"Don't talk like that. I never intended to marry him." She turned toward him. "Didn't you know that?"

"How would I know?"

"Oh, stop it," she said impatiently. "Of course you knew that I was just trying to make you jealous. You went away without telling me and expected me to be waiting, whenever you wanted me. I had to—to wake you up."

"I see."

"Please try and understand. While you were away Jay began coming to the office as a patient—sinus trouble, he thought. He was very friendly, and when he asked me to go with him, I went—to spite you. I hadn't heard from you and he seemed all right. I couldn't see any harm in it. I'll admit I was surprised when he asked me to marry him, but—"

"Kind of sudden, wasn't it?" Chad broke in.

"Yes—but I was flattered. Any girl would be."

"He had a reason."

"I know—now. I don't feel flattered anymore." She shivered a little. "But in some ways he was nice. There was something exciting about him, and yet I was a little afraid of him. His eyes, I guess, and he asked so many questions about Dr. Kerry's movements, and about Mrs. Kerry. But he was always kind and a—a gentleman." She laughed a little nervously. "I felt ashamed of myself, knowing that I would never marry him, and I was beginning to wonder how would tell him." She moved against him. "Must we talk about him?"

"You're talking," Chad said. "Did you tell him?"

"Yes," she said quickly. "I told him tonight, after he picked me up and

brought me here. He asked me to treat the bullet wound, and I refused, and I knew that I'd been silly and—"

"All right." Chad stirred restlessly. "Let's forget about Jay Lawton."

"Yes."

"How was Virginia Kerry when you left her?"

She moved away from him. "Isn't that changing the subject?"

"Yes."

"What's wrong, Chad? You act—different. If it's Jay—"

"Forget Jay. What about Virginia?"

"Still in an alcoholic stupor." There was an edge to her voice. "I gave her a sedative and stayed with her most of the afternoon, except for the time that policeman—Lieutenant McKinney—was with her. She was more coherent when I left, after the nurse from the police department arrived."

"Is she under arrest?"

"I don't know. Lieutenant McKinney didn't say, but there were policemen around the house." She plucked at his sleeve. "Chad, who killed the doctor? Who would do a thing like that?"

"The police took Dr. Hamid downtown for questioning."

"I kind of liked him," she said. "He seemed so sincere and so sad." She paused and added in a cold voice, "But I think I hate Virginia Kerry, for what she was doing to the doctor."

He said carefully, "Where did Walter go last night? After the medical meeting?"

She looked at him quickly. "Why?"

"It's important that I know."

"He left the meeting around midnight. When the hospital called me, I called one of his friends who was also at the meeting—Dr. Holman. He told me there had been a bad accident on the lake highway—a bus load of people and a truck. There was an emergency call for doctors, and most of them at the meeting went out, including Dr. Kerry. That was why I couldn't reach him, and I asked Jay to take me to his house, thinking that he might have gone home in the meantime."

"He wasn't there?"

"No, but she was there, sleeping. I couldn't arouse her."

Chad said, "Doc didn't come home until six-thirty. I saw him drive in. What time did he go out to the accident?"

"Dr. Holman told me he left with the rest shortly after midnight. Dr. Holman couldn't go because he's on emergency call at one of the hospitals."

"I'll check with him in the morning," Chad said. "The coroner estimates that Dr. Kerry died between three and seven this morning." He turned

and placed an arm around her shoulders. "I'm sorry I neglected you."
She came against him. "Don't be," she whispered. "I'm sorry for the way
I acted—about Jay. It was childish, and—"

"Shush," he said.

"Did I make you a little bit jealous?"

"More than a little bit."

She sighed happily. "Then it was worth it." She raised her face to his
and her fingers were soft and cool on his cheek. He kissed her, gently
at first, but as her lips grew warm beneath his he pulled her to him
roughly and her arms went around his neck.

"Listen," he said unsteadily, "let's get married."

"Yes, yes. Chad—"

"Don't talk." His mouth found hers again.

Presently she pushed gently away from him. "Happy?" she whispered.

"Yes."

"So am I. It—it's like old times, isn't it?"

"Yes," he said again and his fingers brushed her hair back from her
forehead. He pulled her to him and he forgot about the death of a sincere
and honorable man, a man who had been his friend. He forgot about
another man without honor, and a sad-faced Turkish doctor, and a
blonde woman tormented by her memories. He forgot about everything
but the soft slim body of Ann Travis, his girl once more, and for a time
he was happy.

They drove to a restaurant, had sandwiches and coffee, and it was two
o'clock in the morning when he left her at the door of her apartment.

"I'll see you tomorrow," he said. "How about lunch?"

"I'd like that."

"I'll pick you up. Here?"

She shook her head. "At the office. I'll stay on, until things are settled.
I can do that much for the doctor." Her eyes shadowed for an instant,
and as she brushed a strand of hair back from her face Chad saw the
glint of the ring on her finger. She caught his glance, removed the ring
and held it out to him. "I don't want this," she said soberly.

He took it and held it up to the light. She saw something in his face
and her eyes asked a question.

"Fake," he said, ashamed of the satisfaction the word gave him.

"Throw it away for me."

"I'll give you a real one," he said. "Small—but real."

She smiled at him. "Is—is everything all right now?"

"Everything's fine." He kissed her.

"Tomorrow," she murmured against his lips.

"About twelve." He patted her cheek and left.

He drove slowly and thoughtfully through the streets to his apartment. On the way he stopped by a vacant lot and took Jay Lawton's ring from his pocket. It looked like a diamond, bright and very acceptable at first glance, something like Jay Lawton himself, and he felt a small sense of pity. People lived the way they were born to live, he thought, and there was nothing they could do about it.

He threw the ring into a high clump of weeds and drove on. The wind whistled softly through the splintered hole in the windshield.

12

In the morning, before he left for his office, Chad looked in the telephone book. There was only one Dr. Holman, and he called him. A cool female voice told him that the doctor was in surgery at the hospital and could not be contacted. Was there any message? No, Chad said, there was no message. When would the doctor be in? Dr. Holman's office hours began at one o'clock. He thanked the cool voice and hung up. The morning paper was outside his door and he glanced at the front page. The headline concerned the bus-truck collision on the lake highway. Three were dead, fourteen injured. Down further, in the middle of the page was a two-column head: DOCTOR MURDERED. The brief story gave only the barest facts, and Chad smiled grimly to himself.

On his way downtown he stopped at a jewelry store and looked at engagement rings. One, a three-hundred-dollar item, caught his eye. He paid a deposit and asked the clerk to hold it until the next day, when he would bring in a finger size. Making the deal gave him a new and oddly happy feeling and he whistled softly as he drove down Northern Avenue. He told himself that he would tell Ann about the ring at lunch.

It was almost ten o'clock when he arrived at the office, Marjorie Betts was typing briskly and both Ben Durstin and Ed Doyle were sitting in chairs along the wall reading the morning paper. Ben had the comics and Doyle the sport page. Both men looked fresh and alert, but there was a small patch of adhesive tape on Doyle's left cheek. Durstin was wearing his usual tan gabardine suit, and Doyle was dressed in a soft brown tweed. His brown shoes were burnished to a saddle-leather glow.

The girl and the two men greeted him. Marjorie Betts stopped typing and said, "Call Lieutenant McKinney."

"Yes, Ma'am."

Ed Doyle lifted a hand, "Hi, boss." The right shoulder of his coat

bulged a little over the bandage covering the wound made by Jay Lawton's bullet.

Ben Durstin stood up and grinned, showing his gold teeth.

"Want me to go out to that machine shop on the north side? Where they're missing them diamond cutting tools?"

"You may as well," Chad said. "Can you run a drill press?"

"Hell, yes, and a lathe, too. I still hold my union card."

"You can't run a lathe in that suit."

Marjorie Betts said, "They'll furnish Ben with overalls. The personnel man called this morning. His name is Sweeney—you report to him, Ben."

"Okay." Durstin handed the comic page to Doyle. "Here, Ed, get some culture." As he moved to the door, he said, "Some fun last night, hey, Chad?"

Doyle raised his eyebrows. "Did I miss something?"

"Not much," Chad told him.

Durstin said, "Hah!" and went out.

Chad said to Doyle, "I thought I told you to take the day off."

"I know." Doyle pretended to leer at Marjorie Betts. "I couldn't stand to be away from Marge."

"Aw, go on, now," she said, and kept on with her typing.

"No sense in my just sitting around," Doyle said to Chad. "Makes me nervous."

"What's the matter with your face?" Chad asked curiously.

Doyle touched the tape on his cheek. "Cut—a flying piece of glass from the left front window of the Ford. Somebody took a shot at me last night."

"Where did it happen?" Chad asked quickly.

"On the lake parkway. I slept all afternoon, and then called up a girl—"

"Isabelle, who likes Brahms?" Chad said, grinning.

"Yes," Doyle said, "the fair Isabelle. We made a date for a few drinks. She lives the hell and gone on the east side. I was headed out there— oh, I guess around nine-thirty, and a car pulls up beside me, and—"

"What kind of a car?"

"Buick convertible—red. I didn't get the license number. He took one shot at me, and barreled away. I damn near lost control of the Ford. When I got it straightened out, the Buick was gone."

Chad sighed. "Well, that makes two of us. The same thing happened to me on Route 20, when I was coming back from Toledo. A red Buick convertible." He paused, and then said thoughtfully, "Both of the agency cars are Fords, black, the same year and model. It looks like he was either after both of us, or mistook one for the other. But he was probably

after me." He smiled at Doyle. "I'm bad company for you, Ed. That's the second time bullets intended for me have been slung at you."

Doyle said quietly, "I do seem to remember a red Buick ..."

"Sure you do. Our man Lawton drives one—he's the guy who winged you at Dr. Hamid's yesterday. He was blackmailing Mrs. Kerry and I caught him at it. He tailed me to Dr. Hamid's and tried to gun me from the fire escape. Then he tried again on Route 20 last night."

Doyle frowned. "Is he still loose?"

"No. Ben and I cornered him last night—that's what Ben was talking about. The cops have Lawton now."

"Did he have anything to do with Dr. Kerry's death?"

Chad shrugged. "I don't know yet. Parts of the deal tie in, but I can't connect them. He had reason to kill Dr. Kerry, if the doctor was wise to the blackmail, but it still looks like Dr. Hamid is our boy."

"Or Mrs. Kerry?" Doyle said softly.

Chad shrugged again.

"I'd hate to think it," Doyle said. "She's—nice."

"Maybe she was once, before the booze got her, and the memories." Chad thought of the tiny life-like doll in the dash compartment of the Ford.

"Yeah," Doyle said. "I know.... What's for me today?"

"You're on detached service for the moment, since you won't take the day off. Wait until I call McKinney." He used the phone on Marjorie Betts' desk.

The lieutenant sounded tired. "Good morning, Chad."

"What's up?"

"This Lawton—he's raising hell and demanding a lawyer."

"You got him there in the pokey?"

"Now we have. He spent the night in a hospital."

"Have you checked the prints on that gun I sent over to you?"

"Yes. I was going to ask you about that. The report from Washington says the prints belong to a joker named Langley. Small time gambler from Kansas City, but now he's wanted for murder. Killed a man down there in a crooked blackjack game and scooted. How did you get the gun?"

"It's Lawton's," Chad said. "My prints are on it, too."

"We figured that, Chad. We'll hold this Langley or Lawton or whatever the hell his name is, and check the Kansas City department. Stop around here sometime today, will you? I think we should have a little talk."

"What about Dr. Hamid?"

"We had to let him loose this morning. A fellow over on Ore Street

swore that Hamid was at his house at six-thirty yesterday—the time
you claim you saw him leaving Dr. Kerry's house."

"But I did see him," Chad said. "I'll swear—"

"I know," McKinney said wearily, "but, this guy, this husband, has
signed a sworn statement that Dr. Hamid was attending his wife at six-
thirty. Says he got there around five-thirty and stayed a couple of
hours. You must have been mistaken, Chad."

"I wasn't," Chad said stubbornly. "I saw him, I tell you. He sneaked
away from Doc's house a few minutes after six-thirty, right after Doc
came home, and I followed him straight to his apartment."

"Wasn't it kind of foggy yesterday morning?"

"Sure, but I know it was Hamid. He's in love with Mrs. Kerry, and—"

"Never mind," McKinney said sharply. "Just never mind. That's the
way it stands now. Maybe the guy on Ore Street is covering for Hamid,
but I can't see any reason for it. Anyhow, you don't have to worry about
it now."

"The hell I don't! Doc Kerry was a friend of mine."

"I know," McKinney said sadly. "Friends come and they go, Chad. The
older I get, the more pals drop off."

"Is it okay if I go out and talk to Mrs. Kerry?"

"Sure. Paul Horgan is there. Tell him I said so."

"Thanks, Abner. I'll see you." Chad hung up and looked at Ed Doyle.
"Want to come along with me to see Mrs. Kerry?"

Doyle shrugged. "Why not?"

Down on the street Chad took the doll from the dash compartment of
the Ford he'd been driving and put it in his coat pocket. Then he drove
the car into the garage beneath the office building and left instructions
for the windshield to be repaired. He and Ed Doyle got into the Ford
Doyle had been using. In spite of his wound, Doyle insisted upon
driving. It was a soft September morning with bright yellow sunshine.
Chad sat quietly while Doyle skillfully maneuvered the car through the
thick downtown traffic. Before they reached Bridge Road, Chad told
Doyle about Dr. Hamid's alibi. Doyle shook his head and said, "I can't
figure it."

"Neither can I. Maybe I dreamed I saw Hamid sneaking home in the
fog."

It was a quarter to eleven when they parked behind a police car in
front of Dr. Kerry's house. Both of them went inside.

The detective named Paul Horgan was tilted on a chair in the hall
smoking a cigar. The house was quiet and hushed. Morning sunlight
shimmered on the polished floor and made a bright reflection from a

wall mirror. Horgan was a medium-sized man with a narrow smooth face and thin black hair. A gold lodge emblem was draped across the vest of his rather shabby brown suit and his scuffed brown shoes were dusty. Chad knew that he had been with the department a long time, and that he was the father of seven children ranging in age from six months to sixteen years.

Horgan waved his cigar. "Hi, Chad."

"Hello, Paul." Chad nodded at Doyle. "This is Ed Doyle, from my office."

Horgan shook hands with Doyle without getting up. "Glad to know you, Ed. Has this old bastard been treating you all right?"

"So far," Doyle said, smiling.

"You gotta watch him," Horgan said. "He's a slicker."

"Paul," Chad said to him, "Abner said I could talk to Mrs. Kerry."

Horgan pointed his cigar at a door. "Go ahead. Maggie Donovan is with her."

As Chad moved down the hall, Doyle said, "I'll wait here."

Chad paused and looked at him. "Come along, if you like."

"No, thanks," Doyle said bleakly. "I've seen her—plenty."

Chad nodded, moved to the door and knocked softly. The door opened and Maggie Donovan's bulk stood before him. She was big and round-bodied and gray-haired, a veteran nurse on the Lake City force. There wasn't much in the way of vice and crime and heartbreak and trouble that Maggie Donovan hadn't seen, and the memories showed in her hard gray eyes. She had a fat red face and a grim jaw, but in spite of her forbidding appearance Chad knew that her eyes could soften and that she had a mother-to-all-the-world heart.

"Hello, Maggie," he said softly. "Abner said I could talk to Mrs. Kerry."

"Sure, Chad." She smiled. "But make it quick." She held a fat finger to her lips and shook her head in a silent gesture of warning.

Chad stepped past her into the room.

Virginia Kerry was on the bed in a half-sitting position with pillows piled behind her head. A blue satin quilt covered her knees, and she was wearing black silk pajamas that buttoned snugly at her throat, mandarin fashion. Chad wondered grimly if the black pajamas were a symbol of mourning for her dead husband. Her eyes were closed and the sunlight filtering through the drawn blinds cast a yellowish glow over her pale face and the blonde hair which fell in soft folds around her face and shoulders. The blue half-moons beneath her eyes were darker than when he'd seen her at Sally's Harbor the previous morning, and her lips were colorless. She had once been beautiful, he thought, and was still beautiful, in spite of the liquor and the thing that tormented her,

and he felt again the quickening within him at the sight of her.

He remembered what Dr. Kerry had told him about the rugged early days, and he tried to picture her as she had been then—the cheerful young wife of a young doctor, serving her husband as nurse, secretary and consultant, helping him in the first years of struggle to establish a practice. He would have liked to have known her then, he thought sadly, before life and the years and the memories had caught up with her, and as he gazed at her the disturbing excitement increased and he remembered vividly the soft lines of her body as she had lain naked on that first night in this same room.

He moved forward slowly until he reached the side of the bed, until he could smell her faint clean fragrance. Behind him Maggie Donovan whispered, "I gave her a hypo a couple of hours ago, but it should be worn off by now."

Chad nodded, touched Maggie's arm, and said in a low voice, "Mrs. Kerry."

She didn't move.

"Virginia," he said.

Her lashes flickered a little, and her lips formed almost soundless words: "Darling, come and get me ..."

Chad leaned over and touched her arm. Her eyes opened and he saw the dullness from the sedative, and the pain and the haunting terror. She gazed directly at him and said in a flat dry voice. "Who are you?"

"Chad Proctor."

Recognition flickered in her eyes. "Walter's friend?"

"Yes."

She closed her eyes and said flatly, "Walter is dead, you know."

"Yes, I know," Chad said. "I'm sorry, and I want to help."

"Help?" she whispered. "What can help now?"

"Nothing, really," he said gently. "All that's left is to find the person who killed Walter. Don't you want that?"

She opened her eyes. The haunted look was still in them, but they were clearer, and he saw another thing, maybe fear, and a veiled slyness. Something like a chill went over him, and he took the doll from his pocket. Her eyes widened and she reached for it, like a child reaching for a toy.

"She's mine," she said distinctly. "Give her to me."

He let her have it. Tenderly she placed it on the pillow beside her and pulled up the quilt until only the small painted head was visible. He saw that the doll's hair was the exact shade and texture as Virginia Kerry's and that the face was her face in miniature. It gave him an eerie sensation, and he glanced around at Maggie Donovan. She had seen it,

too, and she compressed her lips and moved her head silently and sadly.

"That's a pretty doll," Chad said.

The woman on the bed smiled faintly and a tear slid down one cheek. She patted the doll's head gently. "My baby, my little Jeanette," she said in a crooning voice.

"Jeanette?"

"That's what I named her before she was born." She looked at Chad and smiled brightly through her tears, but there was a wildness, a something, in her eyes. "Don't you think she looks like me?"

"Yes," Chad said soberly, remembering that Dr. Hamid had told him the initials stood for his dead wife in Turkey, Josephine Kizza. "Where did you get her?"

She closed her eyes and said wearily, "Questions, questions ..."

Chad felt Maggie Donovan plucking at his sleeve, but he said, "Where, Virginia?"

"From a man in New York," she said in the same tired voice. "An artist. I sent him a photo of myself and some of my hair, and I asked him to make a doll. It took a long time, but finally she came." She opened her eyes, and the wildness was still in them. "Caesarean section, you know."

Chad remembered the long white scar he'd seen on her abdomen. "Yes, I know, Virginia."

"Did Walter tell you?" she asked brightly. "About how I was in labor for twenty-two hours before he permitted them to do a Caesar? Dr. Holman wanted to do it right away, after he saw the X-rays, but Walter wouldn't let him. He said it would be better if I had a normal delivery. So they waited, and my baby died ..." Her face contorted, and she began to cry, as a child cries.

Maggie Donovan said in a motherly voice, "Now, honey ..."

Virginia Kerry stopped crying and looked at Chad. "It was my pelvic structure," she said calmly. "And so now I pretend that the doll is my baby. You can understand that, can't you?"

"Of course," Chad said. "I found the doll in Dr. Hamid's apartment."

Her eyes wavered and she plucked at the satin quilt with long pale fingers. "Thank you," she said shyly, "for bringing her home to her mother." She raised her gaze to his. "Where is he?" she asked plaintively. "Where is Dr. Hamid? He should be with me now."

"He's in love with you?"

"Yes," she said softly. "He's a good and kind man. He's been trying to help me. I let him try, but I didn't tell Walter. He would have been angry." The sly look crept into her eyes and she patted the doll's head tenderly. "We fooled Daddy, didn't we, Jeanette?" A maternal look of love softened her face.

Chad said, "A man named Jay Lawton knew you were seeing Dr. Hamid, and he made you pay to keep him from telling Walter, didn't he?"

"I believe so," she said absently, gently stroking the doll's head.

Chad took a deep breath. "Virginia, you'll have to face it—you're going to be arrested for the murder of your husband."

She turned her head slowly until she looked directly at him. The melting maternal look faded and a black ugly shadow seemed to creep slowly behind her eyes. Her slim fingers plucked at the quilt, and then the fingers bunched the material violently and a scream died in her eyes. Her mouth opened a little, slackly, and her cheeks seemed to sag and crumple. "Go away," she whispered. "Please go away."

"What happened?" he asked softly. "You were here, in this house, with him all the time. Where is the gun?" Maggie Donovan plucked nervously at his sleeve once more, but he shook off her hand impatiently.

"I was drunk," Virginia Kerry said brokenly. "I told the police I was drunk, asleep. I don't remember ..."

"Did you want to kill him?"

Horror was naked in her eyes. "No, no. I—I loved him. He neglected me and left me alone, but I loved him. He wanted me to have a baby, but I can't have any now, not ever, ever. All I have is Jeanette, and they wouldn't even let me see her after she was born. They took her away from me and I didn't know that she was dead, and I never forgave Walter for not letting me see her. He said it was best that I didn't see her, but she was mine. He had no right ..." She began to sob, her face twisted in an ugly mask of sorrow.

Chad touched her hand. "Virginia, I'm sorry."

She jerked her hand away from his, and her voice was thick with the tears and her grief. "Give me a drink, oh please give me a drink."

"No, honey," Maggie Donovan said firmly.

Chad said helplessly, "Virginia, I—"

"Go, go!" she screamed, her hands beating on the quilt. "Damn you, go!"

He turned and looked at Maggie Donovan. The big policewoman pursed her lips and jerked her head toward the door. There was the bright gleam of a needle in her hand as she moved to the bed.

Chad went out and quietly closed the door.

13

Outside in the hall Chad paused to light a cigarette. Paul Horgan and Ed Doyle gazed at him silently. He moved slowly down to them.

Horgan said, "Hysterical, huh? We heard her."

Chad nodded, drawing on his cigarette.

Horgan shifted the cigar in his mouth. "She carried on yesterday, too—when Abner talked to her. I think she's nuts."

"No," Ed Doyle said gently. "She's—" He searched for a word, and then said, "Lost. She's lost in a dark woods."

Chad glanced at him in surprise. Doyle's face was grave as he gazed at the door to Virginia Kerry's room.

"You're right, Ed," Chad said. "She's lost in a dark woods."

"Blah," said Horgan. "Lost, hell. Abner told me about her. She was just boozing and chasing around and her husband got wise, and she killed him." He flicked cigar ashes to the polished hardwood floor. "Happens every day."

"Paul," Chad said to him, "did Abner tell you the name of the man on Ore Street—the guy whose wife Dr. Hamid was supposed to be seeing at the time Dr. Kerry was killed?"

"Yeah," Horgan said from around his cigar. He took a small notebook from a pocket and flipped the pages. "What would you private dicks do without us cops?" He stopped at a page and read. "Alfred L. Newcomb, 1546 Ore Street."

"Thanks," Chad said. "I'll see you."

He and Doyle went out. As they stood by the agency Ford, Doyle thoughtfully fingered the tape on his cheek. "What now, boss?" he asked quietly. "Did she tell you anything?"

"Not much. She admitted seeing Dr. Hamid and that Lawton was blackmailing her, but that's all. Claimed she didn't know anything about what happened the night Doc was shot."

"Do you believe her?"

"I don't know. There's only one thing more we can do; should we run out to Ore Street and see this Alfred L. Newcomb? Dr. Hamid's alibi?"

Doyle shrugged. "It's up to you. Is there anything in it for the agency anymore?"

Chad shook his head. "Not a damned cent. In fact, we'll have to wait now until Doc's will is probated before we can collect what's already owing us." He looked back at the house.

Doyle followed his gaze, and Chad knew that he, too, was thinking of Virginia Kerry. "She's in for a rough time," Doyle said.

"Maybe she deserves a rough time," Chad said harshly.

"Maybe—but I still don't think she killed him."

"You never know ... Want to come along to Ore Street?"

"We'll be doing it for free—for Doc."

"And for his wife?"

"Maybe."

"You and Dr. Kerry were pretty good friends, weren't you?" Doyle asked.

"Yes."

Doyle smiled at him. "What's money, then? Let's go."

Number 1546 Ore Street was a small frame house with a narrow porch in a row of small frame houses with narrow porches. There was a garage in back housing a bright new Chevrolet. A mammoth television antenna towered over the house like a schooner's main sail on a row boat. The lake and the docks were at one end of the street, with a vast industrial area at the other. Beyond was the city, its buildings bright against the blue September sky.

Chad and Ed Doyle left the Ford at the curb and went up a short sidewalk to the porch. An elaborate wooden plaque beside the mailbox bore old English lettering: *Alfred L. Newcomb—Welcome Ye Friends.* From inside the house a nasal voice blasted at their ears above the twanging of a guitar. Chad pressed the bell button, not daring to hope that it would be heard above the thundering sound.

The door remained closed. He pressed the button again and looked at Doyle, who said something he couldn't hear. Doyle made a motion of opening the door. Chad nodded and turned the knob. The door swung open and sound engulfed them in drowning waves. Directly across a small room they saw a man sitting in a sagging overstuffed chair. In one hand he held a beer bottle. He was gazing intently at something out of the line of vision and beating time with one foot on a thin worn carpet.

"Hey!" Chad yelled at him.

The man didn't look at them and Chad yelled again. Doyle stepped inside and closed the door. They could see the television then, a monster set with a giant screen in a gleaming mahogany cabinet which also housed, Chad had no doubt, the very finest radio and record-playing combination. On the screen a toothy cowboy was strumming a guitar and singing a song about a gal who loved a pinto pony. On the floor along one wall was a row of empty beer bottles, and through a door was a kitchen and a table littered with dirty dishes. There was one other chair in the room and on it was piled an assortment of clothing—shirts, socks and overalls. Bread crusts, beer bottle caps and wrinkled newspapers covered the floor.

Chad waved his arms over his head, like an official in a football game signaling a touchdown. The man in the chair saw them then and turned his head suddenly. He was about thirty-five, with a narrow pale face, a thin rodent nose and a shaved butter-bowl haircut. He had on blue denim pants and a soiled and torn T-shirt. His feet were bare and

stiff bristles of chest hair protruded from holes in the T-shirt. He glared at Chad and Doyle suspiciously, but he made no move.

"Mr. Newcomb?" Chad shouted, but his voice was lost in the drowning waves of nasal voice and thumping music.

The man cupped a hand to an ear and his mouth formed an irritable and soundless "What?"

Chad tried again, straining his throat: "ARE YOU MR. NEWCOMB?"

The man shook his head impatiently, got up suddenly, padded over to the television and turned down the volume. He looked at the two men and in the comparatively blissful quiet he said sullenly, "I'm broke until payday."

"Mr. Newcomb?" Chad asked once more.

"That's me, boys, but I ain't got any—"

"We just want to ask a few questions," Chad broke in.

Newcombe looked relieved. "Then you ain't bill collectors?"

Chad shook his head.

"What kind of questions you wanna ask?" Newcomb asked suspiciously.

"Is your wife sick?"

Newcomb took a half-smoked cigarette from his pants pocket and stuck it in his mouth. "Why do you wanna know that?" he asked reasonably.

"We just want to know," Chad said patiently.

"Cops, ain't you?" Newcomb flicked a match with a thumb nail and lit the cigarette butt.

"That's right," Chad said, "Now—"

"Lemme see your badge." Newcomb grinned slyly, pleased at his caginess.

Chad gave him a quick look at his private agency card.

"Okay," Newcomb said grudgingly. "Cops was here yesterday, too—about Dr. Hamid."

"Is he your regular doctor?"

"Oh, sure. He's kind of screwy acting, being foreign and all, but he comes when we want him. The missus has got gall bladder trouble. Had a hell of a time with her the last couple of days. Kept me up all night the night before last."

"Is that when you called Dr. Hamid?"

"Yep. And he came right out—in a taxi, yet. He don't know how to drive a car."

"What time was he here?"

"Them other cops asked me the same thing."

"I know," Chad said. "We're just double-checking."

"Well, like I told them, he got here around five-thirty in the morning and stayed until almost eight. He gave her a couple of shots in the arm, and watched her a while, and finally he said she oughta go to the hospital. But I can't afford that—I didn't pay my hospital insurance last month."

"You're certain about the time?"

"Sure I am. What did Doc do—murder somebody?" He giggled at the joke.

"How long has Dr. Hamid been treating your wife?"

"Oh, four-five months now, on and off. The missus always got something wrong with her. Even when we got married, she was sick then. She had—" He paused and frowned in concentration. "Something with a long fancy word." He took a swallow from the beer bottle and his eyes brightened. "Mal-nu-trition," he said proudly. "That's what she had. Mal-nu-trition."

"Have you been in Lake City long?" Chad asked him.

"About a year. Came up from Kentucky, when the coal mines went on slack time. I work for the Northern Steel Company."

Ed Doyle spoke for the first time. "Isn't it kind of tough on your paycheck? I mean, with your wife sick so much?"

"Tough? Hell, brother, it's murder. I had to lay off the last couple of days to take care of her, and I owe Doc Hamid two hundred bucks, and the finance company is after my car and the TV." He grinned at them, showing broken yellow teeth, "You guys wanna beer?"

"No thanks," Chad said, moving to the door. "We won't bother you anymore."

"No bother," Newcomb said, and pointed at the television screen. "Now watch. Pretty soon he'll do some rope tricks. See them guns he's wearing? Real six-shooters, silver plated. And that belt's got gold nuggets in it. And them boots—genuine cowhide. I'm gonna get me a pair—if I can save up enough box tops." He drained the bottle, "Of course," he explained, "they don't send you real cowhide boots, like his'n, but they got spurs on 'em and everything."

The cowboy on the screen smiled winningly and strummed his guitar. *Now, don't forget, kids—just ask your Mommy to buy that swell, crunchy, delicious cereal called Candy Pops and you eat 'em morning, noon and night, and at bedtime, too, and don't forget—*

From somewhere in the house a woman called angrily in a shrill voice, "Al! Turn it up—I can't hear!"

Alfred Newcomb twisted a dial viciously and it seemed that the walls began to shake with the sound. Chad nodded and smiled at Newcomb, who waved a hand absently. As Chad and Doyle went out, he was seated

once more in a chair, watching the television intently, his foot beating time to the strident music.

It was almost twelve noon when they drove away from the residence of Alfred L. Newcomb.

Doyle said, "Well, what do you think?"

"It looks like Hamid's alibi is airtight. Anyhow, we can't prove that he wasn't at Newcomb's."

"It's your word against his," Doyle said. "You saw Dr. Hamid leaving Dr. Kerry's house at six-thirty in the morning."

"Yes, I know," Chad sighed. "It doesn't add up."

Doyle turned the Ford into Northern Avenue. "You know," he said, "Newcomb owes Dr. Hamid two hundred dollars; could Hamid buy an alibi for that?"

"I've thought of it," Chad admitted. "Maybe we should have talked to Newcomb's wife, too—just to see if the stories checked."

"Hell," Doyle said, "if Newcomb is lying for Hamid, you can be damn sure he had his wife tipped off."

Chad didn't answer, and presently they drove into the garage in the basement of the building where Chad's office was located. An attendant came over to tell them that the windshield had been replaced in the other Ford, the one Chad had been driving, and Chad left instructions for the replacement of the side window in the second car,

As they went up in the elevator, Doyle said, "That was damned queer—both of us being gunned last night. They took a shot at me right here in town, and then jumped you at Seneca Falls." He touched the tape on his cheek. "You think it was Lawton?"

"It was a car like Lawton's. Who else could it be?"

"I've been thinking," Doyle said quietly, "if it wasn't Lawton—then whoever it was is still sneaking around loose."

The same thought had been with Chad for some time, but he had pushed it to the back of his mind. Now he remembered that Lawton had denied shooting at him on the road outside Seneca Falls, and a kind of cold uneasiness crept over him. "It must have been Lawton," he said, "and he's in jail." He hesitated, grinned at Doyle, and added, "But keep your eyes open anyway."

"Sure, boss." They left the elevator and moved down the hall to the office.

Marjorie Betts greeted them briskly, told Chad that he was to call Lieutenant McKinney and also Miss Ann Travis. Then she showed him a letter from an insurance company in Chicago asking the agency to locate a beneficiary to a ten-thousand-dollar policy whose last address

had been in Lake City. The insurance company was a regular client and the letter contained all the necessary information, including data given them by the Lake City post office.

Chad handed the letter to Doyle. "Here's a nice soft job for you, Ed. No blondes to tail, no oriental doctors, no hot lead. Just find a guy and tell him he's got ten thousand bucks."

Doyle grinned, took the letter, moved to a shelf of books and began looking at the latest city directory. Chad entered his office and closed the door. He called Ann Travis first.

Her crisp voice answered. "Dr. Kerry's office."

"Good morning," he said.

"Hi, Chad." Her voice grew warm, and the memory of the night before came back to him. "Listen, would you mind very much if I didn't have lunch with you?"

"Certainly I mind. We have a date, and—"

"Oh, Chad, I can't! This office is a madhouse, and there's so much to do. The phone's been ringing constantly, and all the patients are worried and asking which doctor to switch to, and a lot of them are coming in for treatments and for appointments I haven't had time to cancel."

"It was in the papers," Chad said. "They all must certainly know by now that Doc is dead."

"I know, but they want to talk to me about it, and some of them don't read the papers, and—Chad, I can't get away now. I'm having a sandwich sent up and I'm working straight through."

"All right," he said in a resigned voice. "How about dinner then?"

"Fine. Six o'clock?"

"I'll pick you up there. We'll drive out to someplace along the lake."

"Oh, good. May I have a martini?"

"Champagne," he said.

She laughed softly. "Are you happy, Chad?"

"Yes."

"So am I. Very happy—" Her voice sobered. "Except for Dr. Kerry."

"I know," he said.

"Chad, have they arrested Mrs. Kerry?"

"Not yet."

"Will they?"

"I'm afraid so—unless something turns up."

"I can't feel sorry for her. Is that wrong of me?"

"No, I guess not."

"Chad, I—I loved Dr. Kerry. I mean—"

"I know," he said again.

"Tonight, Chad. I'll be looking for you."

"All right. Good-bye, Ann." He hung up, and then immediately called Lieutenant Abner McKinney.

"Chad, can you come over to the station?"

"Now?"

"If you can."

"What's up?"

"Dr. Hamid has just signed a confession that he killed Dr. Kerry."

"No!"

"Yep. Come over, and I'll tell you about it."

"Ten minutes." Chad picked up his hat and moved to the outer office.

Ed Doyle turned away from the book shelves and tapped a thick volume in his hand. "Last year that guy worked for the Lincoln-Mercury Auto Sales here. I'll start there."

"Good," Chad said. "Listen, Ed—Abner McKinney just told me that Hamid confessed to killing Dr. Kerry."

Doyle stared wide-eyed. "Honest?"

Chad nodded slowly.

Doyle took a deep breath. "Then you were right all along? About seeing Hamid leave the house?"

"Yes. I was beginning to think I'd dreamed it."

"Well, I'm glad," Doyle said. "That leaves Mrs. Kerry out."

"I'm going over to the station," Chad said. "See you later."

14

Lieutenant Abner McKinney faced Chad across a small battered desk in a small battered office. From the squad room outside could be heard the drone of a shortwave radio and the ringing of telephones. McKinney had his coat off and held a short stub of cigar in his fingers. Sunlight glinted on a gold wedding ring. His thin black hair was tousled on his round skull and his blue eyes behind the rimless glasses looked more tired than usual.

"First," McKinney said, "you may like to know that we got a report on this Lawton, or Langley, from the Kansas City department. He's wanted there, all right, and we're agreeing to extradition. Apparently he was small-time around here. Of course, if you want to hold him ..."

"No. Throw him to the boys in Kansas City."

"All right," McKinney said, and he smiled thinly. "I forgot to mention that there's a thousand-dollar reward for him. You'll get it."

"Not me," Chad sighed. "The agency."

McKinney grinned. "You're just a working man, like the rest of us?"

"That's me."

McKinney tapped a paper on his desk. "Here's Hamid's confession, all signed and sealed," he said with satisfaction. "He'll be indicted tomorrow."

"Nice work, Abner. Tell me about it."

McKinney puffed on his cigar. "Not much to tell. This morning the D.A. decided we ought to arrest Mrs. Kerry. She had the motive and the opportunity. Circumstantial, of course, but the D.A. wanted action. We were just bringing her out of the house when Dr. Hamid shows up. He was all excited and wanted to talk to Mrs. Kerry in private, but we wouldn't let him, and I told him that she was under arrest for the murder of her husband. He went kind of wild then and spilled the whole story. Said he was in love with her and had killed her husband. A common motive but a good one. He admitted sneaking into the house to see her and that Dr. Kerry came home and surprised him. Said he had a gun and shot Doc, and that Mrs. Kerry didn't even wake up. Claims he threw the gun into the lake. I've got men looking for it now. Chad, I guess you were right, after all, about seeing him leave the house."

"I didn't hear any shot," Chad said.

"That could be," McKinney said. "He was inside the house, in the bedroom, And maybe you were dozing a little." He grinned.

"The hell I was," Chad said. "What about Hamid's alibi? This Newcomb?"

"Hamid admitted that he'd paid Newcomb to say he'd been at his house treating his wife. Said he canceled a debt Newcomb owed him, and paid him more besides."

"What does Newcomb say?"

"Nothing. He sticks to his story, but he's scared of being slapped with a perjury charge."

"Naturally," Chad said. "Could I see Hamid?"

"Why?"

"Just to ask a couple of questions."

McKinney laughed shortly. "We've asked 'em all. There ain't any more questions." He peered at Chad narrowly through his glasses. "You don't seem happy about it, Chad. Were you hoping it was the wife?"

"No. I just want to be sure it's Hamid."

"Hell, he confessed."

"I know. Let me see him."

McKinney sighed, picked up a telephone and spoke briefly. Neither he nor Chad spoke while they waited. In a few minutes Detective Paul Horgan came in with Dr. Hamid handcuffed to a wrist.

Horgan grinned at Chad and said, "Hi."

Dr. Hamid stood quietly, his liquid brown eyes shifting from Chad to McKinney. His dark gray suit was wrinkled and his pointed black shoes were dusty. He needed a shave and his skin looked dead white against the black stubble.

Chad said, "Hello, Doctor."

Hamid bowed slightly. "Mr. Proctor," he said in his soft rich voice.

"I'm sorry to see you here. Lieutenant McKinney tells me that you have confessed to a murder."

"That is true."

"Why did you kill him?"

Dr. Hamid looked bewildered and glanced at McKinney.

"But I have told the lieutenant ..."

"I know," Chad said harshly. "Tell me, too."

A faint flush showed beneath Dr. Hamid's pale skin. "Very well. I was in love with Mrs. Kerry. I wanted to help her, but I could only see her on rare occasions, when she would come to me in desperation. I wanted her for myself, but she was married. So I killed her husband. He surprised us, when I was attempting to arouse her, and I shot him."

"Your benefactor," Chad said bitterly. "The man who was your friend, who helped you."

"Yes," Dr. Hamid said sadly. "I am sorry that I had to kill him."

Chad suppressed a sudden impulse to rise and smash Hamid with his fist. He said in a tight voice, "Does Mrs. Kerry love you?"

"I do not know. Sometimes I dared hope that she did. But it did not matter. She would have loved me—in time."

"Does she know that you killed her husband?"

"She does not," Hamid said instantly. "She is entirely blameless."

"One thing more," Chad said. "Did you know that I followed you when you left the house—after you killed Dr. Kerry?"

"No," Dr. Hamid said stonily. "I did not see you."

Chad turned to McKinney. "Take him away. If I look at him anymore, I'll be sick."

Chad had lunch with McKinney and returned to the office. He called Dr. Holman, talked briefly and sympathetically about Dr. Kerry's death and learned that his friend had indeed left the medical meeting to go to the scene of the accident on the lake highway. Dr. Holman did not know what time Dr. Kerry had gone home, but he stated that the injured persons had received emergency treatment and had been removed to hospitals very quickly. Chad thanked him, parried some rather pointed questions about the circumstances of Dr. Kerry's death,

and hung up.

He spent the afternoon doing desk work. At five-thirty, after Marjorie Betts had left, he turned off all the lights except the shaded one over his desk, and moved to the window and watched the late September dusk creep over the city. It will soon be October, he thought, and the days are getting shorter. Soon the leaves will all be down and the snow will come in off the lake and I'd better check with the garage about antifreeze for the cars.

Far below the streets were clogged with traffic and the faint continuous hooting of horns came up to him. People, he thought, hurrying to wives and husbands and kids, to a cocktail, to warm lighted living rooms, or to a tenement on the waterfront, to a cold and lonely room.

Outside in the corridor he heard the doors slamming and the sound of footsteps, and the cheery babble of office workers on their way home. Presently the voices and the quitting-time sounds were gone and it was still and hushed. He turned to his desk, took a bottle from a deep drawer, carried it into the outer office and got a paper cup from the dispenser beside the water cooler. He filled the cup, placed the bottle on Marjorie Betts' desk, and sipped slowly at the whisky.

Events of the past slid slowly across his brain, and he was seeing people again and hearing snatches of conversation, a slow parade of the minutes and the hours. He saw again the body of Dr. Walter Kerry, and the haunted eyes of a blonde woman tormented with her own private hell. He saw the long pale face of Dr. Hamid and he heard again the words of his confession. He thought of Ann Travis and of all the lonely years before and of the women he'd known in the past. For the first time in months he thought, with sadness, of his younger brother, dead in a nameless grave on Okinawa, and he thought of his own military service, of the years with the O.S.S., and of a certain *fräulein* with a tiny wicked gun in her hand in a room in Berlin. He thought of his father and mother, dead now, buried together in a grave along the Ohio River, and he remembered the days of their funerals and the rain falling both times in the cemetery. He remembered his training at the agency school in Pennsylvania, and of his first client, the aging, pouting rich woman who had wanted a lover far more than the bodyguard she pretended she needed.

He thought of Ben Durstin, and wondered if he'd nabbed the tool stealer at the machine shop, and of Ed Doyle, searching now for a missing insurance beneficiary, and of Marjorie Betts, who lived alone at the Y.W.C.A. and who never seemed to have much fun. He thought of Jay Lawton, wanted for murder in Kansas City, who had tried to kill

him, and Ed Doyle, too. He thought of all these people and more, and presently it was time for him to pick up Ann for their dinner date.

He was pouring a last small drink when the door opened and Ed Doyle stepped in.

Chad held up the bottle. "Drink?"

Doyle shook his head. "No, thanks. Just wanted to wash up a little before I eat, and to unload this." He took a heavy Colt .38 from the inside pocket of his coat and laid it on the desk. "It weighs me down," he said, grinning.

"Any luck?" Chad asked him.

"A little. I found out he left town about six months ago and moved to Fremont. I'll run down there in the morning." He sighed. "I wish to Christ somebody would hunt me up and tell me I was on the receiving end of ten thousand bucks."

"Me, too," Chad said.

Doyle rested a hip on the edge of the desk and looked across at Chad. "You look beat up, boss. It's been kind of rough the last couple days, hasn't it?"

"Kind of." Chad smiled at him. "You don't look like any daisy yourself."

Doyle lit a cigarette. "Me for a big thick steak, and then home to bed.... Is Ben working a double trick tonight?"

"It's up to him. If he gets a line on the guy who's swiping the diamond tools he might work straight through the graveyard shift." He glanced at a small bronze clock on the desk. Six o'clock. Ann would be waiting for him. "Well," he said, "I've got a date."

"With the cute nurse?"

Chad nodded.

"You're lucky, pal."

"How's your love life?" Chad asked. "How's Isabelle?"

"I'm afraid she wants to get married." Doyle said, grinning.

"Everybody should get married," Chad said, "sooner or later." Suddenly the idea seemed attractive to him and he remembered with pleasure the ring he had picked out for Ann that morning.

The telephone rang, a sudden shrill sound in the quiet office. Chad answered it and recognized Ann's voice. "Chad?"

"Yep. I'm on my way."

"Listen—I just had a call from Mrs. Kerry. She's in a bar at Seneca Falls, and she wants me to come out there. I—"

"She's on her own now," Chad said harshly.

"Chad, she was crying, and she said she was lonely, that she wanted to talk to someone. The doctor's funeral is tomorrow, you know, and she said there were relatives at the house, and that she couldn't stand them,

and so she sneaked out this afternoon. She didn't say so, but I guessed that the police have released her. Is that right?"

"Yes," Chad said.

There was silence on the wire for a moment, and then Ann said, "I— I don't like her, Chad, but I can't refuse her. She should be taken home and kept there, at a time like this. It's not—not decent, with her husband lying dead. I'd better go get her. I can do that much, for the doctor's sake."

"All right," Chad said wearily, "but I'm going with you."

"I wish you would, Chad. We can have dinner later. If you like, we can get some food and take it to my apartment ..." The soft promise in her voice was like a caress.

"That sounds fine. Did she name the bar?"

"No. She hung up before I asked her. She just said Seneca Falls, but it's a small place. I'm afraid she's pretty drunk...."

Ann's voice went on, telling him more about Virginia Kerry, asking him questions, but he only half heard her. Two words were burning into his brain: *Seneca Falls.* A small crossroads town on Route 20 three miles from Lake City, the place where someone in a red Buick had shot at him, tried to kill him. His fingers tightened on the phone and suddenly it seemed that a bleak wind was blowing slowly across the office. The parade was moving in his brain again, and then it stopped, and the words seemed to blink at him like a vast neon sign: *Seneca Falls, Seneca Falls....*

"Chad," Ann Travis was saying, "are you listening?"

"Sure."

"I'll lock the office and wait for you down in front."

"All right."

"What's the matter, Chad?"

"Why?"

"You—you sound queer."

"Never mind. Wait for me."

She was saying something as he hung up. He gazed across the desk at Ed Doyle.

"Trouble?" Doyle asked softly.

Chad took a deep breath, realizing that he was trembling a little. "Yes," he said, his voice sounding tight and queer in his ears. "Bad trouble. We've got to take a ride."

Doyle sighed. "Now?"

Chad nodded.

"Okay," Doyle said. He slid off the desk and stood up straight. "Neither snow nor rain, nor heat nor gloom of night ..."

"That's right," Chad said heavily. "The mail must go through."

"Where are we going?" Doyle asked curiously.

Chad picked up the gun Doyle had laid on the desk. "To the police," he said, "to turn in the murderer of Dr. Kerry."

Doyle looked startled. "I thought that was all cleared up. Hamid confessed, didn't he?"

"Yes, but he's just protecting Mrs. Kerry, because he loves her."

"Then she ...?"

Chad shook his head.

"Then who?" Doyle's voice was desperate, faintly shrill.

"You, Ed," Chad said sadly.

15

The office was very quiet and Ed Doyle seemed lost in thought. He was facing Chad, but his eyes weren't seeing him; they seemed to be looking at something far away and lost forever.

"I'm sorry, Ed," Chad said gently.

Doyle's eyes focused on him then. "It's all right," he said. "I've been rather expecting it, and I'm kind of glad." There was sweat on his forehead and the piece of tape on his cheek looked like a spot of leprosy in the dim light.

"Take off the tape," Chad said. "Your face isn't cut."

"No," Doyle said slowly, "it isn't."

"You faked it," Chad said wearily, "after you deliberately broke the window of the Ford you were driving, to make me think that the same person was after both of us, or had maybe mistaken you for me. You got scared yesterday—you decided I was digging too much, learning too many things, and so you laid for me outside Seneca Falls—in a red Buick convertible—to make me think it was Jay Lawton, in case you missed me. And when you did miss me, you gave me the story about somebody shooting at you, too. Isn't that it?"

"Partly," Doyle admitted. "I had to go to three car renting outfits before I found a red Buick convertible." He paused, and his gaze shifted away from Chad's. "You've got me, haven't you?" he asked in a low voice.

"Yes."

Doyle took a deep breath. "I know it," he said miserably. "I know you. You've got me, or you wouldn't have said anything, not yet." He raised his eyes and Chad saw the pain and the black sadness in them. "I—I'm sorry."

"For trying to kill me?"

"For everything," Doyle said. "For all of it. But I was on the wheel—I couldn't stop. But I didn't try to kill you. I intended to miss—to convince you that Lawton was still gunning for you, to get your mind away from Virginia Kerry and me."

Chad remembered that Doyle had ranked high in marksmanship at the agency school, and he did not doubt that Doyle could have hit him, even from a moving car, if he had wanted to. But the knowledge only made him feel worse, more sad; somehow he wished that Doyle had really shot to kill.

"Thanks, Ed," he said.

"There's more," Doyle said, spreading his hands in a hopeless gesture. "I didn't kill Dr. Kerry—not intentionally."

"His wife did?" Chad couldn't keep the faint mockery from his voice.

Doyle shook his head. "Neither of us. Do you believe me?"

"Maybe."

"Say you do," Doyle said quickly. "It's important to me, that you believe me. I know I won't have a chance with a jury—I can't prove a thing. But I didn't mean to kill him. Maybe, in a way, I was glad that he died—I admit that. But afterward I had to try and cover up, to save Virginia and myself, if I could ... What did I do wrong, Chad? When did I slip?"

"This morning," Chad said, "after we left Newcomb's house. That's when you slipped. We were coming up in the elevator and you mentioned that someone had shot at me at Seneca Falls. All I told you was that it happened on Route 20, a highway that runs clear to New York. But you pinpointed the spot—'Seneca Falls,' you said, because you were there."

"Such a little thing," Doyle said dismally. "What else?"

"Other little things added up; your rage at those men dragging Virginia Kerry out of Sally's Harbor—I wondered a little about that. I wondered, too, about your generosity in offering to work overtime, your refusal to take a day off. You wanted to stick to me, to know what I was doing. I was the one you had to convince, the one you were afraid of. Except for Marjorie Betts, you were the only person who knew I was going to Toledo yesterday and that I expected to return at the time I did. You relaxed after Dr. Hamid confessed and thought you were safe, even though you knew he was lying.... You're really crazy about Virginia Kerry, aren't you?"

"Yes," Doyle said in an unsteady voice. "Crazy is the word, I guess. Ever since that first night when we saw her naked on the bed, I wanted her, knew that I had to have her. Can you understand that?"

"Yes."

"Can you?" Doyle asked wonderingly.

"Yes," Chad said again, remembering Virginia Kerry's slim white body.

A kind of shine crept into Doyle's eyes. "She's wonderful, Chad. She used me, but I didn't care. She used me like she uses whiskey, to help her forget what she is trying to forget. She didn't really care about me, but it was all right. I figure I'm way ahead."

"Even now?"

"Even now," Doyle said quietly.

"How did it happen? About the doctor?"

"It's still kind of foggy in my mind," Doyle said, "like something I dreamed. After you left me that night, I stayed in the car, watching the house, thinking of her. Then the people came in the Buick and after they left I entered the house, as I told you. Virginia was still sleeping, passed out completely, because she'd been drinking steadily until we brought her home. I thought of what you had said about the doctor taking her away, and I—I didn't know if I'd ever see her again. I kissed her—a kind of good-bye kiss, I guess—and I laid down beside her. Maybe I was hoping she'd come out of it. Anyway, I wanted to be near her, for just a minute or two, before I left her. It was a stupid thing to do—I didn't realize how tired I was. I must have fallen asleep right away. The next thing I knew the light was on and Dr. Kerry was standing in the doorway. I—"

"What time was that?" Chad broke in.

"How the hell do I know?" Doyle asked harshly. "Three-thirty, maybe four o'clock in the morning. Does it matter?"

"Go on."

"He just stared at me and he didn't say anything. The sleep had made me groggy and I was too shocked to move or speak. Then I started to get off the bed. He said, 'You sonofabitch,' and walked to a dresser across the room. I didn't know what he was up to. Then he opened a drawer and took out a gun. He turned and pointed it at me. There wasn't any use in trying to talk to him—I knew that he intended to kill me, and I felt that I was dead, right then."

Doyle paused and shivered a little, remembering. "I couldn't jump for him," he went on. "He was too far away and he held the gun straight out, with both hands. It looked queer as hell, awkward, but at the same time as if he wanted to be sure he wouldn't miss. I saw his finger press the trigger hard, and I reached for my gun, expecting all the while to die, waiting for the blast. But I shot anyhow, aiming for his arm or shoulder, just to wound him, to stop him. I heard the shot, and I didn't know if it was his gun or mine, or both, but I felt my gun jump. I was rattled and

groggy and my aim was lousy." Doyle paused and smiled bitterly. "He fell without a sound, and when I went to him I saw that he was dead."

"Then what?"

Doyle turned away slowly and gazed out at the evening sky. "Virginia didn't wake up. She stirred a little and moaned, but she was too far gone to know what had happened. I was glad of that. I picked up the doctor and carried him to the adjoining room and laid him on the bed. My bullet had hit his heart. I—I went through hell for a while. It looked like murder without a doubt, and unless I did something Virginia would be on a very hot spot, and me, too. Then I thought of Dr. Hamid, of what you had told me about his being in love with Virginia, and I had an idea."

"Yes?" Chad said softly.

Doyle turned to face him, his face haggard. "Chad, I want you to know all of this and I want you to believe it, because it's the truth."

"All right, Ed."

"I decided to frame Dr. Hamid. He meant nothing to me, compared to Virginia."

"And yourself," Chad said.

"Yes," Doyle said bleakly. "When the chips are down, we think of our own skins, don't we, Chad?"

"Maybe. It depends."

"Damn it—what would you have done?"

"Probably gone to the law with the truth."

"Like hell you would," Doyle said harshly. "Listen—I wanted to clear Virginia and myself. But the truth wasn't pretty. I'd be damn lucky to get off with manslaughter, very, very lucky. I couldn't tell you about it. I'd already betrayed the agency, and the truth wouldn't be believed anyhow. It was the old messy story; husband catches wife's lover in bed with wife. Lover kills husband. Send the sonofabitch to the chair."

"You never know what a jury will do," Chad said.

"But I couldn't take the chance! Can't you see? I figured everything out. Then I called Dr. Hamid, told him that I was sick and wanted him right away and gave him a phony name and an address way over on the south side, so I'd be sure he'd be gone as long as I wanted him to be. The poor guy said he'd come right away. He seemed glad to come—"

"He needed the money," Chad said. "He doesn't have many patients yet."

"That's what I figured. I went to his apartment, saw him leave in a taxi, and went up and forced the lock on his door. You remember that the lock was broken?"

"Yes," Chad said. "I told the woman in the office there to have it fixed."

"I went inside," Doyle went on, "and took one of his dark suits and a

Homburg hat. I even took some of his Turkish cigarettes, so that I'd smell like him if you got that close to me."

"You knew I'd follow you?"

"Of course. You're a bloodhound, Chad. But I knew that I'd have to stay far enough away from you so that you couldn't get a close look. I carried the suit and hat back to Dr. Kerry's house. Virginia was still dead to the world. Then I went out and drove the doctor's Packard around the block and left it, returned to the Ford and waited for you to relieve me, as you said you would. When you showed up, I told you that Dr. Kerry hadn't come home yet—"

"But he was already there?" Chad broke in. "And dead?"

"Yes. I left you, drove the Ford a couple of blocks and parked it, went to where I'd left the doctor's Packard. His medical bag was in it. Then I drove the Packard past you and into the garage and entered the house carrying the bag. In the fog I knew you would assume that it was the doctor. Inside the house I turned off the lights, put on Hamid's suit and hat and waited. At six-thirty I left, knowing that you would see me and follow. I led you to the Clermont and let you see me enter Dr. Hamid's apartment."

"You took a big chance," Chad said.

"I know," Doyle admitted, "but I had nothing to lose. And I counted on the rain and fog. Hamid and I are about the same height and build." He paused and said in an odd reproachful voice, "It would have worked out, Chad, if you hadn't ..."

"I know," Chad said harshly, "but I can't duck it now. What did you do with the gun? The one the doctor had?"

"I threw it in the lake, off the dock at the foot of Northern Avenue. A funny thing, Chad—the safety catch was still on. Dr. Kerry wanted to kill me and he tried to pull the trigger, but he couldn't, not with the safety on. I can't figure it out. And the way he held it, with both hands—"

"Shut up," Chad snapped. "The poor guy didn't know any better. He spent all his life helping people who needed him, and a gun isn't a scalpel or surgical scissors or a pair of forceps. He never had time to learn about guns, or to even care about them. He told me that he'd never fired a gun in his life. That's what saved you."

"Chad," Doyle whispered. "I'm sorry, so damned sorry ..."

"So am I," Chad said bitterly. "I'm sorry for everything. When Hamid confessed, that tied it all up for you, didn't it? You would have let him go to the chair for murder?"

"Yes," Doyle said. "So would you, for a woman like her. She was marvelous. You've no idea ..."

It seemed to Chad that he'd been standing by Marjorie Betts' desk for

a long time, and he saw that it was now black dark outside. The dim light in the office made hollows in Doyle's lean face and glinted on his eyes. The gun felt heavy in Chad's hand and he felt old and deadly tired. "Ed," he said, "I'd like you to go over to the station with me and walk in with your head up. As a favor to the agency and to me."

"No," Doyle whispered.

"I want you to tell your story to McKinney."

"No," Doyle said again. "He wouldn't believe me—nobody will believe me."

"I do, Ed. You've got to face it."

Doyle laughed suddenly, a brittle sound, and it seemed to Chad that something feral and ugly glittered in his eyes. "I'm in too deep," he said. "They'll pin it on me, first- or second-degree murder, one way or the other, and Virginia will be in it, too—it's made to order for a jury of honorable husbands and jealous wives. I'll run, Chad, and take my chances."

"It'll be an admission of guilt."

Doyle shrugged. "If they catch me, I can still give them my story."

"It'll make it worse for you."

"Maybe—if they catch me."

Chad sighed and hefted the gun. "You're not going anywhere, Ed. I'll call McKinney. He can pick you up here." He reached for the phone.

Doyle's quick voice stopped him. "No, Chad. You've got the gun. You'll have to use it."

"I don't want to do that."

"I'll jump you if you don't."

"Damn it, Ed ..."

Doyle moved slowly forward until only the width of the desk was between them. There was a hot light in his eyes. "There's another way, Chad."

"What?"

"Can we make a deal? Let Hamid take the rap? I'll marry her—I know I can talk her into it—and she'll get a hundred thousand dollars from the insurance company. Name your price, Chad."

Suddenly Chad felt better. The sadness was still with him and the shock, but he felt better. "Thanks, Ed," he said. "That makes it easier."

"No price tag?" Doyle asked bleakly.

"You know better."

"Yes," Doyle said, and his face seemed to crumple. "Chad—" His voice broke. "It—it's Virginia. I'm thinking of her. She's had enough, and they'll blame her, too, sure as hell ..."

"She's in the clear," Chad said shortly.

Rage flared in Doyle's eyes. "How do you know?" he cried. "You weren't there! Who do you think you are—God?"

"Listen," Chad said. "Yesterday morning at Sally's Harbor she paid Lawton money to keep certain information from her husband. But her husband was already dead, and if she had known that he was dead there would have been no need for her to give Lawton the money. Do you see?"

Doyle nodded slowly. "That adds up and I'm glad. You'll swear to it?"

"If I have to."

"Now it's just me," Doyle said.

"Take your chances, Ed."

"No, I can't. I'm washed up with the agency, with everything.... You'll have to use that gun, Chad."

"No."

"You'd better, because I'm coming for you. Shoot fast and straight, Chad."

"Don't be a fool."

"Let me walk out of here, then. Give me a couple of hours."

"I can't."

Doyle's lean body tensed and his eyes were on Chad with a cold intensity. He was measuring the distance, Chad knew, and calculating his chances. Then Doyle smiled and moved forward a fraction of an inch. "I'm coming, Chad."

There was only a tiny space of time left. Chad knew that he would have to shoot, do something, and he hated it.

A shrill sound broke the silence, a startling jangle, the telephone ringing.

At the sudden sound Doyle's gaze shifted for an instant, involuntarily, and in that instant Chad leaned forward and swung the gun. Doyle ducked, but he was too late. The heavy barrel struck the side of his head and he went to his knees. Chad leaped around the desk, grasped the short dark hair of the lowered head and swung the gun again in a short chopping arc. Doyle's body sagged and gently Chad lowered him to the floor.

The telephone rang insistently, shattering the stillness. Chad gazed at it dully. Ann's calling me, he thought; she is growing impatient. Thank you, Ann, he said silently in his mind. I didn't have to shoot him. Thank you for calling me the instant you did.

Abruptly the telephone stopped ringing.

In the dim soft quiet he got a pair of handcuffs from a cabinet along the wall and clicked one of the bracelets around Doyle's right wrist, the other around the leg of the desk. Then he picked up the bottle, took a

long swallow, and leaned against the desk. He gazed out of the window at the dark sky, and had another drink, thinking that there were things he must do. But there was no hurry, and the whisky was hot and comforting.

After a time Doyle stirred and turned over on his back. The handcuffs clinked faintly. He opened his eyes and gazed up at Chad, blankly at first, and then with recognition, and with it came the pain of remembrance.

"Chad," he whispered.

"Yes, Ed."

"I stopped a bullet for you—at Hamid's place. Remember?"

"I remember."

"It—it seems like a long time ago."

"Long ago, but I thank you just the same."

"She was marvelous, Chad."

"I know."

"You can't know. She ..."

"I know," Chad said again, thinking of Virginia Kerry waiting desperate and alone in a bar at Seneca Falls for someone to come to her, to help her. Maybe Dr. Hamid could help her now, he thought, really and truly help her. If love could help, and understanding, Mustapha Hamid, M.D., was the man.

"What now?" Doyle said.

"The cops, Ed."

Ed Doyle closed his eyes and smiled a little, as if he were remembering.

"Right-o," he said.

THE END

DEATH OF A LADIES' MAN

···

ROBERT MARTIN
WRITING AS LEE ROBERTS

1

Saturday Afternoon, Late

The car was a late model black Pontiac sedan. It had been stolen in South Bend and was splattered with mud. Behind the wheel sat an angular man with hot dark eyes, a lean tanned face, and close-clipped black hair growing gray at the temples. He wore a brown leather jacket over a plaid flannel shirt. A soiled, white silk scarf was knotted about his throat, cowboy fashion. Beside this man sat another, a squat, dark man who needed a shave. He, too, wore a leather jacket, a black one, with a ragged tear in one sleeve. A gray checkered cap was pushed to the back of his head. In the rear of the car a third man, younger than the two in front, sat on the edge of the seat. His blond hair was too long and it curled at the back of his neck and over his ears. There was a thin yellow fuzz on his cheeks and his eyes were a pale washed blue. He wore a dirty tan trench coat, belted, the collar turned up.

The three men were gazing at a large brick building on the corner across the sidewalk to their right. A huge sign across the front read: THE FRIENDLY LOAN CO. CAR FINANCING OUR SPECIALTY. PERSONAL LOANS: $10.00 TO $1,000.00. FAST SERVICE. NO RED TAPE.

The man behind the wheel spoke softly. "It's almost time. They'll be closing now. All set?"

The squat man nodded, leaned forward and drummed his fingers on the dash. The young one in back leaned further forward and said, "See if I've got it straight, Steve. You go in. I stay outside by the door to be lookout. Delbert drives." He had a high-pitched, breathless voice.

"Right, kid." The man at the wheel opened the door, got out, and stood on the pavement. Cars moved past and a few people were on the sidewalks. No one paid any attention to the three men and the dirty black car.

The squat man slid across the seat and settled himself behind the wheel. He turned the ignition key and the motor hummed softly. He put the automatic shift lever into drive position and placed a foot on the brake pedal. The car was on the very edge of the corner No Parking zone and no other cars were in front of it. The three men had cruised the block until this space became empty. It was one minute to five o'clock on a Saturday afternoon in April.

The man called Steve nodded at the young man in the car and then

walked around the front bumpers and crossed the sidewalk to the glass door of the building. He paused there a moment, his left hand on the glass, and peered inside. The young one in the trench coat got out of the car, strolled over to the building, and leaned casually beside the door. His name was Ronald, but everyone called him Ronnie. He was Steve's brother.

Now Steve pushed at the door and went inside. The man at the wheel of the car gunned the motor gently and cursed softly and steadily. His name was Delbert Owens and he was very nervous. Ronnie, standing by the building door, glanced up and down the street and then got out a cigarette and lit it with trembling fingers. He was nervous, too, but did not want his brother or Delbert Owens to know it. This was his first big job. One minute went by. Then two. Then three.

The glass door swung open and Steve hurried out carrying a bulky, brown paper shopping bag which had been folded beneath his jacket. "Come on, kid," he snapped. "Hurry, but don't run." He crossed the sidewalk and was inside the car before Ronnie fully realized that it was over. He dropped the cigarette and walked swiftly toward the car, the trench coat flapping about his legs. Behind him the glass door opened again and a slight, gray-haired man in a blue suit ran out to the sidewalk. He raised a revolver and fired at Ronnie three times, the shots echoing all along the street

"Stop, thief!" the gray-haired man cried melodramatically. "Police, police!"

Ronnie stumbled once, but he made it to the car, lurched inside and huddled on the rear seat. As the car swung out from the curb, brakes screeched behind them and horns sounded, but Delbert paid no attention. He fed gas, cleared the cross street. At the next block the light was red, but Delbert picked a hole in the cross traffic and snaked the Pontiac through. Then he swung right on a one-way street leading to the lake road, following their plan.

"Gun it," Steve said. "Get the hell out of here."

"Sure, sure." Delbert was panting and the wheel was slippery with sweat from his hands.

Steve turned in the seat and looked back at Ronnie. "You okay, kid?"

"I—I'm hit, Steve. In the leg, high up. It—it hurts." Ronnie was almost sobbing.

"Just take it easy." Steve turned back in the seat and spoke to Delbert. "We'll be in the clear in a couple of minutes, out of the city. You know where to turn off."

"Sure, Steve, but what about the kid? If he took a slug, he'll need a doctor. Can't we just head for the state line and—?"

"Shut up," Steve said harshly. "You just drive. I'll worry about Ronnie."

"All right, all right! Anybody on our tail?"

Steve turned again and gazed back through the rear window. "I don't think so; not yet." Then he spoke gently to his brother, who was still huddled, gray and shivering, on the rear seat, his legs drawn up. "How is it now, kid?"

"B-bad," Ronnie stuttered. "I—I can feel the blood, Steve."

"Don't worry. You'll be fine, I promise." Steve turned back and spoke viciously to Delbert. "Faster, stupid."

They had made another turn and were on the lake highway now and the car's motor sang a keener song. As he gripped the wheel and nervously watched the road, Delbert asked, "What was the take, Steve? How much?"

"How the hell do I know? Did I stop and count it?"

"I was just asking," Delbert said sullenly. "Ain't that the turnoff up ahead?"

"Yes," Steve said. "You're real smart."

Delbert slowed the car and made the turn from the highway onto a narrow, rutted road leading back through weeds and scrub pine trees. He drove carefully over the bumps and said nothing.

A crowd had gathered on the sidewalk in front of the Friendly Loan Company, but two uniformed policemen kept the curious back from the doorway where the slight, gray-haired man in the blue suit was talking to a tall, bare-headed man in a gray tweed topcoat. This man was Lieutenant John Horner, of the Harbor City police. The gray-haired man, who still held the revolver, was the manager of the loan company. His name was Richard Eversole. Lieutenant Horner, after securing a somewhat incoherent description of the muddy black car and the three men, had phoned crisp orders to headquarters for roadblocks to be set up outside the city. He had dispatched two cruise cars in the direction the robbers had taken and had also alerted the sheriff's office and the state highway patrol. Lieutenant Horner was an efficient police officer and knew his business. Now he poised a pencil over a pad and said, "We'll get 'em, don't worry. Tell me again just what happened, and take it slower."

The manager took a deep breath and began to talk.

Just before closing time he and five assistants were checking the day's receipts, mostly cash in five-, ten- and twenty-dollar bills, and preparing a total to be placed in the night depository at the bank. It was company policy to bank every other day—Tuesday, Thursday and Saturday. Friday and Saturday were their biggest days and they never left much

cash in the office over weekends. He went to lock the door just as this man walked in, a tall man wearing a brown leather jacket. When the man was inside, he took out a gun with his right hand and his left hand produced a large brown paper shopping bag. "Fill it up," the man said. "Quick."

Mr. Eversole filled the bag at gun point while the assistants huddled in a corner. Then the man grabbed the bag, cautioned them all not to move, and left. Mr. Eversole snatched a revolver from a drawer. It was an old weapon which had been there for years because the insurance company required a gun on the premises. Mr. Eversole had never fired it, but he knew it was loaded. He ran out to the sidewalk, saw the man in the brown leather jacket getting into the front seat of a car. Another man, wearing a tan trench coat, was hurrying toward the car. Still another man sat behind the wheel. Mr. Eversole had fired three times at the man in the trench coat. He guessed it had been three times, but he couldn't be sure. He had been pretty excited and had just pulled the trigger until the gun seemed to jam. Then the man in the trench coat got into the back seat of the car and the car drove away from the curb fast, causing cars approaching from the rear to suddenly slow down to avoid hitting it. The car ran through a red light at the corner and kept going.

"Do you think you hit him?" Horner asked.

"I don't know. He seemed to sort of stumble once, just before he reached the car."

Horner held out a hand. "Let's see the gun."

The manager handed it over. Horner took it and with some difficulty swung out the cylinder. "Rusty," he said. "No wonder it jammed. Lucky you didn't get your hand blown off."

"I don't know anything about guns," Mr. Eversole said. "I hate guns."

Horner returned the revolver. "How much did they get?"

"A little over forty-two thousand."

Horner whistled softly.

A light panel truck with POLICE DEPT. lettered on the side stopped in the No Parking zone at the curb. Two men got out and pushed through the crowd to Horner. "Just prints," Horner said to them. "No pix. Take the door first, inside and out." He nodded at the manager. "Mr. Eversole will show you where to lift them inside." Horner sighed. "A needle in a haystack, but we've got to try. The prints inside, if there are any, will be on top of all the rest, though."

"Overlay?" one of the men asked.

Horner nodded and then spoke to Mr. Eversole. "That man wasn't wearing gloves, was he?"

Mr. Eversole shook his head. "No. I'm positive of that."

"Did you, by chance, get the license number?" Horner asked the question without hope.

"No, I didn't," the manager said regretfully. "You see, I was so—"

"I understand." Horner turned to the two laboratory technicians. "The door is our best chance. It's a swinging door, but he might have touched it when he went in or out."

"Okay, Lieutenant." The two men went to the truck to get their equipment.

"Thanks for your help," Horner said to Mr. Eversole. "We'll do our best."

"I'm sure you will." Mr. Eversole sighed. "I've been in the loan and finance business for thirty years, but this is the first time I've ever been robbed. I mean like this, with a gun. Sticky fingers, yes, I've had that." He pushed open the glass door. "I'll have to notify the home office and the insurance company."

"Is the loss fully covered?" Horner asked.

"No, I'm sorry to say." Mr. Eversole shook his head ruefully. "Twenty-five thousand is the maximum."

"Let's hope we get it all back for you."

"Yes," Mr. Eversole said bleakly as he entered the building.

Tuesday Evening

Clinton Shannon, M.D., rested his arms on the restaurant counter and raised tired eyes to the girl in the white uniform. "Just coffee, Sue." It was ten o'clock on a rainy night and his day had begun with surgery at seven-thirty that morning in the Harbor City Memorial Hospital.

The waitress smiled. "You look all in, Doctor."

Shannon nodded and sighed. "I'm a little weary, I admit."

She drew his coffee and set it before him. The only other customers in the small restaurant were a group of teenagers drinking Cokes and giggling in a rear booth. The front window glistened with rain and the light from inside shone brightly on the wet sidewalks. Shannon's light tan raincoat and gray felt hat were sprinkled with raindrops. He removed glasses with amber-tinted frames and began to wipe them on a paper napkin. A faint stubble of reddish beard showed on his cheeks and chin. His coppery hair, showing a tinge of gray, was clipped short. He replaced the glasses, removed his hat and placed it on the stool beside him.

"Quiet evening, Sue?" he asked, stirring the coffee.

"So far, since the supper hour, but it'll pick up when the movies let out."

A big man wearing a gray tweed topcoat came in and sat beside Shannon. "Hi, Doc." He spoke to Shannon, but his gaze went appreciatively over the waitress. He was younger than the doctor, no more than thirty, with a dark handsome face and clear blue eyes. He wore no hat and moisture glinted on his black curly hair. His name was John Horner, but everyone called him Jack, of course.

"'Evening, Jack," Shannon said, sipping his coffee.

The waitress, who was young and blonde, eyed Horner with a faint provocative quirk to her lips. The uniform was too tight for her full figure, and she knew it. "The usual, Lieutenant?" she asked.

"That's right, honey." Horner flung back his coat, reached into his right trouser pocket and placed a half dollar on the counter. The movement revealed the black butt of a revolver protruding from a holster at his belt.

The waitress moved away, moving her hips more than was necessary. Shannon finished his coffee, lit a cigarette and said, "On duty tonight, Jack?"

Horner took his gaze from the waitress. "Not officially, Doc. I'm sort of on my own."

"Do you still think the men who robbed the loan company are holed up near here?"

Horner nodded. "It's just a hunch. We know they headed for the lake highway and I don't think they got clear ahead of the roadblocks. They just—disappeared."

"Maybe they got away in a boat," Shannon suggested.

Horner shook his head. "The harbor patrol and the Coast Guard were alerted right away. Anyhow, they would have had to ditch their car and we haven't found it." Horner thumped his fist lightly into his palm. "I'd sure like to nab them."

Doctor Shannon grinned. "Bucking for that promotion, Jack?"

"I don't have to buck. When Captain Keely retires next month I'm in line for his job."

"You'll get it," Shannon said, thinking that Lieutenant John Horner was one of the best men on the Harbor City police force. Horner's only fault, as far as Shannon knew, was his weakness for female companionship. This was not a fault, for a bachelor, but Horner was married and the father of two children. As a doctor, Shannon was aware of certain extra-marital activities on the part of some of his patients. For example, he had treated Lieutenant Horner for an infection not ordinarily contracted in normal family life. Shannon sighed and reminded himself that it was his duty to heal, to be objective, and not to concern himself with the morals of his patients.

The waitress returned with coffee and two sugar-coated doughnuts, rang up the sale and placed change on the counter before Horner, who said, "That's for you, honey. Buy yourself a pack of cigarettes."

"Thanks, Lieutenant." The waitress pocketed the coins and turned to Shannon. "More coffee, Doctor?"

"Half a cup, Sue, thanks." He pushed the cup across the counter, thinking that he should be leaving. Before going home he wanted to stop at his office and check his schedule for the morning. But he remained at the counter, drinking the coffee, feeling a dull inertia and an aching weariness.

Horner said, "Those boys made a big haul—forty-two grand. And they timed it right. Saturday afternoon late, just before closing time. They knew that with the Friday and Saturday installment payments there would be a big payday bundle."

"So I read in the papers," Shannon said.

"Professionals," Horner said, "from their M.O. We got one good set of prints, though, from the glass of the office door—Steve Donegal's. He's wanted for murder in Indiana and for armed robbery in four other states. He just got careless, I guess. Two men with him. One in the car and a lookout on the sidewalk. Steve made the heist himself. The company manager, Dick Eversole, ran out and fired a couple of shots at the lookout—he was the last one to get into the car—but he's not sure if the guy was hit. I hope he was, because if it's any wound at all he'll have to see a doctor. Maybe that will smoke 'em out." Horner grinned at Shannon. "They might even pick you."

"Have all the doctors in the area been notified?"

Horner nodded. "Sure. We did that right away."

Shannon put on his hat and slid off the stool. "Well, good luck, Jack. But watch yourself."

"I'll do that, Doc."

Shannon went out into the rainy night. Behind him in the restaurant Horner began joking with the waitress.

In his office on the fringe of the city's business district Shannon switched on his desk lamp and read a note that Lucille Sanchez, his combination nurse and secretary, had typed on a prescription form. *Doctor: Dr. Kovici called. Not necessary to assist him with surgery in the morning. Patient expired early this evening. Morning house calls listed in appointment book. Full afternoon schedule beginning at 1:00. Lucille Sanchez, R.N.*

Shannon smiled at the note's formal efficiency. Lucille was the best nurse he'd ever had, but he sometimes wished she'd relax a bit, be more human, and not always address him as "Doctor." But he shouldn't

object, he thought, even though he felt that she deserved more enjoyment from life. She was still young and darkly attractive, but to his knowledge she had no men friends, or any love life whatsoever. But perhaps her work was all she needed, and he should count his blessings. He was sorry about Dr. Kovici's patient, but the poor women had been terminal. Surgery, at best, would have only prolonged her life for a short time. He reached for his desk phone and dialed his home number.

His wife, Celia, answered. "About time," she said. "I was thinking of sending out a search party. Do you realize that I have not seen or heard from you since we went to sleep after the eleven o'clock news last night?"

"I realize," he said, "and I'm sorry."

"Are you coming home now?"

"Instantly, my love."

"Good. Coffee or bourbon?"

"Bourbon, a small one, on the rocks."

There was a short silence, and then Celia said, "Sorry, Doctor, truly sorry. I forgot. I guess I was just overcome by the sound of your voice. Sam Gideon called. Mrs. Gideon is in labor. He wants you to come right out."

Shannon groaned. "Oh, Lord. She isn't due for another week or two. Did Sam say how far apart the pains are?"

"Mr. Gideon did not say. He just said, 'Tell the doctor it's time.' I am now doing that, as a dutiful wife should. Will you be home for that drink, or will you not?"

Shannon sighed. "I will not, I'm afraid. I'd better go out and at least check her."

"Why doesn't Sam take her to the hospital?"

"You know why, my dear—economic reasons. Remember that everyone is not accustomed to luxury. Sam Gideon does not have Blue Cross, or even the price of a doctor. He just lives out there on the marsh, fishing and hunting and procreating, caring for his growing brood as best he can."

"And not paying his personal physician."

"He certainly does pay me. How many pounds of Sam's pickerel and perch fillets do we have in our freezer? Not to mention mallards, pheasants, rabbits and venison?"

"Hundreds, I must admit," Celia said, laughing. "All dressed, too. Sam's a dear, isn't he? Would you like me to go with you? Boil water and stuff like that?"

"You can't leave our son. Lucille will accompany me."

"She's dedicated, isn't she? Poor Lucille."

"Lucille is a very efficient nurse."

"But she needs a man. It just isn't natural."

"Maybe she has one, for all we know. Leave a candle in the window."

"Clint, you sound tired."

"I am. But I swore by Apollo, the physician, and—"

"But you need sleep! What about the morning?"

"John Kovici's patient died," Shannon said quietly. "Maybe I can sleep until nine, at least."

"I'm sorry about John's patient. Do you want me to wait up for you?"

"Of course not. Good night."

"Good night, Clint."

Shannon replaced the phone and immediately dialed the number of Lucille Sanchez, who lived with her parents in an old house on the edge of the city. Her father was a retired city fireman and her mother was a semi-invalid. Shannon suspected that both Mr. Sanchez's pension and Lucille's salary were needed for the family's living expenses, even though he made no charge for his constant medical services to Mrs. Sanchez.

After two rings he heard the nurse's voice speaking in a soft accent, a carryover, perhaps, from her grandparents, who had lived in Madrid. "Yes?" It could have been "*Sí?*"

"Lucille, were you in bed?"

"Yes, Doctor, but I was reading. Mother and Father are asleep. What do you wish?"

"I need you. Sam Gideon's wife is ready, I think, ahead of time. I'm going out there now. It will probably only be a simple obstetrical procedure, but I'd like you to be with me."

"Of course, Doctor. Shall I come to the office?"

"No, no. I'll pick you up."

"I will be ready."

Shannon checked his bag, made certain that it contained everything he might possibly need, and went to his car parked behind the office and drove across the city to the nurse's home. She was waiting for him at the curb, her white uniform protected by a transparent plastic raincoat and hood. As she got in beside him he became aware of her scent, not a scent, really, but an antiseptic odor which was not unpleasant. "Thanks, Lucille," he said. "I appreciate this."

"I am your nurse. We work together, yes?" Again it seemed to Shannon that the word was "*Sí.*"

"*Sí,*" he said, not thinking.

Lieutenant John Horner finished his coffee and doughnuts and then

went to a phone booth in the rear of the restaurant and called his wife. "Honey," he said easily, "I won't be home for a while yet. I'm still working on that robbery thing."

"But you worked last night, too," she protested.

"Yeah, yeah," he said impatiently, "I know."

"Are the other men working on their own time?"

"No, but that's not the point. I want that captain's job."

"You'll get it anyhow. You deserve it."

"Maybe, but it won't hurt for Chief Beckwith to know I'm doing some digging on my own. You go to bed, honey. I'll be home as soon as I can." He hung up before she could protest further and left the booth. As he passed the blonde waitress he said in a low voice, "Let's get together some night, baby."

"Any time, Lieutenant," she said, smiling. "You name it."

Horner, grinning to himself, went out, crossed the street in the rain to his car, a black Chevrolet, and drove northward through the city. When he reached the edge of the business district he turned right into a wide thoroughfare called Dennison Avenue and drove slowly beneath overhanging trees bordering the wide boulevard. Far out, where the houses were spaced farther apart, he turned into an alley and stopped at the rear of a big frame house which had been converted into a duplex. A flight of stairs ran along the outside to the upper apartment, where a light glowed behind two windows of a rear room. The blind at one window was pulled almost to the bottom, while the other blind was only halfway down. Horner, observing the positions of the blinds, smiled in the darkness. All clear, he thought.

He drove the Chevrolet to the edge of the alley, stopped behind a two-car garage, turned off the lights and motor. As he moved up the walk leading to the stairs he noted that the downstairs apartment was dark, but he did not observe a furtive movement behind one of the windows there; he was gazing upward in anticipation. A shadow moved behind one of the windows as he went swiftly up the stairs. At the landing he rapped softly on the glass of a door and peered about as he waited. The entire neighborhood was dark and silent.

The door opened and a woman said softly, "Come in. Hurry."

Horner stepped inside and turned to the woman, who was closing and locking the door. They were in a short passageway from which an arch opened into a living room comfortably furnished and dimly lighted. Against one wall a television was turned on, the volume low, to a popular Western program. The woman said, "I thought you'd never come." She wore pale yellow pajamas beneath a light cotton robe. Her feet were bare.

Horner said, "Sorry, Nina. I couldn't make it any earlier." He pulled her to him. They kissed and then she took his arm and led him into the living room. She was a handsome woman, in her middle thirties, with ash blonde hair pulled severely back from her face and coiled in a bun at the back of her head. Her eyes were pale blue, her skin milky, and her mouth held a look of sullen discontent.

Lieutenant Horner shrugged out of his topcoat and tossed it over a chair. "I didn't want to come until that snoopy neighbor of yours downstairs was in bed. Besides, I wasn't sure he'd be gone, not until I saw the blinds, one at half mast—"

"Our sign," she said with a trace of bitterness. "I've had them that way since dark, hoping you'd come. He left for a sales meeting in Toledo this morning and won't be back until tomorrow night. I've been lonesome, Jack. I almost called you at the station."

"Don't you ever do that, baby," he said softly. "Don't you ever call me."

"I know—you've told me not to often enough. I guess I just feel bitchy." She came against him and pressed her cheek to his chest. "Do you want a drink?"

He smelled the whisky. "How many have you had?"

"Only a couple," she said defensively. "I had to do something. What do you want? I have beer and bourbon."

"Bourbon. But I can't stay too long. The little wife and kiddies, you know."

Her mouth twisted and she stepped away from him. "Yes, I know. Why is everyone married and tied down?"

"You're married," he said. "What about that?"

She shrugged. "It's not a marriage. I'm alone all the time. I get bored."

"Maybe you need some kids."

"Not that. Spare me that." She moved to the television, turned it off.

Horner removed his suit jacket, loosened his tie and shirt collar and slouched into a deep chair. "How's good old Myron these days?"

She made a grimace of distaste. "The same. Still going to Doctor Shannon for his ulcer. Still on the same diet. I know it by heart. God! Milk, milk, milk, nothing fried. No nuts, no sweets, no smoking, no beer, no whisky. No nothing. Myron and his damned ulcer. No wonder I drink alone."

"You're not alone now, baby," he said.

She smiled and for an instant she was more than handsome; she was beautiful. The fine lines around her eyes and mouth did not show in the soft light and there was a kind of wicked glow in her blue eyes. He stood up and she came against him. "Jack," she whispered, "if I ever thought you were seeing another woman, I'd ..."

"You'd what?" he asked softly.

"You'd see what I'd do. I couldn't stand that."

"We're both married," he said.

"I don't mean your wife, Jack. I'm not jealous of her."

"I'm jealous of Myron," he said easily. "All the time." He knew she wanted him to say it.

Her fingers dug into his shoulders. "Don't be, Jack, don't ever be. I— I'll divorce him. Then you and I—"

"I can't," Horner broke in, "and you know it. Not now, with the promotion coming up. We'll talk about it later."

She sighed and her voice was muffled against his chest. "It's always later, isn't it? But I can wait, as long as it's just the two of us. There isn't anyone else for you, is there?"

"Of course not," Horner said sincerely.

"I trust you, Jack. And we're good for each other, aren't we?"

"You bet," Horner said. "Now, about that drink ..."

2

Tuesday Evening and Wednesday Morning

As soon as Doctor Shannon and his nurse arrived at Sam Gideon's place on the edge of the vast marsh the doctor knew it would be a long wait. An examination of Mrs. Gideon told him that the new little Gideon was not quite ready to enter the world, but there was no point in returning the ten miles to the city only to be called out again before morning. So Shannon and Lucille Sanchez waited, with Gideon and the numerous children gathered about. The nurse talked and laughed with the children. She was very good with them and Shannon thought sadly that she should marry.

The husband offered coffee and cold fried fish, apologized for not having whisky or beer, and made frequent trips to the bedroom to speak soothingly to his wife. At four in the morning the pains became regular and Shannon timed Mrs. Gideon's moans. Presently he nodded to Lucille Sanchez and entered the bedroom. The husband wanted to watch, as did some of the older children, but Shannon was firm and closed the door. It was a rather difficult birth and the doctor was glad for the nurse's help. At four-thirty he opened the door and said, "A boy, Sam. You can come in now."

Later, standing outside the house in a chill dawn breeze from the marsh and the lake beyond, Shannon said to the husband, "They'll be

fine, Sam. Get that prescription filled. I'll be out tomorrow afternoon late, but if you think you need me before then, just call."

"Doc," Sam Gideon said, "I sure appreciate this. I know I ain't never paid you no cash money, but—"

"Forget it," Shannon said. "Mrs. Shannon and I enjoy all the fish and game you've given us."

"I'll bring you some more, Doc," Gideon said eagerly. "Spring fishing ain't been too good yet, but I had a pretty good catch yesterday. Could you use maybe ten or twelve pounds of cleaned pickerel and perch?"

"Not right now, Sam. Our freezer is full. But how about some sweet corn in August?"

"You'll get it, Doc, all the ears you want. Sweet potatoes, too. And I'll have some nice green onions before long."

"Thanks." Shannon and the nurse moved over the muddy yard and got into his two-year-old green Ford sedan. As they drove along the narrow, rutted lane leading to the lake highway, the nurse sighed and said, "A long night, Doctor."

"Yes. Thanks for coming with me, Lucille."

"It was my duty. I was proud and glad to come with you."

Shannon hesitated before he spoke. Then he said carefully, "Lucille, I would miss you, but why don't you get married?"

She averted her eyes and there was a brief silence before she said in a low voice, "I do not wish to marry. I am happy working for you."

Shannon said nothing and turned into the highway leading along the lake into the city.

Wednesday Morning, Early

It was one o'clock when Lieutenant John Horner left Nina Faro and went quietly down the stairs to his car parked in the darkness of the alley. As usual lately, when he left Nina, he felt restless and keyed up. She was all right, he thought, but he wished she would stop feeling sorry for herself. All the time harping about what a tough life she had. Hell, what did she have to complain about? Maybe her husband was away a lot, but he provided for her and she had it pretty soft, if she only knew it. But all she did was bitch. And if she kept on hitting the booze, and talking about getting serious, he'd have to do something about her, break off with her completely, maybe. She might make a stink, though, and he couldn't afford that, not now with the captaincy coming up. Chief Beckwith was strict about scandal, a real blue-nose when it came to the Department. If Nina got too drunk some time and let anything slip to

her husband, there'd be hell to pay. He'd have to go easy about breaking it off, at least until after he had that captain's badge. Then maybe he'd figure something out. Maybe her husband would get transferred and they'd leave town. That would be great, but he couldn't hope for it.

It was still raining, a soft April drizzle. Lieutenant Horner backed his car and drove down the alley and did not turn on the lights until he reached Dennison Avenue, where he turned left toward the heart of the city. He was not tired and did not want to go home, not yet, and he wasn't due to go on duty until noon. Wednesday was the one day of the week he worked the noon-to-eight shift.

Horner drove slowly down the broad avenue. The memory of Nina Faro was like a cloying sickness. Why had he ever gotten mixed up with her? Then Horner grinned bleakly. Why, indeed? She wasn't the only one, and it had started as it had with the others. Fun at first, an exciting game, but sometimes it had been too easy. Horner was not really vain, but he knew that he was attractive to women, some women, anyhow, and he did not think of his affairs with remorse or feel that he was actually unfaithful to his wife. He loved her and the children as much as he was capable of loving, and maybe the other women helped him prove something to himself. Anyhow, he asked himself, what harm was there—as long as his wife didn't know? It had nothing to do with Violet and the kids. He wasn't hurting anyone, not really. But that Nina; he'd have to do something about her, and that was for sure.

The night was still young, Horner thought, as he drove along. Would Betty be alone tonight, by any chance? Would that young jerk of a doctor husband, that Nelson Keough, M.D., be called out on a baby case or something? He thought of Betty Keough and felt his pulse quicken. She was a dish, all right, and bored, like the others. He remembered the first time he'd seen her, when she'd entered the station last September to pay an overtime parking fine. The desk sergeant had gone out for coffee and he, Horner, had taken his place. Betty Keough had walked in holding the parking ticket and looking like a child about to cry. She was small and rounded, her little face framed by straggling strands of short red hair, the lipstick on her mouth slightly smeared, tiny beads of perspiration on her upper lip. She wore soiled white shorts and a thin black sleeveless blouse. Harbor City was in the heart of the Lake Erie resort area and such a costume was not unusual for downtown wear. Her legs were tanned and on her feet were fringed white buckskin moccasins. Her head barely came to the top of the high desk.

Horner smiled down at her. "Can I help you, Miss?" He spoke before she placed her little grubby hands on the desk, before he saw the gold wedding ring and the small diamond on her left hand.

"It's mean," she said, slapping the parking ticket to the desk. "It's just hateful." Her voice was thin and shrill, like a child's, and she seemed close to tears. "I parked by the drugstore and I didn't have a nickel for the meter and the children were in the car and I just wanted to run inside for a box of Kleenex and some chewing gum and I was only gone a tiny second and when I came out there was this nasty ticket under the windshield wiper ..."

"I'm sorry." From his position of vantage Horner saw that the two top buttons of her blouse were missing. He could see almost down to her navel. "The officer was only doing his duty. When the red flag on the meter is up he has to give a ticket. It's too bad that he just happened along at that time."

"Well, what do you *want?*" she asked in her small, thin voice. "What do I *do* about it?"

"Just pay a dime," Horner said gently, "and sign this." He pushed a pad and pencil toward her.

"But I don't have a dime!" she wailed. "I never carry any money. I charge everything."

"You can't charge a parking fine," Horner said.

"Then what'll I *do?*" There were actual tears in her eyes.

"We won't put you in jail," Horner said dryly. "Here." He reached into a pocket and placed a dime on the desk.

She smiled through her tears. "That's kind of you, Officer. I'll pay you back."

"Any time. Just sign, please."

As she picked up the pencil he saw that her nails were not quite clean. When she had written her name he tore the sheet from the pad, gazed at her wobbly scrawl. *Mrs. Nelson Keough.* "Oh," Horner said, "the new doctor's wife?"

"Yes," she said breathlessly. "You know my husband?"

"I haven't had the pleasure, but I'm pleased to meet you, Mrs. Keough. I'm Lieutenant Horner."

She ran a small finger across her upper lip and smiled up at him. Her teeth were tiny and milk white, like a kitten's. She plucked at the top of the blouse, but there were no buttons there, and she gave, up and dropped her hand. Horner could see the whiteness of her flesh, where the tan stopped; it was impossible not to stare. Betty Keough saw the direction of his gaze and smiled secretly. She said, "I'll bring the dime tomorrow."

Horner, watching her face now, said carefully, "I could stop by and pick it up."

She laughed. "I wouldn't want to trouble you."

"It would be no trouble."

She laughed again, a trifle nervously, but the secret glint was still in her round black eyes. "You mean you would actually drive way out to our little old house just to collect a dime?"

"From you I would."

"I hope I'm home when you come, Lieutenant."

"I hope so, too. Will you be home tomorrow afternoon?"

The desk sergeant returned then, carrying a container of coffee and a wrapped sandwich. Horner gazed at him, concealing his annoyance, and slid off the chair behind the high desk. Betty Keough said, "Goodbye, Lieutenant," and moved toward the street door.

"Goodbye," Horner said, noting the movement of her small hips.

The sergeant said, "Wow."

"Yes," Horner agreed. "She was paying a parking fine."

"Thanks for watching the desk, Jack."

"You're welcome. Quite welcome, indeed." Horner left the station in time to see Betty Keough drive away in a battered and dusty station wagon. Three children seemed to be struggling with one another in the rear seat. He watched the car turn a corner and then went to his office in the station, where he thumbed through a phone book. Nelson Keough, M.D., lived in a new development near the lake front. He did not write the address down because he knew he would remember it.

The next afternoon he took one of the patrol cars and drove through the city and out to the lake-front development. Dr. Nelson Keough's house was like many others on the street; frame, two-story, pseudo-Colonial, with miniature pillars in front extending to the second story. There were the usual post lamp, black-top drive and two-car garage connected to the house by a breezeway. The garage was empty, but the station wagon was in the drive. The front walk and stoop were littered with children's toys. Horner stopped the patrol car behind the wagon, walked back to the breezeway and saw Betty Keough reclining in a lawn chair beside the garage. She still wore the soiled white shorts and the black blouse with the top buttons missing. She was reading a comic book, munching potato chips and sipping at a bottle of Coke. She wore dark sunglasses which gave her small round face a rather ludicrous bug-like appearance. She sat there, absorbed in the book, drenched in the peaceful afternoon sunlight, alternately raising potato chips to her mouth and sipping Coke. When Horner's shadow fell across her she looked up, startled, and removed the sunglasses.

"Good afternoon, Mrs. Keough," Horner said politely. The sun glinted on his thick black hair and cast a warm glow over his dark, handsome features.

"Oh," she gasped. "My goodness."

"Surprised?" He smiled down at her, noting the grains of salt from the chips on her mouth and small round chin.

"It's Lieutenant—Lieutenant ..."

"Horner."

"Yes. Hi, Lieutenant Horner."

"You can call me Jack."

"Jack Horner." Her voice was reedy and breathless. "That's cute. Little Jack Horner sat in a corner. Only you aren't little."

"I came for my dime," Horner said.

"Oh, yes," she said in her treble child's voice, plucking at the top of the blouse. "I'll get it for you."

"Where are the children?" he asked.

"Asleep. They were driving me nuts and I gave them tranquilizers."

"Would the doctor approve of that?"

"No, but what he doesn't know won't hurt him." She tilted her head defiantly. "I'm entitled to some peace around here, aren't I? Aren't I?"

"Sure," Horner said.

She smiled up at him guilelessly. "Would you like a Coke?"

"No, thanks."

"A cold beer, then? I just drink Coke in the yard, because of the neighbors, but if you want a beer we could have it inside."

"What would the neighbors think about that?"

"It's none of their business." She tilted her small chin defiantly. "I can entertain a friend, can't I?"

"In the middle of the afternoon, while your husband is gone?" From past experience Horner had learned to be practical and somewhat cautious.

"Do you want a beer, or don't you?"

"I'm on duty," Horner said, still being cautious.

"All right!" Betty Keough sprang up from the chair, her face contorted, sudden tears on her cheeks. "I can never do anything I want to do!" She stamped a bare foot on the grass and clenched her fists. "Do this, do that, be dignified, bathe every day, keep your ears clean! You're a doctor's wife, remember? I'm sick of it, sick, sick, sick! Never any fun, never any parties, just the stupid stuck-up country-club crowd and the stupid medical meetings and the stupid medical wives." She stormed across the grass and over flagstones to the kitchen door. "I'll get your goddamned dime!" The screen slammed behind her.

Lieutenant Horner hesitated only a second. Then he moved swiftly to the door and entered the kitchen, hooking the screen behind him. Betty Keough was rummaging furiously in a drawer by the sink,

sobbing and whining shrilly at the same time. "He—he never leaves me any money. I—I can't even pay the bread man and the milk man and the paperboys. He treats me like a baby! But I'll find a dime if I gotta smash Junior's piggy bank. My God, the lousy kids got more money than I have!" She slammed the drawer shut, jerked open another.

"Never mind," Horner said. "Forget the dime."

She whirled to face him, panting with rage. "Who asked you to come in?"

He moved close to her, smiling. "No one, but I'm in."

She beat at him with tiny fists, but he pulled her close and held her. She smelled faintly of sun and potato chips and green grass. He held her tightly, stroking her back and murmuring soothing words, and presently she was quiet. He picked her up then, surprised at her lightness, and carried her out of the kitchen and into a living room littered with newspapers, toys, apple cores and orange peels. An expensive sectional divan was piled with children's socks, jeans and shoes.

"Upstairs," Betty Keough whispered.

"No." Horner spoke from experience. He did not wish to be trapped on a second floor. On his right was a dining alcove and a room beyond, the door ajar. He carried her there, saw that the room was a sort of den. He entered, kicked the door shut. An open screened window faced the drive and he could see the patrol car parked behind the wagon. The room contained a small desk, a tall bookcase, two straight chairs and a deep leather one with a matching ottoman. On a low table beside this chair were a pipe rack, a brass ash tray and a tobacco humidor. A rather battered portable phonograph was on the floor beside the desk. In contrast to the living room this room was clean and very neat.

Betty Keough, one arm around Horner's neck, used her free hand to pluck at his tie. "This is his room," she said sullenly. "He won't allow me or the kids in here. But I don't care. I can come in here if I want to, can't I?"

"Sure you can. The children ...?"

"Just lock the door. *He* does, all the time."

He lowered her into the leather chair and went to lock the door.

3

Wednesday Morning, Early

Now Lieutenant Horner, driving in the rainy April night, dismissed from his memory the woman he'd just left and thought with pleasure of Betty Keough and that first meeting with her on a September afternoon. He slowed at an intersection and eyed a huge, lighted service station on the corner, noted the glass-enclosed phone booth on the edge of the cement apron, and on an impulse turned in and stopped. An attendant wearing a black raincoat came out and greeted him. "Hi, Jack."

"Just want to use the phone," Horner said, getting out of the Chevrolet.

He called Dr. Nelson Keough's home number. It was after one in the morning, he knew, but if the doctor answered he would hang up. But if *she* answered....

Betty Keough answered in her thin child's voice, speaking mechanically, as if by rote. "Doctor Keough's residence. Mrs. Keough speaking."

"Is the doctor there?" Horner asked, just to be on the safe side.

"Who is calling, please?"

"You know damn well, Betty."

"Jack?"

"Yes," he said impatiently. "He's not there, is he?"

"I am very sorry, but the doctor was called out on an emergency. If you will leave your name and phone number I will tell the doctor—"

"Stop the act, baby," Horner broke in. "Is it okay if I come out?"

"I just don't know about that," she said airily. "I don't know if I wish to see you. It's been a month since the last time and you haven't even bothered to call me. My goodness, you can't expect a girl to just—"

"I've been tied up. How long will he be gone?"

"I just don't know if I want—"

"Oh, shut up," Horner said impatiently. "How long?"

"I don't know, Jack, honey," she breathed. "He's at the hospital. Emergency, his note says. He always leaves me a note. It might be hours."

"All right," Horner said. "Fifteen minutes, baby. Unlock the back door." He hung up and left the booth.

The attendant stood by the pumps in the drizzle. "Say, Jack, with them gangsters loose I feel a little jittery. I'm alone here all night."

"They won't bother you."

"How do you know? They might need gas, see? And if they pull in here—"

"Don't worry about that. They've got plenty of unmarked money. If they get gas, they'll pay for it. They won't want to attract any attention. But if you do see any suspicious characters, call the station right away."

"Sure, Jack."

As Horner drove away he thought that what he'd told the attendant was true. If Steve Donegal and his men were still in the area they would most certainly try to be inconspicuous. The police had Donegal's prints and a photograph, which hung in the post office. The other two men were not known. They would be the ones Donegal would send out for food or on any other errand. Horner was certain they would not expose themselves at any of the big markets in the city or at the shopping centers; they would pick a small, out-of-the-way store. He had expressed this belief to Chief Beckwith and Captain Keely and had mentioned as an example a small all-night store at the city limits operated the year 'round by a man and wife eager for the tourist trade. During the season the store did a brisk business, because vacationers were apt to want T-bones, beer, aspirin, hamburger and frankfurters, even charcoal for a barbecue, at three or four in the morning. The summer people might want anything at any time of the day or night. Even in April there were the early spring fishermen and the cottage owners who spent weekends at their haven all months of the year.

Lieutenant Horner passed this store on his way to the development where Doctor Keough lived. A lighted sign in front read: CONNIE'S CORNER—BEER—WINE—MEAT—GROCERIES—FISHING TACKLE—BEACH SUPPLIES—DRUGS. OPEN 24 HOURS WINTER AND SUMMER. The store faced the lake at an intersection where the highway branched inland to the south and was so named because it was situated on a corner and also because it was operated by Emil Tomescek and his wife Constance, a fat, blowsy woman known all along the lake as Big Connie. Horner saw that even at this hour a few cars were parked in front and in the parking area in the rear. Then the store was behind him and he turned at the corner and stopped the car on a quiet street a block from Doctor Keough's home. He turned up the collar of his topcoat and walked in the drizzle to the house, made certain that only the battered station wagon was in the garage, and then crossed wet flagstones to the kitchen door, opened it and stepped quietly inside. The only light was a small one over the electric stove. He moved into the dark living room and through the archway.

Betty Keough was waiting for him in the study. She had turned off the

light Doctor Keough had left burning and was curled up in the big leather chair. He could barely see her small, pale face. "Hi, baby," he whispered, removing his coat.

"Listen for his car," she said. "Watch for his lights. If he comes, sneak out the front door."

"I've done it before." Horner grinned in the darkness.

"I don't like this," she said plaintively. "You don't really care about me. All you want is—"

"Shush, baby." He went to her.

At a little past three in the morning Lieutenant Horner stopped his car in front of Connie's Corner. Now he would have liked going home to bed, but he was a good policeman and it seemed to him that he could afford to take a few minutes to check the store, as long as he had to pass it on his way home. It would be something to report to Chief Beckwith and Captain Keely; on his own time he had been out hunting for the robbers. Also, it would be something to tell his wife, who had lately questioned him rather closely about his evening activities. She sometimes shopped at Connie's Corner and it was quite possible that she might casually ask Emil or Connie if her husband had stopped in. Horner was clever about such things; it never hurt to have something concrete to back up his account to her about where he had been. Besides, he really wanted to get a lead on Steve Donegal, if one were to be had. Stopping at Connie's Corner was a long shot, but Horner knew that a cop sometimes scored by playing a long shot, a hunch.

Inside the store a few fishermen were buying beer and other supplies. Horner knew one of them and nodded. Big Connie was behind the counter scrutinizing a cash register tape. She smiled at Horner and smoothed a white apron over her broad hips. "Good morning, Lieutenant. You working the night shift now?"

He moved close and spoke in a low voice. "Any strangers in here tonight?"

"Strangers? Hell, we get 'em all the time—on this road. Tourists stopping for cigarettes, candy and pop for the kids. Driving all night, you see."

"No strangers buying bread, meat, milk, coffee—stuff like that?"

"One," Big Connie said. "Maybe an hour ago."

"What did he look like?"

"Little man. Black leather jacket. Dark, needed a shave. He paid and went right out."

"Did you see his car, or which way he went?"

"No. I was busy then."

"He just bought groceries?"

"No," Big Connie said. "He also bought cigarettes, iodine, adhesive tape and a big box of surgical gauze."

Horner's eyes narrowed and he drummed fingers on the counter, remembering that the loan company manager had fired at one of the robbers. Maybe he had hit him, after all. "Listen," he said, "if that man comes in here again, call me right away and try and stall him."

"Sure, Lieutenant."

"Any men on the force around here tonight?"

"Captain Keely stopped in."

"Keely?" Horner was surprised. "When?"

"A while ago. He bought some cigars and just stood around. Excuse me, Lieutenant." Big Connie moved away to wait on a customer.

Horner thought bitterly that Captain Keely was taking his advice about watching outlying food establishments. And doing it personally. To Horner it meant that Keely wanted credit for any arrest. And Horner knew why; Keely did not want to retire, wanted to hang on to his job as long as possible. By making a good showing to Chief Beckwith and the city council he might make a case for an extension of his retirement date. Horner hoped there wasn't a chance of that. Beckwith would never ask the council to make an exception and revise the city code. Age sixty-five was the end. Then it was compulsory retirement for members of the Police and Fire Departments. And he, John Horner, was the only man on the force qualified for the captaincy. He had studied, passed the exams. His record was good. He was ready. Beckwith knew it and so did Keely. No other man on the force could qualify for at least two years, maybe longer. Horner knew that Beckwith had been plagued with the resignations of young policemen deciding to take higher paying jobs in industry and elsewhere. Law enforcement was an honorable, respected and necessary profession, but to make it a career one had to love the work. Horner loved it. And he knew that if he should leave the force, which was unthinkable, Beckwith would have no choice but to retain Jason Keely as captain until a suitable replacement could be trained, and the city council would have no choice, either.

John Horner knew that Keely disliked him, resented his youth and aggressiveness, but he tried not to antagonize Keely in any way. He was courteous, efficient, and carried out Keely's orders without question. He could afford to wait. It was only a month now until Keely retired and then he, Horner, would be captain. And if he was smart, stayed out of trouble and played things right, he would be in line for the chief's job when Beckwith retired. Horner wanted that more than anything else.

As Big Connie returned to the cash register, Horner asked, "Did

Keely notice that stranger?"

"I don't know. I was busy. I remember that the captain was here then, though."

"Save the stranger for me. Call me if he comes in again."

The woman gave change to one of the early morning fishermen, thanked him and then turned to Horner with a mocking smile on her wise, fat face. "Okay, Lieutenant. What's in it for me?"

Horner grinned crookedly. "Connie, I know you've got two girls upstairs. Chief Beckwith likes a nice, quiet town. I've been looking the other way, because I like you, but I could tell the chief that I cruised past here one night and heard a ruckus. If I testified to disorderly conduct, you'd be closed up tight."

The woman rested her fat, ringed hands on the counter and gazed at him thoughtfully. "You know something, Lieutenant? You're a bastard."

"Sure," Horner said amiably. "Just remember that the stranger is mine."

"You'll be captain anyhow," Connie replied, "when Keely retires. Everybody knows that. What the hell you worrying about?"

"I'm not worrying. I just don't want Keely nosing in right now."

"You mean you don't want him to grab any of the credit."

"That could be. Just remember what I told you. So long Connie." Horner left the store.

When he reached his home he was surprised to see a light in the kitchen. Maybe one of the kids is sick, he thought uneasily as he left the car port and entered the kitchen. His wife was sitting at the table there smoking a cigarette. An ash tray before her was filled with stubs. On a breakfast bar were a coffee percolator and an empty cup. The hands of an electric clock on the wall stood at ten minutes to four. Horner removed his topcoat and asked, "Why are you up?"

"I'm waiting for you." Violet Horner was a short woman beginning to get fat. She had once been pretty in an elfin way, but now her small brown eyes were dull and there was a puffiness beneath her chin. Her sand-colored hair was uncombed and her rather large mouth held a sullen, accusing look.

"Why, honey?" Horner asked as he hung his topcoat in a closet off the kitchen.

"Where have you been?"

Horner left the closet, dropped his suit jacket over the back of a chair, loosened his collar and tie and grinned at his wife. "I've been working. I called you, remember?" He leaned over and patted his wife's plump cheek.

She struck his hand away.

"Now, baby—"

"A woman called here for you," she said in a dull voice. "About a half hour ago."

"Oh?" Horner raised heavy black brows. "Who?"

"She didn't say. She just asked if you were home. She sounded drunk. I said, 'No,' and she hung up."

Horner frowned. "Probably police business," he said, "but she should have called the station—not here at this time of morning."

"That's what I thought. The phone woke up the kids and after I got them settled I couldn't get back to sleep. Jack, I—I..." Her voice broke. "I trust you, but—"

"Damn it," Horner broke in angrily, "what's the idea? Here I've been out working my tail off, for you and the kids, on my own time yet, and all I get—"

"There's lipstick on your shirt," Violet Horner said.

Horner looked down at his white shirt front. It was there, all right, a pink smear over the left pocket. Damn, he thought, damn, damn. He knew that either Nina Faro or Betty Keough had made the stain, but he grinned at his wife. "Now, look, honey. If it's lipstick, it has to be yours."

"I wash your shirts, Jack. That shirt was clean when you left last evening. I haven't seen you since." Mrs. Horner crushed out her cigarette and a tear slid down one cheek. She began to cry softly, her lips quivering.

Cursing silently to himself Horner patted his wife's trembling shoulders.

"D-don't touch me," she sobbed.

"You've got to trust me. You know that my work takes me out at night."

She raised wet eyes to meet his gaze. "I do trust you. I—I did, anyhow. But you've been away so many nights, and that woman called for you, and the lipstick ..."

He pulled her to her feet and put his arms around her. "You're upset and imagining things. I wouldn't cheat on you, don't you know that? Come on, let's go to bed."

She allowed herself to be led from the kitchen, through the living room and down a passageway past the children's room to their small bedroom. Horner got a sleeping capsule from the bathroom and brought it to his wife with a glass of water. "Take this and get some sleep. In the morning you'll see how silly you've been."

"I—I hope I'm wrong, Jack." She put the capsule in her mouth and sipped some water.

"You should know me better than that." He took the glass, gently

pressed her to the bed and pulled up the sheet and blanket. "Sleep now."

She smiled wanly up at him. "I love you, Jack. I can't bear think of you—being with someone else."

"Just forget it, will you? Get some rest now. I'll take care the kids' breakfast and take Jackie to school."

"You need rest, too." Violet Horner's voice seemed drowsy.

"I don't have to be at the station until noon." Horner turned off the light and went to the bathroom, where he undressed and put on pajamas. He dawdled there and smoked a cigarette. When he returned to the bedroom he heard his wife's even breathing but he waited a few minutes, listening intently, to make certain that she was sound asleep. Then he quietly closed the bedroom door, moved softly on bare feet to the kitchen and picked up the phone.

After five rings Nina Faro answered in a thick, husky voice. She did sound drunk, Horner thought, as his wife had said. She would have to be drunk to call him at his home at three-thirty in the morning. "Listen, Nina," he said in a low, intense voice, "that phone call of yours did it. We're through, do you understand?"

"Jack, I—I'm sorry. I didn't realize. Please, please forgive me. I'm so lonely. I just wanted to hear your voice ..."

"I warned you about calling me," he said, feeling rage, "and I may as well tell you right now that I'm sick of you."

"Jack, don't—don't talk like that. Where have you been?"

"It's none of your business," he said brutally.

"You—you weren't working, were you?"

"No." He took a savage satisfaction in saying it.

"Who—who is the woman?"

"Not you, Nina, not anymore."

"Jack" she said desperately, "not like this. I—I'm sorry. Listen, please, please! I said I was sorry I called your home."

"Goodbye," he said coldly.

"I won't let you do it!" she screamed. "You can't !"

He slammed the receiver into the cradle and stood there a moment, waiting for her to call back. She was hysterical enough to do anything. But it was best to break with her cleanly and get it over with. When the phone did not ring immediately he turned away. And stopped. His wife stood in the kitchen doorway watching him. Horner was startled. "I thought you were asleep."

"I know," she said in a curiously dead voice. "I wanted you to think that."

"But you took a sleeping pill ..."

"I only pretended. I didn't swallow it. Who were you talking to?"

"I had to call the station."

"Don't lie, Jack, not anymore. I heard it all. Is she the one you were with tonight?"

He grinned, a sickly attempt, moved forward, reached out to touch her. "Now, listen, baby—"

She struck his hand away viciously and he was shocked to see the hate in her eyes. Behind him the phone began to ring shrilly.

4

Wednesday Morning, Early

Nelson Keough, M.D., was annoyed when the hospital called shortly after midnight. His wife and children were asleep upstairs, but he was smoking his pipe and reclining in his leather chair in the little room he called his study and listening to Brahms on the portable phonograph he'd had since college. The little room was the only sanctuary he had in the cluttered and mismanaged house and he personally kept it neat and tidy. His books were there, the medical volumes and the set of Shakespeare, the slim books of poetry. On a low table beside his chair were a bronze ash tray, a tobacco humidor, a pipe rack and the latest *Time* Magazine. Another table against one wall bore a cut-glass decanter of port wine and one of sherry. Dr. Keough seldom drank whisky or beer, but he did indulge his wife by usually keeping a supply of the latter in the refrigerator. Betty Keough loved beer, but the doctor was careful to control her consumption. Moderation in all things was his motto and he often stated a chemical fact to the effect that every action had a reaction, whether it applied to eating, drinking or making love.

Dr. Keough was a young man who had completed his internship a year before and begun practice in Harbor City. His training was sound but he was inclined to over-cautiousness and over-treatment, known in medical circles as the shotgun method. But he was nevertheless a competent general practitioner, and to his credit he was not hesitant about calling in consultation when he was uncertain of a diagnosis or procedure. His practice was small as yet and he performed only minor surgery, leaving the major operations to Dr. Clinton Shannon, Dr. John Kovici and several other older men, but he hoped eventually to work into surgery. He was a slight man with the thin, pale face of a poet, which he had once, in his early youth, aspired to be. He wore tri-focal glasses with heavy dark frames and affected a tweedy, professorial appearance; gray flannel slacks, loose gray herringbone jacket, soft oxford shirts and

solid-colored knit ties, usually dark blue or black. With slight variations his clothes were almost like a uniform for him.

He had met Elizabeth Smith while attending pre-med at Ohio State. She had been a major in home economics, which had attracted Nelson Keough to her. He was fastidious himself and liked things to be orderly, tidy and clean. But as soon as they were married, in his junior year of medical school, he learned immediately that his wife had absorbed practically nothing of her training.

They lived at first in a student housing development on the campus and the babies came fast, too fast to suit Nelson Keough who had tried without success to teach his wife the elementary rules of feminine hygiene and birth control. He wanted children, but not until after he'd completed medical school and had started practice. After the third baby was born, during his internship at Miami Valley Hospital in Dayton, Ohio, he took matters into his own hands and the babies had stopped. Nevertheless, it had been a struggle, even with financial help from both his wife's parents and his own, and he had begun his career in Harbor City heavily in debt for his office equipment, instruments and supplies, plus the mortgage on his home and the note payable to his father-in-law, who had loaned him the down payment.

His wife, he learned with a growing hopelessness, was no help to him at all. She was not only a slovenly housekeeper and incompetent mother; she was childishly extravagant. She had no money sense whatever. For this reason Dr. Keough had been compelled to handle all financial matters himself, even to personally paying the newspaper boys, the butcher, the grocer, the utility companies, all expenses connected with the household. Nelson Keough realized early that his wife was still a child. She resembled a child in appearance and actions, although she was almost twenty-six years old. He was often required to gently tell her to take a bath, brush her teeth or clean and clip her fingernails. Yet he loved her very much, even though he sometimes felt he was more a father than a husband. He loved the three little boys, too, but he wanted a girl. When he was on his feet, he thought, firmly established, with his home paid for and a solid practice, he and Betty would try for a girl. If it was another boy, fine, but there would be no more children after that. Four were enough.

Now, as the phone rang, he sighed, pushed himself up from the chair and went to the kitchen, where he turned on a light above the sink, noting with distaste the stack of unwashed dishes, the congealed grease in a frying pan, the crusts of bread lying about, the open jars of peanut butter and jelly, the empty soft-drink bottles on a littered counter. Spilled sugar and coffee grounds crunched unpleasantly on the too-

seldom-washed linoleum beneath his feet as he moved to the phone.

"Doctor Keough speaking," he said quietly.

"This is Miss James at the hospital," a voice said crisply. "I'm sorry to call you at this hour, but we have an emergency. Doctor Kovici is doing an appendectomy and would like you to administer the anesthetic."

Keough frowned. "Kovici? Doctor Shannon usually assists him."

"I know," the nurse said. "It's really Doctor Shannon's patient, but he's out on a case."

"I see," Keough said, somewhat bitterly. "Who is the patient?"

"Jill Beckwith, the young daughter of the Chief of Police. Can you come right away?"

"Yes, of course," Keough said, thinking that neither Shannon nor Kovici would have called him if either of the others had been available. The two doctors were a sort of team.

"Thank you. I'll tell Doctor Kovici."

Keough replaced the phone, took a pen from his shirt pocket and wrote on a prescription pad: *Called to hospital. Emergency.* He carried the note upstairs, entered the dark bedroom he shared with his wife and propped it against the extension phone on the bedside table. He always did this when he was called out at night and had patiently trained his wife to answer the phone when he was not at home. The dim light from the hall shone on her sleeping figure and gazing down at her he felt a moment of tenderness. In sleep she was more than ever like a child. He pulled the blanket up over one bare shoulder and quietly left the room. After looking in on the three small boys, he went down to a closet beside the front door, took a jacket from a hanger and put it on. The metal earpieces of a stethoscope protruded from a side pocket of the jacket. He also put on a raincoat and then got his bag from the study where he always left it. He went out the kitchen door, leaving the light burning beside his leather chair.

It was almost one o'clock in the morning when he parked his four-year-old Mercury behind the hospital in the space reserved for doctors and entered by a rear door. Miss James was at her desk in the corridor looking neat and efficient in her white uniform and cap. She was a plump, dark-haired woman in her early thirties. She smiled at Doctor Keough and said, "Doctor Kovici has gone to surgery."

Keough nodded and walked down the wide corridor to the doctors' lounge and dressing room. It took him only a few minutes to change. He emerged and moved quickly toward the operating room in the east wing of the building. As he passed the visitor's waiting room he saw a man and woman there. He recognized the man as Chief of Police Chad Beckwith and assumed that the woman was Mrs. Beckwith. The chief

was a big man with a broad, heavy face and thick, graying hair. He was pacing the room slowly, smoking a cigar. Mrs. Beckwith, a sturdy pleasant-faced woman, sat quietly holding a purse on her knees. Dr. Keough knew that the Beckwiths were Doctor Shannon's patients and thought that it really must be an emergency, since Doctor Kovici was operating on the Beckwith girl in Shannon's absence.

Remembering his training, Dr. Keough paused at the door and smiled reassuringly at the couple. Chief Beckwith turned and said, "Good morning, Doctor. You're helping John?"

Keough nodded. "I'm sure your daughter will be fine. Please don't worry." Then he hurried away, thinking somewhat grimly that he really did not know if there was no reason to worry; any surgical procedure is a serious business and he was not yet aware of the girl's condition. But if it was an emergency that meant that the appendix had ruptured, or was about to, or that there were other complications. Doctor Keough pushed through the door leading to the operating room and was soon scrubbed and ready.

Doctor Kovici and a nurse were waiting for him under the white light. As the nurse adjusted Doctor Keough's surgical mask, Doctor Kovici said, "Thanks for coming, Nelson. I appreciate it."

Doctor Keough felt a warm glow. He admired Doctor Kovici almost as much as he did Doctor Shannon, who had been so kind in helping him get his practice started. "Glad to help," he said.

Then it was all cold, antiseptic seriousness. Doctor Keough was skillful with the anesthesia and there were only cryptic words from Doctor Kovici to the nurse. Doctor Keough knew what was required of him and twice he had the satisfaction of an approving nod from the surgeon.

At last it was over. The girl was wheeled away and the two men, masks hanging loosely beneath their chins, went in to the anxiously waiting parents.

"She'll be all right," Doctor Kovici told them. "Just a matter of time and rest now."

"Thanks, John," Chief Beckwith said. "Clint told us over a year ago that it would have to be done, sooner or later. I appreciate your taking over for him."

"Don't mention it," Kovici said. "You've met Doctor Keough?"

"Yes." Beckwith's smile was friendly. "How long have you been in town now, Doctor?"

"Almost a year."

"Got all you can handle yet?"

"Not quite, I'm afraid." Keough smiled somewhat ruefully.

"Maybe I can help," Beckwith said. "Old Doc Conners is retiring and moving to Florida. He's always taken care of the city employees—accidents on the job, physical examinations, things like that. I think I could get the council to appoint you city physician. Would you take it?"

"Of course," Keough replied. "I'd be glad to."

"Good. I'll be in touch."

Keough felt the warm glow again. The faint resentment was gone. He was glad now that Doctor Kovici had asked him. This could be a door opening for him in Harbor City. Suddenly he wanted to tell his wife, even though he knew it would not mean too much to her, but he hoped that she would understand a little.

Mrs. Beckwith asked Doctor Kovici, "Could we see Jill now?"

"Not just yet. The nurse will let you know." Doctor Kovici smiled at the couple and then nodded at Doctor Keough. "Come on, Nelson. I'll buy you a cup of coffee."

An accident case was brought to the hospital while the two doctors were still there and Doctor Keough again assisted Doctor Kovici with surgery. At three-thirty in the morning Keough drove home feeling tired, but happy and contented. This was the break he'd been waiting and hoping for. He'd assisted Doctor Kovici twice in emergency surgery and had had coffee with him in the hospital cafeteria. The nurses and aides had seemed to regard him with a new respect. And Chief Beckwith had offered him the post of city physician. Maybe everything would be better now. He would wake Betty and tell her and maybe she would realize what it meant to them. He would have a long, serious talk with Betty. She was an adult and it was time she began thinking and acting like one. He was going to be a respected member of the community, in a respected profession, and Betty would have to conduct herself accordingly.

Keough turned into the drive at his home and stopped the Mercury in the garage beside the old station wagon. Carrying his bag, he went to the kitchen door and entered. After turning on a light, he hung his jacket and raincoat in the front closet and carried the bag to his study. He stopped there, frowning. The little room was dark and he distinctly remembered leaving the light on by his chair. He moved slowly to the doorway and peered in. There was an unusual smell; the odor of stale cigarette smoke. Betty did not smoke and he himself smoked a pipe. He entered the room and touched a wall switch. As the overhead light came on he saw his wife huddled in the leather chair, sound asleep. The light did not seem to bother her. She was naked. Her nightgown was on the floor beside the chair.

Nelson Keough dropped his bag to the floor and moved toward his wife. Then he stopped, staring at the bronze ash tray on the table beside the chair. In the center of a little pile of pipe ashes was a cigarette stub, half smoked, bent double. He leaned down and touched his wife's cheek. She stirred and made a protesting, plaintive sound, like a kitten mewing. He grasped her bare shoulder then and shook her. She blinked and turned her face away from the light. "Betty," he said, "why are you down here? Why aren't you in bed?"

"Go away, Jack," she mumbled. "Go on, get out. He'll be coming—" She jerked her head around, clamped a little hand over her small child's mouth and her eyes grew round with horror. "Nelson!"

He shook her savagely. "Betty, what is this?"

She cringed beneath him, sobbing wildly. He released her, picked up the nightgown and threw it over her. It was a flimsy covering for her small, rounded body. She plucked at the gown, trying to cover her nakedness, avoiding his shocked gaze. "I—I couldn't sleep," she whimpered. "I woke up and—and saw your note and I—I came down here to wait for you, honest...."

He stood rigidly. "Who's Jack?"

"J—Jack?" Her voice was terrified, thin and shrill.

"Yes. He smoked a cigarette." Keough kept his voice under control.

"Cigarette ...?" Betty squirmed helplessly, drew up her be knees. Her fingers worked nervously at the nightgown.

He slapped her then, stingingly, on both cheeks. He never thought he could do it, because he loved her. He was amazed at the will and the strength which he had summoned up. He slapped her again and stood over her, his hand raised menacingly. "Who's Jack?"

From upstairs a child began to cry. Keough paid no attention. He slapped his wife once more, this time across the mouth. She sprang up screaming and ran for the door, dropping the nightgown. He caught her and held her arms. She struggled, but he held her tightly, aware of her familiar, faintly musky scent. The child's crying grew louder.

"The—the kids are awake," Betty gasped.

"Tell me." Keough felt cold and detached. His fingers dug into his wife's flesh. "Who is he?"

She stood trembling in his grasp and made no answer. He released her, moved quickly, closed and locked the door and turned to face her. She began to whimper at his expression. There was a smear of blood on her lower lip. "Don't hit me again, Nelson, please...."

He unbuckled his belt, pulled it from the trouser loops and whipped it across her thighs. She screamed and scurried away, hugging the walls. He stalked her, noting with satisfaction the red welts on her white skin.

Maybe this was something he should have done long ago, he thought, as he slapped the belt at her hips. From beyond the closed door he heard the muffled crying of the children. They must all be awake now, but it didn't matter. Betty, sobbing wildly, ran to a corner and huddled there. She was confused and terrified. This man was not Nelson. He was going to kill her....

The children's crying was shrill now. The chorus outside the door rose to a caterwauling. Above the din Keough said, "You may as well tell me, Betty. I'll kill you if you don't." He now felt quite calm. Would he really kill her? It was an interesting thought. He owned a .32 revolver which had been given to him by his father years ago. It was upstairs in a dresser drawer beneath his socks and handkerchiefs. He flicked the belt at Betty's ankles. She danced away and then rushed to him, hugging and patting him with her small, stubby hands.

Nelson Keough smiled to himself and stood stiffly, holding the belt, ready to push her clear and slash away. He had never known Betty to be afraid of him, but then she had never had reason to be. He had been indulgent, preoccupied, treating her like a pretty, spoiled child. And suddenly, as her small, naked body pressed against him, he felt a surge of self-reproach. If she had done wrong, it was as if a child had disobeyed. Did she know right from wrong? Had she been like a child greedily eating a chocolate bar just before dinner, knowing it was wrong and wanting it anyhow? He ran fingers through her short tangled hair and said gently, "It's all right, Betty. Just tell me about it."

"You—you won't hit me anymore?" Her voice was small and muffled against his chest.

"No. I'm sorry I did that, Betty. You can tell me now. I won't hurt you."

She took a deep shuddering breath and began to talk, thinly and rapidly. She told it all just as it had happened, from the September day in the police station, when she didn't have the dime for the overtime parking fine, to what had happened on that early morning in April. She told it simply and clearly, as a child would, and her words bore the ring of truth. She was not mentally capable of improvising; she could not gloss over or twist events. Nelson Keough listened calmly, almost dreamily, still feeling the self-reproach. Was it mostly his fault?

When Betty finished she said in a small timid voice, "Are—are you mad at me?" It was as if she'd burned a roast, or forgotten to do something he'd told her to do, like sending a suit to the cleaners.

"I'll have to think about it, Betty. His name is Horner? On the police force?"

She nodded silently, still clinging to him.

He felt a slow, cold rage. Horner. Police force. It was rape, really. Or

almost, anyhow. "I'll kill him." He had meant to only think it, but knew he'd spoken the words aloud.

Betty sighed and clung to him.

He pushed her gently away. "Put on your nightgown, Betty." He turned and unlocked the study door, opened it part way. The three little boys stood there, tears on their faces. Keough stepped out and closed the door, so that they could not see their mother, and smiled at his sons. "What's the idea, you guys? Back to bed."

"What's wrong with Mommy?" the oldest boy asked. "We heard her yelling down here."

"She didn't feel well, but she's fine now." He clapped his hands. "Scoot."

When they had trooped back upstairs he entered the study. Betty had put on her nightgown and stood by the leather chair. Her short red hair was tousled and her eyes were large in her small pale face. He stared at her silently for a moment and then, sighing, he stooped down and opened his bag. "Lift your nightgown, Betty," he said.

She obeyed wordlessly and watched him with wide eyes as he knelt at her feet and applied soothing ointment to the welts his belt had made on her body.

5

Wednesday Morning

Myron Faro awoke in his hotel room in Toledo feeling weak and ill. Sales meetings were always murder for him because he couldn't eat and drink like the others, especially like Charles ("Red") Buchanan, the regional sales manager for the Tip-Top Auto Supply Company. Buchanan was a big, jolly, red-haired man with a booming laugh and an enormous capacity for bourbon and a sneering contempt for more temperate men. The kick-off dinner in the hotel's main dining room the evening before had been preceded by a cocktail party during which Buchanan had circulated among his men, glass in hand, urging one and all to drink up, boys, it's on the company, you know. Because of his ulcer Myron Faro had sipped plain ginger ale until Buchanan came by with a bottle and said, "That drink looks pretty pale to me, Myron, old pal," and had filled the glass with bourbon before Faro could protest. Buchanan knew that Faro's physical condition did not permit him to drink, but he had pretended to forget and said, "bottoms up." He laughed, but there was cold contempt in his eyes.

Faro drank, feeling his stomach contract, knowing that he would be

ill. He also knew that Buchanan was just drunk enough to insist if he did not comply. He hated Buchanan, but the big man was the boss and a job was a job. Faro had been a high school mathematics teacher and had quit to take the selling job with Tip-Top Auto Supply because the pay was better. But now he was forced to attend sales meetings and had a duodenal ulcer. He often thought of his teaching career with regret and longing.

Buchanan clapped him on the back. "Atta boy, put hair on your chest." He moved away laughing.

After the dinner there had been a peppy speech by Buchanan, followed by what he called the "Tip-Top Table Talk" during which the sales representatives in the various territories were invited to unburden themselves of any special problems. Myron Faro had no sales problems; he was always above his quota. He sat in the swirling cigar and cigarette smoke feeling ill and wishing he could get away. He had eaten very little dinner and the whisky was like fire in his stomach. The pain persisted, even after he'd taken two of the tablets Doctor Shannon had given him. He should have refused to drink for Buchanan, he thought. It had been weak of him to allow himself to be cowed by the sales manager.

When the Table Talk was over Buchanan adjourned the meeting until nine the next morning when he would present his famous Chalk Clinic and identify on a blackboard the salesmen's territories by female names, after the manner of designating hurricanes, such as Mabel Alice, Rosemary and Elaine, and discuss the previous quarter's sales effort of each. Myron Faro's territory was labeled Annabelle and was near the top of the names on the blackboard. The weaker territories were at the bottom and the respective salesmen would squirm as Buchanan said, "Now Alice, here, has got herself in a rut. She's not getting out there and beating the bushes. And look at Mabel; she's really slipping. She has the potential, but ..." The female names were supposed to conceal the identities of the salesmen involved, but all the men knew each other's labels. Once an intoxicated gentleman had wandered into a Tip-Top sales meeting, heard the representatives addressing each other as "Alice," "Rosemary" and "Elaine" and had staggered out muttering something about a "damned bunch of queers."

After the Table Talk the men scattered in search of entertainment. They were away from home, billeted at company expense in a deluxe hotel, and were now on their own at last. Some repaired to the hotel bar, others streamed out into the night to see what the city offered and a large group went to "Red" Buchanan's suite to play poker. The meeting would officially adjourn after the next day's sessions followed by the "All

for One, One for All" dinner in the grand ballroom and the closing inspirational speech by the regional sales manager.

Myron Faro declined a number of invitations from his fellow salesmen to accompany them to the bar, to the sales manager's suite, to night clubs featuring undressed girls, and slipped away to his room where he took more of Doctor Shannon's tablets, undressed and got into bed. The pain in his stomach had dulled somewhat and he smoked a forbidden cigarette as he lay in bed listening to the radio. He slept at last, but badly, and was compelled to take more medication before morning.

Now he stared at the hotel room ceiling knowing that he could not face the morning meeting, the luncheon, the afternoon meeting and the final dinner. He simply could not. He wanted to go home, to his wife, Nina, and he would go home, even if Buchanan fired him. Not that it was likely; his sales record was solid. Buchanan needed him, despite the contempt in his eyes when he'd forced the whisky on him. And he'd had enough of that, too. To hell with Buchanan from now on. As long as he maintained his quota he would have a job. The dealers and distributors liked him. He did not high-pressure them and gave prompt service. If a garage owner needed a '53 Chevy carburetor in a hurry he could count on Myron Faro for fast delivery, even though it meant that Faro would make a special trip to the warehouse. It was the little touches that counted.

He got out of bed, called room service for a pot of tea and some dry toast and then entered the bathroom. He was a tall, slender man in his early forties with a lean, hollow-cheeked face. His complexion was gray and there were dark folds of flesh beneath his deep-set brown eyes. He wore a graying mustache and his hair was gray over the temples. If his color had been better he would have been distinguished-looking, a perfect model for a gentleman in a whisky advertisement, or perhaps in one for a filter-tip cigarette.

He shaved with an electric shaver and showered before his breakfast arrived. His head throbbed wickedly and the pain in his stomach seemed to spread to his chest and loins. He drank most of the tea and ate half of the toast and took two more tablets. Presently the pain lessened, but he knew from long experience that it would return when the soothing effects of the food, tea and medicine wore off.

He lit a cigarette, knowing that he should not. There were so many things Doctor Shannon had forbidden him; cigarettes, whisky, beer, fried or fatty foods, all condiments and spices, chocolate, nuts, pastries. The list was endless. Except for smoking, Myron Faro adhered strictly to his doctor's orders. There was a new surgical technique that Doctor Shannon had talked to him about and they had decided that if his

condition did not improve within the next few months the operation would be undertaken. But Doctor Shannon had gravely pointed out that in the meantime there was always the danger of intestinal perforation and hemorrhage. Myron Faro was intelligent enough to recognize this danger and conducted himself accordingly, except for the smoking, about which he felt guilty. But he had smoked cigarettes all of his adult life and it was his only indulgence. Doctor Shannon had called him "a good patient" and commended him for obeying his diet instructions so carefully.

Before Myron Faro dressed he called "Red" Buchanan's room. The sales manager's voice was thick but his "Good morning" was cheerful and hearty. Faro had long marveled at Buchanan's recuperative powers. The man had no doubt drunk and played poker until early morning, but Faro knew that he would be on hand for the morning meeting as alert and aggressive as ever.

"Red," Faro said, "this is Myron. If it's all right with you, I'll skip the meeting today and go on home. I feel pretty rough."

"Hell, man, you can't do that. I feel rough, too, believe me. On top of that those monkeys took me for sixty bucks last night. We start at nine, on the dot."

"I won't be there," Faro said. "I'm sorry, Red."

"But you're receiving a merit pin for placing third in the regional sales contest. You be there, Myron. That's an order."

"Send me the pin," Faro said, feeling the slow, coiling beginnings of pain.

"What's the matter? Getting anxious to see that good-looking blonde wife of yours? Is that it, Myron, old boy?" Buchanan laughed suggestively.

"I really do feel lousy, Red." Faro was beginning to sweat. "I've been taking medicine, but—"

"All the other boys will be there. They'd better be." Buchanan's voice now held an edge. "You be there, too, Myron. After the meeting we'll have a few drinks—little hair of the dog, you know?—and then a nice lunch. You'll be fine."

"You know I don't dare drink," Faro said, ashamed of himself for pleading with Buchanan. "And I couldn't eat a thing. Really, Red—"

"My God," Buchanan broke in. "All of us feel rough this morning. But this is Tip-Top business and the company comes first, don't forget that. I'll expect you, Myron."

Faro took a deep breath and said firmly, "I won't be there, Red."

There was a short silence. Then Buchanan said softly. "I can replace you, Myron. How old are you now? Forty-five? Forty-six?"

"Forty-three," Faro said, hating himself for the defensive tone of his voice.

"A little old to start all over. You'd better think about this, Myron."

The pain flared within Faro and with it came a sudden, cold rage. He said distinctly, "To hell with you, Red."

There was another silence, a shocked one. Then: "Listen, you goddamned peddler. I'll—"

Faro slammed the phone into the cradle and sat a moment, breathing heavily. Presently, when he was calmer, he began to dress. The phone rang before he was finished. He paid no attention, but hurried his movements. When he was ready to leave, neatly clad in a sober brown suit, tan top-coat and brown hat, and holding his bag and briefcase, he glanced about to see if he had forgotten anything. As he stepped out into the hall and closed the door he heard the elevator stop on his floor and he hurried to a stairway. It could be Buchanan, he thought, coming in person to throw his weight around. He walked down to the next floor, took an elevator to the lobby and checked out. A number of his colleagues were there, freshly shaven but bleary-eyed. One of them called, "Hey, Myron, where do you think you're going? The meeting will start pretty quick and Red won't like it if—"

"Goodbye," Faro said grimly and went out to the street. He got his car, a two-year-old Buick, from a parking garage a block away and drove out of the city over the Cherry Street bridge. His head still throbbed and the pain within him was now full blossomed. He stopped once at a gas station and took more of Doctor Shannon's tablets with water from a paper cup. It was a little after ten when he reached Harbor City.

He parked the Buick in the garage at the rear of the converted duplex on Dennison Avenue and went up the walk to the outside stairway leading to his upper apartment. Maybe he should have called Nina, he thought, to tell her, that he was coming earlier than he had intended. But it didn't matter. He would surprise her. He would have to tell her, though, that he might very well lose his job. She wouldn't like that, but he hoped she would understand how he felt about Buchanan. He shouldn't have talked to the sales manager as he had, but he wasn't sorry. He felt good about it. Even if he was fired and didn't find another job right away he and Nina could get along for a while; he had over two thousand dollars in a savings account and the last installment on the Buick had been made months ago. Suddenly all Myron Faro wanted was his wife, his slim, cool, golden-haired Nina. She would make him some tea and he would tell her how he had defied Buchanan. He moved eagerly toward the stairs, carrying his bag and briefcase.

A woman emerged from the back door of the downstairs apartment

and called, "Mr. Faro."

He stopped, his hand on, the railing. "Hello, Mrs. Kennedy."

"May I speak with you a moment?" Mrs. Kennedy was a widow, a thin wrinkled woman with a thin pursed mouth and sharp black eyes. Her only income was from Social Security and the rent from the upstairs apartment, and her only diversions were radio, television, neighborhood gossip and spying. A gray shawl was slung over her shoulders, concealing the upper half of a shapeless house dress. Bony hands hugged her bare elbows.

Faro, concealing his impatience, said, "What is it?"

She came closer, her expression grim and righteous. "This ain't nice to talk about, Mr. Faro, but there's something you should know."

He frowned. "About what?"

"About Mrs. Faro. I hate to say it, but she's been seeing a man—when you're gone. He was here last night again." Mrs. Kennedy watched him narrowly.

"A man?" Faro was startled and confused. "Who?"

"You've been a good tenant, Mr. Faro, and I will admit there's never been any trouble. But the neighbors are beginning to talk and I decided it was my duty to tell you. Not only that, if I must say so, I can't have such goings on in my house and on my property. I'd hate to lose you as a tenant, but all I ask is that *she* conduct herself properly. It's shame, with a good husband like you—"

"Wait a minute." Faro passed a hand over his forehead, felt the cold sweat there. What was the woman talking about? "If a man came here it was probably a city employee to check the meters, or maybe a television repair man."

"Hah!" Mrs. Kennedy said scornfully. "A meter-reader or a repair man coming late in the evening? And staying until all hours of the morning?" She knew that this little talk with Mr. Faro might result in losing tenants, but she could easily rent the apartment again. She had always resented Mrs. Faro's superior and indifferent attitude. It served her right. Mrs. Kennedy had wanted to do this for a long time and was enjoying herself. Not that she had anything against Mr. Faro. He was a polite man, coming and going quietly, and always paying his rent on the dot. Mr. Faro was all right, but his wife, that snooty, cheating ...

Myron Faro said coldly, "You're talking nonsense, Mrs. Kennedy. You are mistaken." He started up the steps.

"I got his license number," the woman said slyly.

Faro stopped and turned slowly. "Whose number?"

"The man's." Mrs. Kennedy's sharp eyes glistened. "I got it last night, after he went upstairs. I went out with the garbage. His car was parked

in the alley. I wrote down the number."

"Why did you do that?" Myron Faro's left hand gripped the wooden railing tightly and the pain flared within him.

"I thought you'd want to know, is all," Mrs. Kennedy said with satisfaction. "It's the same car that's been coming here since last summer, always at night and when you're gone. Today I checked the number at the court house. It belongs to—" She stopped and smiled, showing sparkling dentures. "But I'd better not tell you. I don't want to cause any trouble."

"I'm sure you don't," Faro said quietly. "Who owns the car?"

Mrs. Kennedy became coy. "I really don't know if I should—"

"Tell me." Faro's voice was low and intense.

Mrs. Kennedy's hands fluttered, causing the shawl to slip. She plucked at the shawl and her gaze skittered. "The car is a Chevrolet and is registered to John Horner. I've heard of him. He's on the police force."

"Thank you." Myron Faro turned and went steadily up the stairs.

Mrs. Kennedy, a little frightened now at what she had done, entered her house and hurried to the living room. She crouched against the wall where the chimney came up from the basement, a spot which she had learned long ago carried best the sounds from upstairs. With an ear against the wall, she listened intently, her eyes glinting avidly. But she was disappointed; there was no sound whatsoever from the upper apartment.

On the landing at the top of the stairs Myron Faro received no response to his knock. He got out a key, unlocked the door, moved through the short passageway to the living room and stood gazing about. The room was in disarray. The divan cushions were scattered about, the ash trays were overflowing with cigarette stubs, an empty bottle with a bourbon label stood on the low coffee table beside two glasses, also empty. It was quiet, even though the television was turned on; the volume was so low that the performers' lips moved almost soundlessly. Faro placed his bag and briefcase on the floor. "Nina," he called.

When she did not respond he crossed the room slowly and turned off the television set. Then it was really quiet. He moved into the kitchen, saw empty ice cube trays and a few dishes in the sink, and entered the bathroom, which was between the kitchen and the bedroom. There was a towel on the floor by the shower stall, but otherwise the room was neat and clean, as it usually was. Faro stepped into the bedroom. It was dusky there, the blinds drawn against the gray morning, but he could plainly see his wife lying on the bed, on her side, knees drawn up, the open robe revealing one slender leg and a white thigh. She was breathing quietly

and peacefully, her face composed. In sleep she was beautiful, even without makeup.

Myron Faro smelled the whisky fumes and he uttered small sound, not a moan, but a tiny cry of pain. He did not go near his sleeping wife, but returned quietly to the living room, where he sank to the divan. The empty bourbon bottle and the two glasses seemed to leer at him. She had not expected him home until late in the evening, he thought dully. Then the apartment would have been spotless, there would have been no trace of her midnight visitor. Horner? Police force?

He bent forward, aware that he was still wearing his hat and topcoat and not caring, and pressed hands to his face. He shuddered, racked with dry sobs.

6

Wednesday Noon

Captain Jason Keely, of the Harbor City police, gloomily surveyed the calendar in his office in the municipal building. On May 26th Captain Keely would be sixty-five years old. The date was circled heavily in black pencil on the desk calendar. It was time for lunch and Keely wanted a couple shots of rye first, but he couldn't leave until Lieutenant Horner reported for duty at twelve o'clock. It was now eleven-fifty-five.

Jason Keely looked his age, and more. He was too fat, because he loved rich foods, and his high blood pressure was evident in his red-veined eyes and florid, heavy-jowled face. Also, he was sometimes bothered by pains in his chest and a sudden shortness of breath. These symptoms worried him periodically but he would not see a doctor, mostly because he was afraid to hear what the doctor might tell him. In addition to food, he loved rye whisky, but he did not permit his drinking to interfere with his job, although many mornings he reported for duty with a searing headache and general jittery feeling of illness. He smoked strong cigars, too many a day, and stubbornly refused to cut down. He and his younger wife had five children and six grandchildren. Two daughters, seventeen and eighteen, were still at home in a rented frame house not far from the police station.

Captain Keely did not want to retire; he couldn't afford to, not on the police pension, not with a wife and two daughters to support. And he could not get another job, at least not one with the pay of a police captain. Because of his self-indulgence and free-handed mode of living he had saved nothing, and the only life insurance he owned was a ten-

thousand-dollar policy his wife had insisted he keep up and a five-thousand-dollar one through the police department. Fifteen thousand, he realized, would not support his family very long, and he hated it. Almost thirty years in the department with nothing to show for it, except his record, which was good. He had been promoted to captain ten years previously and was noted for being tough and strict. He had gone by the book, but had been wise enough to temper the law with fairness and common sense. Even so, he had few real friends in Harbor City, whereas his superior, Chief Beckwith, was very popular.

Keely thought bitterly of Beckwith. The chief had it made; his home was paid for, his son doing well as a lawyer in Cleveland, his older daughter married to one of the city's most successful young insurance men. Beckwith had only to worry about his younger daughter, Jill, who would graduate from high school in June. And Beckwith was only sixty-one years old. He had four more years to collect his chief's salary and salt away a big chunk of it. Also, he had plenty of insurance, plus investments. But he, Keely, owed for a new television set, a hi-fi for the girls, a new washer and dryer his wife had bought just a month ago. He was up to his neck in installments, even for the family car. Keely knew that he drank more than he could afford and therefore felt guilty about refusing things to his family, even though it meant going deeper into debt. All his life he had thought that when the time came he would be able to retire comfortably. But he had made no plan, had not prepared for it. Suddenly the time was now. He was old, not just middle-aged, and could not go back. Where had the years gone?

Captain Keely looked up at the clock on the wall. Five minutes past twelve. Where in hell was that cocky young Horner? He moved restlessly in his chair. Damn it, he would put it in the book that Horner was tardy today. Then he sighed, knowing that it wouldn't detract very much from the lieutenant's excellent record. A tardy mark would mean nothing to the chief or the city council. Anyone could be late for work once in a while. It would have to be something more serious than that.

At ten minutes past twelve Horner hurried in, smiling, hatless, removed his gray topcoat and hung it on a rack in a corner. "Sorry to be late, Cap." He turned to face Keely and added apologetically, "I'm kind of beat. Worked late last night and this morning the wife didn't feel so good and I had to take over—the kids' breakfast, you know, and getting them off to school. After that I tried to get some shuteye, but forgot to set the alarm,"

"What do you mean about working last night?" Keely asked coldly. "You were off duty."

"I know, Cap," Horner said easily, "but I've got this thing, this idea,

about those hold-up boys. I figure they've got to be hiding out somewhere around here—thought maybe if I prowled around a bit I might get a lead."

"I'm still captain," Keely said, "and I'll assign your duties. Remember that."

Horner spread his hands. "But it was on my own time, Cap. I told you and the chief that if they're holed-up they've got to eat, show themselves sometime."

"I've alerted all the food markets." Keely's voice was still cold. "I have men patrolling the store areas." He patted the cigars in his front pocket and stood up. He rarely wore his uniform and was dressed now in a wrinkled blue suit. His big stomach bulged over his belt. He took a soiled gray felt hat from the rack and moved to the door.

Then Horner said slyly, "I hear you've been doing a little work on your off time, too."

Keely turned slowly and his heavy face darkened. "What was that?"

"Big Connie told me you were in her place last night."

"I see," Keely said evenly. "What were you doing there?"

"The same as you—looking for leads." Horner grinned, thinking that he would not have to be too careful with Keely anymore. Keely was done and he, Horner, would soon have his job. Beckwith had practically promised him the captaincy. He added, "Frankly, Cap, I was a little surprised. You don't have to go snooping around at night."

"That's my business," Keely snapped. "I don't work by the clock, never did." His lips curled a little. "Did you go to Big Connie's directly—or did you just happen to pass there on your way home from one of your lady friends?"

Horner attempted to cover his surprise and shock with a frown. "I don't get it, Cap."

Keely said grimly, "Feel like needling me a little more, Lieutenant?"

"Gosh, Cap, I didn't mean anything. It's none of my business what you do at night. You're the captain. I just meant that you could have a detective check Connie's for you, if that's what you wanted. You've got enough to do without going out at night yourself." He smiled. "Hell, Cap, if you'd asked me I'd have done it. But you, the captain—"

"Shut up," Keely said. "You make me sick." He took a deep breath. "You're zealous as all hell, the rising young officer slated for promotion— my job. You stop at a store in the middle of the night, on your own, without orders. But I had also been there, personally. That's duplication of work. You should have been home sleeping so that you could report to work on time today."

"Gee, Cap," Horner said helplessly, regretting his arrogance, "don't get

in an uproar. You were there, sure, but one of those hoods could have come in before or after—you couldn't be on deck all night. I just figured it was worth checking, as long as I was out anyhow. How was I to know that you—"

"To hell with you," Keely said bitterly. "I've got that covered. I told Connie to call the station if anyone suspicious came in, and all the other food places have the same orders."

"Then why did you bother to go to Connie's in person?" Immediately Horner knew the question was a mistake.

"That's none of your damn business," Keely snapped. "Were you coming from Mrs. Keough's? She lives over that way. Or did you drive out to Connie's after you left Myron Faro's wife?"

Horner began to sweat. "Cap, I—I don't know what you're talking about."

Keely spat an obscene word. "Don't give me that! If I told Chad Beckwith what I know about you, you'd never make captain. You might even get kicked off the force."

"But I'm qualified," Horner said desperately. "I passed the exams. They haven't got anybody else."

"They'll find somebody, don't worry," Keely said with satisfaction. He hitched at his belt and added, "It might even be me."

John Horner pulled himself together. "Stop dreaming, Cap. I know you don't want to quit, but you're at the retirement age. And you can't prove a thing about me."

"It'll be my word." Keely thought of the nights he'd followed Horner, hoping to discredit him in any way he could. He knew he had no proof, unless one of the women would talk, which was highly unlikely, but he added, "Chad will believe me. I've seen you park your car in the alley behind the house where Myron Faro lives, and I've seen you park a block away from Keough's and walk to the house, when the doctor is out. And there've been a couple of others, but not lately. Two all you can handle anymore, lover boy?"

Horner couldn't speak. It was unthinkable that Keely, or anyone, had actually followed him. He himself had tailed many a criminal suspect and prided himself on his technique. He had thought confidently at all times that no one saw him, that he could spot any possible person intent upon spying. And then he remembered bleakly that Jason Keely had been a policeman when he, Horner, was a sixth-grader. Keely's accusation, coming on top of the early morning scene with Violet, left Horner scared and bewildered.

Keely said, "You want to hear more, Lieutenant?"

"Cap," Horner said unsteadily, "are—are you going to tell the chief?"

Keely grinned wickedly, showing the yellow edges of his teeth. "It all depends."

"I don't understand."

"It's simple," Keely said. "I want to work a couple more years, get myself on my feet. You just go to Chad Beckwith and tell him you don't feel you're quite ready for the captaincy and ask for a retention of your present rank. There's nobody else in line, as you said, so they'll be forced to keep me on until they can find and train somebody else."

"I can't do that," Horner said. "I've worked hard for this promotion."

"Okay." Keely flapped a hand carelessly. "I'll just tell Chad what I know about you. He won't approve the promotion of a man with the morals of an alley cat. This is a big city and growing bigger all the time. Public opinion, you know. What I'll have to say about you will be in the papers, whether I can prove it or not."

"You wouldn't do that," Horner said, thinking that it couldn't be happening to him.

"Oh, yes, I would," Keely said blandly. He hadn't meant to bring the matter up just at this time, but Horner's attitude had angered him. Keely opened the door and gave Horner a benevolent smile. "Think it over, lover boy." In the hall he felt a twinge in the region of his heart and stopped at a fountain for a drink of water. The twinge went away by the time he reached the street, but he told himself uneasily that he really should see a doctor.

Lieutenant John Horner went to the desk, sat down and lit a cigarette, his hands shaking a little. He felt as if the world had fallen in on him. It had been bad enough since his wife had seen the lipstick on his shirt and caught him talking on the phone to Nina Faro. He didn't know if he could ever square it with Violet. She had become hysterical, babbled about divorcing him, of taking the children to her parents' home in Columbus, Ohio. By making promises and begging forgiveness he thought he'd talked her out of that, but he couldn't be certain. And now he had that damned sneaking Keely on his back. What was he going to do about him?

Lieutenant Horner began his day's work. Captain Keely returned at a quarter of two, smelling of whisky. He greeted Horner jovially and thanked him for holding down his desk.

"You're welcome," Horner said grimly and went to his own office, a cubby hole off the squad room, where he busied himself with paper work and handled some cases of a minor nature. At five o'clock Chief of Police Beckwith paused at his doorway, smiling. "Good afternoon, Jack."

Horner looked up. "Hi, Chief."

"Hard at it, I see."

"Just routine stuff. By the way, how's your daughter coming along?" The entire force knew, of course, that the chief' daughter had undergone emergency surgery the night before.

"Fine," Beckwith said, "but it's a good thing we got her to the hospital when we did. The appendix was about to rupture."

"I suppose Doc Shannon operated?" Horner asked.

Beckwith shook his big, gray-thatched head. "Nope. Clint was out on a case. John Kovici took over. That young Keough helped him."

"Keough?" Horner raised his eyebrows. So that's where he'd been last night, he thought, while he had been with Betty.

Beckwith nodded. "He seems all right, quite capable. And well-trained, John says. He's new, you know, not too much practice yet. I offered him the job of city physician when old Doc Connors leaves. Do you think you can work with him—when you're captain, I mean?"

Horner grinned. "Chief, I can work with anybody. Just so he's on the ball when we need him in a hurry."

"I think you can count on him. He's a rather serious young fellow."

"I've seen him," Horner said, "but never met him."

"How's the family?" Beckwith asked pleasantly.

"Fine, Chief, just fine."

Beckwith nodded and left.

Horner worked on. At six o'clock he took over the desk while the sergeant went across the street to get sandwiches and coffee for both of them. At a little after eight the station quieted down. There was only the mutter of the shortwave radio, mostly cruisers reporting in. The first night-shift patrolmen were all on their beats and both Chief Beckwith and Captain Keely had gone home. Behind his high desk the sergeant read a ragged copy of *Life*. In his little office Lieutenant Horner lifted the phone, grinned at the annoyance of the sergeant who was obliged to drop his magazine and plug in the call. Horner's grin faded when he had his home number and his wife answered sharply, "Yes?"

"Hi, honey," Horner said. "It's me."

She said nothing.

He forced a laugh. "Didn't you hear me?"

"I heard you." The words dripped ice water.

"Look, honey, I told you I was sorry. It didn't mean a thing to me, honest."

"It meant a lot to me."

"You've got it all wrong. Are the kids in bed yet?"

"What do you care?"

"Oh, come on," Horner said. "It isn't that bad. Look, I'll be home in a little while and we'll talk things over."

"I don't want to talk to you."

"Maybe I'd better not come home at all." There was an edge to his voice.

"That's up to you. I don't care what you do." The phone banged in his ear.

Horner replaced the phone slowly, feeling anger. To hell with her, he thought. She'll get over it. But she'd never acted this way before. But then, he thought wryly, she'd never caught him as she had last night. He sighed, thinking that he would give her time to cool off. And, after all, what could she do about it? A woman with two kids?

Horner put on his gray topcoat and was about to leave when his phone buzzed. He picked it up, glanced out of the door across the squad room at the sergeant, who was holding a palm over the mouthpiece of the desk phone. "Some dame," he said in a low voice.

Horner nodded and said, "Lieutenant Horner speaking," noting that the sergeant had returned to reading his magazine

"Jack, don't hang up." It was Nina Faro.

Horner's face darkened with anger. "I told you never to call me," he said in a low voice from between clenched teeth. "Aren't you satisfied with what you did to me last night? My wife—"

"Jack, listen, please." Her voice was hurried, desperate. "Everything's gone wrong. Jack, Myron—knows about us."

"What?" Horner's blunt fingers gripped the phone tightly.

"I—I couldn't help it. He came home this morning, before noon. The apartment was a mess—I thought I had plenty of time to clean it up, but he got sick in Toledo and left before the meeting was over. He found me in bed, sleeping it off. I drank a lot after you left last night and I know I made a fool of myself. I should never have called your home. But this is serious. Myron *knows*."

"Did you tell him?"

"No, no. That snoopy bitch downstairs, that Mrs. Kennedy, told him."

"How did she know?"

"She's been watching you come here—spying. She got your license number and checked it at the courthouse. She told him. It's been terrible, Jack. When I woke up in the afternoon Myron was in the living room, still wearing his coat and hat, just sitting there. He—he scared me. He didn't talk much, just told me what he knew. Then he went into the bedroom and locked the door."

Horner felt sweat dripping down his ribs. "Where is now?"

"He just left. I—I couldn't call you before. I'm afraid, Jack. He took his gun, a pistol he's had for years, and he acted so strangely. I've never seen him like that."

"Did he say where he was going?"

"No. He wouldn't talk to me. He just—walked out."
Horner took a deep breath. "All right, Nina, thanks."
"I—I thought I'd better tell you, warn you ..."
"Sure," Horner said, feeling numb. "Goodbye."
"Jack, I'm sorry."
He laughed bitterly and hung up. As he crossed the squad room he nodded a goodnight at the sergeant and went out to the street. He stood on the sidewalk in the April evening, gazing at the passing cars, at the people moving by. It was raining again, very lightly, more of a falling mist than rain. He got his car from the parking area behind the station, drove out to the lighted street and across the city. The windshield wipers swished gently and the rain fell gently and Lieutenant Horner drove aimlessly, thinking.

And watching.

7

Wednesday Evening

He had a few drinks of whisky, straight, with water chasers, at several small bars where he was not known. At ten o'clock he was driving aimlessly again, feeling like a man in limbo. He thought of calling Betty Keough, but could not hope that the doctor would be out two nights in a row. And he did not want to see Nina Faro, certainly not now, not ever. There were several other women he knew, but they did not interest him any longer and he impatiently dismissed the thought of them. In fact, on this night Lieutenant Horner was not really in the mood for any female companionship.

He should go home, he thought, and try and make his peace with Violet. It was all that was left for him to do. If Nina's husband, that Myron Faro, was really gunning for him, he wished he would make his move. But maybe Nina had just been trying to scare him. You couldn't tell about Nina. How much of what she had told him had been the truth? Still, Horner thought, he'd better be careful. Maybe Faro was following him right now. He glanced in the rearview mirror. There were several cars behind him, but none really close, and they seemed to be proceeding in a normal manner.

Horner came to the fringe of the city and turned right on the lake road. Up ahead he saw bright lights and realized that he was approaching Connie's Corner, the all-night market. On an impulse, and because he had nothing better to do, he turned into the parking space behind the

building, left his car in the darkness there and walked around to the lighted front entrance. Through the window beyond stacks of canned food he saw several customers in the store and Big Connie herself at the check-out counter. Then, with a start, Horner saw Jason Keely standing at one side near the entrance. Horner stepped back from the light and watched the interior of the store. A man stepped away from the counter carrying a bulky brown paper bag. He was a small, dark man, a stranger to Horner, and wore a black leather jacket and a gray checkered cap. As the stranger left the store, Horner move further back into the shadows and watched as he got into an old and battered gray Plymouth sedan parked in front. Horner eyed the rear license plate, noted the number, which was local, and the dealer's name attached to the top: HI-DOLLAR TOM. Horner frowned and then, as the Plymouth's motor started, stepped forward quickly and rapped sharply on the window glass on the driver's side. The man inside rolled down the window and regarded Horner with ferret eyes. "You want something, bud?"

"Police," Horner said curtly. "Your driver's license please."

"Sure, Officer." The man made a move to reach inside his jacket. Then the Plymouth's motor roared and the car lurched away, spewing gravel from the rear wheels. It hit the lake road, gathering speed, still in second gear, and rocketed away into the night. Horner drew his revolver but the car, without lights, was already out of sight. Cursing softly, Horner holstered his gun and turned. Captain Keely stood on the steps in front of the store chewing on a cigar and regarding Horner sourly from beneath his hat brim.

"Did you see that man?" Horner jerked his head toward the road.

"Still snooping on your own time, I see," Keely said.

"Damn it, I asked you a question."

"I'm still captain," Keely said softly. "Watch your tone, lover boy."

"Sorry, Cap. You saw him, didn't you?"

"Who?" Keely asked blandly.

Horner restrained himself and spoke in a level voice. "That punk who just tore out of here in the beat-up Plymouth."

"I observed that," Keely said. "Reckless driving."

"I asked to see his license and he took off."

"Probably drunk."

"I don't think so," Horner said, eying the police chief. "Would you mind sticking around until I make a phone call?"

"Why? I was just going home."

"It'll only take a minute. This is police business." Horner entered a glass-enclosed phone booth in front of the store and thumbed a directory hanging by a chain. He knew that Hi-Dollar Tom's used car lot was

closed at this time of night, but he was acquainted with the owner, Tom Delgrado, and he called the car dealer's home number. Through the glass he saw Captain Keely watching him, chewing on his cigar. Delgrado answered and Horner said, "Tom, this is John Horner."

"Hello, hello," Delgrado said jovially. "How about trading in that Chevy of yours? I got a nice, clean Ford, late model, one owner, new rubber—"

"Listen, Tom," Horner cut in, "I need some information. I can get it from the courthouse in the morning, but I want it now."

"Sure, sure. But I don't think I've got any hot heaps on the lot right now. You know I always cooperate with the cops."

"Yeah, I know. Tom, did you sell an old Plymouth sedan, gray, four-door, in the last couple of days? A '47 or '48?"

"Plymouth? Gray? Oh, yeah. Unloaded it yesterday. That was really a dog. But it ran, and a steal for fifty bucks. Traded it from a farmer for a '51 pick-up."

"Who bought the Plymouth?"

"Jason Keely," Delgrado said. "Said he wanted it for his daughters."

"Thank you, Tom," Horner said. "Thank you very much." He left the booth and faced Keely.

The captain's red-veined eyes bore on Horner. "Well, what's on your mind?"

"Plenty," Horner said. "That stranger was here buying groceries and medical supplies. I think one of them was wounded. And you were on hand, covering for him. You bought that car from Delgrado and gave it to those hoods, because their getaway car is hot. The Plymouth has local plates and they can move around without being noticed. How much of that forty-two grand are they kicking back to you?"

Keely removed the cigar from between his teeth and regarded the glowing end. He seemed bemused, detached, and smiled gently to himself. His smug, faintly superior manner angered Horner, who said harshly, "I'm going to Beckwith. You're done, Cap. You won't get a pension. All you'll get is a jail sentence. Where are they hiding out?"

Keely spoke then and his voice was calm. "I can break you for this, Jack."

"You can like hell! I'll—"

"Be quiet," Keely broke in sternly, "and listen to me, for your own good. I don't have to explain anything to you, but I'll do you a favor—to keep you out of trouble. I did buy an old Plymouth from Tom Delgrado—for my daughters. It was stolen before I got it home."

Horner's lips curled in a sneer. "I didn't see any stolen car report filed by you."

"I'll tell you why I didn't report it," Keely said quietly, "There would have been cheap publicity in the news about a police captain's car being stolen. Besides, it only cost fifty dollars. Are you certain about the license number?"

"You're damn right. And I'm going to Beckwith."

Keely smiled. "You just do that," he said pleasantly. "Make a fool of yourself. And tell Chad what I know about his bright, upstanding, married, captain-to-be."

"You can't prove a thing about me, but I can prove that you bought that car. And now all I've got to do is scout around until I spot a gray beat-up Plymouth parked in the woods, or maybe even at a motel or tourist place." Horner gestured toward the lake highway. "They're out there someplace. I'll find them now. And you'll be done, Cap, finished, no matter what you blab about me. Beckwith won't buy it anyhow, not after what he'll know about you, not after I nab those hoods. I'll be a hero, Cap, and you'll be nothing but an old cop who finally sold out. I'm going to call Beckwith right now."

"Go ahead." Keely's yellow teeth showed in a wolfish grin. "You go right ahead, lover boy. You just call Chad—and listen to him laugh. And tell him he can reach me at home if he wants to talk to me. I'll be glad to put him straight about the car—and about you. Think it over." He moved away, puffing calmly on his cigar.

Horner entered the phone booth once more. He was all policeman now, his mind efficiently ticking off the things to be done. Roadblocks first; pick the men he wanted with him; machine guns and tear gas, searchlights, shotguns, rifles and plenty of ammo. The bastards might make a stand of it. He was faintly uneasy about Keely's unruffled reaction to his accusation, but he called Beckwith nevertheless.

"Chief, this is John Horner. I'm sorry to bother you at home tonight, but it's important. I'm out at Connie's Corner, on the lake road, and I'm sure I got a hot lead on those finance company robbers. I think they're holed up east of here, not too far away. I want your permission to—"

"Wait a minute, Jack. Captain Keely is still your immediate superior. Have you contacted him?"

Horner hesitated. In spite of what he'd told Keely, he was not quite ready to reveal his suspicions to Beckwith. He said cautiously, "No, sir. I couldn't reach him at the station or at his home. And this is urgent. Can I go ahead?"

"All right, Jack, I'll take your word. But be careful. And good luck."

"Thanks, Chief." Horner hung up and then called the police station, gave crisp, detailed instructions. "Get the men and equipment lined up," he finished. "I'll be there right away."

"Has this rumble been cleared with the chief?" the sergeant asked politely.

"Yes," Horner snapped. "I couldn't reach Keely, but Beckwith told me to go ahead."

"Okay, Jack."

As Horner left the booth he noted vaguely that a few additional cars had parked in front of the store while he'd been on the phone. He strode rapidly around the building to the dark parking area in the rear where he'd left his car. He had the ignition key in his hand and was opening the door of the Chevy when a soft voice called to him.

"Hey."

Horner turned slowly, peered into the gloom, saw a shadow move between two cars parked ten feet away. He couldn't tell if the voice belonged to a man or woman; it had just been a low, hoarse whisper. "Yes," he said loudly, peering. "Who is it?"

"Goodbye," the voice said.

Horner took one step forward. "Come out of there—"

Flame stabbed the darkness then and the *crack, crack, crack* of exploding bullets echoed in the misty April night. Horner felt the impacts of the bullets; the pain was no worse than if he'd been struck by crisply hit tennis balls in rapid succession, but he was slammed back against the car. He hung there, bewildered, and then felt himself slipping downward. He flopped awkwardly sideways, turning, hands slipping on the wet surface of the car, his legs buckling oddly. He sank to his knees, felt his forehead strike against a cold wet fender, gazed stupidly at the dull gleam of a chrome hubcap and the moist blackness of a tire. He knelt there briefly, aware of the hot beginnings of pain, and he said aloud, "I've been shot, sure, but it can't be too bad ..."

He coughed after uttering the words, saw the bright dark splatter on the hubcap metal. A sudden terrible fear struck him and he fought against it, physically and mentally, as he felt his forehead slip downward from the fender. He couldn't help himself. His brain fiercely demanded, but his body could not obey. He sank to the wet asphalt, huddling beneath his topcoat. The pain was worse now, but not really bad. He would be all right, he thought dimly, and could bear the pain until a doctor came. Then they would take him to the hospital, and Doctor Shannon, or Doctor Kovici (not Doctor Keough, thank you) would take care of him. And he and Violet would get squared away. She would forgive him, now that he was hurt. He had never meant to hurt her, though. Maybe she would even sneak a cold beer into his hospital room. They would laugh and it would be like when they were newly married. And the kids; he loved those kids ...

John Horner stirred feebly and thought plaintively, *Where are the people? Why isn't somebody here?* "Hey, here I am," he called. "Help me, please." He did not realize that his voice was only a sibilant whisper in the misty night.

People entered and left the establishment known as Connie's Corner, cars pulled up in front and drove away, and one car, driven by a fisherman who needed some spinners and gut leaders for early-morning trolling off the islands, parked in the rear. His headlights picked up the body of John Horner lying by a rear wheel of the Chevrolet. The fisherman, being kind-hearted and also curious, got out of his car to investigate, thinking that the man was intoxicated, dead drunk. But when he leaned over the still figure and saw the blood glistening in the glow of the headlights he knew that the man was not dead drunk.

He was just dead.

8

Wednesday Evening

Dr. Clinton Shannon ushered out his last patient at a little before eleven o'clock and sat smoking a cigarette before going home. He'd had only three hours sleep since delivering the baby at Sam Gideon's home on the marsh and was very weary. There was a soft knock on his door and he said irritably, "Come in, come in." Why did she always have to knock? he thought. Only the two of them were in the office now.

The nurse entered, removed her white cap and fluffed slender fingers through her black hair. She regarded him gravely and spoke in her soft accent. "It has been a long day, Doctor."

"*Sí*," Shannon said, forcing a smile. "I'll take you home."

"It is not necessary. I will call a cab. You must be very tired."

"So are you." Shannon crushed out his cigarette. "Let's go."

The nurse protested, but he was firm. She owned an old car, but it was in the garage for repairs. "It is kind of you," she said softly and went to get her coat. Shannon removed his white jacket, put on his suit coat, raincoat and hat, turned off the lights. The nurse joined him at the rear entrance, just beyond the X-ray room, and her hip brushed his fleetingly.

Shannon was aware of the physical contact, but thought it accidental. He said, "The front door is locked?"

She nodded and they went out and got into his Ford parked behind the office. As usual when they were alone, Lucille Sanchez had little to say. Shannon drove across the city making idle remarks about the

weather, about patients, his family, her parents, about anything which came to his mind. He sometimes felt a little uncomfortable in her presence; she was so cool and formal, often so distant and aloof, but he thought wryly that he should not hope for an efficient assistant who was also a jolly conversationalist. Tonight, however, she seemed more quiet and restrained than usual. When he stopped at the curb in front of her house she made no move to get out of the car and sat quietly staring straight ahead.

There was a short, strained silence. Then Shannon said, "Well, I'll see you tomorrow, Lucille."

Without looking at him the nurse spoke in a low voice. "Would—would you like to come in for a while? My parents are asleep."

Shannon was surprised, almost shocked, and for a moment he could think of nothing to say in reply. When he did speak he tried to make his voice matter-of-fact, as if she often asked him in. "Thanks, Lucille, but it's pretty late and—"

"It is all right," she broke in, gazing at him now, her face a pale oval in the gloom. "No one will know." She paused and then said, "I—I love you. I cannot conceal it any longer."

"Lucille," Shannon said gently, "listen—"

"There is no need for you to say anything," she said quickly. "I know you do not love me. I do not care. I have thought about this for a long time. I—I am not a virgin."

"No?" Shannon said stupidly.

"There was a man, a long time ago, before I came to work for you. He was killed in an auto accident."

"I'm sorry," Shannon said.

"I loved him, too, but not as I love you. You are everything—kind, wise, gentle." She spoke swiftly in her faint, soft accent. "I think you will like me, even if you do not love me. I did not think I would ever have the courage to tell you, but I could not go on being with you every day and not tell you. And please do not think me—cheap."

"Never." Shannon turned off the motor. This was something he could not brush off, he thought. He had to face it, now. He tried to think of the right words.

"You can have me," Lucille Sanchez said quietly. "Any time, and always. I do not ask anything more."

Shannon turned on the seat, tilted her chin with a forefinger and kissed her. She came against him eagerly and her lips were warm and full of promise. It was an abandoned, wanton kiss and Shannon, being male, felt the stirring of desire, a basic human emotion which had nothing to do with his love for his wife. But he drew away and said,

"Thanks, Lucille. That was—nice."

"Then you will come in with me?" she asked gravely.

"I can't," he said, still groping for the words. "It wouldn't be right, not for you, or for me. You deserve better than that."

"It is all I ask," she said. "I—I think I would please you."

Shannon was confused. Were there any right words for this? He said carefully, "Lucille, I'm flattered. And touched. Really. And I'm probably a fool. I like you very much, but—"

She placed cool fingers on his lips. "I understand. It is all right."

"But it's not all right," he said. "I can't tell you how sorry I am."

She moved away from him and placed a hand on the door latch. "I will stay with you until you can get another nurse."

"I don't want another nurse," he said. "I want you."

"Even now? After what I have confessed?"

"Certainly. Goddamnit—"

"Do not curse." She smiled gently. "I have upset you, and I am truly sorry."

"Lucille, you'll meet someone," he said lamely, "fall in love again. And it will be better than—than ..." He moved his hands helplessly.

"Than having an affair with my employer?" she finished for him.

"That's what it would be, and you're too fine a person for that."

"Am I?" she asked sadly.

"Yes. Will you stay with me, Lucille?"

"If it is your wish, Doctor. I am sorry for my shameless action. It will never happen again."

"Don't ever be sorry. And why don't you stop calling me 'Doctor'?"

"I cannot. I respect you too much."

"Oh, hell." He lit a cigarette and wished he had a drink.

"You *are* upset," she said softly. "Please forgive me."

"Let's both forget it. Okay?"

"I will try very hard. Good night, Doctor. Thank you for bringing me home." She opened the door and got out of the car.

"You're welcome."

She crossed the sidewalk and he waited until she had entered the house and then drove to his own home on the edge of the city. The phone on the wall by the breakfast bar was ringing as he entered the kitchen. It stopped just as he lifted the receiver from the hook and he heard his wife's voice on the bedroom extension. "I'm sorry, but he isn't here. He may still be at the office."

"I just called there," a man's voice said. "This is Chad Beckwith. We need—"

"Hello, Chad," Shannon broke in. "I just came in. Hi, honey."

"Are you talking to me or to your wife?" Beckwith asked dryly.

"Both." Shannon heard the click as Celia hung up.

"Clint," Beckwith said, "we've got trouble. I'm out here at Connie's Corner on the lake road. Somebody pumped three slugs into Jack Horner and he's dead."

"Horner? I saw him only last night. Said he was working on that loan company robbery."

"I know he was." Beckwith sighed heavily. "Jack was eager, too eager, maybe, but one of my best men. In fact, he was the only qualified man in line for the captaincy when Jason Keely retires next month. Can you come out here right now?"

"If you want me, yes."

"You're the coroner, Clint. The lab crew and photographer are finished. I want you to see him before he's moved." Beckwith sighed again. "A wife and two kids. They don't know it yet."

"Have you any idea who shot him? Did he get too hot on that robbery thing?"

"Maybe," Beckwith said. "Anyhow, I'm working on that assumption. He called me tonight, claimed he had a lead on it and asked my permission to set up roadblocks and take out a search crew. Knowing Jack, I think it is quite possible that he tangled with Donegal or one of his men."

"I'll be right out." Shannon hooked the phone and turned to see his wife standing in the kitchen doorway. Her short, black hair was tousled and her gray eyes were sleepy. She smiled at him as she tied the cord of her light robe around her slender waist. "Hello, stranger."

Shannon went to his wife, kissed her and said, "How about some coffee? I've got to go out again."

"Oh, no! Not really!"

He nodded. "Chad Beckwith just told me that one of his men—a lieutenant named John Horner—was shot to death tonight."

Celia's eyes widened. "Do you mean the one they call Jack?"

Shannon nodded again.

"But that's—terrible. Who shot him?"

"They don't know yet."

Celia placed a teakettle on a burner. "If the poor man's dead, why must you go?"

"I'm still the coroner, remember?"

When the water was hot enough for the coffee he drank a cup hurriedly and picked up his bag.

"Will you be long?" Celia asked.

"I don't think so. If I decide to do an autopsy, morning will soon enough."

"I'll wait for you. I want to hear about it."

"Good. Have a short bourbon waiting for me." Shannon grinned, patted her cheek and left.

Thursday Morning, Early

At a quarter of one Doctor Shannon, wearing pajamas, sat with his wife in their bedroom sipping a glass of bourbon and water. "It's a shame," he said. "He was young and healthy, with a future before him. He died instantly, or almost. Two bullets in the right lung, one in the stomach. Missed the heart, but it didn't matter."

"Are you going to do an autopsy?" Celia asked.

Shannon sighed. "I'd better, I guess, for the record. The body's at the Hoyt Funeral Home. Beckwith told Mrs. Horner—I didn't envy him his job. You've got to give Chad credit. There was a mob out there, but he kept everything under control."

"Does he have any notion yet who—?"

"No," Shannon said, "but he's got the whole force working on it, and the state patrol. Just before Horner was shot he called Beckwith, all excited about a lead he said he had on those finance company robbers. Chad gave him a free hand—roadblocks, men, equipment, the works. He had a lot of confidence in Horner. But we'll never know now what Horner had found out."

Celia sighed. "It's just too bad. When I think of that poor man's family ..."

"Yes," Shannon said, sipping his drink.

"Well," Celia said briskly, "let's not be morbid. Life goes on, and all that. And you should be asleep, Doctor Shannon."

He smiled and lifted his glass. "As soon as I finish this."

"How's Sam Gideon's wife? Did you see her today?"

"Yes. I went out after office hours this afternoon. She's fine, and so is the baby."

"How many does that make for Mrs. Gideon?"

"I've lost track."

"Sam paid you, I'm sure." Celia's voice was mocking.

"He wanted to, with fish. I said I'd settle for sweet corn in August."

"Clint Shannon, you're an easy mark. I'll bet no other doctor in town would go out there to the marsh, deliver a baby in the middle of the night and go out again for a post-birth examination—for nothing."

He grinned at her over his glass. "Sam Gideon was one of my first patients here. Remember?"

"Oh, sure," Celia said scornfully. "A non-paying patient."

"But think of the experience. Invaluable."

"Since when do you need OB experience? You can catch a baby with your eyes shut—and get a nice fee for it, too."

"Please don't be mercenary, my love. Besides, have I ever paid Sam for his professional services? In cash, I mean?"

"What on earth are you talking about? Sam's a professional no-good."

"You do him an injustice. He's a professional guide, fisherman and hunter. And I'm his favorite client, for free. When I hunt or fish on Sam's place I always get my limit. His land is posted, you know—not open to the common public."

Celia moved her hands impatiently. "Ducks, pheasant, rabbit, fish. Gad! Why don't you and Sam open a market? We have enough in the freezer right now to start one."

"That's an idea," Shannon said, grinning. "You can never tell when my patients will switch to some of these sharp new young men setting up practice in my bailiwick."

"Like Doctor Nelson Keough?" Celia asked. "That fellow who appears in public with a stethoscope sticking prominently from his coat pocket, as it did last Friday at the country club dance? From his *tuxedo* pocket?"

"Don't sneer at him for that," Shannon said. "It's probably a carry-over from his interne days, when he wanted to impress the nurses and the cute little probies. Did it myself. He'll get over it. Besides, he seems competent and I know he's had sound training. John Kovici told me he did a first-rate job with the anesthesia for Chad Beckwith's daughter."

"It was surgery you should have had," Celia said. "The Beckwiths are your patients, but you were not available. You were out on the marsh being noble and dedicated."

"No professional jealousy, please. I'm grateful to John for taking over."

"Of course," Celia said, smiling. "I'm sorry. But that young Keough, who did such a first-rate job with the anesthetic, had better keep an eye on that child wife of his. I observed her the other day, wearing too-tight shorts and a sloppy blouse, chatting cozily with a new young pharmacist at the drugstore. They may have been discussing toothpaste, but it didn't look that way to me."

"Merely harmless conversation, I'm sure." Shannon finished his drink and stood up.

"Bad schedule tomorrow?"

"Not particularly. No surgery in the morning and I can sleep until eight. I'll do the autopsy first, before the house calls. I don't know what Lucille has lined up later."

"Poor Lucille," Celia said. "Does she have a boyfriend yet?"

"Not that I know of." Shannon had already decided not to mention to

his wife the incident with Lucille Sanchez. It would serve no good purpose and he wanted to forget it.

"It's too bad," Celia said. "She's quite attractive. Or haven't you noticed?"

"I've noticed. She's also a very fine nurse. I'd hate to lose her."

"For professional reasons?" There was a teasing quirk to Celia's lips.

"Hell, no. Lucille and I are having an affair. Haven't you suspected?"

"So that's the reason for all these late office hours. How is she?"

"Not bad."

"Better than me?"

"Let's not be clinical," Shannon said, grinning. "Anyhow, it's too late to make a comparison."

"I could change your mind," Celia said softly.

"Yes, I know. I'll try and get home early tomorrow night. Do we have a date?"

"I'll think about it," Celia said. "Would you mind checking our son on your way to the bathroom?"

"Be glad to. Anything else, madam?"

"Yes. You're supposed to attend a Cub Scout meeting tomorrow evening. One of the parents must accompany the cub. Scout regulations."

"You're a parent," Shannon said. "I'll be tied up with emergency surgery."

"But I always go," Celia protested, "and besides, I'm a den mother. You're shirking your responsibility as a father. Can't you get away long enough to go to the meeting? What emergency surgery? And if it's an emergency, why wait until tomorrow night?"

"I'll think of something," Shannon said, as he left the bedroom, carrying his glass.

"Shirker," his wife called after him.

A few minutes later when they were in their respective beds in the darkened room, Celia spoke in a small voice. "I can't stop thinking about that—that murder. And the wife, and the children, without a father now ..."

"Yes," Shannon said, gazing upward into the darkness.

"Little Jack Horner sat in a corner," Celia said drowsily. "That's Mother Goose, isn't it?"

"Little Jack Horner *died* in a corner," Shannon said. "Connie's Corner."

"Only he isn't little. He's big and handsome."

"Was," Shannon said gently.

Celia sighed and presently slept, but Shannon lay awake for a while, thinking. He had rather liked John Horner, even though he had not known him very well. He thought also of Lucille Sanchez and hoped that

what had happened that evening would not mar his professional relationship with her.

Thursday Morning, Early

It was almost two in the morning when Chief of Police Chad Beckwith reached his office at the station. After receiving the report of Lieutenant Horner's murder he had called Jason Keely, but the police captain had not been home. Beckwith had then personally taken charge. Bearing in mind what John Horner had told him on the phone just before he had been shot, Beckwith had gone ahead with the roadblocks, even though he was afraid it was too late, and had sent a search crew east on the lake road. He wished he knew more of what Horner had learned, but the least he could do was act on the little information he had.

The men at the road blocks stopped many cars, but the occupants were not criminals. The search crew as well as the state highway patrol had reported no suspicious persons in the area along the lake highway east of the city. Maybe when it was daylight, Beckwith thought, they would have more luck. Lieutenant Horner had not been a man given to hasty action; he must have learned something definite.

Suddenly Beckwith realized that Captain Keely was not aware of Horner's death. In the confusion and activity following the discovery of the body, and after Beckwith had called Keely's home, the police chief had forgotten about Keely. Now he picked up the phone and called the captain's home number.

After several rings Keely answered and Beckwith said, "Jason, this is Chad. I'm sorry to—"

"It's all right. What's up?"

Beckwith told him quickly, not permitting Keely to interrupt, and finished by saying, "I called you as soon as I got the report, but your wife said you weren't home yet."

"I was on my way. My wife told me you called, and I called the station and your home, but couldn't reach you. I figured if it was important you'd call again."

"I didn't think," Beckwith said. "I was pretty busy."

"I understand, Chad. My God, I saw Jack out at Connie's tonight. I stopped there for some cigars. Have you told his wife?"

"Yes, I told her," Beckwith said wearily.

"Look, I'll get dressed and come right down."

"No need, Jason. We can't do any more until morning. What time did you see Jack?"

"Around ten-thirty. He was going into Connie's as I came out."

"He was killed shortly after that," Beckwith said. "He called me at twenty minutes of eleven."

"He should have notified me," Keely said stiffly.

"Yes, Jason. I asked him why he didn't. He said he couldn't reach you, and seemed to be in a big hurry. He must have stumbled onto the information, whatever it was, after he saw you. Otherwise he would have told you." Beckwith was a veteran diplomat when it came to soothing the delicate feelings arising from rank and the chain of command "You go back to bed, Jason. I'll see you in the morning."

"All right, Chad. There are some things I want to tell you about Jack. Did he mention me when he called you?"

"Only that he couldn't contact you. Why do you ask?"

"Frankly, I've had a little trouble with Jack," Keely said "I'll tell you about it in the morning. He was a good man, though. We'll miss him."

"Yes," Beckwith agreed. "His death creates a real problem for the force. I want to discuss it with you, Jason."

"All right, Chad. You can count on me."

"I know I can. Good night, Jason."

After instructing the desk sergeant to inform him of any developments, Beckwith went home to bed.

9

Thursday Morning, Late

At ten-thirty Chief of Police Chad Beckwith sat behind his desk smoking a cigar. Two men sat facing him. One was Captain Jason Keely and the other was a young laboratory technician named Franklin Hobbs, who held a bulky manila envelope. Beckwith wore a gray suit, a crisp white shirt, a sober blue tie. His thick graying hair was neatly combed and his heavy blunt face was smoothly shaven. He puffed slowly on the cigar and tapped a paper on his desk with a thick forefinger. "I have Doctor Shannon's autopsy report," he said. "John Horner died of three bullet wounds, two in the right lung and one in the stomach—I'll omit the medical terms." He nodded at the laboratory man. "You take it from there, Frank."

Franklin Hobbs said, "The slugs were .32 caliber, fired from fairly close range—not more than ten feet. The lead in inches and the groove diameter indicate that the gun was a Smith and Wesson. We didn't get too many clear fingerprints, because of the rain, but they were all from

parked cars and don't mean much. We went over Horner's car. His prints were on the wheel, gear lever and dash, and there were other—"

"Excuse me, Frank," Beckwith broke in. "I know you and your men did a thorough job, but I don't think fingerprints are important. The killer had no reason to be near Horner's car, or to touch it. He just blasted away and lammed out of there."

"Right, Chief." Hobbs opened the clasp of the envelope. "We picked up everything we could find in the parking lot and dried it out, but it's just the usual junk—burnt matches, cigarette and cigar butts, chewing gum wrappers, stuff like that. You want to see it?"

Beckwith nodded. Hobbs stood up and dumped the envelope's contents on the chief's desk. As the laboratory man had said, it was junk, trash; burned matches, smashed and crumpled cigarette and cigar butts, flattened cigarette packages, a small collection of soft-drink and beer-bottle caps, an empty pint wine bottle, two hairpins, a small wax-paper package containing three salted peanuts, a flat wooden stick from an ice cream bar, a soggy comic book, a scattering of Ohio sales tax stamps. Attached to each article was a tag.

Beckwith grimaced in distaste. "Looks like the city dump. How often does Connie sweep out the parking lot in the rear?"

"Every morning," Hobbs said. "I asked her."

"Then this trash accumulated yesterday and last night?"

"That's right, Chief."

Beckwith sighed. "None of it means a thing to me. Put it back, Frank."

As Hobbs began to scoop the articles into the envelope, Captain Keely said, "Wait a minute—where did you find that peanut package?"

Hobbs peered at the tag. "I picked that up myself. It was about ten feet from Horner's body."

"In the direction the shots came from?" Keely asked sharply.

Hobbs nodded.

Keely looked at Beckwith. "Chad, I remember something. Maybe it doesn't mean a thing, but I'd better tell you about it."

The police chief nodded and said to Hobbs, "Thanks, Frank. Keep that stuff on file."

The lab man nodded, folded the envelope flap over the clasp and left. Beckwith said to Keely, "All right, Jason, what's on your mind?"

"This ties in with what I told you about Horner. I warned him and I would have mentioned it to you before, but I hoped to get him straightened out without bothering you." Keely paused and then added quietly, "Jack Horner was chasing, Chad. It's not just gossip. I followed him personally."

"Why?" Beckwith asked grimly.

"Damn it, it was my responsibility. It's bad for morale when an officer conducts himself improperly. When I first heard the rumors, I didn't believe them—I always liked Jack. But the talk about him continued and I decided to check on him myself. The rumors were true. I spoke to Jack about it yesterday and warned him. He didn't like it at all."

"Then that's why he by-passed you last night," Beckwith said. "After he got the tip-off on the robbery, whatever it was, he came to me directly, because he was sore at you. Is that it?"

"I'm afraid so, Chad. I was going to tell you, but hoped I could clear it up first. There was also another matter between Horner and me, but there's no point in discussing it now."

"Who are the women Horner was seeing?"

"A Mrs. Faro," Keely said. "Blonde, not too young, but attractive. Husband is a salesman for an auto accessory outfit, away from home a lot. They live in the top half of a duplex out on Dennison. There were a couple of others, both married, but he dropped them a while ago. The newest one is a Mrs. Keough—little woman, three kids. Her husband is a doctor, M.D."

"I know him," Beckwith said grimly. "He helped Tuesday night when John Kovici operated on my daughter." Beckwith hunched forward, drawing on his cigar. "What else is on your mind, Jason?"

"That peanut package," Keely said. "When I was buying the cigars at Connie's last night, this Faro came in—I think his first name is Myron— and just stood around. I happened to see him get a package of salted peanuts from a vending machine. He was eating them as he went out."

"Do you know this Faro personally?" Beckwith asked.

Keely shook his head. "Only by sight. Tall, thin fellow, has a mustache. Doesn't look too healthy. When I left Connie's, he wasn't in sight. Horner came around from the parking lot then and wasn't too friendly. I figured he was still peeved about my jumping him for his woman-chasing. He went into the phone booth. When he came out we had a few words and I left."

"Could this Faro have gotten wise about his wife and Horner?" Beckwith asked. "And maybe followed Horner to Connie's?"

"It's possible. I think Horner was getting a little careless."

"What about Keough? Do you suppose he knew that Horner was seeing his wife?"

Keely spread his hands. "I don't know, Chad. It's a hell of a mess."

Beckwith picked up the phone and said, "Get me Frank Hobbs at the lab." As he waited for the connection, he spoke to Keely. "We'll start with Faro, hear what he has to say about last night. And we'll keep Doctor Keough in mind. It'll be touchy in both cases. If either or both of them

were wise about Horner, okay. If not, they're not suspect." He grinned wryly. "I'd hate to let something out of the bag and cause a family row." He turned away as a voice spoke in his ear. "Frank, this is Beckwith. Did you try for prints on any of that junk you picked up at the parking lot?"

"Not yet, Chief."

"Give that peanut package a going-over, will you? And let me know?"

"Sure, Chief, but it was raining, you know, and—"

"Yes, but do your best. It may be important." Beckwith replaced the phone and turned to Keely. "If they get even a smudge of prints, and they match with Faro's, we're in business."

"It would help if we knew whether or not Faro was wise to his wife and Horner," Keely said.

Beckwith nodded. "And the same with Keough. But Faro was at the right time. Do you know Doctor Keough?"

"Only by sight, the same as Faro. But I didn't see him at Connie's too. It was just luck that I spotted Faro—and remembered about the peanuts." Keely stirred his heavy body in the chair. "But Horner told you he had a line on those hold-up boys. It could have been one of them. Maybe they knew Horner was on their tail and ambushed him in the parking lot."

"Maybe," Beckwith admitted, "but Faro was *there*. We know that for certain. We'd better pick him up." As he spoke, the phone on his desk began to ring. Beckwith answered it. "Chief Beckwith speaking." Then he listened intently for perhaps a minute, after which he said, "I see. Thank you very much for calling."

Beckwith cradled the phone and met Keely's curious gaze. "I think you've got something hot, Jason. That was a woman named Mrs. Kennedy. She owns the house the Faros live in, a duplex, as you said. She's downstairs, they're up. Yesterday she told Faro that his wife was entertaining John Horner when Faro was away. She knows it was Horner because she checked his license number. Claims she tattled to Faro because the neighbors were gossiping and because she didn't want any 'indecent goings-on'—her words—in her house. Last evening around eight o'clock she saw Faro leave the house and drive away. He didn't return until after midnight. This morning she heard on the radio that Horner had been murdered. She felt it her civic duty to inform me." Beckwith paused, his eyes bleak.

Keely said, "Do you believe me now? What I told you about Horner and Mrs. Faro?"

"I didn't doubt you, Jason." Beckwith pulled thoughtfully at his lower lip and added, "Mrs. Kennedy also told me that Mr. Faro did not go to work today. He is still in the apartment."

Keely stood up. "Then what're we waiting for?"

"Not a thing, Jason," Beckwith said gently. "Let's go."

Thursday Morning, Late

Nina Faro placed a soft poached egg and a slice of dry toast beside a cup of hot tea on the kitchen table before her husband and said, "Anything else?"

"Just my pills," he said.

She got them from a cabinet over the sink, three different kinds, white, pink and green, and lined them up beside the tea cup. She wore the light blue robe over her nightgown and her ash blonde hair was combed smoothly back into a gleaming bun. Her thin face, with the delicate nose and prominent cheekbones, bore a waxy pallor. There was no lipstick on her full mouth. Slender white fingers plucked nervously at the cord of the robe as she said, "I didn't hear you come in last night. I waited for you, but it got so late I took a sleeping pill and went to bed."

"That's all right." He took a bite of toast and a sip of tea. He wore red-striped pajamas, the jacket hanging loosely over his thin shoulders. He needed a shave, but his graying hair was neatly combed.

"What time was it?" she asked.

"I don't know. Late, I guess." He sipped more tea.

She stood watching him, fingers working at the cord. "Where did you go?"

"I just drove around, thinking and thinking."

"About us?"

"Yes." He tasted the egg, and then put his fork down. "It's too hard."

"Sorry. I'll poach you another."

"Don't bother. I'm not hungry." He took the pills with a glass of water, shook a cigarette from a pack on the table and placed it between his lips.

She struck a match and held it for him. "You shouldn't smoke so much. Doctor Shannon said—"

"Yes, yes. Does it matter?"

"Yes," she said soberly. "It matters to me."

"Why?" His eyes were sardonic.

"Because I love you."

He turned his head and gazed out of the kitchen window, drawing on the cigarette.

"I mean it, Myron. That—that man means nothing to me. Less than nothing. Believe me, please. Last night, after you left, I was afraid—for you, not for him. But I called him, Myron, to warn him. I—I didn't want

anything to—to happen. You were so strange, so—so frightening. You took the gun, didn't you?"

"Yes." He was still gazing out the window, saw the barren backyards below, the sodden brown April grass showing patches of new green, the fences, the alley, the garage in back.

"Where is it now?"

"I threw it away," he said. "The gun wasn't the answer."

"I was lonesome, Myron, and bored, and bitchy. And stupid."

"Yes," he said again.

"I know now what he is. And I know what I am. But I love you, Myron."

He drew on the cigarette, gazed out the window and did not answer.

She said, "What're you going to do?"

He turned his head slowly to look at her, his thin, lined face as bleak as death. "I don't know, Nina. Give me some time."

"I wasn't—unfaithful. Not really."

"How unfaithful can a wife be?" he asked bitterly.

"It wasn't love. Believe me, please." Her hands were clenched now and she watched him with a bright intenseness.

"Twelve years," he said. "I thought you were happy."

"I was, Myron. I am. Maybe if we'd had a child ..."

"That's not my fault." He saw the pain in her eyes and added quickly, "I'm sorry, Nina." It was one of Myron Faro's faults; he was too kind, too honest, too sensitive to the hurt of others.

"It's all right," she said quietly.

He crushed out the cigarette, taking longer than was necessary, and at last he said, "We're all alone, Nina, just you and I. No one to go to. I've thought and thought. It's my fault, too. I hate my work, I'm sick, I've left you alone too often and too long and not caring, worrying about myself, about what *I* want. I can see how it could happen."

She watched him silently.

He moved a hand helplessly. "Hell, I don't know. I'm supposed to be the wronged husband. I left here last night wanting to kill, to smash at somebody or something. But it was silly, juvenile. It would solve nothing and erase nothing. It wouldn't even be fair. I—" He stopped abruptly and lit another cigarette with a hand that trembled.

"What are you trying to tell me?" she asked in the same quite voice.

"There was a woman in Saginaw," he said harshly, "and another in South Bend. They didn't mean anything, either."

She closed her eyes and seemed to sway slightly.

He took a deep, ragged breath. "I had to tell you." His mouth twisted. "Maybe we deserve each other."

She opened her eyes. "No. We need each other."

He pushed back his chair and stood up. "Come here, Nina."

She moved forward and stood within the light embrace of his arm. "Let's both forget," he said. "Or try to. Okay?" She nodded silently and his lips brushed her cheek. They stood together for maybe a minute and then he said, "It'll be like starting all over again."

"Good," she said. "I want that."

"I'm going to call Buchanan and resign."

"If it's what you want, I'm with you."

"There'll be a vacancy on the teaching staff at Central High," he said. "I think I can land it. We have enough money to get along until September. What will we do until then?"

"Just be together." She averted her gaze. "Those women—were they pretty?"

"No. Let's not talk about them."

"Good." She smiled at him. "Call Buchanan. Now."

He touched her cheek, entered the living room where the phone was and placed a call to Mr. Charles Buchanan, regional sales manager of the Tip-Top Auto Supply Company, Toledo, Ohio. When Buchanan was on the wire, Myron Faro said, "Hello, Red. This is Faro. I—"

"Hi, Mike, old boy! How you doing, pal? Got a juicy order you want expedited?"

"No, Red, listen—"

"By the way," Buchanan cut in, "I just remembered you left the sales meeting yesterday morning, after I personally requested you to be present."

"I know, Red, but I didn't feel well at all."

"You could have stayed a little longer, Mike, in the interest of that old do or die company spirit. A lot of the boys missed you and wondered what happened to old Annabelle down there in Harbor City." Buchanan paused and when he spoke again his voice held a sharp edge. "Also, Mike, I seem to remember that you told me to go to hell."

"I'm sorry about that, Red. I was sick and upset." Myron Faro heard soft music from the kitchen and knew that his wife had turned on the radio out there. "I just wanted to tell you that—"

"It's okay, Mike. No need to apologize. But I can't have insubordination. I'm jumping your quota for May. Gotta have discipline, you know. You better make that quota, boy."

"I'm afraid I won't," Faro said. "I'm quitting, Red."

"You're what?"

"As of now. I'll service the territory until you can send someone in, but no longer than two weeks. Will that be satisfactory?"

"You kidding, Mike?"

"No, Red. I've just decided that I can't work any longer for a stupid, arrogant, bullying—"

"You're talking to Red Buchanan. By God, I'll—"

"Shut up. I offered you a two-week notice. Do you want or don't you?"

There was a shocked silence on the wire. Then Buchanan spoke in a calmer tone. "Mike, we can fix this up. All right, all right—I know you've got an ulcer, but I thought you we just using it as an excuse to skip the meeting yesterday. It was nothing personal, Mike. Hell, you're one of my top men."

"I know that," Faro said.

"Okay, okay. Now listen, Mike. This is top secret stuff; the company is going to promote you to regional sales manager—my job—and is moving me up to the entire Midwest slot. I wanted to talk to you about it after the luncheon yesterday, but oh, no, you had to goof off. I'm sorry I was kind of rough on you, Mike, but it's my job, see? I'll run down there tomorrow and we'll talk this over. Okay, pal?"

"No," Faro said. "I'll be in the territory until the middle of next week, winding up my accounts. If you want me to stay longer, maybe take the new man around to meet the customers, let me know."

Buchanan said desperately, "Now, wait a minute—"

"Goodbye, Red."

"You stinking, lousy, ungrateful, stinking jerk, you goddamned peddler, you—!"

Faro laughed and replaced the phone. He felt good. And then he thought of his wife. It would be hard, but maybe they could work it out. He would try. He went to the kitchen, where Nina was washing dishes. She gave him a half-shy smile. "What did Buchanan say?"

"He was mad."

"Don't worry. It'll be all right."

Faro sighed. "I hope so. I'll see about the school job tomorrow." He hesitated a moment. "Nina, do you want to stay here? In this house, I mean?"

"No," she said soberly.

"Neither do I. We'll look for another place before the end of the month." Faro nodded at the radio. "Did you feel like some music?" Somehow, it seemed to him that dance melodies were out of place at this time.

"Just habit, I guess. The eleven o'clock news will be on in a minute. I always listen. It helps pass the time."

"Yes," he said, thinking for the first time how his wife must have spent the lonely hours when he was away.

She held a cup under running water and spoke without looking at him.

"Myron, you didn't have to tell me about about those women."

"Yes, I did. I couldn't condemn you when I was guilty, too."

She turned. There were tears on her lashes.

He wanted to hold her, kiss her, but he felt strange and awkward. He said unsteadily, "Nina, let's go away for a few days."

"But don't you have to work? I mean, until Buchanan replaces you?"

"Not really. I'll see my customers, of course, but Monday is soon enough. We can rent a nice place along the beach this time of year. We'll be alone and it'll be quiet."

"Like Catawba Island that October, when we were married?"

"Like that," he said. "It's April now, but it'll be the same."

"I love the lake out of season. No people around and the waves roll in. Maybe we'll have some rain. I loved the rain in October." Nina Faro had forgotten the dishes.

"Let's go," he said eagerly. "Right now. No one will know where we are. I don't want to talk to Red Buchanan again."

"But you said you wanted to see about the school job tomorrow."

"It can wait until Monday, too. Let's get out of this place. Nina, I—" A voice coming from the radio stopped him. Neither of them had realized that the music had stopped, that a commercial for a local bakery had preceded the news broadcast. Now a man's crisp voice seemed to echo hollowly in the suddenly quiet kitchen.

... the murder of Lieutenant John Horner, of the Harbor City Police Department. As we reported earlier today, Lieutenant Horner was shot about eleven o'clock last evening in the parking area behind Connie's Corner, an all-night market and carry-out at the intersection of the lake highway and State Route 42. He was shot three times in the chest and stomach and died almost instantly, according to Dr. Clinton Shannon, coroner of Island County. The body was discovered by Milton Koslo, of 1436 Lake View Place, who had driven into the lot behind the store intending to purchase fishing equipment. Mr. Koslo immediately called police. Police Chief Beckwith has made no comment as to the possible identity of the killer, but stated that he has thrown all the facilities of the force into the investigation and search. This station will report developments as they occur. Lieutenant Horner was twenty-nine years old, married, the father of two small children. He joined the Harbor City force as a patrolman eight years ago. Funeral arrangements are as yet incomplete, but—

Myron Faro moved to the radio, shut it off and turned to face his wife. She stared at him with stricken eyes. He said, "Don't look like that." "But—but you were out last night," she stuttered. "You had a gun ..." "I didn't kill him." Faro rubbed a trembling hand across his mouth. A buzzer sounded from the small passageway beyond the living room. Neither of them moved. The buzzer sounded again, impatiently.

"The door," Nina Faro said.

He hesitated a moment, his thin mouth twitching. Then he abruptly left the kitchen, crossed the living room and entered the passage leading to the door at the top of the outside stairway. He paused at the door, his hand on the knob, gazing at the solid blank wood. After a second he turned the knob and pulled the door inward. Two men stood there. Both were past middle age. One was a sturdy, neatly dressed man with heavy graying brows, who stood a little to one side, his right hand in a topcoat pocket. The other man was taller and looked older. His eyes were liquid and red-rimmed and his ruddy face seemed bloated. This man spoke in a faintly rasping voice. "You're Myron Faro?"

Faro nodded, watching the two men silently.

"Police. I'm Captain Keely." The tall man nodded at the other. "This is Chief Beckwith. We'd like to ask you a few questions."

"What about?" Faro asked. "I—I don't understand."

"You will. May we come in?" Even as Keely spoke he was already over the threshold, followed by Beckwith.

Faro backed away and then stood aside, waiting for them to enter so that he could close the door. Keely passed him and Beckwith said, "You go on in, Mr. Faro. I'll close the door."

Faro obeyed, saw that his wife was standing in the kitchen doorway watching silently. He avoided her gaze, moved to the center of the room and turned. He felt the beginning of the familiar gnawing pain in his stomach and hoped that he would not be sick. Keely, the tall one, stood just inside the arch. Faro heard the outside door close and Beckwith came through the arch into the living room and stood still. Both men nodded politely at Nina Faro, but neither removed his hat. Beckwith kept his right hand in his coat pocket.

Nina Faro said, "What's this all about?"

"Police, ma'am," Keely said. "We just want to ask your husband where he was last night." He looked at Faro. "Will you tell us, please?"

Faro's eyes were bewildered. "Why do you want to know it?"

"Just answer the question," Keely said gently.

Faro shot a quick glance at his wife. Then his gaze shifted to the silent Beckwith and back to Keely. He took a deep breath and said, "I—I was here, all evening." He took a package of cigarettes from a pocket of his

robe. His fingers trembled a little as he placed a cigarette between his lips and struck a match.

There was a short silence, during which Faro turned and dropped the match into an ash tray on a low table.

Keely said, "Can you prove that, Mr. Faro?"

Faro turned back and straightened. "Why should I have to prove it?" His face was gray. "What is this, anyhow?"

Keely and Beckwith exchanged significant glances. The chief nodded, almost imperceptibly. Keely returned the nod grimly, sighed, and said to Faro, "I'm sorry, but we want you to come to the station with us."

"But *why?*" There was sweat on Faro's temples and high forehead.

Nina Faro spoke then. "My husband was at home last evening," she said quietly. "He was here with me since shortly before noon and didn't leave at all. I don't understand why you want to know, but that's the truth. Now will you please give us an explanation?"

"We'll explain to your husband at the station." Keely turned to Faro. "Please get dressed."

"No, Faro said sharply. "You can't take him away, not like this."

"Do you know a man named John Horner?" Keely asked her abruptly. She did not hesitate. "No, I do not."

"Do you?" Keely pointed a long finger at Myron Faro.

"No," Faro said. He seemed grayer than before. "No, I—I don't."

"He's a policeman," Keely said grimly. "A good one. He was a policeman. He was murdered last night." His keen gaze moved back and forth from the woman to the man. "Does that mean anything to either of you?"

"Not to me," Nina Faro said firmly, "nor to my husband. We never heard of him."

Keely sighed heavily and looked to Beckwith for guidance. The chief said quietly, "Save it for later, Jason. We have witnesses, remember." Then he addressed Faro courteously. "We're sorry about this, but it will be easier if you will come with us. There are no charges against you at this time, but if you wish to call an attorney you are free to do so."

Faro hesitated, looking from Beckwith to his wife. Then he asked the chief, "What if I refuse?"

Beckwith said dryly, "I wouldn't advise that."

Faro pulled a trembling hand down over his face and then spoke in a strained voice. "I—I'll go with you. We may as well get this over with, whatever it is."

"Thank you," Beckwith said. "Get dressed, please."

Faro turned and moved slowly toward the kitchen door, which led to the bath and bedroom beyond. He did not look at his wife, who stood aside as he passed. Keely started to follow Faro, but Beckwith stopped

him. "No need, Jason. The outside door is the only way out."

Keely stood still and the three of them, the woman and the two men, were silent. Keely coughed, moved to a window and stood looking out, his hands clasped behind his back. Nina Faro said to Beckwith, "You're making a mistake."

"I hope so, ma'am."

There was another short silence. Presently Keely turned away from the window, nodded at the door Faro had entered and said to Beckwith, "Maybe I'd better go in there, Chad. If he had a gun last night, he might—"

"I don't own a gun," Myron Faro said quietly.

The three of them turned, Faro stood in the doorway fully dressed in a tan flannel suit, white shirt, dark brown tie, light raincoat and brown hat. He moved to his wife, touched her arm and said in a low voice, "It's all right. I'll be back soon."

"I'll wait for you, Myron."

"Good." He hesitated and then added, "And thank you, Nina." He turned to face Keely and Beckwith. "Ready, gentlemen?"

The three men left the apartment and went down the outside steps. As they passed Mrs. Kennedy's kitchen window, Faro saw the curtain move and smiled secretly and bitterly, thinking that Mrs. Kennedy was no doubt one of the "witnesses" Chief Beckwith had mentioned. He walked between the two officers around to the front of the house where the police car was parked at the curb.

Faro was pleased that they had not handcuffed him.

10

Thursday Morning, Early

Betty Keough was like a child who had been spanked and who was now attempting to get back into the good graces of her elders. On Wednesday morning she had risen before her husband and prepared breakfast, in spite of the few hours' deep she'd had. After the scene in the study he had ordered her to go to bed alone and she had missed him. It was the first time since their marriage she'd slept alone, except when she had the babies in the hospital. But even though she missed Nelson, she thought, it was kind of nice to be able to spread her legs and move about without fear of disturbing him. He was a very light sleeper and became very cross when she turned over or moved in bed. Her thighs still burned, even though her husband had applied ointment, and

the smooth cool sheets had felt good on her bare skin. Betty liked to sleep raw, as she termed it, but her husband considered it immodest.

Early Wednesday morning, after awakening in bed alone, she had crossed the hall and found her husband asleep on the studio couch in the oldest boy's room. He had made no comment when he later appeared in the kitchen to find Betty there and breakfast ready. The few words they exchanged had been strained, and neither mentioned what had happened in the study in the early hours of the morning. After Doctor Keough left Betty did not see him until dinner time, when he hurried in to get a sandwich before returning to his office for the evening hours. Because she was tired from lack of sleep the night before Betty had gone to bed early on Wednesday evening, hoping that her husband would join her when he returned. But he had not. She had gone to sleep and sometime in the gray dawn she had awakened to find his side of the bed empty. She stumbled sleepily into the oldest boy's room, thinking that he was sleeping there again, but the studio couch was not occupied. Betty had become confused. Where was he? Asleep on the divan downstairs? She was too dazed and sleepy to investigate and returned to the double bed in their room. She hoped that Nelson would not continue to stay mad at her, even though she realized she had not been a good wife. She resolved to try and do better in the future. Then she had slept again.

Now, on Thursday morning as she awoke at seven-thirty, she knew immediately that she was still alone in bed. She stretched and yawned, slipped from the bed, put on a nightgown and robe and crossed once more to the oldest boy's room. The studio couch was still vacant. Faintly alarmed, she hurried down the stairs and saw with relief that he was sleeping on the divan in the living room. He had removed his coat and shoes, but looked uncomfortable. Quietly she got his topcoat from a closet and gently covered him. Then she went to the kitchen, where she made coffee, set the table, got out orange juice and cereal and washed the dishes from the previous evening. The sight of the clean sink pleased her and in a burst of energy she swept the kitchen floor, which needed it badly, and decided that she would mop and wax it as soon as Nelson had gone and the children were dressed. Then she would start cleaning the house and when Nelson came home that evening she would be bathed and smelling nice, with lipstick on and wearing the little print dress which Nelson had bought for her birthday last year. She would stop screaming at the boys and, oh, she would do so many things to please him. She hadn't really meant to do wrong; it had nothing to do with her love for Nelson. Maybe he would forgive her. She hoped he would.

Tears slid from Betty's eyes and dripped from the tip of her short, freckled nose. Brushing the tears away with the back of a hand she turned the switch of the kitchen radio just as the morning news came on from the Harbor City station. She heard the name, "Horner," and then listened intently to the newscaster's account of the murder. When it was over she turned off the radio and her expression grew ugly. "Goody," she breathed in the silence. "Goody, goody, goody."

The boys came tumbling down the stairs then and she was giving them their breakfast when she heard the sound of the shower upstairs in the bathroom and knew that her husband had awakened and gone up to dress without speaking to her, even though he must have heard her moving about in the kitchen. The children were still eating when Keough appeared, dressed for the day. His delicate poet's face seemed drawn and there were dark, sunken areas beneath his eyes which the thick-framed glasses could not entirely hide.

"Good—good morning," Betty said breathlessly. "I—I waited for you last night, but I guess I went to sleep. I didn't hear you come in. What time was it?"

"I don't know," he said shortly. "Late."

"I see. What do you want for breakfast, Nelson?"

"Just coffee." He gazed at her suspiciously. "Why are you down here so early again?"

"Oh, I have lots to do." She poured coffee and avoided his gaze.

"What, for instance?" he asked coldly.

"Clean the house, wax this floor—oodles of things."

He frowned. "But why, all of a sudden?"

She pretended to pout. "Can't a woman take care of her house properly?"

He shook his head slowly. "It won't do you any good now, Betty."

"Are you still—mad at me?"

"Not mad, Betty." His mouth twisted. "Just sick."

"I can't stand it when you're mad at me, Nelson. You won't even sleep with me—two nights now. I—I missed you. Why didn't you come to bed last night? Where were you?"

"I had some late house calls. When I got home I sat in my study for a while. When I got sleepy I stretched out on the divan. I've been thinking, Betty."

"About me? About—us?"

The three small boys left the table and ran shouting past them into the living room. In a minute the blare of the television could be heard. They were all pre-school age and regularly watched certain children's programs in the mornings.

"Yes," Keough said.

"What—what're you going to do?"

"I don't know, Betty. I've got to think about it some more." He left the kitchen abruptly and returned in a moment wearing his hat and topcoat and carrying his bag.

"It's going to be all right," Betty said. "He's dead."

Keough, almost to the door, swung and said sharply "Who's dead?"

"That—that man. Horner. I heard it on the radio. Somebody shot him last night."

Keough stood very still and then exhaled a deep breath "Who—who killed him?" His voice was shallow.

"They don't know yet." Betty came against him and snuggled her face on his shoulder. "I'm glad." Her thin child's voice was muffled. "I'm glad he's dead, Nelson. He was bad. Now we can forget him. I didn't mean to do anything wrong. It was just—"

He pushed her away violently, strode to the kitchen door and went out, the door slamming loudly behind him. Betty heard his car start and the sound of it backing swiftly down the drive and then the squeal of tires as it stopped and turned in the street, and the diminishing roar as it sped away.

Betty Keough began to cry, her eyes squeezed shut, her small round face contorted. She beat little fists against her thighs and her shrill sobbing rose above the sound of the television. Her youngest son, still in his pajamas, toddled to the kitchen door and gazed up at her solemnly. "Why Mommie cry?"

"Shut up!" Betty screamed. "Shut up, shut up, shut up!"

Thursday Evening, Late

It had been a long, tiring day for Dr. Clinton Shannon, beginning with the autopsy on Horner, followed by house calls, a visit to the hospital and then afternoon and evening office hours. It was now a few minutes before eleven o'clock. Lucille had performed her duties with her usual crisp efficiency and Shannon, of course, had carefully refrained from any mention of the previous evening when they'd sat in his car in front of her house. He was acutely aware of it, however, and so was she; it embarrassed them both, but they tried not to show it. Also, Shannon was annoyed. He liked Lucille personally, admired her professionally, and wanted her to stay with him, but he knew that if their strained relationship continued he would be forced to replace her. He could not be concerned with her emotional state, especially since he was involved,

and still give full attention to his patients.

Now in his quiet office, after the last patient had left, he sat at his desk smoking a cigarette and making notations on case-history cards. There was a soft knock on his door and he looked up, still feeling the annoyance. She always knocked, just as she always addressed him as "Doctor," which was proper in the presence of patients, but he felt that she could be a little less formal when they were alone. Then he remembered the previous evening and reproached himself with the thought: *How informal could the poor girl get?*

"Come in, Lucille," he called.

The door opened slowly and the dark-haired nurse stood there. She made no move to enter his office and said quietly, "I'm leaving now, Doctor." Her raincoat was folded over one arm.

He forced a smile. "Okay, Lucille. Good night."

"Good night, Doctor." But she didn't move.

He drew on his cigarette and said, "If you'll wait a few minutes, I'll take you home." Immediately he knew it had been a mistake. Why had he made such a stupid offer?

Her dark eyes wavered for an instant and then her chin came up a trifle. "Thank you, but I have my car. The man from the garage brought it over this afternoon."

"What was wrong with it?" he asked, just to say something, to cover his tactless remark.

"It needed a new muffler and there was something wrong with the ignition. It is an old car, Doctor." And still she stood there.

"Look, Lucille," he said, "let's be friends. When we're alone I wish you would call me Clint. That's my name, you know. How long have you been with me now? Three years, four?"

"Four years and two months," she said. "I came to you right after I finished my training. I have never worked for anyone else, Doctor."

"So it's still 'Doctor'?" he said sadly.

"That is proper."

Shannon crushed out his cigarette. "All right, Miss Sanchez, let's both be formal as hell. What's my schedule for tomorrow, Miss Sanchez?"

The hurt showed in her dark eyes but her voice was firm and precise. "It is in your book." She nodded at a leather-bound appointment book on his desk. "Surgery in the morning, starting at seven-thirty. Mrs. Appleby, hemorrhoidectomy; Mrs. Morris, breast tumor, biopsy; Mr. Woods, left inguinal hernia, industrial. I have the workmen's compensation forms ready for your signature."

"Thank you," Shannon said. "Good night, Miss Sanchez."

"Good night, Doctor." She turned, her dark eyes remote, and quietly

closed the door.

Shannon sighed, lit another cigarette and returned to the cards. It was an awkward situation, and one that he could not allow to continue. He sighed again, finished the cards and telephoned his wife.

"About time," Celia Shannon said. "I thought you were coming home early tonight. We have a date, remember?"

"I remember, but things sort of jammed up tonight. I'm leaving now. Want me to pick up anything on the way? Beer, cigarettes, pizza, ice cream?"

"Just pick yourself up and get home. Shall I make you a drink?"

"By all means. I'll be there in fifteen minutes." Shannon cradled the phone and got ready to leave. He was certain that the nurse had locked the front door before she left, but he checked it anyhow. It was locked, of course. He turned off the lights and moved to the rear door, carrying his bag. When he stood outside in the small dark area where he parked his car he gazed upward at the April moon, hazy behind drifting clouds. A brisk night breeze fanned his face as he went to his car.

His hand was on the door handle when a soft voice said, "Wait a minute, Doc."

Shannon turned, saw two men standing in the shadow of the building just beyond the moonlight glow. They moved forward slowly and when they stood close he could see them quite clearly. Both were hatless. One was tall and angular, the other short and squat. Both wore dark leather jackets. A white scarf was knotted about the throat of the tall one, who held a revolver close to his side. Moonlight glinted dully on the blue metal of the short barrel. This man, the tall one, untied the scarf with his left hand and flicked it idly at his side. "Don't get scared, Doc," he said, smiling. "We're just going to take a little ride." His face was young-old, sculptured in hard planes, and he badly needed a shave. The other, the short one, was also unshaven. He had a mean, pinched, ferret face, close-set eyes, and he wasn't smiling. His little eyes glittered as he watched Shannon.

"What is this?" the doctor asked. "Who are you?"

"The name is Donegal," the tall one said. "Steve Donegal. You've probably heard of me."

"Yes," Shannon said, remembering. "You robbed the finance company."

"Forty-two grand," Donegal said. "A nice take."

"You can say that again," the short one said.

"Well," Shannon said, "what do you want of me?"

"Your professional services," Donegal said. "We've got a buddy who's in kind of a bad fix."

"Where is he?"

"You'll see, Doc. Just turn around, nice and easy." Donegal moved the gun. "Don't make any trouble and you won't get hurt. Okay?" He smiled brightly.

"If someone is sick, I'll come," Shannon said, "but you don't need the gun."

"I'm afraid I do, Doc. By the way, this is my friend, Delbert Owens." Donegal nodded at the short man.

"Hello, Delbert," Shannon said.

"Hi," the short man said sullenly.

"Turn around, Doc. I told you before." Donegal prodded Shannon gently with the gun.

The doctor hesitated, and then turned slowly. Immediately he felt smooth silk whipped across his eyes and tied securely. He was startled, but resisted the urge to struggle, and stood quietly, knowing that his hat had been knocked off, not caring. He stood there, blindfolded with Donegal's scarf, still holding his bag and wondering what he should do. The gun prodded his back and he heard Donegal's voice. "Don't be scared, Doc. Just do as I say. Now walk, nice and easy."

Shannon walked, felt a guiding hand on his arm, felt himself being pushed gently into a car. He sank back on a seat, heard a door slam and then another, the whirring sound of a starter, the uneven mutter of a tired motor. He felt movement, was aware of rasping gear-shifting sound, and he thought, *It's an old car, real old. What am I doing here?* He reached a hand up to the scarf, but the gun prodded his ribs and he knew that the tall one, Donegal, was beside him "Don't get nervous, Doc," he heard Donegal say. "Just relax."

"Why me?" Shannon asked from the blackness, like a blind man. "There are other doctors in town."

"We just picked you from the phone book," Donegal said "Shannon is a good Irish name, like mine. Then we went to your office, saw your car in back and waited."

"I see." Shannon sat stiffly, holding the bag on his lap, his head tilted back like a man peering through bifocals. Celia would be expecting him, he thought, and he hoped she wouldn't worry. But she would, of course, because he had said he'd be home in fifteen minutes. It had been that long already. And now the car was moving swiftly and the stops were more infrequent. They must be on the outskirts of Harbor City, heading for open country. But in what direction? Along the lake, to the beaches; or inland to the big marsh and the farming country south?

"I'm all Irish," Donegal said. "Black Irish. My mother always said I'd come to no good."

"Your mother was right. Where are we going?"

"Don't worry about it, Doc. We'll be there pretty quick." The cold gun muzzle playfully brushed Shannon's chin.

They rode on a smooth road, the old car rocketing along. After a while it slowed almost to a stop and turned and the smoothness was gone. It rocked and groaned over ruts and depressions. The motor struggled in second gear and presently coughed and stopped. In the sudden silence Donegal said, "End of the line. We get out here, Doc."

They left the old car and walked on sand through underbrush which pulled at Shannon's trousers. At last they stopped. Donegal laughed softly as he removed the scarf from Shannon's eyes. "Here we are, Doc."

Shannon blinked in the moonlight. As his eyes adjusted he saw a wide expanse of weeds and marsh grass, a stretch of water ruffled by the wind, gnarled branches and twisted roots, the utter desolation of the Erie marsh south of the shore. He heard the soft whisper of the wind in the budding trees on the higher ground, the faint, whimpering cries of the night birds. Somewhere in a lagoon nearby a fish surfaced and submerged with a splashing sound. Then, on his right, he saw a small wooden structure with two broken windows partially boarded up and a sloping tin roof. He recognized the place then; he had often hunted in this section with Sam Gideon. The shanty had been erected by a lumber company to house tools and equipment until the area had been cleared of marketable timber. Sam Gideon's home was less than two miles away. Shannon smiled grimly; Steve Donegal's precaution with the blindfold had been useless.

Delbert Owens moved ahead to the shanty and opened the door. Shannon saw a tiny glow of light. "Go on in," Donegal said.

Shannon walked slowly to the shanty, stepped inside. Donegal entered behind him and closed the door. The doctor took in everything with one sweeping glance; bare wooden floor, bare rotting walls still bearing rusty nails from which tools had once hung, shelves at one side. Holes rusted in the low corrugated tin roof admitted faint shards of moonlight. A candle flickered on one of the shelves. Glowing charcoal in a punctured oil can more than adequately heated the small enclosure. In addition to the candle the shelves bore cans of food, bread in bright waxed wrappers, a tall thermos bottle, several whisky bottles. A man lay on a blanket against the far wall. He was partially covered by a dirty tan trench coat. He seemed to be asleep and was breathing loudly and laboriously. In the closeness and warmth Shannon could smell the sickness, the fever.

"There he is," Donegal said, motioning with the gun. "Bullet wound in the left leg, high up."

Shannon went to the man, knelt down and flung back the trench coat.

The man was young, under twenty, Shannon guessed, with silky blond hair and a yellow stubble of beard. His face was flushed and he seemed to shudder with every breath. He wore a soiled gray pullover sweater, faded tight blue jeans and short, muddy motorcycle boots. The left leg of the jeans had been slit to the waist, exposing a crude bandage on the thigh.

Donegal and Owens stood silently by while Shannon opened his bag, took out scissors and cut the bandage. When he saw what was beneath he sighed and shook his head. There was an ugly black hole in the thigh, close to the hip, sunk in the flesh and almost enveloped by a vivid red swelling which stretched the skin from knee to hip. The inflamed flesh was shiny, like that of a basted turkey. Gently Shannon turned the man until he could see the underside of the thigh, grimly noted the absence of a wound there and knew that the bullet had not gone through. There was no need for him to use a thermometer; he knew that the man's temperature was dangerously high, a hundred and three or more. His fingers closed over a limp wrist. The pulse was weak and ragged.

"Well, Doc?" Donegal asked softly.

"Blood poisoning, infection. He might have a chance in a hospital."

"No hospital. Why the hell do you suppose we brought you out here?" Shannon looked up at him. "There's not much I can do here. He'll die."

"Don't give me that. You've got to do something."

"Who is he?" Shannon asked.

"His name is Ronald. I call him Ronnie. He's my kid brother."

Shannon stood up. "I'm sorry."

Donegal slapped Shannon across the cheek and the doctor stumbled backward, holding a hand to his face. There was a short silence, broken only by the wounded man's hoarse breathing. Delbert Owens gazed at Donegal, his little eyes glittering uneasily in the feeble candlelight. He spoke timidly. "Watch it, Steve. You know how you get ..."

"Shut up." Donegal's voice was vicious. Then he took a deep breath and spoke to Shannon. "This is the way it is Doc; if that kid dies, you die, too."

11

Thursday Evening, Late

A coldness crept over Shannon, but he kept his voice steady. "The bullet's got to come out. I have no anesthesia, except a local one, which doesn't last long enough. Also, the infection is already widely spread. He

needs emergency attention under general anesthesia, in a hospital. Not here." He moved a hand, indicating the filthy interior of the shanty. "If he doesn't get it, he'll die before morning. It may be too late now."

There was another short silence, during which Delbert Owens shuffled his feet. Then Donegal spoke from between his teeth. "No. You're stalling. Use what you've got and get that slug out."

Shannon said, "I wouldn't do it to a dog."

Rage blazed in Donegal's eyes and he fired a bullet into the boards at Shannon's feet. The shanty rocked with the blast. Delbert Owens jumped back with a small frightened squeal and the man on the floor stirred and moaned. Shannon flinched, but stood still. The echo of the shot died away and the wind off the marsh rustled around the shanty.

Owens said in a small voice, "Listen, Steve, maybe—maybe we could take Ronnie into town and dump him off at a hospital ..."

"And leave him for the cops?" Donegal asked harshly.

"It's better than dying," Shannon said.

Donegal pointed the gun at Shannon's face. "You get to work right now, and it better be good. I'm sick of talking." He waggled the gun. "It's up to you, Doc. You help Ronnie—or take a slug in the eye."

Shannon sighed. During the war, in the medical corps, he had performed much more serious surgery under more adverse conditions. But that had been war. This was a sort of war, too, he thought bleakly, and above all he was a doctor, an M.D. A human being was hurt and he, Shannon, had taken an oath. He had known from the start what he must do but had demurred in the best interest of the patient. He had done his best from both ethical and humane viewpoints, but now he had no choice. He said, "I'll need hot water, boiling."

A deep sigh of relief escaped Donegal. "We can heat it on the charcoal." He turned to Owens. "Get that coffee can and go out and dip up some water."

"Sure, sure, Steve." Owens snatched a can from a shelf and hurried out.

Shannon knelt by the wounded man, his brain coolly and professionally ticking off medication, procedure and needed equipment. He forgot Donegal and the gun as he made his preparations. Local anesthesia was no good—he would have to probe too deeply—but sodium pentothal in a vein would do the trick, at least for fifteen or twenty minutes. For the first time he wished he carried ether in his bag, even though the shanty would have been a tricky and dangerous place to administer it. Conditions were not sterile, to say the least, but he would hope for the best. Alcohol, iodine, probe, scalpel, gauze, tape, penicillin. He had those. They would have to do.

Delbert Owens returned with the water and placed the can directly

over the charcoal. When the water was boiling Shannon dropped in the instruments, stripped to his shirt and rolled up his sleeves. Donegal stood in the shadows against one wall, holding the gun, watching Shannon. Delbert Owens took a whisky bottle from a shelf and tilted it to his lips.

Shannon worked swiftly and deftly. The bullet was not as deeply imbedded as he had feared. Within a few minutes, in spite of the swollen and inflamed flesh, he had plucked it out, a little, ugly, misshapen chunk of lead, not more than .25 caliber, Shannon guessed. He used iodine on the wound and it was then that Ronnie aroused and screamed. "Steve!" The boy's eyes rolled wildly.

Donegal stepped forward quickly, stood over Shannon and Ronnie and spoke in an oddly gentle voice. "I'm here, kid. It's okay."

"It—it hurts, Steve," Ronnie gasped.

"I know, kid. Take it easy."

Shannon swabbed Ronnie's upper right arm with alcohol, pumped in the penicillin. The boy lay back on the blanket, breathing heavily. There was sweat on his face and his half-closed eyes were glassy. "I'm hot, Steve," he muttered, "so hot...." His eyes closed. "Where—where's Mom?"

"She's dead," Donegal said. "Don't you remember?"

"I—I didn't swipe the wine from the icebox," Ronnie babbled. "Pop did. Mom blamed me and whipped me. Hey, Steve, let's knock out a few, huh? Pitch 'em to me, Steve. Where's Blackie, Steve?"

Shannon stood up slowly and faced Donegal. "Delirious," he said. "Fever. All we can do is wait."

Donegal smiled sadly, his eyes remote. "Blackie is a dog we had once, back in Zanesville. A little black mutt with a bushy tail. Killed by a truck. Blackie never would stay out of the street."

"I've done all I can for your brother," Shannon said. "What now?"

"We wait, as you said." Donegal grinned crookedly. "Ronnie and me had an unhappy childhood. Pop was a drunk, and so was Mom. Because of our sordid home life we drifted into crime, as they say. We're victims of our environment and all that jazz."

"Maybe," Shannon said, "and maybe not. I think you're what you want to be, and your brother is what you made him."

Donegal nodded. "You could be right, Doc." He motioned carelessly with the gun. "You may as well sit down. Want a drink?"

"Thanks," Shannon said. "I can use one."

The three of them, Shannon, Donegal and Owens, sat on the floor against a wall and passed a bottle around. The whisky was hot and raw, but Shannon didn't mind. It soothed his ragged nerves somewhat and

dulled his fears a little. Once he glanced at his wrist watch, saw that it was past two in the morning. Celia would be worried, and he hated that. Ronnie Donegal slept, still breathing heavily. Occasionally he would stir and moan. The wind grew stronger, rustled and whistled around the shanty. The coals in the oil can died down and Delbert Owens got up to add more charcoal. Ronnie grew more restless and Shannon went to him to administer a sedative. Presently the boy slept quietly.

Shannon said to Donegal, "You can't hide here forever."

"We can stay as long as we need to—until Ronnie is able to travel."

"Listen, Steve," Delbert Owens said uneasily, "don't forget that cop who jumped me at the store last night. If I hadn't hauled out of there—"

"Shut up," Donegal said impatiently. "So some cop gets nosey? It doesn't mean anything. Nobody knows where we are."

"Nobody?" Owens asked softly, jerking his head at Shannon. "What about him?"

"He don't leave until after we do," Donegal said. "And if Ronnie don't make it, he won't leave at all." He grinned at Shannon. "Sorry, buddy."

"What good would that do you?" Shannon asked.

"Hell, that's simple. You can identify us. Besides, if Ronnie—"

"You've been identified," Shannon cut in. "The police know you were in on the hold-up."

Donegal's eyes narrowed. "How do you know?"

Shannon remembered what Lieutenant Horner had told him in the restaurant on Tuesday evening: *Professionals, from their M.O.... One good set of prints ... Steve Donegal's ... Wanted for murder ... armed robbery....* He said, "A policeman told me. They have your fingerprints. Also, it's been in the papers and on the radio."

Donegal swore softly. "I had to ditch my car—too hot. And that clunker we've got now doesn't have a radio. You telling the truth, Doc?"

Shannon shrugged. "Why should I lie about it?"

"How soon will the kid be able to travel?"

"In a few days—if he lives."

"He's got to live," Donegal said.

"That's not for me to decide."

"You're a doctor," Donegal said harshly. "What's the score?"

"I've done all I can. As I told you, he should be in a hospital. I'm not equipped to give him the additional medication and treatment needed."

"Like what?"

"More penicillin, for one thing. I don't have nearly enough with me."

"Write me a prescription, I'll send Delbert into town to get it."

"The drugstores are all closed now."

"All right!" Donegal shouted. "We can get it from your office. Give

Delbert the key."

Shannon shook his head. "That's only part of it; the wound should be thoroughly cleansed and sterilized, under general anesthesia. And he may need oxygen. When the infection hits the pulmonary—"

"Mumbo-jumbo," Donegal snapped. "What are his chances?"

Shannon said evenly, "With proper treatment he could recover. Without it he may live until tomorrow, or the day after. I can't tell exactly."

Donegal stood up and began to pace the floor.

Delbert Owens got up, too, and said cautiously, "Steve, maybe we'd better leave the kid with the doc and pull out now, while we got a chance."

Donegal whirled and struck Owens across the chin with the revolver muzzle. The little man uttered a small cry of pain and staggered back against the wall. He crouched there and made no further sound.

Donegal turned slowly to face Shannon. "Doc," he said heavily, "I appreciate what you've done for my brother, or tried to do. I know he should have had attention sooner, but it couldn't be helped and I'm not blaming you." He passed a hand over his beard-stubbled face. "It's been rough, Doc—over six days now. But I'm not leaving here without the kid—not if he's alive."

"Why don't you face it?" Shannon asked. "Let's get your brother to the hospital. You can't run forever."

"Are you kidding?" Donegal asked bitterly. "Murder in Indiana means the chair, the straps, the old electrodes. What've I got to lose?"

"Your brother's life," Shannon said, answering the question. "Take us in to the hospital now. I'll handle it from there and you can start running, if that's what you want."

Donegal's mouth twisted. "And give you a chance to tip off the cops?"

"I'm concerned about your brother," Shannon said quietly. "I'm a doctor, not a policeman. I give you my word."

"But the kid will be nabbed for armed robbery."

"And he can die, if that's better," Shannon said. "Make up your mind."

Donegal's face was twisted with indecision. Delbert Owens pleaded from the shadows. "Listen to him, Steve. He makes sense. Let's take the kid to the hospital, and then you and me can lam. I—I can't stand it out here anymore, Steve. I—" Owens' voice cracked as he dabbed at his bloody chin with a dirty handkerchief.

Donegal ignored Owens and eyed Shannon narrowly. "All you want is to get out of here, save your hide. You don't give a damn about Ronnie."

"You're wrong," Shannon said quietly. "It's my duty to help the boy in any way I can."

Donegal said an obscene word. And then he laughed. "It was a good try, Doc, but I don't buy it. I didn't just get off the boat. No hospital. You take care of Ronnie right here. If the kid makes it, fine. We'll pull out and let you loose on the highway. If he don't make it, I'll kill you. Simple, huh, Doc?"

"That's stupid," Shannon said. "I've done all I can for your brother."

"So you say, so you say." Donegal's eyes were wild. "You can do a little more, can't you? To put him over the hump? To keep me from shooting you?" His voice softened. "You married, Doc? Wife and kids?"

"Yes. One son."

"Think of him and your wife, then. I was married once. No kids. She went on a job with me and got herself shot. Dead. She wasn't a moll—she was just with me. Goddamn trigger-happy cop—it was only a gas station heist. Twenty-three bucks and forty-six cents. It was the same with Ronnie. It wasn't his fault the stinking finance company guy ran out with a rod, a big stinking hero. Bad luck, is all." Donegal waved the gun angrily. "You fix Ronnie up good, real good. Or else."

Shannon said nothing, knowing there was no point in talking to Donegal now. He turned away, moved to the figure on the blanket and knelt down. His hands moved expertly. Fever higher, he noted grimly, much higher. Skin burning to his touch. Respiration shallow and faint. Shannon reached into his bag, filled the needle again and administered the last of his penicillin. It was all he could do.

"How is he?" Donegal asked.

"He's much worse."

"Okay." Donegal's teeth glinted in the candlelight as he cocked the gun. "We'll just wait and see."

12

Friday Morning, Early

Celia Shannon sat numbly in the quiet house wondering what else she could do. When her husband had failed to come home by midnight she had called his office, thinking that perhaps a patient had come in after he'd called her, but had received no answer. Then she had called the hospital, learned that Doctor Shannon had not been there since early in the evening. She put away the whisky and glasses, which she had gotten out in anticipation of her husband's arrival, and made a cup of tea. She drank the tea and smoked a cigarette at the kitchen table and told herself that he could have had an emergency call from one of his

patients, but it was unlike him not to let her know. At a little after eleven he had said he'd be home in fifteen minutes. Maybe there was no phone where he was, Celia thought, but she was certain that he would have called her from the office or gotten word to her somehow that he had been delayed. He had always been very particular about telling her where he could be reached.

Now, at one in the morning, Celia fought against worry and fear. She crushed out her cigarette, left the table and looked in on her son, who was sleeping peacefully, and returned to the kitchen. By a quarter after two, after she had called the office and hospital once more, she knew that something was definitely wrong and called the police station. The desk sergeant was polite. "I'm sorry, Mrs. Shannon. I haven't seen the doctor all evening."

"I don't suppose Chief Beckwith is there now?"

"No, ma'am."

"Would—would it be all right if I called him at his home?"

"For you, yes. You just hang on, Mrs. Shannon. I'll call him for you. We have a direct line."

"Thank you very much." Celia waited, aware of the rapid beating of her heart. Presently she heard Beckwith's deep, calm voice.

"Hello, Celia. What's wrong?"

"Chad, I—I'm sorry to bother you at this hour, but—"

"You know me better than that," Beckwith said sharply, "What's the matter?"

"It's Clint. He called me from the office a little after eleven and said he was coming home. He isn't here, Chad, and no word from him. I called the office twice, and the hospital, too. I—I'm worried."

"He was probably called out into the country, maybe a baby case. A lot of the farmers don't have phones, you know. He'll be along, Celia."

"Did you see him today?" Celia asked. "I mean yesterday?"

"Just for a few minutes in the morning, when he left the autopsy report on John Horner." Beckwith paused, and then added, "Look, Celia, if it will make you feel better I'll put it on the radio. If any of the men in the patrol cars spot Clint's car, maybe parked at a house where there's sickness, I'll have them call you—if Clint's too busy to call himself. Of course, if he's tied up out in the country someplace ..."

"I don't want to make a fuss," Celia said, "but Clint never did this before."

"I know how you feel," Beckwith said soothingly, "but I'm sure he'll be home. If he doesn't show up pretty soon, you call me, hear?"

"All right, Chad, thanks. I'm sorry to have bothered you."

"No bother. Goodnight, Celia."

Celia hooked the wall phone and stood in the silent kitchen listening for a car in the drive. After a few minutes she put the teakettle on a burner, thinking she would have more, but changed her mind abruptly. She poured a small glass of whisky, added a little water and entered the living room, where she turned on the television and then sat in a deep chair. The television screen flickered and glowed and was eventually filled with the antics of a famous comedian in a film which was fifteen years old. Celia sipped the whisky and tried to concentrate on the movie, but her attention kept slipping away and a cold knot of fear and worry grew and tightened within her. At last, when she'd finished the drink, she turned off the television and all the lights except one lamp in a far corner, got a light blanket from a closet and curled up on the divan beneath a wide window overlooking the street. She closed her eyes and tried to relax, but whenever she heard a car go past she would get up and peer out. None of the few cars slowed or turned into the drive.

At a quarter after four Celia went to the phone in the kitchen once more and called Miss James, the head night nurse at the hospital. "Has Doctor Shannon been there yet?"

"No, he hasn't," Miss James said. "Is anything wrong, Mrs. Shannon?"

"I—I don't know. He hasn't come home, and I expected him hours ago. And he hasn't called, or—or anything...."

"Have you contacted Lucille Sanchez?" Miss James asked. "Maybe the doctor was called out and told her to let you know. She may have forgotten, but it wouldn't be like Lucille. Or maybe they're out on a case together and got tied up. Anyhow, you might call Lucille's home. If she isn't home, then you'll know that she's probably with him and—"

"Of course," Celia said, feeling a flood of relief. "I didn't think of that. Lucille's mother will know if she went with the doctor. Maybe there was an emergency of some kind."

"That's probably it," Miss James said soothingly. "It's a shame, though. Doctor Shannon has a full schedule of surgery in the morning and he needs his sleep."

"It's almost morning now," Celia said.

"Do you think I should postpone the surgery?" Miss James asked. "All of it is routine and can wait. Even if the doctor comes home soon he won't get much rest. Shall I do that?"

"Maybe you'd better. Thanks, Miss James."

"You're welcome. And don't worry."

As soon as Miss James hung up, Celia dialed Lucille Sanchez's number and waited breathlessly, not wanting it to be the nurse who answered. She wanted it to be Lucille's mother, explaining in her Spanish accent that her daughter and Doctor Shannon had gone out in

the country to a remote farmhouse to care for a very sick lady, or a man, or a child, and that she, Mrs. Sanchez, was to have telephoned Mrs. Shannon, but she had forgotten, was so sorry...

The nurse answered in her clear, precise voice.

Celia closed her eyes and said faintly, "Lucille?"

"Yes."

"This—this is Celia Shannon. Clint hasn't come home, and I'm worried. I thought—"

"He has not?" Lucille asked sharply. "Where did he go?"

"I—I don't know. He's never done this before, Lucille. Did he say anything to you about—about a patient? Where he might be going? After office hours, I mean?"

"No, he did not. He was still at the office when I left. He said he wanted to do some desk work before he went home."

"What time was that?"

"Shortly before eleven. I do not understand."

"Neither do I. Well, thanks, Lucille."

"If there is anything I can do ..."

"No, no, thanks." Celia's voice was faint again. "Goodbye, Lucille." She lowered the phone, missed the hook, grasped the cord and then put it in place. She stood in the silence, the back of her hand to her mouth, letting herself succumb at last to the fear which had been with her since midnight.

"Where is he?" she whispered in the silence. "What *happened?*"

After a few minutes she lifted the phone once more. When Chief of Police Beckwith was on the wire, she forced herself to speak calmly. "He's not home, Chad. No calls, nothing. Clint wouldn't do this."

"All right, Celia," Beckwith said briskly. "We'll find him don't worry. You just try and—"

"Sure," Celia said. "Thanks, Chad." She left the kitchen, went into the long living room. She lay on the divan, rigidly, until seven o'clock. Then she went to her son's room and gently awakened him. "Time for school, baby."

Later, as she gave the boy his breakfast, she said, "Daddy isn't here."

"Out on a case, huh?" he asked, spooning cereal.

When she didn't answer, he said, "Gee, Mom, I don't wanna be a doctor. Do I have to?"

"Not if you don't want to. Hurry now. You'll be late."

When the boy was bundled against the raw April morning and had left the house, shouting at classmates on their way to the nearby school, Celia washed dishes mechanically and then made a pot of coffee. The sudden ringing of the phone caused her to start nervously

and she literally ran to lift it from the hook. "Yes?" she said breathlessly.

"This is Chad Beckwith, Celia."

"Oh," she said in a dead voice. "No word from Clint, huh?"

"I would have called you."

"Yes." She heard Beckwith sigh. "Celia, I'm sorry, but he's just—gone. We found his car—"

"Where?"

"Parked behind his office. His hat was on the ground there, too—Clint's initials are on the inside band. After you called, went to his office right away. Everything inside is okay."

"But how did you get in?"

"We got a key from Lucille Sanchez—didn't want to bother you."

"Yes. But Chad, if his hat's there, and he didn't take the car ..."

"I can't figure that out," Beckwith admitted, "but try not to worry."

When she had replaced the phone, Celia decided that she did not want the coffee, after all. She knew she needed to rest, to sleep, in order to better face the day and what it might bring. She was a practical woman and realistic enough to realize that her husband's disappearance meant that he was involved in something serious, to say the least. The very fact that he had disappeared without a word to her was sufficient cause for alarm. He could be injured, ill, or even dead. Celia tried to think it through rationally; she tried to steel herself against any eventuality, but in the end she was shuddering with dry, choking sobs, her head pressed against folded arms on the kitchen table.

At nine o'clock she attempted to calm herself and turned on the radio. Her missing husband was the first item of news. *Dr. Clinton Shannon, coroner of Island County and prominent Harbor City physician, has been missing since late last evening. Members of the city Police Department and the county sheriff's office are conducting an extensive search and the state patrol has been alerted. Doctor Shannon was last seen by his office nurse, Miss Lucille Sanchez ...*

Celia turned off the radio and almost immediately the phone began to ring. Friends, neighbors and even strangers called to offer sympathy and aid and to ask curious questions. Celia tried to speak calmly to all, but it seemed that a hammer was beating at her brain. The seventh call was from Chief Beckwith. "I'm sorry, Celia. That damned radio station reporter was hanging around the desk when the sergeant broadcast it to the state police. You've been pestered, I suspect?"

"Yes, but it's all right, Chad."

"No, it's not," Beckwith snapped. "You need rest. Look, Celia, Maude's on her way out. You need somebody until Clint shows up."

"Yes," Celia said, thinking of Maude Beckwith, wife of the police chief,

plump, friendly and capable. "Thank you, Chad."

"Maude will take over," Beckwith said. "Don't try to stop her. You get some rest, hear?"

"I'll try." Celia hooked the phone and immediately it rang.

It was Melissa Kovici, wife of Dr. John Kovici, Doctor Shannon's friend and colleague. "Celia, what can I do?"

"Nothing, Melissa. I'm just waiting. And Maude Beckwith is coming."

"Do you want John to stop? Give you something? I know you must have been up all night."

"Thanks, Melissa, but I'll be all right."

"Try not to worry."

"I'll try." Celia felt light-headed. "Goodbye, Melissa."

And the phone rang again. Celia did not answer it. She couldn't. Maude Beckwith strode into the kitchen then, not bothering to knock. Celia went to her, was comforted by plump arms and soothing words. "The phone," Celia mumbled. "It keeps ringing."

"I'll handle the phone, honey. What time does your boy come home for lunch?"

"Eleven-thirty," Celia said. "But, Maude, you have trouble, too. Your daughter ..."

"Jill? My goodness, she's fine. Just a little old appendectomy. I'm not worried about Jill. I'm worried about you. Do you have any sleeping pills?"

"Yes."

The phone rang shrilly.

"Let the damned thing ring," Maude Beckwith said. "You take two pills and get in bed. Don't worry about anything. I'll give your boy lunch and send him back to school with his face clean. Scoot now, honey." Gently she pushed Celia toward the door.

As Celia left the kitchen she heard the police chief's wife talking on the phone. "No, ma'am, Mrs. Shannon is not available. Goodbye."

In the bathroom Celia took two pink capsules from a bottle and swallowed them with water. *I look terrible, she thought, gazing in the mirror. Clint would not like my looking this way. I must comb my hair and put on some lipstick before ...*

She moved down the short hall to their bedroom and stood in the doorway gazing at the two beds, both neatly made and undisturbed. How long had it been since they'd been slept in? Not very long, she realized; only one night, last night. It seemed much longer than that. Celia pulled the blinds against the gray April morning and removed her robe. Then she got into bed and stared at the ceiling. The phone on the bedside table rang and she reached out and pressed a switch which

disconnected it. After a while the sleeping capsules numbed her and she closed her eyes. Presently she slept. It was not a quiet sleep. Celia dreamed that her husband was lying dead in a water-filled ditch.

Friday Afternoon

She moaned and stirred, opened her eyes. Maude Beckwith stood over her, smiling.

"He's home," Celia said instantly, half rising.

"No, honey," Mrs. Beckwith said gently, "but no news is good news."

Celia sank back. "What time is it?"

"A little after one. I fed your boy and sent him back to school. He's a nice little boy, very polite."

"Thank you." Celia rubbed her eyes, aware of a dull headache.

"You'd better eat something," Mrs. Beckwith said. "I brewed some tea and I'll poach you an egg and make some toast. Sound good?"

"Yes," Celia said. "Thank you."

13

Friday Morning

At ten-thirty Chief of Police Chad Beckwith sat at his desk in his office at the police station. The flesh beneath his eyes was puffy, his thick, iron gray hair was not as neatly combed as usual and his cheeks and chin were covered with a white stubble of beard. Captain Jason Keely sat slouched in a chair before a window overlooking the street. He, too, appeared weary and somewhat disheveled. Both men had been up since early morning directing the search for Shannon.

Keely shook his head. "Nothing to do but wait now. We've got all the men we can spare looking for him, and so has the sheriff. On top of that, I'll bet there are a hundred civilian volunteers out combing the beaches and the back roads."

Beckwith sighed. "Clint was well-liked in this town."

"Is." Keely corrected him gently. "You're not giving up yet, are you, Chad?"

Beckwith moved a hand impatiently. "Of course not. We have no reason to think that Clint's not alive." He removed a cigar from between his teeth and gazed at it with distaste. "Everything comes at once. Have you talked with that Faro this morning?"

"No."

Beckwith sighed again. "Well, as long as we can't do anything about Clint right now, we may as well talk to Faro again. Maybe he'll crack some more."

"He's all we've got," Keely said, "and he's already admitted that both he and his wife lied to us yesterday when they claimed he was at home Wednesday night—and he confessed to carrying a gun in the bargain. If we work on him, maybe we can break him down all the way. I don't buy the rest of his story at all."

"Neither do I," Beckwith said. "Too bad the lab couldn't raise any prints from that peanut bag."

"Yes," Keely agreed, "but I really didn't expect any. It was raining and that paper is slick."

Beckwith lifted the phone from his desk and spoke to the desk sergeant. "Have Faro brought to my office, please." As he replaced the phone, he said to Keely, "I'll do it this time. You just listen for him to slip up."

"Okay." Keely leaned back and crossed his legs.

"I think he killed Horner," Beckwith said.

The police captain nodded. "So do I. No alibi at all. Motive and opportunity. And he lied to us in the beginning and I think he's still lying. But we can't crack him."

"We will," Beckwith said grimly. "That negative paraffin test on his hands doesn't mean a thing. After he admitted that he *had* gone out on Wednesday night he said he was wearing leather gloves—which would eliminate finger prints. He's slippery, Jason, but if we had the gloves we could run a test for powder residue on them."

Keely grunted and said, "Only he claims he lost the gloves."

"Convenient," Beckwith said.

There came a knock on the door and Beckwith called, "Come in."

A young policeman entered with Myron Faro. Another policeman stood outside in the corridor. Faro wore no coat, tie or belt. His shirt collar was unbuttoned. His lean face held a gray tinge and he needed a shave. Beckwith told the policeman to wait outside and spoke pleasantly to Faro. "Good morning, Mr. Faro. Please sit down."

Faro's gaze shifted from Beckwith to Keely, who nodded lazily. Faro then sat in a chair facing the desk. Beckwith leaned forward and spoke in a friendly voice. "We're sorry to detain you, Mr. Faro, but we have no choice. As you know, you are now being held on suspicion of murder. I hope you won't mind if we ask a few more questions about your activities Wednesday evening."

"Would it do me any good to mind?" Faro asked bitterly.

"You can refuse to answer," Beckwith said mildly, "but for your own good I think you'd better cooperate."

"I've told you everything."

Beckwith nodded. "We have appreciated what you have told us so far, but we thought you might have remembered more details." Beckwith coughed delicately. "After all, you did remember that you left your apartment Wednesday night—and that you had a gun."

"I've told you my reason for that," Faro said quietly. "I lied at first, sure, because I'd just heard on the radio that Horner had been murdered. And when you and Captain Keely arrived right afterward I got scared. I knew the spot I might be in and I didn't think straight." He smiled wryly. "Protective instinct, I guess. But it was stupid. I later realized that our curious landlady, Mrs. Kennedy, had no doubt seen me leave the apartment and had informed you—after she learned of Mr. Horner's death, and I decided to tell the truth, all of it, even the fact that I was carrying a gun. Also, my attorney advised me to do so. I should have in the first place."

"And Mrs. Faro?" Beckwith said quietly.

"She's my wife. She wanted to protect me."

"I see," Beckwith said. "Are you quite certain you can't remember other things you haven't told us?"

"Like what?"

"Like where you threw away the gun," Beckwith said gently.

"I told you—"

"I know," Beckwith broke in, lifting a hand. "You said you don't remember. That just doesn't seem reasonable to me."

"It was dark," Faro said with faint desperateness, "and raining. I was upset, disturbed, very much so, just driving aimlessly. I don't remember just where I was at the time. I rolled down the window and threw the gun out. I didn't even stop the car. I think I was crossing a bridge. There was water, I know that."

"There are many bridges around the city," Beckwith said. "A number of small streams empty into the lake and the marsh. Perhaps you can recall a landmark, a house, maybe, or trees. A road sign?"

"No," Faro said. "I'm sorry."

"All right," Beckwith said. "Maybe something will come to you. Let's go back a bit; you returned from a sales meeting in Toledo Wednesday morning, around ten o'clock, long before your wife expected you to. Your landlady, Mrs. Kennedy, told you that your wife had been—ah—seeing a man in your absence. She told you the man was Lieutenant Horner. You went up to your apartment, found your wife asleep. What did you do then?"

"Nothing," Faro said in a dead voice. "I told you. I waited until she woke up."

"When was that?"

"In the afternoon some time. I told her what I had learned. At first she denied it, and then admitted everything." Faro spoke in a monotone as if he were reciting from memory, like a child who has learned the lines but not the meaning. "We quarreled, naturally. Then I calmed down a bit. I wanted to think. I blamed myself partly for what had happened, but I hated Horner." Faro took a deep breath and sat with his hands clasped between his knees.

"You hated him enough to kill him?" Beckwith asked gently. "Is that right?"

"Yes. I loved my wife. I—I love her now. This morning we came to a sort of understanding. We planned a, well, a new life together. That sounds trite, but it's true. I forgave her—and she forgave me."

"This is new," Beckwith said, leaning still further forward. "You didn't tell us this yesterday. What had your wife to forgive you for?"

"I was guilty, too," Faro said. "There were—other women. When I was away on trips."

"But your wife didn't know about these women?"

"No."

"Then why did you tell her?"

"Because I had to," Faro said simply. "It wasn't fair to her. I couldn't condemn her when I—"

"I understand," Beckwith broke in. "I admire your sense of justice."

"Thank you," Faro said bleakly.

Beckwith placed the dead cigar in an ash tray and folded his hands. "All right. What were your intentions when you left your apartment around eight o'clock on Wednesday evening?"

"I don't know," Faro said. "I was confused and upset. I just wanted to get away for a while, to think."

"But you took a gun?"

"Yes."

"Why?"

Faro moved his bands helplessly. "I hated Horner. Maybe I even wanted to kill him. But after a while I knew it would be senseless. It wouldn't solve anything and only make trouble. So I threw the gun away."

"So you wouldn't be tempted?"

"Perhaps," Faro said. "I don't know. I only know that I realized that nothing would be gained by Horner's death."

"Was the gun loaded?"

"Yes."

"Describe the gun."

"I did yesterday."

"Again, please."

"It was a Harrington and Richardson .22 revolver, nine shot, with a long barrel—five or six inches."

"Where did you get it?"

"I bought it in Cleveland several years ago. It was a sort of target pistol. I used to like to shoot. I—" Faro paused, closed his eyes and opened them. "I—I don't feel well."

"I am aware of your condition. Can we get you anything?"

"Just some water." Faro reached into his shirt pocket. "I have some tablets here...."

Beckwith nodded at Jason Keely, who got up and left the office. Neither Beckwith nor Faro spoke until the captain returned with a paper cup filled with water. Faro swallowed two white tablets, crumpled the cup and tossed it into a basket beside Beckwith's desk. "Thanks," he said weakly.

"Do you feel up to a few more questions," Beckwith asked kindly.

"No, but let's get them over with."

"What time did you return home on Wednesday evening?"

"Shortly after midnight."

"Was Mrs. Faro waiting for you?"

"No. She had gone to bed."

"When you were driving around, did you stop at a food market known as Connie's Corner?"

"Yes. I bought some cigarettes there, from a vending machine."

"And a package of peanuts?"

"No, I—"

"Captain Keely saw you," Beckwith cut in sharply. "Don't lie, Mr. Faro. You followed Lieutenant Horner to the store, waited for him in the parking lot and then shot him dead."

Faro moved his head slowly from side to side. "No, I did not."

"But you admit that you had a gun?"

"Yes."

"And you threw the gun away? But you can't remember where?"

"Not exactly, no."

"Would it help you to remember if you attempted to retrace your route on Wednesday evening?"

"It might," Faro said. "I think it was on a bridge, not far from town."

"Would you be willing to go with Captain Keely and try and locate the spot?"

"Certainly."

"You realize, do you not, that if the gun is found it might directly connect you with the murder?"

"Not my gun," Faro said quietly. "It hadn't been fired."

"But you will cooperate in a search for it?"

"Yes."

Captain Keely stood up and said to Beckwith, "I'll get a couple of men. We'll need rakes and wading boots. If the water's too deep, we'll need a diver—that is, if we find the right place."

"All right," Beckwith said.

Ten minutes later Myron Faro rode in the rear seat of a cruise car beside a uniformed policeman. Captain Keely sat in front beside the driver, a second officer whose name was George Romano. They drove slowly through the city, Romano following directions from Faro. "It's hazy," Faro said, "but I'll do my best."

"Just try and remember the bridges you crossed," Keely told him. "Especially the one where you threw out the gun."

It seemed that Faro had crossed a number of bridges, several inside the city limits and others on roads in the country. They passed the market called Connie's Corner and Faro leaned forward. "Keep going out the lake road," he said.

"Starting to remember now?" Keely asked.

"Maybe."

"It figures," Keely said. "You wanted to ditch the gun right after you shot Horner back there." He jerked a thumb toward the store, which was now behind them.

"I didn't shoot him," Faro said.

Keely half turned in the seat. "You sure you weren't drinking Wednesday night?"

"I can't drink," Faro said. "Doctor's orders."

"Tough." Keely turned back and gazed at the road ahead. "There's no bridges on this road, not until you get to the Island. Did you drive out that far?"

"No," Faro said. "I'm sure I didn't. I think I turned off and circled back to town."

"I see," Keely said. "Then it could be Duckpond Road. There's a bridge there, over Deer Creek."

"Does the road make a circle through woods and then dip down over the creek?" Faro asked. "With a deserted farm house just up the hill beyond?"

"Yes," Keely said. "The old Klinghorn place. Been empty for years."

"I think that's it," Faro said quietly.

"Good." Keely turned to the driver. "You know where it is, George?"

"Sure, Cap. I used to live near there. We kids called it the haunted house." Officer Romano increased the speed of the car and soon turned off onto a gravel road leading down through scrub pine woods. They reached a wooden bridge with iron railings over a narrow stream muddy with the April rains. On a hill above the stream, between green-budding trees, was a gray, rotting, broken-windowed ruin of a house. "There she is." Officer Romano pulled the police car to the side of the road and stopped.

Keely turned and asked Myron Faro, "Which side?"

Faro motioned toward the left rail of the bridge.

Keely told Romano to come with him and instructed the officer in the rear of the car to stay with Myron Faro. Keely and Romano walked to the bridge and gazed down at the muddy water. "Too bad it's not clear, Cap," Romano observed.

"How deep is it through here?" Keely asked.

"It's shallow, not over a couple of feet."

"What kind of bottom? Mud? Sand?"

"Mostly rock," Romano said. "We used to wade in here, getting minnows and crabs."

Keely pointed to the sloping bank leading from the road down to the water's edge. "We can go down there."

"No need for you to go wading, Cap."

"Two's better than one," Keely said. "Let's go."

"Kind of a needle in the haystack job, isn't it?" Romano asked. "I mean, with the water so muddy."

"We can try," Keely said. "If he really threw the gun in, it should still be here. The current's not swift enough to carry it away."

The two men returned to the car, put on waist-high rubber wading boots and moved down to the creek bank carrying long-handled garden rakes. Romano waded in first and began to pull his rake carefully over the creek bed near the left side of the bridge. Captain Keely stepped gingerly into the water and began to perform a similar operation a few feet further out.

A number of times both men reached into the water, soaking their sleeves above the elbow, and lifted out stones of varying sizes and threw them to the bank. Fifteen minutes went by as the search continued. More stones were lifted from the creek bottom and tossed to the bank. At last, after more than a half hour, at a spot ten feet from the center of the bridge, Keely straightened and gazed at a dripping revolver in his hand. "I found it," he called softly to Romano.

Romano lifted his head, saw what Keely held and thrashed through

the water. "By golly, you did!" he cried gleefully.

"Luck," Keely said shortly. "We'll get it to the lab right away." He waded toward the bank. Officer Romano followed, making huge splashing ripples in his wake. At the car they took off the boots, stored them with the rakes in the trunk of the cruiser. Keely carefully wrapped the gun in a handkerchief, placed it in the inside pocket of his coat and then got into the front seat of the car as Romano slid behind the wheel.

"Did you find it?" Myron Faro asked quietly.

"Yes," Keely said.

"May I see it?"

"Later. It goes to the laboratory first."

"I see." Faro sank back in the seat and closed his eyes. He was in pain, but knew that he couldn't take any medication now. Not under four hours, Doctor Shannon had said. He had taken the tablets in Chief Beckwith's office around eleven o'clock and it was now only twenty minutes past twelve. No more tablets until three. But it would help if he ate something. Usually, after he ate, the pain was subdued, sometimes for as long as two hours. But he couldn't eat the jail fare. Faro wondered if Chief Beckwith would authorize a soft-boiled egg and tea. Maybe some dry cottage cheese, a broiled lamb chop, a small portion of roast chicken? Skim milk? Dry toast? Anything bland that was on his diet. Beckwith had impressed him as a kind and sensible man. Perhaps he would understand about his diet and see that he had the proper food. Even in jail, Faro thought bitterly, if a man was sick he was entitled to some consideration.

And he wanted to talk to Nina, his wife. Maybe they would permit him to call her when they returned to the station.

14

Friday Afternoon, Early

At one-thirty Myron Faro reclined on the bunk in his cell smoking a forbidden cigarette. He had promised Doctor Shannon that he would stop smoking, or at least cut it to a minimum, not more than five or six cigarettes a day, but he was smoking his sixth right now and was already worrying about how he would get through the balance off the day and evening. In every other respect he had followed Doctor Shannon's orders faithfully—except at the sales meeting in Toledo when he'd allowed himself to be bullied by Buchanan into drinking whisky. He was ashamed of that, but was glad that he had severed

connections with the auto supply company.

Chief of Police Beckwith had been sympathetic about Faro's diet and had seen to it that Faro's lunch consisted of two lean broiled lamb chops, a baked potato, cottage cheese, dry toast and tea. Also, he had permitted Faro to telephone Mrs. Faro. The conversation had taken place in a phone booth off the squad room with a policeman standing by.

"Hello, Nina."

"Myron, I—I ..."

"Don't cry, Nina. I'm fine. I just wanted to talk to you."

"Myron—Mike ..."

"You haven't called me that for a long time."

"I know. I'm sorry. When can I see you?"

"I don't know," Faro said. "I suppose they permit visitors here, but I can't tell you when."

"I'll find out. But it—it's horrible. You shouldn't be there. What does Fenzel say?"

"He's working on it, trying to get bail," Faro said. "If it isn't too high, we can make it." Lyle Fenzel was Faro's attorney, a reputable man well known in Harbor City.

"I don't care what it costs," Nina Faro said. "I just want you out of there."

"There's something else," Faro said. "I told the police the truth—that I was out Wednesday night, that I had the gun."

"You did?" Her voice was shocked.

"Fenzel told me to. In fact, he refused to take my case unless I did." When she did not reply, he said, "Nina, did you hear what I said?"

"Yes, Myron." She sounded faint. "Why did you tell Fenzel?"

"Because I wanted to. Because I had to. We should not have lied, Nina. It was wrong."

"I did it for you," she said.

"I know that. I'm not blaming you."

"Did—did you tell Fenzel *all* the truth?"

"Of course. My God, Nina, you don't think that I—?"

"Never mind," she broke in quickly. "Please don't excite yourself. I do want to tell you this: Mrs. Kennedy asked us to move. She said she didn't want a—a murderer in her house."

Faro's jaw tightened. "What did you say to her?"

"Nothing. I just slammed the door in her face."

"Good for you. We'll move as soon as we get this thing settled. Nina, they found the gun today, but they didn't show it to me. I'm not worried, though. I didn't shoot Horner... That man ..." Faro's voice faltered.

Nina Faro didn't speak for a few seconds. Then she said quietly, "You

don't like to think of him, do you?"

"No. What about you?"

"I'm sorry he's dead, that's all. Can't we forget him?"

"Let's try," Faro said. "I want to try, Nina."

"So do I, more than anything."

"All right, Nina. Goodbye." Faro left the booth and the waiting policeman escorted him back to his cell.

An hour later he sat again in Chief Beckwith's office. Captain Keely was present, as were the laboratory technician, Franklin Hobbs, and the young officer, George Romano, who had helped Keely search the creek. Faro sat quietly, facing Beckwith, but his gaze kept straying to a manila envelope on the chief's desk. The envelope bulged and Faro was certain that it contained his gun. He stirred and wished he had a cigarette, but refrained from lighting one because he knew that he had already smoked too many that day. His gaze shifted from the envelope to Chief Beckwith.

The chief spoke gravely. "Mr. Faro, do you know Mr. Hobbs?" He nodded at the lab man.

Faro glanced at Hobbs and shook his head.

Beckwith said dryly, "Mr. Faro, Mr. Hobbs." The two men nodded at each other as Beckwith went on. "Mr. Hobbs is one of our technicians. Among other things, he is a ballistic expert. Do you know the meaning of the word 'ballistic'?"

Faro nodded. "Bullets, caliber, trajectory—things of that nature."

"Yes." Beckwith cleared his throat. "Would you please describe once more the gun you say you had in your possession Wednesday evening? The weapon you tossed into a creek east of the city? To be explicit, a stream of water known as Deer Creek."

Faro replied mechanically. "It was a Harrington and Richardson .22 revolver."

"And it was the gun you threw into the creek?" Beckwith asked sharply.

"Yes."

"Do you own any other revolvers?"

"No."

Beckwith hunched forward. "How many chambers in the cylinder? What caliber?"

"Nine chambers. Twenty-two caliber."

There was a short silence during which the lab man, Franklin Hobbs, moved in his chair and gazed up at the ceiling. Jason Keely sat quietly, his hands folded over his bulging stomach, watching Beckwith.

"Why did you buy this gun?" Beckwith asked Faro.

"I've told you that, too," Faro said wearily. "I used to like to shoot, go out in the country and plink away. Tins cans, bottles, crows. But I hadn't used it for a long time."

"Why did you take it with you Wednesday evening? Why did you lie to us in the first place?"

Faro felt the pain returning, knew that he was going to be sick, but managed to speak calmly. "I've already gone over that with you."

"So you have." Beckwith's blunt fingers opened the clasp of the envelope and drew out a blue steel revolver with a white tag tied to the trigger guard. He placed the gun on top of the envelope and asked Faro, "Is this your gun?"

Faro gazed at the weapon, saw the short barrel, not more than four inches long, the checked black grip, the fat cylinder, the wicked hole of the muzzle bore, larger than a .22, and said distinctly, "No, it is not."

"But you did throw a revolver into the water from the bridge over Deer Creek?"

"Yes, but not that one," Faro said, fighting the pain and the nausea and an ugly fear.

"Mr. Faro," Beckwith said softly, "this gun was found in the water beneath the bridge over Deer Creek. Do you honestly think that more than one revolver was discarded there?"

"I—I don't know." Faro now felt weak and dizzy and sweat stood on his face. "That—that's not my gun."

Beckwith thumped a fist to the desk. "But you told us where to find it!" He snatched up the gun and swung toward Captain Keely. "Is this the gun you found in Deer Creek by the Duckpond Road bridge?"

"It is," Keely said grimly.

Beckwith turned to Officer Romano, "You were a witness, were you not?"

"I sure was, Chief."

"And you and Captain Keely made a thorough search?"

"Yes, sir."

"And you found no other gun?"

"We did not."

Beckwith, his lips compressed, slowly turned to face Myron Faro. "Do you have anything further to say, Mr. Faro?"

Faro passed a hand over his face and said faintly, "It—it's not my gun."

"How do you explain that?" Beckwith snapped.

"I—I could be mistaken about the—the location. Wednesday evening I was—was not myself. I just drove aimlessly, not paying any attention to my surroundings, or where I was. I ..." Faro moved a hand helplessly.

"Mr. Faro," Beckwith said evenly, "are you suggesting that we conduct

a search beneath every bridge in Island County?"

"No, no ..."

"Are you certain you threw the gun from a bridge? Did you perhaps toss it into a ditch, or into the lake? Maybe from a pier at the harbor?"

"I know I threw it into water."

Beckwith spoke in a tired voice. "Listen, Mr. Faro, you picked the spot where the gun was found, not us." He held up the revolver. "The bullets which killed Lieutenant Horner were fired from this gun."

Slowly Myron Faro raised his head to stare at Beckwith. His thin face was ravaged, dissolute; it seemed to crumble and sag. He lifted a shaking hand and pointed. *"That is not—my gun."*

Beckwith leaned forward and said kindly, "I can see you're becoming upset. Why don't you make it easy for yourself and tell us all of the truth? Why did you say you owned a Harrington and Richardson .22 when it was a Smith and Wesson .32? Were you so certain it could not be found? And then did you become confused and lead Captain Keely to the correct spot by mistake? And are you now attempting to deny ownership, to cloud the facts, to conceal your blunder?"

"No, no," Faro gasped. "I—I ..." He leaned slowly forward, pressing hands to his face. The others in the office thought that a sob escaped him, but it was a groan of physical pain.

The lab man's lips curled in contempt. He nodded knowingly at Beckwith and formed a circle with a thumb and forefinger. Captain Keely made no move and said nothing. Beckwith spoke to Faro sharply but not unkindly. "Don't you feel well?"

"No," Faro whispered, bending lower. Something in his stomach seemed to be trying to chew its way out. "I—I ..." Blood reddened his mouth and chin in a sudden spurt and he lurched forward to the floor.

Beckwith sprang up from his chair, hurried around the desk and knelt beside Myron Faro. The lab man got to his feet, but made no move toward the stricken man. Captain Keely, seeing the blood spreading on the floor beneath Faro, got up from his chair, moved quickly to Beckwith's desk and telephoned for a doctor.

Friday Afternoon, Late

The Harbor City jail had no facilities for caring for sick prisoners and Myron Faro was therefore rushed to Memorial Hospital in an ambulance with Dr. John Kovici sitting beside him. Doctor Kovici had left an office filled with patients to respond to Captain Keely's urgent call. Now, at four-thirty in the afternoon, the doctor stood in the hospital

corridor talking to Chief Beckwith. Two plainclothesmen loitered outside Myron Faro's door. Mrs. Faro had been called and was inside with her husband.

Dr. Kovici said, "Perforated ulcer, massive hemorrhage. He'll need more transfusions, but I think he's in the clear now."

"Good," Beckwith said. "How long will he be here?"

"It'll be a week, maybe longer, before he can go home."

"He's not going home," Beckwith said grimly. "He's going back to a cell."

Doctor Kovici was a short, thick man with bristly black hair. He raised heavy brows. "Oh, a prisoner? What's he charged with?"

"Murder—or rather suspicion of murder. Don't you read the papers?"

"Not lately. I know his name is Faro, though. One of Clint Shannon's patients; Mrs. Faro told me. What murder?"

"John Horner's."

"Oh, really?"

"Really," Beckwith said, and sighed.

"Any news about Clint?" Kovici asked.

Beckwith shook his head. "So you did hear about him?"

"My wife told me. She heard it on the radio this morning. I can't imagine what could have happened to him."

"Neither can I," Beckwith said. "And Celia is worried sick. My wife is with her now." He paused and regarded Doctor Kovici thoughtfully. "I'm a good friend of Clint's, understand, but maybe you know him better than I do. Did he ever, well, take off on a binge? Anything like that?"

Doctor Kovici shook his head. "No. Clint's as steady as a rock. He takes a drink, sure, as we all do, but he wouldn't—Damn it, Chad, something's happened to him."

Beckwith nodded slowly. "I'm afraid so."

As the two men moved down the hospital corridor, Doctor Kovici said, "That Mrs. Faro is quite attractive."

"I agree," Beckwith said. "That's the trouble. She was fooling around with John Horner when her husband was out of town."

"Oh? And Faro got wise? And killed Horner?"

Beckwith nodded.

"Did Faro confess?"

"Not yet, but we found the gun he used. He claims it isn't his—even after taking my men right to the spot where he threw it away. I figure he intended to lead them on a wild goose chase and became confused. Anyhow, we have the gun which killed Horner. Also, when Jason Keely and I first talked to Faro, he denied that he had been out of his apartment on Wednesday night and his wife backed him up, naturally. But later, after he'd talked to Lyle Fenzel, he admitted that he'd gone

out that night carrying a gun. And there's other evidence, all of it pretty conclusive."

"Fingerprints, I suppose?" Kovici asked. "And a paraffin test?"

"What do you know about a paraffin test?"

"Hell, right after I interned in Cleveland I was on police emergency call and learned, among other things, that you can tell if a person has fired a gun recently by the powder residue on his hand. The paraffin picks it up."

"Well, well," Beckwith said. "I can use you on the force."

"No, thanks, Chief. Then you do have proof?"

"Enough. No prints, though, and the paraffin test was negative. But Faro admitted he was wearing gloves."

"You ran a lab test on the gloves?"

"Unfortunately, no. Faro claims he lost them."

"Hmm."

"Yes," Beckwith said. "A couple of hmm's."

"Maybe you can't blame Faro too much. The unwritten law, you know."

"I just enforce the written ones," Beckwith said wearily.

It was almost six o'clock when Nina Faro left her husband, after responding to his weak smile and promising that she would return in the evening. She knew that he was very ill and regretted that Dr. Shannon had not been available. Not that the other doctor—Kovici?—was not competent. On the contrary, Nina Faro had been favorably impressed by Doctor Kovici and was certain that he was doing everything possible for her husband. As she left the room the two plainclothesmen outside the door politely touched their hat brims and watched appreciatively as she walked down the corridor with a free, long-legged stride. "Nice," one of them observed.

"You said it, buddy. I can't say I blame the lieutenant."

"I wouldn't want to die for it, though."

"Me, either. But it's nice to think about. How many kids does Jack have? I mean did he have?"

"Two, I think. And his wife isn't bad at all."

"Do you think this Faro killed Jack?"

"Sure I do."

"The Faro dame wasn't the only one."

"We all know that, buddy. I don't just cruise around this town looking for drunks and stop-sign violators. I see what goes on. Jack's had a department car parked in Dr. Keough's drive more than one afternoon. And I've spotted his Chevy a block away at night."

"Keough? She's a mess. Like a little kid. Whining voice, dirty face, even.

Always paying parking fines."

"When she's got a dime. Most times we put it in the uncollected file and the doc comes in and pays. He's kind of a queer bird."

"Smart, I hear, though. And a good doctor."

"I'll take Doc Shannon. He delivered all my kids. I still owe him for the last one."

"What the hell do you suppose happened to him?"

"Probably holed up in a motel with a bottle and a babe."

"Not him. I could be wrong, though. You true to your wife, buddy?"

"I gotta be. She checks on me. Even calls the desk when I'm on night duty."

"Well?"

"Well what?"

"It could happen to any of us. Look at that Faro in there. His wife was cheating and he got wise. What would you do?"

"Kill the bastard."

"Well?"

"Oh, shut up. So Faro blasted Jack Horner? So what? I know Faro. He's not a pal, but I know him. He got me some tires at a discount once. Always friendly, a nice guy. My dogs are tired. Let's get a couple of chairs."

"Can't. Too conspicuous."

"Hell, the whole damn hospital knows why we're here. We're not fooling anybody. Did the chief say when we'd be relieved? My in-laws are coming for supper tonight."

"You're on duty, buddy. What more excuse do you need?"

"I'd still rather be home."

"Okay, take off. That Faro won't go any place."

"I can't, you know that. The chief said to stay until relieved."

"That means eight o'clock, buddy. Just relax. We're a team, remember? I'm out of cigarettes."

"Here. Got a light?"

"No."

"Should I spit for you, too?"

"You're a scream. What if that Faro climbed out a window?"

"He's not in shape. Anyhow, this is the second floor."

"Oh, yeah, I forgot. Cute little nurse coming this way." Both plainclothesmen touched their hat brims as a dark-haired nurse moved briskly past them. They turned in unison to watch her retreating figure.

"Stacked," one said.

"Yeah, but that Mrs. Faro was better. I like 'em older."

"Me, too."

"Here comes another. See? Carrying the bedpan. Kind of skinny, though."

"The closer to the bone the sweeter the meat, they say."

They both laughed and continued their bored vigil outside Myron Faro's hospital room.

15

Friday Afternoon, Late

Nina Faro drove the Buick into the garage behind the house on Dennison Avenue. As she got out, she saw a pair of light pigskin gloves almost obscured on the cement floor between two empty paint cans. She picked them up and smoothed them with her hands. They were her husband's, she knew. He must have dropped them without noticing when he'd come home on Wednesday night. Carrying the gloves, she left the garage and went up the walk leading to the stairway to the upper apartment. Mrs. Kennedy, the landlady who lived downstairs, had been watching from her kitchen window. Now she appeared on the back porch with a dust mop just as Nina Faro reached the outside stairway. She shook the mop vigorously over the porch railing and pretended not to notice Nina Faro, who stopped and spoke quietly. "Hello, Mrs. Kennedy. My husband is very ill. He's in the hospital."

Mrs. Kennedy stopped shaking the mop. "Oh, it's Mrs. Faro! I didn't see you came up the walk." She gazed at the other woman in mock surprise. "What did you say?"

"My husband is in the hospital. Is it all right if we keep the apartment until he recovers?"

"Your rent is paid until the first, which is Monday, but I could give you a refund and order you out now."

"I hope you won't do that."

"You slammed the door in my face. In my own house."

"I'm sorry. I—I was upset."

"I thought your husband was in jail." Mrs. Kennedy eyed Nina Faro narrowly.

"He was, but he became ill."

"The same trouble? His stomach?"

Nina Faro nodded.

"I heard the phone ring upstairs this afternoon and I just happened to see you leave shortly after. I wondered where you were going. So it

was to the hospital?" Mrs. Kennedy's eyes were very sharp.

"Yes," Nina Faro said. "I'm going back this evening. Is it all right if we keep the apartment until—"

"No, it's not all right. I have a lovely couple who want it. You be out by Monday. I don't want any loose women in my house, and no murderers. Besides, nobody slams a door in my face and gets away with it."

Nina Faro's slender fingers tightened around the thin pigskin gloves. "I said I was sorry. And my husband is not a murderer."

"Don't get high and mighty with me!" Mrs. Kennedy's voice was shrill, vicious. "I know what you are, and your husband, too! I won't have you in my house!"

Nina Faro's face went white and she said distinctly, "To hell with you, you old hag." Then she turned and started up the stairway.

Mrs. Kennedy screamed after her, waving the mop. "Monday, you hear? I'll get the police to evict you! You hear me?"

Nina Faro did not answer and continued up to the landing. Mrs. Kennedy was still screaming as she entered the passageway and closed the door. She moved into the living room and stood gazing at the gloves in her hand. After a minute she walked through the kitchen into the bedroom and placed the gloves in a dresser drawer beside her husband's socks and handkerchiefs. Then she removed her coat, hung it in a closet and went to the kitchen. She poured herself a drink of bourbon, added ice cubes and water and carried the glass into the living room, where she sat by a window and sipped the whisky slowly. It was very quiet.

After a while she turned on the television, but none of the programs interested her. She returned to the kitchen, made another drink and sipped it while she opened a can of vegetable soup and heated it. She ate a bowl of the soup with crackers and a glass of milk and then washed and dried the pan, glass, bowl and spoon, after which she went into the bedroom, turned on a small radio there and smoked a cigarette as she sat at a dressing table and combed her pale blonde hair. In the soft light from lamps on each side of the mirror she was beautiful. She was applying lipstick when the seven o'clock news broadcast came on from the Harbor City station. An opening sentence caused her to jerk the lipstick from her mouth and stare at herself with stricken eyes.

> ... *murder of Lieutenant John Horner, of the Harbor City police. The missing gloves are an important clue, according to Chief Beckwith. Myron Faro, who is being held on suspicion, has stated that he was wearing light leather gloves on the*

night of the shooting but that he had lost them. A paraffin test on Mr. Faro's hands was negative, but police state that if he was wearing gloves when the fatal shots were fired the gunpowder particles in the gloves could be identified by laboratory tests. If the gloves can be found, tests would strongly indicate Mr. Faro's guilt or innocence. And now to other local news: There have been no developments in the strange disappearance of Dr. Clinton Shannon, who ...

The newscaster's voice droned on, but Nina Faro did not listen. She crushed out the cigarette, went to the dresser, took her husband's gloves from the drawer and carried them to the kitchen, where she dropped them into the sink. Then, moving swiftly, she got a can of lighter fluid from a cupboard and thoroughly soaked the gloves with the inflammable fluid. She struck a match and held the flame to the gloves, shielding her eyes with a forearm from the flare-up. They blazed instantly and briskly, but it was necessary to squirt on more of the fluid before they were burned completely. The process made some acrid smoke in the kitchen, but she turned on the exhaust fan over the stove and the fumes were soon dissipated. With a damp paper napkin she cleaned the sink, wiped out the black, crisp ashes and then tossed the crumpled napkin into the bathroom toilet and flushed it down. Then she washed her hands carefully and returned to the bedroom.

By seven-twenty Nina Faro was smartly dressed and groomed and ready to leave for the hospital. When she had descended the outside stairs and was moving toward the garage the back door opened and Mrs. Kennedy called after her, "Monday, don't forget!"

Nina Faro paid no attention and continued to the garage, where she got into the Buick and backed out. At seven-forty she was walking down the hospital corridor toward her husband's room. Evening visiting hours began at seven-thirty, and she had planned to be there on the dot, but the glove-burning had delayed her. She hoped her husband would not worry and perhaps think she wasn't coming, because he had told her how much he looked forward to her visits. As she reached the door, the two plainclothesmen stepped aside and politely touched their hat brims. She smiled at them and entered.

At first she thought her husband was asleep, but when she moved to the bed he opened his eyes and smiled at her. She sat beside him and held his hand. "I'm sorry I'm late," she said.

"That's all right. I knew you'd come."

"I had two drinks before dinner tonight," she said.

"Good."

"We won't have any more secrets, will we?"

"No, Nina."

"Having the drinks didn't make me late," she said. "There was something I had to do."

"What was that?"

She avoided his mildly curious gaze and said in a low voice, "I—I burned the gloves, Myron."

He frowned. "Gloves? What gloves?"

She raised her eyes to his. "Yours. I found them where you hid them in the garage."

He pushed himself to an elbow and his eyes were bewildered. "But I didn't hide my gloves. I lost them, Nina. Just where in the garage did you find them?"

"Behind some paint cans along the wall. It wasn't a very good hiding place. If the police—"

"Look," he broke in, "I must have dropped them when I got out of the car. I didn't miss them until the police asked me about the—the shooting, and I remembered that I'd worn them. Why on earth did you burn them?"

She touched his cheek. "Please don't get excited. It's bad for you."

He brushed her hand away impatiently. "I'm sorry, Nina, but I don't understand this."

Her eyes grew sad. "No secrets, remember?"

"What's this about the gloves?" He was still supporting himself on an elbow and his voice was harsh.

She told him swiftly about the news broadcast and finished by saying, "I burned the gloves for you, Myron, for us." Gently she pressed him back to the pillow. "Just forget it."

He closed his eyes and sighed deeply. He was silent for a moment, and then he said wearily, "Nina, they wouldn't have found any powder marks on those gloves. I didn't shoot the gun that night. And you burned them."

"I'm sorry, Myron," she said softly. "I just did what I thought best for us. And I understand."

He opened his eyes, turned his head on the pillow and gazed at her steadily. "You still think I killed him, don't you?"

"I don't care. I believe whatever you say. But I don't want you hurt anymore."

He closed his eyes again and said nothing.

"I only wanted to help, to protect you," she said.

He opened his eyes and said dully, "Nina, I didn't fire the gun that night."

"Of course not," she said soothingly and caressed his face with her fingers. "I believe you."

He sighed again. "There's nothing we can do about it now." Then he gave her a crooked grin. "Anyhow, we couldn't have proved that the gloves were mine. The police would think, after they tested them, that you bought a pair and faked a story about finding them in the garage—to help me. I guess I can't blame you for wanting to help me, but I did not—"

"I know." Swiftly she changed the subject. "Mrs. Kennedy says we've got to be out by Monday."

"She might have waited until I leave here."

"It's all right. I don't want to stay there anymore."

"You can go to a hotel for now," he said.

"All right. I'll pack our things, put the furniture in storage and move out on Sunday."

"I'm sorry I can't help."

They talked of other matters then, but neither of them again mentioned the murder of John Horner or the burned gloves. At eight-thirty the lights dimmed momentarily, signalling the end of the evening visiting hour. Nina Faro said she would return the next afternoon, kissed her husband and left. The two policemen outside were as polite as ever. She smiled coolly and strode away, her chin high.

Friday Evening, Late, and Saturday Morning

The sound of the wounded man's labored breathing filled the shanty. Dr. Clinton Shannon, his cheeks and chin covered with a reddish stubble, got slowly to his feet and faced Steve Donegal. "He's much worse," he said. "The wound's got to be opened and drained. I can't do it here."

Donegal drew on a cigarette and eyed the doctor narrowly. The flickering flame of the candle cast moving shadows against the shanty's walls and over the figure of Delbert Owens, who sat hunched against a wall with his head resting on arms folded over drawn-up knees. Apparently he was asleep. Donegal dropped the cigarette to the rotting wooden floor and ground it out with a heel. The butt of the revolver protruded from his waist band. He said, "Don't lie to me, Doc."

"I'm telling you the truth. Your brother is dying and there's nothing I can do for him here."

Rage flared in Donegal's eyes and he shook a fist. "Damn you, you're stalling." He stepped close and slapped Shannon across the face. The

doctor stumbled sideways, caught his balance and then rushed for Donegal, who jerked the gun clear and cocked it. "Oh, no, Doc," he said from between his teeth.

Shannon stopped. He was taller than Donegal, and heavier. Also, he had been on a boxing team in college. But the gun was between them. He felt himself tremble, not with fear but with hate. It surprised him, because never in his life had he really hated anyone. But he hated Donegal for what he was, for what he was doing to Ronnie, for holding him and causing Celia to worry. Now he hated Donegal with a pure intensity. Shannon said, "If I get a chance, I'll kill you."

Donegal laughed shortly. "You won't get a chance."

Shannon nodded at the man on the floor. "You're letting your brother die. It's murder."

"You're the doctor here. Let's see how smart you are."

Shannon began to curse Donegal in a low, intense voice. He called him all the filthy names he could think of, including words he'd forgotten and some he'd never uttered in his life. He cursed Donegal until he was ashamed of himself, but when he was finished he felt better.

Donegal eyed him quizzically. "Say, you're really in an uproar, Doc."

"Scum," Shannon said, "dirt."

Delbert Owens stirred, raised his head and watched the two men silently. The wounded man began to babble incoherently. Owens spoke in a pleading voice. "Please, Steve, let's leave the kid here with the doc and you and me pull out. It's our only chance. Please, Steve."

Donegal turned slowly, sauntered over to Owens and then suddenly and viciously kicked the sitting man in the side. Owens yelped with pain, lurched to his feet and stood crouched against the wall holding a hand to his side. "Jeez, Steve, what the hell—?"

"Shut up," Donegal shouted. He turned to Shannon. "I'm through fooling with you." He tapped a wrist watch. "It's almost midnight. You've got twelve hours—noon tomorrow. If the kid's not better by then, I'll kill you." His teeth glinted in the candlelight. "And I won't mind it at all."

"He'll die," Shannon said.

Donegal shrugged. "All right. So will you."

"Steve," the wounded man called loudly and clearly. "Hey, Steve, where are you?"

Donegal moved over and stood above his brother. "I'm here, kid."

"Hey, Steve, pass the catsup, will you? You know I like catsup on my French fries. And maple syrup on my pancakes and jelly on my bread and peanut butter, too, and butter on my sweet corn and the heap needs new rubber all around. The six ball in the side pocket and here comes

the snake eyes. You're faded, bud, and my point is eight the hard way. We got a rumble tonight and boy, oh, boy ..." The words merged and stumbled along and at last died into thick mumbling. Ronnie screamed then and his breathing became rasping and strangled. He turned on his side and chattered wildly to the wall.

Donegal swung toward Shannon. "Help him," he said harshly.

"I can't. My penicillin is gone. He's burning up with fever. He might like some water."

"Give it to him, then!"

Silently Shannon got the can of boiled water, knelt beside Ronnie, lifted his head and shoulders with his left arm and placed the can to the swollen, fever-blistered lips. Ronnie choked and strangled and the water ran over his chin, making rivulets in the blond, downy fuzz of beard. Shannon gently lowered him to the blanket and stood erect.

"Beer," Ronnie mumbled. "Man, I dig that brew ..." His voice broke into a cracked song. "Jesus wants me for a sunbeam ... To shine for Him each day, a sunbeam, a sunbeam ..." And then he was silent, except for the terrible sound of his breathing.

Delbert Owens edged along the wall toward the door. "I—gotta go, Steve," he stuttered. "We—we'll split the take later, when the heat's off. I—I just gotta get out of here."

"Stay," Donegal said, as if he were commanding a dog.

"I can't!" Owens screamed. "I'm going nuts!" He lunged for the door.

Donegal raised the gun and fired. The blast seemed to rock the shanty. Owens jerked, slammed blindly against the wall and thudded clumsily to the floor. His legs moved feebly and then he was still. Shannon moved swiftly to Owens and knelt down. In a moment he straightened and faced Donegal.

"He's dead."

"Sure," Donegal said. "He had it coming."

"Not that. You didn't have to kill him."

"He was a stupid punk. He'd get it sooner or later anyhow. Besides, I didn't want to split with him."

"Are you just going to leave him there?"

"Why not?" Donegal said carelessly. "It'll be a few days before he starts stinking. I'll be gone by then."

Shannon stared at him and said, "What now?"

"We wait. Tomorrow noon. No longer."

"You'll have to sleep sometime," Shannon said.

"Not me. I can go forever. You sleep, Doc. You'll need your strength."

"For what?"

"To save my brother."

"I can't save him. Not here."

"You'd better. It's like this, Doc; I don't think you're doing all you can for the kid. I think you're holding out, stalling. But if you get him in shape so we can pull out by tomorrow noon—just so he's able to travel—okay. I know a doctor over the state line. He'll take care of Ronnie for a grand or two, no questions asked. But I want the kid in as good a shape as possible for the trip. That's up to you. If he isn't in shape, you'll stay here to keep Delbert company." Donegal spoke calmly, but Shannon saw the glint of desperation in his eyes.

The doctor said nothing. He knew there was no point in talking anymore. He went to the dead man, removed the leather jacket, straightened the limp arms and legs, and placed the jacket gently over the still, slack face.

"Don't expect me to lay you out like that, Doc," Donegal said.

"I won't." Shannon moved to Ronnie, knelt over him, felt the hot face. Ronnie was quiet now, not mumbling or chattering. The fever was consuming him, burning away his life. Shannon soaked a handkerchief with water from the tin can and bathed Ronnie's face. Maybe, the doctor thought, if he goes into a coma, the wound could be opened without anesthesia. If Donegal would help, hold Ronnie firmly, maybe it could be done. Nothing would be sterile, Shannon knew, but that couldn't be helped.

Shannon turned his head. "Donegal."

"Yeah, Doc?"

"I'm going to open that leg. When I start cutting, I want you to hold him." Shannon stood erect, removed his coat and shirt and began to tear the shirt into strips. Then he pulled his undershirt over his head and stood naked to the waist in the yellow glow of the candle. "Remember this, Donegal; what I'm going to do is not for me, or for you. I'm doing it because I'm a doctor, because I must, even against my better judgment. I want you to understand that."

"What do you want me to do?"

"Just hold him—tightly."

"You won't try anything? With me, I mean?"

"I can't promise you a thing."

"If this is just a stunt, I swear I'll—"

"Shut up." Shannon took a scalpel from his bag, knowing it was not sterile and not caring anymore. Nothing else was sterile, either. "Bring the candle over here, put it on that box and hold his legs." He knelt on the floor, placed the torn strips of shirt and his undershirt on the blanket beside Ronnie.

Donegal placed the candle on the box, stooped down and grasped his

brother's ankles firmly. Shannon said, "Now."

The scalpel moved expertly and firmly, moved again, cutting deeply and cleanly. Ronnie aroused and screamed, began to struggle. Donegal moved swiftly, swung the gun against his brother's head. Ronnie fell back with a sigh and was still.

"Good," Shannon said, panting. "Thanks." He wadded his undershirt over the wound. "Turn him on his side. It's got to drain."

Donegal obeyed silently. Shannon's hand went to Ronnie's head, felt the rising swelling there where the gun had struck him. Then he checked the boy's pulse. It was feeble and ragged. Shannon stood erect and sighed, holding the bloody scalpel. "It's crude," he said, as if talking to himself, "but I couldn't help it." He tossed the scalpel into the bag and pulled his jacket on over his naked shoulders.

Donegal straightened, holding the gun. "Will he be all right now?"

"Probably not. The infection is advanced."

"We wait until noon. You may as well get some sleep, Doc."

"All right, but I've got to dress that boy's leg the best I can, after it drains. Call me in an hour." Shannon moved past the body of Delbert Owens, threw his topcoat over his shoulders and sat down against the wall. He folded his arms, dropped his chin to his chest and closed his eyes. He didn't really sleep, but dozed intermittently. He was in a kind of haze, induced by fatigue and tension, and for a while the nightmare of the shanty and the past twenty-odd hours receded somewhat. He knew vaguely that Ronnie was muttering again, that the boy had regained consciousness, but he did not stir until Donegal called softly, "Hour's up."

Shannon got stiffly to his feet, went to his patient and did what he could, which was not nearly enough. Then he sighed, returned to his place by the wall and hunched down with the coat over his shoulders.

"Well?" Donegal said.

"He's bad. You're not being fair to your brother, Donegal. He'll die if he isn't taken to a hospital. He may die anyhow."

"Noon," Donegal said softly. "You have until noon."

Shannon didn't answer. He didn't care anymore. There was nothing more he could do. He closed his eyes and was almost immediately asleep. He had learned during his intern days, and when he'd been in the army medical corps, to sleep when he had an opportunity, regardless of what went on around him. And so he slept now.

Sunlight streaming through the cracks of the boarded windows awakened him. He stirred painfully, knew that he'd slipped down to his side. He struggled to a sitting position and rubbed his eyes. His head ached and there was a bitter taste in his mouth. His fingers rasped over

the stubble on his face and he saw his hands. They were filthy. He winced, thinking of the surgery he'd performed the night before. He turned his head, saw the still figure of Ronnie lying on the blanket against the far wall of the shanty. A corner of the blanket had been folded over Ronnie's face.

"He's dead, Doc."

Shannon jerked his head, still not fully awake. Steve Donegal was sitting against the wall nearby, the gun resting on one knee. Shannon squinted until Donegal came into focus. He saw the bearded face, the sunken eyes, the glint of teeth.

"You put on an act," Donegal said, "tried to fool me. But you didn't really try. You let the kid die."

"No." Shannon struggled to his feet and stood swaying slightly.

"You don't need to look at him. He's gone."

"Why didn't you wake me?"

"What was the sense? For you to cut him, hurt him more? To tell me he had to go to a hospital, so you could get clear? You didn't care about Ronnie at all."

Shannon's foggy brain cleared. "I had to open that wound," he said. "It was the only chance he had. Are you sure...?" He moved toward Ronnie's body.

"No." Donegal raised the gun threateningly. "Don't you touch him, you butcher. Keep your hands off him."

Shannon stood still. Donegal did not get up, but sat reclined against the wall, the gun muzzle leveled across a knee, his eyes hooded and lazy. "It's not noon yet, but I'm not waiting. No point in it now. I'm pulling out, with all the money from the job. You killed the kid, Doc. You let him die. You can stay here with him, along with Delbert."

Shannon said, "I'm sorry about your brother, but I guess this is what you wanted from the first. You like to kill, don't you?"

Donegal smiled lazily and cocked the revolver. "Goodbye, Doc," he said.

16

Saturday Morning

In the Harbor City morning newspaper, the *Independent Observer*, the story of Lieutenant Horner's murder was greatly enlarged from the meager accounts in the Thursday and Friday editions. Chief of Police Chad Beckwith had at last bowed to increasing pressure and had reluctantly released all the facts he had. The *Observer* made the most

of them on Saturday morning, gleefully getting the jump on the *Evening Sentinel*.

LOCAL MAN CHARGED WITH POLICEMAN'S MURDER, Evidence Mounts Against Auto Parts Salesman... Myron Faro, 43, was arrested shortly before noon on Thursday by Chief of Police Chad Beckwith and Captain Jason Keely and charged with suspicion of murder in connection with the fatal shooting of Lieutenant John Horner, of the Harbor City Police Department, and was held without bail in the city jail. While being questioned on Friday afternoon Mr. Faro suffered an internal hemorrhage and was taken to Memorial Hospital where he is under police guard. His condition this morning was reported improved, but it is uncertain how long he will remain in the hospital.

Lieutenant Horner was shot to death in a parking lot behind a food market known as Connie's Corner near the city limits at the intersection of the lake highway and State Route 42. Mrs. Emil (Constance) Tomescek, who operates the market with her husband, has stated that Lieutenant Horner was in the store shortly before the shooting took place, and that Faro was there at the same time.

Yesterday Faro led police to the bridge over Deer Creek on Duckpond Road, where he said he threw the gun he was carrying into the water. Police recovered a .32 caliber revolver from the creek and Chief Beckwith has stated that laboratory tests prove that it is the murder weapon. After the gun was found Faro denied that it was his and claimed that his gun was .22 caliber. It was understood early this morning that there were other material witnesses as well as additional evidence strongly implicating Mr. Faro.

Also on the first page of the *Observer* was an account of the disappearance of Dr. Clinton Shannon.

HUNT CONTINUES FOR MISSING DOCTOR. Police announced today that there have been no developments in the strange disappearance of Dr. Clinton Shannon, prominent Harbor City physician and surgeon, who has been missing since late Thursday evening. Dr. Shannon apparently left his office shortly after eleven o'clock, after telephoning Mrs. Shannon that he would be home in a few minutes. Nothing has been heard from him since. His hat was found by police beside

his car at the rear of his office. There is no apparent motive or reason for his disappearance. "He is just missing," Chief of Police Beckwith stated. "That's all we know at this time. We are doing everything possible to find him."

On that bright and sunny Saturday morning in April Sam Gideon and his oldest son, Samuel, Jr., who was fourteen, trudged happily over the sandy earth and through the dry marsh grass of their domain on the fringe of the great marsh area south of Lake Erie and east of Harbor City, a barren and forbidding country, dry and bleak in winter, lushly green in summer. Now, in April, the waving brown marsh grass was turning a pale green and the sandy soil on the high ground was beginning to soften. The spring rains would form lagoons and swell the numerous streams leading to the vast lake, which stretched to Canada. Sam Gideon and his son walked freely over the dry, springy loam and watched for pheasants or mallards, rabbits and even deer. Not many people entered the marsh, or wanted to, not even the summer people who swarmed the beaches from May until September. The vacationers on the south Erie Shore were not interested in a narrow sandy lane leading back from the highway through puddles and waist-high grass; they were only interested in the blue water, the beaches, the motels and cottages.

Two ring-necked pheasants were tied by the legs and slung over Sam Gideon's shoulder. They were hen pheasants and the fact that shooting hens was illegal, even in season, did not bother Sam at all. He considered the swamp his personal domain and he was rarely challenged, not even by the game wardens, who mostly confined their spying to the duck blinds on more civilized terrain. To them the swampy marsh was a wasteland, and catching one lone poacher who had lived there for years with his family could not compare to nabbing a U.S. senator red-handed with more than his limit of ducks or with a pheasant or rabbit shot out of season. The only people who penetrated the swamp were Sam's few friends, Dr. Clinton Shannon among them.

Sam, Jr., said, "Hey, Pop, what's that old jalopy doing there?"

The father stopped and frowned. His face was lined and leathery, but his blue eyes were bright and youthful. He wore a plaid cap with ear tabs, an old thick mackinaw and blue jeans tucked into high felt boots. A double-barreled 12 gauge Winchester shotgun rested easily in the crook of his right arm. His son carried a .22 Savage bolt action rifle and wore a tan parka, the hood lined with rabbit fur.

"Where?" the father asked.

"Over there." The boy pointed.

Sam squinted in the April sunshine and saw the car parked off the narrow, rutted lane and half obscured by dry marsh grass and a clump of stunted pines, and then walked forward grimly. He did not like strangers in his territory. They reached the car and inspected it. "Fair rubber," Sam said, kicking a rear tire. "Island County plates." He moved to the front of the car, an old Plymouth sedan. "Ignition key's gone. They must be around somewhere." He turned and swung his gaze over the barren land.

"Kids, maybe," his son said.

Sam grunted, his keen eyes searching the vicinity.

"Maybe they got girls with 'em. This is Saturday. No school. Maybe they got girls and took 'em to that old lumber camp shanty."

Sam Gideon gazed down at his son and said sharply, "What for?"

"Maybe they wanted to play house." The boy put a hand to his mouth and giggled.

"What do you know about stuff like that?"

"Plenty, Pop. I'm fourteen, you know." Sam, Jr. pointed to the ground. "They went that way. See the tracks? I'll bet they're in the shanty right now. Oh, boy."

"Shut up," Sam Gideon said sternly. Then he studied the impressions in the sand. "If it's kids, they're big ones. And no females. Just three men. There's other tracks, but older. These are fresh."

"Let's follow 'em, Pop," the boy said eagerly.

"All right. This is my land. I don't like trespassers."

"You don't own it, Pop."

"You talk too much." Sam and his son followed the tracks over a rise and down into a hollow and then through a sea of dry, coarse grass. On a knoll ahead they saw the abandoned shanty with its loosely boarded windows and surrounded by underbrush and rotting stumps.

The boy said, "That new baby brother is cute, Pop. You and Mom gonna have any more?"

"I don't know. Shut up."

"Doc Shannon is a nice guy, ain't he? He even brought—"

"Shut up," the father said again. "Please shut the hell up. And don't say 'ain't.'" He knew now that the footprints led directly to the shanty and he moved more slowly, frowning again. When he and his son were twenty yards away the fresh tracks in the sandy soil told him that no one had left the shanty recently to return to the car. There were tracks leading away, but his keen woodsman's eyes told him that they were older. The persons who had made the fresh tracks were still inside.

Sam motioned to his son to stay back and went forward to the shanty and peered through a narrow section of dirty window glass between two

nailed boards. He could see the entire interior and it took him a couple of seconds to adjust to what he saw. Two men were lying on the floor, a blanket folded over the face of one, a leather jacket over the other. Another man sat crouched against a wall holding a short-barreled revolver on his knee. The man was grinning and Sam's expert eye saw that the gun was cocked. Sam's gaze swung to a fourth man, who was standing, facing the one with the gun, and for a second he was shocked and bewildered. What was Doc Shannon doing in there? Then he saw the other man raise the revolver from his knee and point it carefully at the doctor.

Sam Gideon did not know what was happening, but he knew it was wrong and his reaction was violent and immediate. He shrugged the brace of pheasant from his shoulder and rammed the muzzle of the shotgun between the boards and through the window. Above the sound of splintering glass he yelled furiously, "You son of a bitch!" His finger was tight on the trigger of the shotgun, but he was not ready for the evil, swift swivel of the revolver and the *crack, crack, crack!* But he ducked instinctively as the bullets tore through glass and wood. When he cautiously raised his head again he saw that the man with the gun was standing behind Doctor Shannon. Both men stared at Sam's face at the broken window.

"Don't shoot, Sam," the doctor said quietly.

"I'll kill the bastard." Sam leveled the shotgun.

The man behind the doctor laughed. "Listen to the doc, friend. That scatter gun would get him, too. You wouldn't want that, would you?"

"I can wait," Sam said grimly.

"Sure, but I can shoot you now."

"Try it," Sam said.

The man leveled the gun over the doctor's right shoulder and Sam ducked as a bullet splintered a window board. Sam crouched beneath the window, cursing softly, and gazed about for his son, but he was not in sight. "Sammy," he called softly. There was no answer. Then he heard a tinkling sound from the rear of the shanty and cautiously raised his head to peer once more through the broken, boarded window. The scene inside was the same, except that now a rifle barrel protruded between the boards of a window in the far wall. The man behind Dr. Shannon swung and aimed the revolver, but the rifle went *spat!* and the man whirled and stumbled away. Sam Gideon leveled the shotgun, but saw that he was not needed. Dr. Shannon moved swiftly and there was a blur of movement and Shannon stepped clear with the man's revolver in his hand. Sam ran to the door then and kicked it open.

The rifle barrel poking through the opposite window was steady and

Sam, Jr. said, "I got him covered, Pop. You can kill the bastard now."

"Watch your language, damn it." Sam moved to the doctor. "You all right, Doc?"

Shannon nodded and spoke to the man, who stood unsteadily, holding his right wrist. "You're hit, Donegal?"

"In the wrist, yes."

"Do you want me to look at it?"

"To hell with you," Donegal said bitterly.

Shannon sighed and turned away. "Nice shooting, Sammy," he said. "Thanks."

"That's all right, Doc," the boy said from the window. "When I saw that Pop couldn't use the shotgun I figured I could pick off the bastard with my rifle and not hurt you."

"Listen, you brat," Sam Gideon said, "I told you to watch your language."

"Sorry, Pop. Should I wing him in the other arm?"

Donegal moved nervously backward, holding his wrist "Don't overdo it, kid."

"Stand facing the wall," Shannon said to Donegal.

As Donegal sullenly obeyed, the doctor spoke to Sam Gideon. "I'll explain all this later. Right now you go to your place and call the police. Tell them to come out here and to send an ambulance."

"Okay, but what about him?" Gideon nodded at Donegal.

Shannon grinned, but it was only a flash of teeth in his haggard, bearded face. "Sammy and I can handle him. Hurry."

Sam handed the shotgun to the doctor. "It'll cut him in two at this range."

Shannon dropped the revolver into a coat pocket and took the shotgun. Sam, Jr., spoke from the window. "You got him covered good, Doc?"

"Sure. Come on in, Sammy."

Sam Gideon, Senior, left the shanty and hurried toward his home two miles away. The boy appeared in the doorway holding the rifle steady at his hip. Shannon said to Donegal, "This boy can shoot straight. Don't try anything."

Donegal stood facing the wall and said nothing. Shannon moved quickly to the body of Ronnie Donegal, knelt down and gently lifted the blanket from the youth's face. After a brief examination he stood erect and said to Donegal, "Did you really think he was dead?"

Donegal half turned and spoke over a shoulder. "Sure, Doc. He—he looked dead to me."

"He's still alive," Shannon said harshly. "If you had let me look at him I could have told you that before. He may still have a chance."

"Honest to God," Donegal blurted, "I was *sure*. He didn't move and was so—so still, and you kept saying how bad he was. I wouldn't lie about it, not about my brother."

"I wonder," Shannon said grimly. "You said you'd kill me if your brother died, but you didn't need a reason. You could have killed me any time."

"I made a deal with you," Donegal said in a surprisingly quiet voice. "Believe it or not, I keep my word. I was sure the kid was gone."

"All right," Shannon said wearily. "It doesn't matter now."

"Will he make it?"

"I hope so. If he doesn't, you're to blame."

"Honest, Doc ..." Donegal started to turn fully around.

"Don't, mister," the boy said sharply, moving the rifle.

Donegal faced the wall once more.

Shannon said, "You're both going to the hospital."

"Why bother?" Donegal asked bitterly.

"If your brother lives, maybe he can start over again."

"Maybe," Donegal said to the wall. "Not me, though. I've had it."

"You have, indeed." Shannon's gaze went to the body of Delbert Owens.

The boy also glanced at the dead man, and then nodded at Donegal. "Did he kill him, Doc?"

Shannon nodded.

"Why?"

Shannon looked at Donegal and said grimly, "Ask him."

Steve Donegal faced the wall and said nothing. Blood seeped in slow drops from his wrist and between his fingers to the floor.

Shannon met the police at the door of the shanty. Chief Beckwith and Captain Keely stared at him. "My God, Clint," Beckwith said, taking the shotgun from the doctor's hand, "you look like hell. You sure had us worried. We—"

"Yes, yes," Shannon broke in wearily. "Did you tell Celia?"

"Sure I did, as soon as Gideon called. Then we tore right out here. The ambulance came in as far as it could. Sam didn't make much sense, except that you were here and—"

"Inside," Shannon said. "A boy in bad shape, and a dead man...." He passed a hand over his face and swayed on his feet.

Beckwith steadied Shannon with a burly arm as Captain Keely and two policemen entered the shanty with drawn revolvers. Shannon took a deep breath and stood erect. "I—I'm all right, Chad. Get the boy to the hospital. Surgery. Tell John Kovici. The other one, Donegal, is wounded,

not seriously. He—"

"Donegal?" Beckwith cut in sharply. "You mean to say you were out here with *him?*"

"Where's Sam?" Shannon asked stupidly, ignoring Beckwith's question.

"Right here, Doc," Sam Gideon said from close by.

"Thanks, Sam."

"To hell with that. You thank my boy."

"Yes, Sammy. Samuel, Jr. I remember well the night he was born." Shannon was dimly aware of movement around him, of men moving out of the shanty, of two prostrate forms carried on stretchers, of Donegal walking away between two policemen, of young Sam Gideon standing by, the .22 rifle now toted in the crook of an arm, of the older Gideon peering at him anxiously, of Captain Keely's bloated ruddy face floating in the haze. He heard Keely say exultantly, "It's Donegal, all right, Chad. We got him and the money, too, most of it, I think, from the hold-up. He had it stashed away in this shopping bag. We'll count it at the station. His partner, the other one, not the kid—"

"Owens." Shannon felt giddy, but he spoke distinctly. "His name is Delbert Owens. Donegal shot him. I saw it."

"Come on, Clint," Beckwith said, leading the doctor away. "It's all right now."

"Where's my bag?" Shannon asked.

"I have it, Clint," Jason Keely said. "Watch your step here."

Shannon felt friendly and helping bands on his arms as he stumbled over the soft earth and through the dry, rustling grass and weeds.

Inside the car Shannon leaned back and closed his eyes. He was aware of a gentle rolling as they moved slowly along the narrow, rutted lane and he knew when the car stopped. He heard Beckwith say, "Here you are, Sam. Thanks, again."

Shannon opened his eyes and saw Sam Gideon standing by the open door of the car peering in at him. "Doc," Gideon said soberly, "they tell me there's a reward for that fellow—Donegal? You sure earned it."

"Not me, Sam. It's all yours—and your boy's."

"I won't argue about it now, but maybe that money will partly pay you for all you've done for the missus and me and the kids."

"You don't owe me a cent," Shannon said. "You'll never owe me anything." He closed his eyes again as the car moved away and was asleep before they reached the lake highway.

17

Saturday Afternoon

The last rites for John Horner were held in the Hoyt Funeral Home at one o'clock and by two his casket was ready to be lowered into the grave at Evergreen Cemetery. Organ music from a portable phonograph pealed softly and died without an echo in the April sunlight. Attendance had been large at the service, but only a comparatively few persons accompanied the body to the cemetery. Mrs. Horner, surrounded by her parents and the parents of her dead husband, stood sobbing near the grave. The children had not attended the funeral, but had been permitted to view their father in the casket the evening before. They were too small to understand the finality of death and the younger boy had commented that "Daddy's asleep in a box." Mrs. Horner had forgiven her husband for his infidelity and her grief was true and deep.

Chief of Police Chad Beckwith and Captain Jason Keely stood with bare, bowed heads as the minister uttered the final words of the burial service. Other members of the police force were present, as were delegations from the Fire Department, two fraternal organizations and the various city and county offices. The mayor of Harbor City had attended the services at the funeral home, but due to a severe head cold had not gone to the cemetery.

Dr. Clinton Shannon was not present; he was at home bathed but still unshaven, and sound asleep. Nina Faro was also absent. She had not even paid a call at the funeral home to view the body and sign the visitor's register. Nina Faro was at the hospital talking to her husband and making plans for their future. She was certain that her husband would be cleared of the murder charge, but she did not know of the accumulating pile of incriminating evidence.

At the edge of the gathering around the grave were Dr. Nelson Keough and his wife, Betty. There were also three women standing alone and trying to appear inconspicuous and anonymous. They were present for sentimental reasons. Each, in her own way, had loved John Horner and regretted his passing. All were attractive and had held a certain degree of appeal for John Horner. And he, in turn, had added something to their lives not provided by dull and complacent husbands. These women, while sorry that John Horner was dead, were thankful that their connection with him had not been made a subject of public gossip,

as it had been with Mrs. Faro. All three were thankful, indeed, especially since Horner had been murdered. Of course, each knew that her husband had not killed Horner, because the husbands had been ignorant (as far as they knew) of Horner's attentions. Mr. Faro had, in effect, avenged all the husbands. Poor Mr. Faro. Only one of the three women knew Mrs. Faro by sight and she furtively eyed the graveside gathering, wondering if Mrs. Faro would be brazen enough to attend. But of course she could not; Mr. Faro was suspected of murder and his wife could not be seen at the victim's funeral. One woman thought smugly, *I'm sure glad Herman never got wise, like that Faro did....*

Betty Keough stood stiffly, her small fists clenched, her chin tilted, and spoke from a corner of her little girl's mouth.

"Why did you make me come here? Why, why, why?"

"Therapy," Dr. Nelson Keough said. "Rub your nose in it, dear. See, the man is dead. They are burying him."

"You're glad," Betty said bitterly. "You're glad and happy."

"Certainly I am. He deserved to die." Dr. Keough's sensitive face held a look of exultation, almost of ecstasy.

"You shouldn't talk that way about the dead."

"I hope his soul burns in hell."

"Nelson!" Betty Keough was not a religious woman, but she was shocked at her husband's words and tone.

"Watch closely now," Dr. Keough said.

"They won't put him down in the grave now, will they? When people are still here?"

"They'll do it some time. We'll stay and watch."

"I—I don't want to." Betty's lips quivered.

"I'm afraid you must," her husband said softly. "You've got to be taught a lesson."

"I—I told you I was sorry. I promised I'd never—"

"Shh," he hissed as the minister's voice died away.

The graveside services were over. Mrs. Horner and her entourage turned away and she moved sobbing between her mother and father, supported by them, to the black limousine parked in the cemetery drive behind the hearse. Other persons walked over the soft April earth to their cars. The minister, carrying his Bible, accompanied the pallbearers, six uniformed policeman, to a second black limousine provided by the Hoyt Funeral Home. When the last car of the funeral procession had wound down the narrow curving drive, and when Mr. Hoyt and his assistants had completed their final duties and left, two cemetery employees appeared. One began to take down the three-sided tent and canopy, while the other busied himself at the grave. This man noticed

Dr. and Mrs. Keough standing close by in the thin sunlight and gazed at them curiously.

"Are you going to lower the casket now?" Dr. Keough asked.

"Yes," the workman said. "You folks relatives?"

"No," Dr. Keough said.

"Just friends, huh?"

"Not exactly." Dr. Keough's fingers dug into his wife's arm. "Do you mind if we watch?"

The workman shrugged and went about his duties. Betty Keough averted her face and closed her eyes when the casket began to sink downward, but her husband clutched her chin with his free hand and turned her face toward the grave. "Look," he said in a low, intense voice. "Watch him go down."

She kept her eyes closed in spite of the cruel pressure of his fingers on her chin and cheeks, which made a grotesque pink figure-eight of her lips. Her small body trembled beneath a blue coat trimmed with muskrat, but she would not open her eyes.

"Look," Keough insisted, shaking her face and jerking at her arm. He was panting a little.

The workman by the grave looked up and said gently, "If she doesn't want to watch, she don't have to, does she?" He was a young man, sturdily built, with a rugged, weathered face.

"Shut up," Keough snapped. "Just go on about your work."

The workman straightened and smiled. Ignoring Keough, he spoke to Betty. "If you don't want to watch, I'll wait until you go."

Betty opened her eyes slowly, saw the smiling, rugged face, the glint of admiration in the gray eyes, the small white scar at the corner of the mouth. She wanted to smile back, but could not because of the rigid grasp of her husband's fingers. Keough released her face then, but kept a hand clamped to her arm and spoke coldly to the workman. "I'll report you."

"Go ahead, Doc. I'm just helping my buddy this afternoon. I work for the telephone company, not the cemetery association. Who you going to report me to? And for what?"

"For insolence," Keough said. "What's your name?"

"The name is Zeller, Doc. Harold Zeller. Call me Harry."

"You seem to know who I am."

"Sure. You're Doctor Keough." Zeller turned his head slightly, so that Keough could not observe, and winked at Betty.

"All right," Keough said. "Are you going to finish your work?"

"Not while the lady's here. I can understand why she doesn't want to watch. A lot of people don't." Zeller grinned at Betty. "I'll wait until you

and the doctor leave."

"Thank you," Betty said gratefully. "Thank you very much."

"You're welcome."

Nelson Keough released his wife's arm. He had lost, and knew it. By bringing Betty to the cemetery he had hoped the experience would mould her, make her more aware of life, its dangers and responsibilities. He had wanted Betty to see her lover lowered into the grave, a final act, to force her to realize that she was an adult and had contributed to a man's death. For a queer reason he had not been pleased to hear the gossip about John Horner seeing another woman also—that Mrs. Faro. He was oddly resentful that Horner's infidelity had not been confined to Betty. If Betty alone was not good enough for him ... It was all an insult, really,

Keough thought. Still, he was grateful that Horner's attentions to Betty had not been made public.

Keough said to Zeller, "I'll remember you."

"Sure, Doc." Zeller smiled easily.

The smile enraged Keough. He began to curse Zeller shrilly. He trembled with his rage and knew he was out of control, but he couldn't stop. He was aware that Betty had moved away, but he kept on, feeling ashamed and depraved, and the terrible thing was that he couldn't help it. He ranted, spittle on his chin. Zeller was a hated symbol of something.

Dr. Keough screamed obscenities.

Zeller slapped Keough sharply on the cheek then, and stood waiting for the reaction. Keough's raving stopped abruptly and he glared at Zeller, too stunned, to speak. Zeller said quietly, "That's better, Doc. Now get the hell out of here."

The other workman had lowered one section of the canopy and now stood beside Zeller eyeing Dr. Keough curiously. "What the hell, Harry? This guy going nuts, or what?"

"He acts like it," Zeller said. "He's supposed to be a doctor, but I wouldn't take my dog to him."

Keough opened his mouth, but no words came out. He swung abruptly and strode away.

Zeller said to the other workman, "Damnedest thing I ever saw. He was forcing that little babe to watch me lower the coffin. I saw she didn't want to and I had a few words with the doc. Then he started screaming at me and I slapped him. The babe was cute, wasn't she?"

"Looked like just a kid to me."

"She's married to him, I guess. Anyhow, she's wearing a ring." Zeller shook his head and returned to his work.

Dr. Keough drove carefully out of the cemetery and onto the highway leading into Harbor City. There was chill sweat on his face and he gripped the wheel tightly in an effort to control his trembling. His wife sat huddled on the seat as far away from him as she could get. She stared straight ahead and said nothing. By the time they reached the city Keough was calmer and spoke for the first time since they'd left the cemetery. "I—I'm sorry, Betty."

"You shouldn't have tried to make me do that."

"I just wanted you to realize how serious ..."

"You'll never touch me again," she said, without turning her head. "Never. No time. No place."

He attempted a laugh. "What do you mean? You're my wife, Betty."

"I was never your wife. You've always treated me like a kid."

"You're upset." He leaned over and placed a hand on her knee.

She brushed his hand away viciously and turned to face him. There was a coldness in her eyes he'd never seen before. Uneasily he looked away and watched the street ahead. As they stopped for a traffic light, she said, "You killed him, didn't you?"

Keough did not answer.

"Don't worry," she said. "I won't tell on you, but I know you killed him. You said you would. You weren't downstairs in your study Wednesday night, were you?"

As the light changed and the car moved ahead, Keough said, "Yes, I was, Betty."

"Part of the time, maybe. But you went out and killed him that night."

"The police have arrested the man who killed Horner," Keough said. "They have proof." He glanced at his wife. "You're talking nonsense. Let's go home and you can have some beer and then you get a sitter and we'll have dinner somewhere alone, just you and I. Wouldn't you like that?"

"It's too late," she said. "It's no use now for you to try and treat me like a—a woman. A wife."

"I love you, Betty." Keough was worried; she had never acted this way before. She was so—so firm. Always he had dominated her, directed her every action, and suddenly he felt a small panic as he realized that what he had said was true. He did love her, in spite of what she had done, and he didn't want to lose her.

"Did you hear me, Betty?" he asked anxiously.

"Oh, shut up," Betty said. "Go peddle your pills, Doctor."

"Don't talk like that," he said sharply. "What's come over you?"

"I just grew up," Betty said. "You don't own me, Nelson. When you treated me like that back there, in front of that man, I hated you. I'm glad he slapped you."

"We'll talk about it later," Keough broke in curtly.

"We'll talk now," Betty said. "And I don't want beer. I want a Martini cocktail. And I want my own money and I'll do my own shopping. I'm going to hire a woman to keep the house clean and one to take care of the kids when I go out. I want lots of new clothes. From now on you just mind your own business. The house is my department and if you don't like the way I'm going to run it you can move out. Is that clear?"

"Listen," Keough said angrily, "I whipped you the other night and I can whip you again."

"Oh, no, you won't," Betty said calmly. "Never."

He didn't speak for a moment. Then he said in a tight voice. "I don't understand you, Betty."

"You will, you will."

"You said you didn't want me to touch you. Did you mean that?"

"I'll think about it," Betty said.

18

Saturday Afternoon, Late

Dr. Clinton Shannon slept until five o'clock and awoke feeling stiff and somewhat sore but otherwise greatly refreshed. After he had shaved, his wife brought a Scotch-and-soda to the bedroom and he sipped at it and smoked a cigarette as he dressed.

Celia asked, "How do you feel?"

"Fine. A little stiff, though. That shanty floor was hard."

"Clint," she said soberly, "I—I almost went out of my mind."

"It's over now." He touched her cheek. "Where's your drink?"

"In the kitchen. Are you hungry?"

"Starved."

"What do you want?"

"Anything. And some milk. And coffee."

They heard the door chimes and Celia left the room. In a moment Shannon heard voices in the living room and Celia called to him, "It's Chief Beckwith and Captain Keely."

"Be right out." Shannon finished buttoning his shirt, left the collar open and went down the hall to the living room carrying his drink. Beckwith and Keely greeted him gravely and shook hands as if he'd returned from a long absence. "Drink, gentlemen?" Shannon asked.

"Well," Beckwith said, "we're supposed to be on duty, but this is an occasion. Bourbon and a little water and ice for me."

"Coming up." Celia looked inquiringly at Keely.

"Do you have any rye?" the police captain asked.

"I think so." Shannon turned to his wife. "Look in the back of the cupboard, behind the vermouth."

"Straight," Keely said. "Water on the side. Thanks."

Celia left and Shannon said, "Sit down." He took a deep chair by a round coffee table while the two officers sat on a divan facing him.

"You look okay now," Beckwith said to Shannon.

"I'm all right. How's that boy?"

"Donegal's brother? John Kovici thinks he'll make it. The kid was in bad shape, though. John says he'll know for sure tomorrow."

"I did all I could for him out there."

"I know. But Donegal thought you were stalling, huh?"

Shannon nodded, remembering. "If Sam Gideon and his son hadn't come along when they did ..."

Celia brought the drinks then and the men stopped talking. "Don't mind me," she said. "I'm just the wife of a hero."

"I was scared blue," Shannon said.

Celia touched his arm and left the room. Shannon asked Beckwith, "Is Donegal locked up here?"

The police chief nodded. "For the present. John Kovici fixed up the bullet wound in his wrist. And we found his car in a woods where he'd ditched it. He's wanted for murder in Indiana. We'll go along with extradition."

"What about the other one?" Shannon asked. "The man Donegal shot?"

"Owens? Small-time hood. A couple of convictions for stealing cars and holding up gas stations. He teamed up with Donegal just before the loan company robbery." Beckwith grinned wryly and sipped at his drink. "Wanted to better himself, I guess."

"Donegal shot him in cold blood," Shannon said.

"All right, but I don't think we'll need your testimony. The Indiana murder charge should take care of him. If it doesn't we'll sock it to him here, with your help."

"I'll be available. What about the boy?"

"Reformatory for a couple of years, maybe. He's only seventeen."

Captain Keely placed his glass on the table and Shannon said, "Bring me up to date on the Horner thing. Has Myron Faro confessed to the killing?"

"Not yet," Beckwith said. "He's in the hospital, by the way. Yesterday afternoon, when we were questioning him in my office, he started hemorrhaging."

"I'm sorry to hear that. He's one of my patients, you know. Who's taking care of him?"

"John Kovici."

"Good old John. Lately it seems he's doing more of my work than I am."

"You couldn't help it, Clint. But tell me, how serious is Faro's condition?"

"He's not good. Long ulcer history, duodenal. I saw him about a week ago and thought he was improving, though. Tension and worry could have brought on the hemorrhage."

"He should have thought of that before he killed Horner," Beckwith said.

"Yes, if he did kill him. I rather like Myron Faro. He didn't seem the type."

"I agree. A nice, quiet guy," Jason Keely said. "It's still murder, though."

Beckwith said to Shannon, "Clint, everything points to Faro. He had a strong motive, and the opportunity. He was on the scene. And he took Jason to the exact spot where he threw away the murder gun, but when the gun was really found he denied that it was his—claimed his gun was a Harrington and Richardson nine-shot .22 pistol, but that didn't cut any ice with me. *He knew the spot.* Also, he claimed he was wearing gloves that night, but that he had lost them. We took a paraffin test of his hands anyhow. Negative. I don't know why he admitted wearing gloves. Maybe he was confused and told the truth without thinking. But if he *was* wearing gloves you can bet he got rid of them, because the powder marks would be on them."

The police chief leaned forward and went on in a lowered voice. "There's one thing that clinches it—for me, anyhow. Horner was killed in the parking lot behind Connie's market, as you know. Faro was seen there, just before Horner was shot. We have witnesses. Also, Faro bought a package of peanuts from a vending machine and stood around eating them until Faro left. Apparently he knew Horner by sight, but Horner did not know him. All right. Horner left, Faro followed. Boom, boom, boom. And near Horner's body, at the spot where the killer must have stood, was a little wax paper bag with a few peanuts still in it. The lab men found it, but they couldn't lift any prints, which doesn't mean a thing to me—it was the only peanut package found on the premises. It points to—"

The telephone began to ring. "I'll get it," Celia called from the kitchen. In a moment she appeared and said to Shannon, "It's Mrs. Newmyer. Her husband just fell down the basement steps. He's in pain and she's afraid to move him."

Shannon got swiftly to his feet. "Tell her to keep him quiet. I'll be right

there."

"Right." Celia hurried back to the kitchen.

"Sorry," Shannon said to Beckwith and Keely. "Stay and finish your drinks."

"I want to talk to you later," Beckwith said.

"All right." Shannon walked quickly down the short hall to a closet, put on a topcoat and entered the kitchen where he picked up his bag from the floor by the door.

Celia turned away from the phone. "While you were sleeping I took your bag to the office and Lucille stocked it again. All of your penicillin was gone."

"Good girl. I'll be at Newmyer's first, and then probably the hospital." Shannon hurried out to the garage, got into the Ford and backed out of the drive.

Captain Jason Keely drove the police car back to the station from Doctor Shannon's house. Chief Beckwith sat beside him smoking a cigar. Beckwith said, "I forgot to tell you that Tom Delgrado called me today. Told me about selling that old car to you—and about Horner calling him Wednesday night."

Keely sighed. "I guess Jack thought he had something on me. By the way, can I claim the car now?"

"Yes, we're finished with it."

"The girls have been pestering me about it. I told them I was buying it for them and they were pretty unhappy when it was stolen before I even got it home from Delgrado's lot."

"I can imagine," Beckwith said, and added, "Donegal's car was hot, but I'll bet he wouldn't have picked that old Plymouth to steal if he'd known it belonged to a police captain." He laughed softly.

"Owens probably stole it," Keely said. "It was my own fault, I guess. On the way home from Delgrado's I stopped at Ricco's Café for a—uh— for some cigars. I shouldn't have left the key in it, but I was only inside for a couple of minutes."

"You should have reported it stolen, though."

"Hell, I only paid fifty bucks for it," Keely said. "And how would it look in the papers? Police Captain's car stolen?"

Beckwith laughed. "I see what you mean."

"You know, Chad," Keely said thoughtfully, "Horner *could* have had a lead on Donegal and wanted to hog the glory for himself. It was something he would do. He was real ambitious."

"Yes," Beckwith agreed.

"Okay. Maybe he stumbled onto something hot and pushed it—and got

blasted."

"No." Beckwith shook his head. "Faro's our man."

"What about Keough? His wife was cheating with Horner, too."

"Are you certain about that, Jason?"

"Certainly," Keely snapped. "I tailed Horner myself. I told you. Damn it, Chad—"

"All right, all right," Beckwith said soothingly, "but we haven't got a thing on Doctor Keough. As far as we know he was unaware of Horner's attentions to his wife. He would therefore have no motive."

"Maybe he found out," Keely said.

"We don't know if he did. And he was not seen at Connie's place that evening. Faro was."

"I still think we ought to talk to Keough," Keely said stubbornly. "He could have been hiding in the parking lot waiting for Horner."

"Jason," Beckwith said patiently, "we know that Faro learned on Wednesday morning that his wife had been seeing John Horner. We know that he left his apartment on Wednesday evening with a gun. Those facts are a matter of record. I can't go to Keough and say, 'Look, Doctor, we know your wife has been cheating with another man. Where were you on Wednesday evening between ten and eleven o'clock?' I can't do that—not yet, at least."

"You mean that what Keough doesn't know won't hurt him?"

"That's right, Jason. Far be it from me—"

"But what if he did know?"

"I've thought of that, but we have absolutely no indication that he did. Jason, without any evidence or reason for suspicion, I can't question a man and maybe break up his marriage. If I had reason, yes. But I think Faro will crack."

"Okay," Keely said, "but what the hell were Keough and his wife doing at Horner's funeral this afternoon?"

"What?" Beckwith asked sharply.

"Didn't you see them?"

"No."

"I did. They were still standing by the grave, both of them, when everybody was leaving."

Beckwith puffed thoughtfully on his cigar. "Why would they attend Horner's funeral?"

"It looks queer," Keely said. "Damned queer."

"Maybe they were friends of the Horners, for all we know, only Keough wasn't aware that Horner was more than a friend to his wife."

Keely made a snorting sound of derision.

"Well," Beckwith said, "I'll keep it in mind—and maybe have a little

talk with Keough, as tactfully as possible."

"And while you're at it, why not question Mrs. Faro some more? She may have learned that she was not the only lady friend Horner was seeing. She would have stood still for a wife, because she's married too, but maybe not for another woman. She could have killed him because of jealousy."

Beckwith shook his head. "No, I don't think so. That Mrs. Kennedy, the landlady, said that Mrs. Faro did not leave the apartment last Wednesday night."

"She could have sneaked out," Keely said stubbornly.

"That outside stairway is the only exit. Don't worry, snoopy Mrs. Kennedy would have spotted her." Beckwith said.

"It's not that I'm not trying to defend Faro," Keely said, "but I've been a cop for a long time and I've seen evidence pile up before—on the wrong man."

"So have I," Beckwith said quietly, "but Faro will get a fair deal."

"It would help if he'd confess."

"Give him time. He's still pretty sick." Beckwith drew on his cigar and added, "I meant to tell you before, Jason; I talked to the mayor today, and the president of council. We'd like you to continue as captain until further notice."

He smiled at Keely. "Does that suit you? I know you want to stay in harness for a while."

"It suits me fine. I'll be glad to stay on as long as you need me."

"Good."

"There's one thing bothering me," Keely said. "If Donegal really got away with forty-two thousand, the money we found is about ten thousand short."

"I've been thinking about that, too, Jason. At first I figured that maybe Dick Eversole at the loan company had miscounted, or maybe even padded the total, hoping to collect the extra money from the insurance company. Dick's a sharp operator, you know. But he couldn't very well do that, because the insurance people would want proof. Also, I remembered that the loss is only covered for twenty-five thousand. So that angle is out. I think now that Donegal stashed away the extra ten thousand—holding out on his partner, that Owens, you see? The money could be hidden out there on the swamp some place."

Keely stopped the car for a red light. "Maybe you're right. Anyhow, we've got Donegal and the kid and a big chunk of the money. Has Donegal made any kind of statement?"

"You know he hasn't. You were there when we interrogated him." Beckwith smiled. "That's a good police word."

"Then you haven't talked to him alone?"

"No. Why should I? He'll be off our hands by tonight. The Indiana police are picking him up, but I'd like to try again to get him to talk, maybe tell where he hid the rest of the money—if he did hide it. Then Indiana is welcome to him."

"You want him in your office?" Keely asked, as the light changed to green and the car moved forward.

"Yes. I want you there, too, Jason."

"Okay." Keely drove two blocks and turned into the parking area behind the police station. The cells were in a wing of the building bordering this section and in good weather prisoners were often led across the court from the cells rather than down the long corridor leading to the squad room and the ranking policemen's offices. As Keely and Beckwith got out of the car, Keely said, "I'll get him for you."

"You'd better take somebody with you."

"Hell, I can handle him."

"All right, but be careful." Beckwith entered the station and paused a moment to talk to several citizens standing by the desk paying parking fines.

Then Beckwith moved on back toward his office. On the way he stopped and spoke to a young policeman just reporting for duty. It was George Romano, who had helped Captain Keely search the creek for Myron Faro's revolver.

"George, go across to the jail and accompany Captain Keely. He's bringing a prisoner to my office."

"Right, Chief." Romano hurried away.

Beckwith was almost to the door of his office when he heard the shots, two of them, close together. They were not loud, but they sounded like the *bam, bam!* of a police revolver. He swung around and walked swiftly back. The door to the parking area was open and Officer Romano stood there, his service revolver poised in his hand, the muzzle up-tilted. At first Beckwith thought that Romano had fired the shots, and then he saw Captain Keely standing alone in the court. Beckwith brushed Romano aside and ran out. Keely stood swaying, his right hand holding his left arm at a point just above the wrist, his teeth bared in pain. At his feet was a man in a brown leather jacket, his legs sprawled awkwardly, his left arm doubled under him, his right arm flung outward. There was a white bandage on the right wrist. The man's face was turned away, but Beckwith knew it was Steve Donegal. A police revolver lay at Donegal's feet.

Beckwith reached Keely. "Jason! Are you all right?"

"No. Hit in the arm. He—he made a break...." Keely was panting. "I

grabbed him, got my gun out. He tried to get the gun, twisted my arm. It fired, hit me. Then he jumped away and I shot him, close range. I—"

Beckwith whirled and bawled at Romano. "Get the captain inside." Then he knelt by the fallen man, gently turned him over and felt for a pulse. There was none. Beckwith knelt there, aware of movement and voices around him.

"I saw it, Chief," Romano said excitedly. "I opened the door just when Donegal made the break. I saw him—"

"Shut up!" Beckwith roared as he stood erect. "Do as I say!"

Romano gulped and led Captain Keely into the station. Other policemen were there, waiting for Beckwith's orders. A curious crowd gathered from the street. Beckwith stooped to pick up Keely's police revolver and spoke to the two nearest policemen. "He's dead. Carry him inside." Then he turned to the crowd and said angrily, "Move on, move on, the show's over." He turned abruptly and entered the station behind the two officers carrying the body of Steve

Donegal. "Put him on the bed in the dispensary for now," he ordered.

"Yes, sir," one of the officers said.

Captain Jason Keely was lying on a bunk in the squad room propped up with pillows. His coat had been removed and his left shirt sleeve rolled up. A young officer with a first aid kit was already applying a bandage to Keely's forearm.

"Is it bad?" Beckwith asked.

"Just a crease," the young officer said, "and some powder burn."

"I'll take you to a doctor, Jason," Beckwith said.

"Hell, I'm all right." Keely hunched upward on an elbow. "What about Donegal?"

"He's dead."

Keely sank back and sighed. "I'm sorry, Chad. I couldn't help it. I had him by the arm and all of a sudden he jerked away. I grabbed him, got my gun out, but he twisted my arm and the gun went off, and I—"

"I know," Beckwith broke in. "Romano saw it all. Don't feel badly." He paused and added grimly, "You just saved the State of Indiana the cost of a trial." He peered at Keely. "You look kind of pale, though. I'll take you to a doctor. You should at least have a tetanus shot."

"If you say so, Chad." Keely said.

The desk sergeant appeared in the doorway. "Want me to call Doctor Shannon, Chief?"

"No. He's on an emergency call. I'll take Captain Keely to Doctor Kovici."

"I mean for Donegal."

"Hell, I don't need a coroner to tell me how Donegal died. All Shannon

has to do is sign the death certificate."

"Yes, sir." The sergeant went away.

Later, as Beckwith drove Keely to Doctor Kovici's office, he said, "You should have used cuffs on Donegal."

Keely sighed. "Yes, I suppose so. But his right wrist was bandaged, and it was only a few feet from the jail to the station. I never thought he'd make a break for it."

"He had nothing to lose," Beckwith said.

"I guess you're right."

"Jason, we've worked together for a long time. How many men have you killed in the line of duty? Donegal was the third, wasn't he?"

Keely nodded soberly.

"You're one up on me now." Beckwith sighed as he spoke.

"We have a nasty job, don't we?"

"Somebody's got to do it."

"Amen," Beckwith said.

19

Saturday Evening

The news spread fast that Steve Donegal, notorious criminal and gunman, had been shot and killed while attempting to escape from a police officer. Reporters from as far away as Cleveland, Toledo and Detroit telephoned Chief Beckwith for details and the following morning Captain Jason Keely was a hero on the pages of dozens of Sunday papers. The wire services picked it up and the news went clicking out over the nation. Two plainclothesmen, on their way to Harbor City to get Donegal and take him back to Indiana for trial, heard it on the car radio and looked at each other in amazement.

"What'll we do?" one asked. "Turn around and go back?"

"Heck, no. Use your head. We don't know anything about it until we get to Harbor City, see? Then I'll call South Bend and report it. That way we'll collect our allowance for meals and a hotel room tonight and go back in the morning."

"But we could make it back to South Bend before midnight," the other said dubiously. "It's only about two hundred miles from here."

"Yeah, and it's only twenty-five or thirty miles to Harbor City. Besides, we ought to talk to the chief there, get an official statement and go through the red tape. We're on an expense sheet, remember? We'll have us some fun tonight. Maybe those Harbor City cops can line up a

couple of women."

"I don't want any woman."

"Go to a movie or something then," the other said disgustedly.

News spread fast in Harbor City and Doctor Shannon learned of Donegal's death from an orderly at the hospital. As soon as he could leave his patient, Mr. Newmyer, he telephoned Chief Beckwith, who gave him a brief account of the incident, including the fact that Captain Keely had been slightly wounded, and ended by saying, "Can you come down here, Clint? The body's at Hoyt's but you won't have to see it, unless you want to. All I need is your name on the death certificate."

"I'll come as soon as I can." Shannon returned to Mr. Newmyer, stayed with him ten minutes longer and then left, after giving instructions to the special nurse on duty. He called his wife from the hospital and told her he'd be home after his visit to the police station.

"But you haven't eaten yet!"

"I'll eat when I get home."

"Will you have to go back to the hospital."

"Probably."

"Oh, my," Celia sighed.

"You should have married a dermatologist. Office hours by appointment, nine to five. No emergencies, no night calls. And your patients never die and they never get well."

"Oh, pooh," Celia said. "Have you heard about that—that gangster being killed? After Captain Keely was wounded?"

"Yes. That's why I've got to see Beckwith. Any calls?"

"A few, none important. I wrote 'em down. Nothing for you to do tonight."

"Good. See you soon, I hope."

Shannon drove to the police station. When he entered Chief Beckwith's office he was surprised to see Captain Keely there. "I thought you'd be home taking it easy," he said to Keely.

"Just a crease," the police captain said carelessly. "John Kovici fixed me up."

"Good." Shannon turned to Beckwith. "I want to go home and eat. Let's get this over with."

"It won't take long," Beckwith said. "I knew you were tied up, and I asked Kovici to examine the body." He pushed a blue form across the desk. "It's all there. Death from a bullet wound in the aorta. The left ventricle—"

"John's statement is good enough for me." Shannon removed the cap from a fountain pen and signed the form. "Is that all this evening,

Chad?"

"One thing more; has Mrs. Faro asked you to take care of her husband?"

"No."

"He was your patient, wasn't he?"

"Yes, but I told you John Kovici's on the case now. Apparently the Faros are satisfied. John called me about it."

"Ethics, huh?" Beckwith asked softly. "You won't go near Faro now—unless asked. Is that it?"

Shannon nodded. "John suggested that perhaps they would want me, now that I'm available again, as it were, but she asked him to stay on since he was good enough to respond to the emergency. I've told my nurse to give Faro's record to John."

"So they're switching doctors?"

"It would seem so." Shannon grinned. "But it's all right. John's patients switch to me, too. It also happens to the other men in town. People shop around for doctors, you know."

"Some people," Beckwith said. "Sometimes because they owe money to one and are ashamed to call him when they need him. So they go to another doctor. Isn't that right?"

"That happens," Shannon said. "Not Myron Faro, though. He was billed once a month and I had a check in the mail the next day. He was a very good patient in all respects. A quiet, pleasant man. And fully cooperative, which is important with an ulcer case. The diet is strict." Shannon moved toward the door, then turned, snapped his fingers and stopped. "Diet. That reminds me," he said to Beckwith. "It's been bothering me since you and Jason were at my house—before I was called away. You said you had a witness who saw Myron Faro buy a package of peanuts and eat them just before John Horner was shot. That doesn't make sense to me, Chad."

"Why not?" Beckwith asked sharply. "That package is important evidence."

Shannon moved his head slowly from side to side. "Your witness is mistaken. Myron Faro would never eat peanuts. They were strictly forbidden, and he knew it."

"Maybe he disobeyed doctor's orders," Beckwith said.

"Not Faro. He wanted to get well. Who is the witness?"

Beckwith nodded at Keely and said quietly, "Jason saw him do it, Clint."

Shannon turned to Keely. "Are you certain?"

"I sure am," Keely said, nodding. "Of course, somebody else could have dropped a peanut package in the parking lot behind Connie's place, but

it was the only one the lab men found—and Faro had the package when he left. Figure it out."

"Maybe Faro bought mints, or chewing gun," Shannon said.

"No," Keely said stubbornly. "Peanuts. I saw him."

Shannon shrugged. "All right. It's too late now to run any tests on the contents of Myron Faro's stomach and bowels last Wednesday night, but I'd swear in court that he did not eat any peanuts."

"You calling me a liar, Clint?" Keely's voice was mild, but his eyes held a sudden hardness.

"Of course not. I just think you are mistaken." Shannon turned back to Beckwith. "I'm not trying to defend Faro. The other evidence seems conclusive, but it's circumstantial. Faro took you to the spot where he said he threw the gun away. The gun you found is the gun which killed Horner?"

"Beyond doubt."

"But Faro claims the gun is not his, not the one he threw into the creek?"

"He claims that, yes."

"But if you searched the creek again and found the gun Faro said he threw in, would that prove him innocent?"

"It would be strong evidence in his favor," Beckwith admitted.

"Then you'd better search again," Shannon said. "Faro is entitled to that much."

"*Two* guns?" Beckwith said incredulously. "Hell, Clint, that's silly."

"Think it over." Shannon nodded at the two men and left.

There was silence in the office for a moment, and then Beckwith sighed heavily and said, "Maybe Clint's right."

"Maybe," Keely said, "but Romano and I searched the creek beneath the bridge pretty thoroughly. There was only one gun."

"It won't do any harm to look again. It's too late today—you can't do a good job in the dark, even with floodlights. Why don't you take a crew out there in the morning and search every inch of the creek bed near the bridge? It's fairly shallow there, isn't it?"

"Yes," Keely said. "Muddy, though."

"Maybe it'll be more clear in the morning, if we don't get any more rain. Take six or eight men. I don't think you'll find anything, but at least we'll have given Faro that much of a break."

Keely shrugged. "Okay, Chad. Nine, ten o'clock early enough?"

"Suit yourself. There's no tearing rush." Beckwith grinned crookedly. "I guess maybe I'm just doing this for Clint—if you leave Faro out of it. After all, Clint's the coroner. How does your arm feel, Jason?"

"Burns a little yet."

"Don't you go splashing around in the water with that wound. Let the men do it."

Keely laughed. "Don't worry. I've had enough of that creek." He stood up, moving his left arm carefully. "Guess I'll knock off for the day."

"You'd better. It's been kind of rough for you."

"The same for you."

Beckwith shook his head and said quietly, "I didn't get wounded in the line of duty. I wasn't forced to kill a man. I know how you feel, Jason, but try not to let it worry you. It couldn't be helped."

"Did you notify South Bend?"

"Yes. Their men are on their way to pick up Donegal. I called as soon as I could to tell them he was dead, but they had already left. I'll stick around to see them. Besides, it's Saturday night."

"Hell, let the men handle the drunks and the saloon fights."

"I would, if we still had Horner on duty. He was a good cop, Jason, in spite of his personal life."

"I agree," Keely said. "Well, goodnight, Chad."

"Goodnight. Call me at home tomorrow if you find anything out there in the creek."

"I will, but don't hold your breath. We'll give it a good try. If there's another gun there, we'll find it." Keely nodded and left the office. Before he went home he had two doubles ryes at Rico's Café. There was pain in his chest again and the whisky helped to soothe it somewhat.

Saturday Evening

Nelson Keough, M.D., gazed uneasily at his wife, Betty, who sat across the table drinking her second Martini. They were in the main dining room of the Perry Hotel in downtown Harbor City. After their return from John Horner's funeral Betty had immediately arranged for an elderly widow lady who lived nearby to stay with the children. Then she had looked in the Work Wanted ads in the morning paper and had contracted for another lady to do housework three days a week, Monday, Wednesday and Friday. Then she had consented to accept a glass of her husband's sherry (there had been no beer in the refrigerator, after all) and had insisted upon drinking it in his study, his sanctuary, where she sat in the leather chair, the throne.

Betty's strange new behavior had angered Dr. Keough at first, but when he realized how serious she was, how firm and confident, he decided to humor her, for the immediate present, at least, partly because he was truly ashamed of his actions in the cemetery that afternoon. It

was after the funeral that Betty had changed from the obedient but untidy and careless wife to the creature she now was; cool, demanding, impossibly sure of herself. Keough was uneasy, even fearful, but determined to regain the upper hand.

He said briskly, "We'll order now, Betty. Would you like the prime ribs, or the chicken?"

"I would like another Martini. When it comes I will order my dinner." Betty spoke very precisely. She was not accustomed to Martinis.

"All right," Keough said, controlling himself, "but what do you want to eat?"

"The beef, rare, mashed potatoes and lots of gravy, hearts of lettuce with Italian dressing. Creamed peas. For dessert I would like the strawberry shortcake and whipped cream. I read the menu, Nelson."

Dr. Keough motioned to their waitress, asked her to bring another Martini and another sherry, although he really did not want any more wine. When the drinks came he ordered their dinner, chicken for himself. When the waitress had left, he said, "Let's be sensible, Betty."

She lifted her small, round shoulders. "All right, Nelson, you just go ahead and be sensible."

"You've done a very bad thing. I want you to realize—"

"Oh, shut up," Betty said crossly. "You did a bad thing, too."

"But not what you did!" Keough hunched forward, his eyes burning. "You must understand that what—" He stopped abruptly, realizing that a senseless bickering at this time was futile. He took a deep breath and started over. "Betty, I'm sorry I forced you to attend the funeral. I have explained my reason for it, and hope that you are mature enough to understand. Now we must think of us, of the children, what we're going to do. Divorce is not the answer. I can't afford any scandal now, just when I'm getting started here. I'll do my best to forget what you did. It's all I can do. But in return you must try and accept your responsibilities as a mother, as the wife of a physician, and conduct yourself properly. If we are to save our—"

The waitress brought the drinks then and Dr. Keough waited until she had left before he went on. "If we are to save our marriage there are certain terms we must discuss."

"I have told you my terms." Betty spoke even more precisely now. She picked up her fresh drink and smiled slyly over the rim of the glass. "Part of them are already in effect. I have a woman to do housework. I have another woman to stay with the children when I want to go out. I have a Martini. We are dining in a nice hotel. The only bad thing right now is that you made me go to Jack's—to that funeral."

Dr. Keough's face went white. "Don't push me, Betty," he said in a low,

intense voice.

Betty smiled serenely, drank from her glass and said, "I think I would like another Martini with my dinner."

"No. You've had too many now."

"I'll scream." Still Betty smiled.

"You tramp," Keough said, losing control. "You dirty little tramp."

At that moment the waitress brought their soup and Betty spoke to her politely. "Would you please bring me another Martini, extra dry?"

"Yes, ma'am." The waitress glanced at Dr. Keough, who waved her away impatiently.

Betty took a spoonful of soup. "Oh, chicken and rice. Delicious."

"You're drunk, Betty," Keough said. "Try and behave yourself."

"Hmm." Betty spooned the soup daintily. "Try some, Nelson." She placed the spoon beside the bowl and buttered a cracker. "Did Jack know that it was you who shot him? I mean, did he recognize you before he died?"

"For God's sake, I didn't kill him!" There was sweat on Keough's high, white forehead.

"You said you were going to," Betty said pleasantly. "The night you whipped me with your belt you said you were going to kill him. Murder is worse than what I did."

"You're drunk," Keough said again. "I'll take you home."

"Oh, no, Nelson. I want my dinner and another drink. Then I want to see a good movie, a love story. One is playing at the Riverview. I saw it advertised in the paper. There are also two cartoons. You know how I love cartoons."

"No," Keough said harshly. "We're going home and have this out. Where did you get the ridiculous notion that I killed that man?"

"I just guessed it, Nelson," Betty said precisely, giving him a bright, glassy smile. "Please eat your soup. It will be cold."

Dr. Keough felt the wild, unreasoning rage which had overcome him at the cemetery when the laborer had refused to lower the casket while they were present. He remembered the slap on his cheek and he hated the man, and he hated his wife for causing it all. He started a harsh, bitter speech but checked himself with an effort; their dinners were being served.

"Don't you want your soup, sir?" the waitress asked.

Dr. Keough shook his head and silently permitted her to remove the bowl and serve the meal. He merely toyed with the chicken, but his wife ate the beef hungrily. "My goodness," Betty said between mouthfuls, "those Martinis certainly gave me an appetite. I think I will have them every evening before dinner from now on." She poised her fork and

smiled at him across the table. "Please eat your food, Nelson, and please stop looking so grim. You won't enjoy the movie on an empty stomach."

"We're not going to the movie. We're going home and have a talk."

Betty Keough smiled and her eyes were oddly soft. "You must humor me, Nelson." She still spoke precisely. "I am pregnant."

He stiffened. "You can't be!"

"Maybe it will be a girl, Nelson. You always wanted a girl."

Dr. Keough pressed palms to his eyes. Horner's child, he thought. It had to be. She had admitted seeing Horner since the previous September. He peered at his wife from between spread fingers and muttered, "How far along?"

"You know I'm not good at keeping track of things, Nelson," she said plaintively. "It's two months, maybe three." Then she smiled at him. "We have three boys and we always wanted a girl. Maybe it *will* be a girl this time."

"Just don't talk anymore." Keough fluttered thin, pale hands. "Just be quiet. I—I've got to think." He was breathing heavily.

Keough couldn't eat, but Betty finished her dinner serenely, licked up the last of the shortcake, dabbed at her small mouth with a napkin and announced, "The feature starts at eight o'clock, Nelson."

"No movie, Betty, please," he pleaded.

"But I want to go," she said firmly.

He shouted, "All right, all right!" and was immediately ashamed. Other patrons in the dining room were staring at him in startled curiosity. He summoned the waitress, paid the check and took his wife to the movie. Before the feature picture began, Betty went to sleep. Dr. Keough sat stiffly beside her, afraid to awaken her. In her present mood she might make a scene. He had never seen Betty really drunk and her cool, precise manner had surprised him. Knowing her as he thought he did, he had expected her to be hilarious and giggly, as she had been on a few occasions in the past, but her reaction to the cocktails had been exactly the opposite. It worried him. And the remarks she had made worried him. And was she really pregnant?

He thought grimly that when he had Betty home he would give her a pelvic examination, if he had to tie her down, and that would be that, one way or the other. But there was nothing he could do about her accusation of murder, not at the present. Perhaps he should not have pushed her so far at the cemetery, but he had really felt that she needed it, for her own good. If only that stupid laborer had not interfered. Zeller, that was his name.

Nelson Keough, M.D., did not see the brilliant moving images on the

screen. He sat in a kind of a stupor beside his sleeping wife and his thoughts circled endlessly.

20

Sunday Morning, Early

Dr. Clinton Shannon slept soundly until six in the morning, when he had a telephone call from a family who lived in the country on Duckpond Road. One of the children, an eight-year-old boy, had been suffering severe abdominal pain since the evening before. Shannon asked a few questions, decided tentatively that it was appendicitis, and said he would come right out. He wanted to examine the boy before sending him to the hospital for tests and possible surgery. He told his wife, Celia, who had also been awakened by the phone, where he was going and that there was no need for her to get up. She protested weakly and was asleep before he finished dressing. He had a glass of orange juice and a cup of instant coffee and was on his way by six-twenty.

The family in the farm house on Duckpond Road greeted him anxiously. A brief examination of the boy confirmed the doctor's tentative diagnosis. He called the hospital in Harbor City, gave instructions and made arrangements and then said to the boy's parents, "It's appendicitis, all right, but I want to do a blood count and make some other tests." He smiled at the man and woman. "Don't worry. It's not serious. Take him to the hospital and I'll be there a little later."

"Whatever you say, Doc," the man said. "We'll take him right away. He can stretch out on the back seat."

Shannon reassured the parents again and left. On the way back to the city, as he crossed the bridge over Deer Creek, he saw a man wearing high fisherman's boots and carrying a long-handled garden rake wading slowly and unsteadily from the middle of the stream toward the bank. An old gray Plymouth sedan was parked by the road on the opposite side of the bridge. It had not been there when Shannon had crossed the bridge earlier. He did not recognize the car but as he reached the end of the bridge he saw that the man in the water was Captain of Police Jason Keely. Shannon slowed his car and stopped beside the Plymouth. Keely appeared to be unaware of Shannon's presence as he reached the bank and stumbled up the slope, his head down, the rubber boots slipping on the grass. Once he fell flat, lay there a moment, and then pushed himself upward and lurched on. Shannon frowned, got out of his Ford, moved to the side of the road and peered down. "Hello, Jason," he called.

Keely stopped and squinted up at the doctor in the bright, early-morning sunlight. He stood unsteadily, holding his left hand behind him and did not speak. Shannon said curiously, "Up kind of early, aren't you, Jason?"

Keely stared at him stupidly and still did not speak.

"What's the matter?" the doctor asked sharply. "Are you all right, Jason?"

"Sure." Keely drew in a deep breath. "I'm fine." His voice was thick and he peered uneasily from side to side, avoiding Shannon's gaze.

"So you took my advice about searching the creek again?" Shannon asked.

"Yeah, yeah," Keely said.

"You should have brought men to help."

"They—they're coming later. Thought I'd come on ahead and get started." Keely waved the rake. "Get started, see?"

Shannon's frown grew deeper. He knew that Keely was a heavy drinker, although he had never actually seen him drunk. But the police captain was drunk now, the doctor knew, at seven o'clock in the morning. Shannon said, "I don't quite understand this."

"Just mind your own business." Keely gazed at Shannon directly now and his voice was ugly. "Just go on about your business."

"Jason, you're drunk. Let me take you home. You can send someone for your car."

"Hell with you," Keely said thickly. "Mind own business." There was a stubble of white beard on his ruddy, bloated face and his red-lidded eyes were pink-veined and watery.

"You're in no shape to drive," Shannon said gently.

Anger flamed in Keely's eyes. "By God, Clint, if you don't get the hell out of here I'll hit you with this rake!"

"You wouldn't do that," Shannon said, smiling. "We're friends." He stepped forward and touched Keely's arm.

Keely jerked away and stood swaying on the sloping bank. His left hand was still at his back and he held the rake handle in his right, the steel prongs resting on the soft creek bank. Shannon smelled the whisky fumes in the soft morning air. "Go away," Keely said from between his teeth. "Right now. You hear?"

Shannon shook his head slowly. "No, Jason. If you want to get drunk, that's your business. But I'd hate to see you have an accident. In the shape you're in ..."

Keely took a deep, shuddering breath, squared his shoulders in an attempt to steady himself, but weaved on his feet. And still he held his left hand behind him. "I can drive all right. Been drunker than this and

drived—drove."

"Did you find another gun in the creek?" Shannon asked.

"Hell, no. That was your dumb idea. If it wasn't for you, I wouldn't be here. We found Faro's gun, the one he killed Horner with, the only goddamned gun in the creek."

For several minutes Shannon had been aware that Keely was concealing something behind him. He moved sideways to peer around Keely, but the police chief turned quickly to face him. "Damn it, Clint, I—I'm warning you." He was panting and lifted the rake menacingly. "Go on about your business."

"Chad won't like this, Jason."

"He knows I get drunk once in a while."

"But he doesn't know you're out here by yourself this morning. What are you holding behind you, Jason?"

Keely cursed and swung the rake viciously. Shannon moved quickly, grasped for the rake, missed, and stumbled on the grassy slope. Keely whirled and swung the rake like a saber and Shannon felt a stir of air as the prongs whistled past his face. Anger struck him then and he lunged for Keely, reached for the rake. Keely turned, lost his footing and stumbled backward, flailing his arms in an attempt to keep his balance, but sprawled on his back at the water's edge. Shannon saw the dark metallic glint of the gun in Keely's hand and leaped forward, wrenched the gun from Keely's grasp. Then he stood erect and backed away, holding the gun. Keely floundered on the bank, and then struggled slowly to his feet. He stood with his head down, shaking it from side to side, as if to clear his brain.

Shannon gazed at the gun, a long-barreled, small-caliber revolver which balanced nicely in his hand. Ignoring Keely, who still seemed dazed and bewildered, Shannon peered closely at the gun, flicked out the cylinder. There were nine chambers and each held a cartridge. None had been fired. Engraved on the left side of the barrel were the words MODEL 929 H & R INC. WORCESTER, MASS. U.S.A. Shannon clicked the cylinder shut and said to Keely, "This is a Harrington and Richardson nine-shot .22—the exact gun Myron Faro said he threw into the creek."

Captain Keely looked up at Shannon. He seemed to be having trouble breathing. "Clint, I—" He paused, gasping for breath. "I—I'm sick." He clawed at his chest with both hands and sank slowly to the grass.

Shannon went to him instantly, knelt down and felt Keely's pulse. It was rapid and irregular. He lowered the captain to the grass, loosened the shirt collar and said gently, "Take it easy, Jason." Then he hurried up the bank to his car and returned with his bag.

Keely gazed up at Shannon, fear in his eyes. "My—my heart, Clint?"

Shannon nodded as he filled a hypodermic needle. "Just lie quietly."

"Pain ..." Keely gasped. "Left arm ..."

Shannon jerked open the stricken man's coat, ripped the shirt, inserted the needle and depressed the plunger. Above him he heard the rumble of planks on the bridge as a car crossed. He stood up and waved his arms. The car stopped and Shannon went up to the road. It was the farmer and his wife taking their son to the hospital. The boy was on the rear seat covered by a blanket, his mother beside him. The couple stared at him and the man said, "What's wrong, Doc?"

"I've got a sick man here. Stop at the next place and call Harbor City for an ambulance. Tell them to bring oxygen. Hoyt has it. Hurry."

The man asked no questions. "Okay, Doc." The car zoomed away.

Shannon went back down the grassy slope to the creek bank and knelt once more beside Jason Keely. A soft morning breeze sprang up and rippled the water of the creek, plucked gently at the budding willows. Birds sang in the willows and the sunlight sparkled. Keely's face was gray and composed. His eyes fluttered open and his lips moved. "Clint," he whispered, "am I—dying?"

"No, Jason. You'll be all right."

"Don't—don't kid me. Had these spells before. Did—didn't tell anybody. Bad, huh?"

"I don't know yet. Just be quiet. An ambulance is coming."

"Tell—tell Chad I—I'm sorry."

"Don't talk now, Jason."

"Got to. Been a good cop all my life. Went—went bad at the end. I ..." Keely's voice weakened and he mumbled thickly, the words blurred together. Shannon's fingers were on Keely's wrist and his eyes were intense. Keely stirred and his lips moved. Shannon leaned close, barely heard the whispered words. "I—I killed Horner."

Sunday Noon

Chief of Police Chad Beckwith and Dr. Clinton Shannon sat in the hospital cafeteria drinking coffee. Beckwith's broad face was drawn and his eyes were bleak. He sighed heavily and said, "He really went bad."

"So he made a full confession?" Shannon asked.

Beckwith nodded. "He thinks he's dying. Will he?"

"It was a pretty bad attack."

"Coronary?"

"A big one. He's had mild attacks before, but didn't tell anyone."

Beckwith sighed again. "When you nabbed him out there alone with

Faro's gun, he knew he didn't have a chance. And the heart attack
clinched it, made him want to repent his sins, I guess. We have it all on
record."

"Poor Jason."

"Poor Jason, hell," Beckwith said bitterly. "He killed Steve Donegal,
too—in cold blood."

Shannon was startled. "But I thought Donegal tried to escape."

"It looked that way to anyone watching, but what Jason really did was
push Donegal away and shoot him dead. Then he laid the gun muzzle
on his arm and grazed himself—to make it look good. He told it all. You
see, Jason needed money. He was being forced to retire and had saved
nothing; in fact, he was heavily in debt. He met and recognized Donegal
in Ricco's Cafe and together they set up the loan-company robbery.
Jason's cut was ten thousand. It was in his locker at the station—as safe
a place as any to hide it. Jason arranged for the hide-out on the marsh
and promised Donegal protection until the heat was off. He bought an
old car for Donegal's use, because Donegal's own car was hot, and
promised him protection. He told Donegal to buy their food and supplies
at Connie's Corner and was on hand where they came in—to make
certain that no other officer became suspicious or interfered. But John
Horner did both. He learned that the old Plymouth, driven by a strange
suspicious character, had been purchased by Jason and suspected the
truth. He accused Jason, said he was going to tell me. So Jason waited
for Horner behind Connie's and shot him."

"But why did he kill Donegal?" Shannon asked. "Was he afraid that
Donegal, after his capture, would implicate him?"

Beckwith nodded. "Donegal wanted Jason to help him escape from jail.
Jason refused because he was afraid—he'd taken too many chances
already. Donegal threatened to spill the whole deal, drag Jason down
with him. So Jason had to get rid of him."

"And Jason tried to pin Horner's murder on Myron Faro?"

"That's right." Beckwith finished his coffee and lit a cigar. "Faro was
a natural for framing. Only Jason overdid it—with that business about
the peanuts. He didn't know then that Faro had an ulcer and was on a
strict diet. You questioned that, but it didn't seem important to me at
the time. I just figured that Faro liked peanuts and had disobeyed your
orders. And everything still pointed to him."

"What about the gun Jason used on Horner?"

"It was an old .32 Jason bought one time at a pawnshop in Toledo. It
couldn't be traced to him. He started carrying it right after he made the
deal with Donegal. Jason was smart enough to know that a thing like
that could go sour, anything could happen. He didn't trust Donegal and

wanted protection—other than a police revolver. When Faro said he'd thrown his gun into Deer Creek, Jason pretended to search the creek. He faked the finding of a gun, his own, the .32 he'd killed Horner with. Then, yesterday, when I decided to have the creek searched again— thanks to you, Clint—Jason got panicky. If Faro's gun was really in the creek he didn't want it found, for obvious reasons. He started drinking and then, early this morning, he went to Deer Creek alone to look for Faro's gun. He found it, just as you came along. That ruined it for Jason." Beckwith paused and drew thoughtfully on his cigar.

Shannon sighed and stood up. "Then you're releasing Myron Faro?"

"Yes. He's been told. He asked me to call his wife, but she's moved— her ex-landlady, that Mrs. Kennedy, didn't know where." Beckwith grinned wryly. "At least, she wouldn't tell me."

"Does Mrs. Keely know about Jason?"

"Only that he had a heart attack. She's in the visitor's lounge now, waiting to see him. His daughters are there, too." Beckwith shook his head sadly. "I sure hate to tell them."

Shannon lit a cigarette and said soberly, "You may as well know, Chad; Jason can't live. It's just a matter of time."

"How much time?"

"A few hours. Tomorrow at the latest. Nothing can be done for him."

Beckwith drew on his cigar and didn't speak for a moment. Then he looked up at Shannon and said, "Maybe it's just as well."

"Yes," Shannon agreed bleakly.

Jason Keely died quietly at five minutes past ten that evening.

Sunday Afternoon

Nina Faro entered the hospital room, motioned toward the door and said to her husband, "Those—those policemen are gone."

"Yes." Myron Faro smiled up at her. "It's all right now. They have the man who killed Horner. Chief Beckwith told me."

She sat beside him on the bed and reached for his hand. Tears were on her cheeks and she couldn't speak.

"Don't cry," he said. "Didn't Chief Beckwith call you?"

"No." She touched his cheek. "I moved, and there's no phone yet. I found a nice apartment for us, near the lake. I think you'll like it."

"I'm sure I will."

"Red Buchanan called last evening, while I was packing. He wants you to reconsider. He promised—"

"What did you tell him?"

"I said you weren't interested."

"Good."

"There's something else," she said. "I met Mr. Donaldson down at the desk just now. You know—head of the school board? He said he'd heard you'd left Tip-Top and wants to talk to you about that opening for a mathematics instructor. Do you feel well enough to see him?"

"Of course." Myron Faro smiled wryly. "The word must be out already that I'm not a murderer. Go tell him to come up."

"In a moment." She averted her face and asked in a low voice, "Who—who killed him?"

"Horner?" Faro said the name without bitterness. "Chief Beckwith didn't tell me. He just said I was no longer in custody and shook my hand."

She gazed at him directly. "It doesn't matter. Do you love me?"

"Yes."

She leaned down and kissed him.

Monday Afternoon

Betty Keough noticed the gray pickup truck turn into the drive from the street, saw the lettering on its side: UNION TELEPHONE CO. Frowning, she answered a knock on the back door. A tall young man smiled at her and touched the bill of his cap. "Telephone Company, ma'am. We had a report about a phone out of order." He wore a wide leather belt from which various tools were suspended.

"You must be mistaken," Betty said. "Our phones are working all right."

"Then you have more than one phone?"

"Yes. One here in the kitchen, and another in a bedroom upstairs."

"As long as I'm here," the young man said, "I'd be glad to check them for you. My name is Zeller. Do you remember me?"

"Of course," Betty said. "You were at the cemetery on Saturday afternoon. How are you?"

"Just fine."

"I want to thank you again for what you did. It was very kind of you."

"It was nothing," Zeller said. "I just saw that you didn't want to see the coffin lowered. I hope your husband isn't sore at me."

"It doesn't matter about him. You did right."

"Thanks," Zeller said. "Was that Horner a friend of yours?"

"Yes, sort of."

"And the doctor thought you should see the coffin go down?"

"Let's not talk about it anymore."

"Sorry," Zeller said. "Is the doctor at home?"

"No."

Zeller stepped inside. "Do you want me to check the bedroom phone first?"

"Not today." Betty placed a small hand on his broad chest. "My cleaning lady is here. She comes on Monday, Wednesday and Friday."

Zeller smiled and stepped back. "Tomorrow is Tuesday. I can come back then—to check the phones. You have kids, don't you?"

"Three little boys. They take naps in the afternoon until around three-thirty."

"I'll be here about two," Zeller said. "Okay?"

"Okay," Betty said carelessly, closing the door.

Monday Afternoon

Doctor Shannon parked his car behind his office and entered by the rear door, passed through the drug room and the big room filled with X-ray equipment. It was a quarter after one and he wondered how many patients were waiting for him. There were two doors to his private office, one opening directly into the waiting room and the other into the X-ray room. This door was ajar. As Shannon entered, Lucille Sanchez, trim and neat in her white uniform, turned away from the window to face him. She smiled and said, "Good afternoon—Clint."

He placed his bag on the floor and squinted at her suspiciously. "Well," he said, "well, well."

"I have been silly. Please forgive me."

"Forget it," Shannon said, feeling a sense of relief. "How many do we have this afternoon?"

"Seven so far." She nodded at the thin neat stack of case history cards on his desk. "Mrs. Longstreet is first."

He nodded. Mrs. Longstreet was a weekly visitor. Anxiety neurosis resulting from menopause.

Shannon removed his hat and topcoat, hung them in a closet, replaced his suit coat with a starched white jacket and entered a lavatory beside the closet to wash his hands. "Send Mrs. Longstreet in," he said.

"In a moment, Clint."

He came out into the office, drying his hands on a paper towel, and regarded her curiously.

"Thank you," she said quietly.

"For what?"

"For being the man you are. For being so kind and so—so

understanding." Her dark eyes wavered for a moment, and then she gazed at him steadily. "I know now that I do not love you. But I admire you very much. There is a difference. I am fine now. I want to continue to work for you. That is all I want."

"Good. That's what I want, too. You'll find someone, Lucille. Someone will find you."

"Yes," she said softly, and again it seemed to Shannon that the word was *Sí*. "I will not fight that anymore."

"Never fight it, Lucille. And when you pick the guy, I want to look him over." Shannon grinned and added, "But please don't get married right away and leave me."

"No. I am happy now."

"Fine." He tossed the crumpled paper towel into a wastebasket beside his desk. "Let's get the show on the road."

"Shall I bring in Mrs. Longstreet?"

"*Sí*," Shannon said.

Monday Evening

Doctor and Mrs. Clinton Shannon were in their respective twin beds. Their son was asleep in his room across the hall. Celia was reading and Shannon was listening to the eleven o'clock news. Celia lowered her book and sighed. "I keep thinking about Jason Keely. What will his family do now?"

Shannon turned off the bedside radio. "He had ten thousand dollars' life insurance on his own, and a five thousand group policy through the Department. With the widow's pension it should keep them until the daughters finish high school."

"I simply can't understand why he would do such a thing. All those years on the force ..."

"He did it for money," Shannon said. "And then suddenly he was in too deep and got scared. I'm sorry about Jason."

Celia turned to face him, her eyes flashing. "Sorry? He tried to kill you with that rake!"

"He was drunk," Shannon said gently, "and desperate. He wasn't thinking straight." He reached across and touched his wife's hand. "And he's dead."

Celia sighed and said soberly, "People."

"Yes," Shannon agreed, "people."

THE END

Robert Martin Bibliography
(1908-1976)

NOVELS

Jim Bennett series:
Dark Dream (Dodd Mead, 1951; Pocket, 1952).
Sleep, My Love (Dodd Mead, 1953; Dell, 1953)
Tears for the Bride (Dodd Mead, 1954; Bantam, 1955)
The Widow and the Web (Dodd Mead, 1954; Bantam, 1955)
The Echoing Shore (Dodd Mead, 1955; Bantam, 1957, as The Tough Die Hard)
Just a Corpse at Twilight (Dodd Mead, 1955)
Catch a Killer (Dodd Mead, 1956; abridged in *Mercury Mystery Book Magazine*)
Hand-Picked for Murder (Dodd Mead, 1957)
Killer Among Us (Dodd Mead, 1958; Detective Book Club, 1959)
A Key to the Morgue (Dodd Mead, 1959; Detective Book Club, 1959; Ace, 1960)
To Have and To Kill (Dodd Mead, 1960; Ace, 1961, abridged)
She, Me and Murder (Hale UK, 1962; Curtis, 1971)
A Coffin for Two (Hale UK, 1962; Curtis, 1972)
Bargain for Death (Hale UK, 1964, Curtis, 1972)

As by Lee Roberts

Little Sister (Gold Medal, 1952)
The Pale Door (Dodd Mead, 1955; Detective Book Club, 1955; Bantam, 1956)
Judas Journey (Dodd Mead, 1956; Popular Library, 1957)
The Case of the Missing Lovers (Dodd Mead, 1957)

Dr. Clinton Shannon series:
Once a Widow (Dodd Mead, 1957; Detective Book Club, 1957; Dell, 1959)
If the Shoe Fits (Dodd Mead, 1959; Crest, 1960)
Death of a Ladies' Man (Gold Medal, 1960)
Suspicion (Hale UK, 1964; Curtis, 1971)

THE PALE DOOR

Dr. Kerry hires Chad to ke_ _ _ _ _ _ _ _ _ _ _ _ _ _
wife, who has fallen apart after the stillborn death of
their child. Chad puts his best men on the case to
keep her out of trouble while he handles a case out of
town. Virginia Kerry is a determined drinker, and
she keeps Chad's men busy. When Chad returns, he
takes over the watch. He observes the doctor
returning home late. He even follows Dr. Hamid, a
fellow doctor and friend of Dr. Kerry's, who leaves
their house suspiciously late. So when Chad
discovers that Dr. Kerry has been shot through the
heart that night while Virginia lay passed out in the
next room, he knows the murder must has been
committed by either the wife or the late night visitor.
But nothing about this case is as simple as it seems.

DEATH OF A LADIES' MAN

It starts with a robbery. Three men steal $42,000
from a finance company, and one of them is shot. This
event sets the wheels in motion—and proves fatal for
Lt. John Horner. Horner has been seeing two women
on the side while bucking for a promotion. Captain
Kelly is about to reach retirement age, and Horner
wants his job so bad he can almost taste it. However,
Horner has made some enemies lately. The husbands
of the two women both find out the same night that
Horner has been seducing their wives while they
were on the job. They both want to kill him. Horner is
too busy investigating the robbery to notice the
danger he's in. Until one night, when it all catches up
with him.